THE RIVER OF NO RETURN

Other books by the Author:

Lion of Scotland (1952, 1974, 1998)
To the Ends of the Earth (1997, 1999)
Not as Strangers (1967)
James Fletcher, Builder (1970).

THE RIVER OF NO RETURN

NEIL ROBINSON

A Novel

Samahani Press Auckland

Dedicated to the Memory of
Neil's father

George Henry Robinson

Published by:
Samahani Press Auckland
Email: zamahani@yahoo.co.nz

ISBN 0-473-09294-8

Pen and ink drawings on pages 236-242 from Neil Robinson's archives

Printed by Premier Print Services, Auckland, New Zealand, December 2002

A Note To The Reader

There was indeed a Norman McLeod who led several hundreds of Highlanders from Scotland to Nova Scotia, and thence to Australia and a final home in New Zealand. And there were among his followers men who worked in the kauri forests, or traded in goods and human lives among the islands of the Pacific Ocean.

But that was all a long time ago. Norman McLeod, revered by many, rejected by others, died in 1866. It is perhaps a measure of his greatness that after all those years his personality is still alive to many descendants of those who had known him; and that legend is still decorating the plain but dramatic facts of his life.

Norman McLeod, one of the last of the great Highland leaders, has his place in this story partly because the many conflicting aspects of his character have always fascinated me; but chiefly because no tale set among his people would be complete without him. Most of the other characters are fictitious, but not, I hope, too far from the truth.

Neil Robinson

Acknowledgments

I'd like to extend my appreciation and thanks to all those who helped bring this book into being, especially to my old dad, Neil, who let this remarkable secret lie in the drawer of his writing desk for over fifty years. Publishing his work has allowed me to develop an understanding of who he was in a way that never really happened while he was alive. For that I am very grateful.

My brother, Peter, typed the manuscript and spent many hours proofing the copy. He carried tremendous enthusiasm for Neil's writing and has been a significant force of support and wisdom.

Betty Powell, genealogist at the Waipu Heritage Centre, read the manuscript, lent her support, and quietly encouraged me to publish it for the 150th celebration.

I'd like to acknowledge the importance of the Waipu Heritage Centre as being the container that holds the ends of the threads of the Scotland-Nova Scotian-New Zealand migration.

I know that Neil set great store in the Waipu House of Memories, as it was called in his day, and especially in the work of Betty Powell as genealogist and historian. In acknowledgment of this, the trustees of the Neil Campbell Robinson estate are pleased to make available a fifty percent net profit royalty from the sales of this edition to the Waipu Heritage Centre.

The detailed knowledge and inspiring organisation of another Nova Scotian descendant, Betty Nelley at The Kauri Museum, was invaluable. She provided photographs from The Kauri Museum's collection, including those of Tudor Collins.

Neil's friends and colleagues have helped me in various ways, from offering advice and reading proofs to printing the book. To all, I extend my sincere thanks.

The publishing of this book has brought to completion the work that Neil started fifty years before. And it is with gratitude and pleasure, Neil, that I offer your work of fiction, The River of No Return, to the reading public.

Alistair Robinson
November 2002

Part One: The Land

Chapter One

THE MOUNTAIN RANGE WAS LIKE A CURLING GREEN WAVE FROZEN before it toppled. Curling, so it seemed to Donald McKinnon, around the great outcrop of ironstone on which he stood. Frozen into a silence that embraced not only the forested hills but the young morning, the cloudless empty sky.

He settled himself on the ledge of rock, his pack comfortable in the small of his back, and looked into the sun's winking, liquid eye. It rested on the rim of the sea, fiery and dazzling, but its heat had not yet reached him. He stretched his legs in front of him and yawned.

Already there was a good day's walking behind him, and the sun only now out of his bed. In the dark and heavy night he had followed the river until it became a stream, twisting through steeper hills. When the profiles of the mountains were high against the sky he had left the valley by a track that tunnelled deep in the forest, climbing a long spur familiar to him from other years. Morning had been a long time coming; and then, with one stride it seemed, he had left the night behind him.

He turned his head and watched the last shreds of night slip from the western hills. Day came in like an invading army. It moved swiftly from hilltop to hilltop, leaving pockets of darkness that were defeated at leisure. Even as he watched, in the space of minutes, the forest stood out clear and clumpy, the night dissolved from its limbs. And the sun, which had not been able to stop him shivering, was warming his face and clothes. Midsummer sun, born with a giant's strength.

He made to get up but instead slumped back as if he had nothing to do but watch the sun come up and think happily about the year's work that had ended and the homecoming that was a few hours away.

'Stir yourself, Donald,' he said. 'If you wanted to rest why did you pack up and leave camp last night, when you could have had a soft enough bed and a walk home in daylight? Don't you know it's Sunday and church this morning, and little enough time for a meal even if you hurry?'

At that he stood up, easing his pack onto his shoulders, setting his broad leather belt around his waist; a tall young man, big boned, loose-limbed, with a dark hank of hair lying across his brown forehead. His hands big, with quiet, powerful fingers. His shirt and trousers moulded to a frame that would grow thicker and heavier in a year or two.

'Talking to yourself, Donald? It's time you were home, isn't it now?' He grinned. 'Don't answer that one, Donald!'

But he paused again before plunging into the last green valley between him and the coastal plain. He threw his head back.

'Hullo there! Hullo!' he called. 'This is Donald McKinnon, coming home from the forest!'

His voice was lost in the great silence. Not even an echo answered him. Suddenly he felt that the silence was an enemy. He laughed and waved one arm defiantly. Then, with grating boots, he slid down the rock until the bush track swallowed him again.

Donald McKinnon paused for breath again on a long, eastward-running spur, black and vivid green from a year-old forest fire. Charred, tumbled logs, the bones of burnt trees grotesquely heaped; tree ferns bursting with new life, their furled fronds unrolling towards the sun. Behind him the mountains, covered with forest that, in the sunshine, had a deceptive softness. Six miles away the sea, shining like polished metal. Across it was spread a chain of islands, drowned mountain peaks, drenched with a misty blue that could not hide the harshness of their ragged profiles.

And at his feet the land where his people lived. Smoke was rising from the chimney of a cabin, a cheerful homely sight. The forest pressed in on all sides. A mile or so away another clearing with tiny figures of cattle, another pale plume of smoke that only emphasised the loneliness of the upper valley. Further away still, a bright curve of river that lost itself in the bay that swept like a sickle blade to the north.

A strange, strange land, he thought. Here is the New Year coming, a time when the world should be stirring hopefully for spring; instead there is a blazing sun, high summer and harvest-time on its way! Think of those other new years in Nova Scotia. Snow on the ground, ice in the bay, the singing, the dancing, and a little food in the storehouse. But you are no exile in this strange land, Donald. This is your home, and these are your people. He cast a stubborn glance at the silent hills and went on his way.

*   *   *

Even though it was Sunday, the dogs could still bark. Long before he reached the house, old Jock came bounding out, sniffed suspiciously at his heels and hands, and then recognised him with lolling tongue and wagging tail. Donald sprinted the last fifty yards, scattering the fowls that fossicked about the door, and was inside before his mother knew he was coming.

Already she was in her Sunday clothes; a gown of sober black, a touch of white lace at her throat showing her mild rebellion against the ordinance that denied frivolity in women's wear.

'Well, Donald, at last!' He moved towards her and kissed her forehead. 'You've grown. I'm sure you must be six inches taller!'

'There's no need to tell me that, mother,' he laughed. He pointed ruefully to his trousers which ended some distance above the heavy boots.

'But you still have some socks, I'm glad to see,' his mother said. 'The other boys came home with none. They must surely have sold them or given them away, for they could certainly not have worn out in only twelve months.

'But never mind. Your father's suit will fit you for today, and doubtless you will need no other for a long time again. And now, Donald, come to your breakfast.'

He took a basin of water from the barrel that stood by the door and sluiced his head, neck and hands with much blowing and splashing.

'It's a whale you should have been, little Donald,' Anne McKinnon said merrily, her eyes warm and proud with love. 'But surely I cannot keep calling you little Donald now!'

She watched him as he dried his face. How tall he was growing, and broad too, though his frame had not yet filled out. Suddenly it seemed to her that a stranger was in the room: a stranger with big, powerful, sunburned arms; dark hair that needed cutting and long legs clad in heavy tweed; alien shoulders, with muscles that moved dangerously as he rubbed himself dry. There was something ruthless, even cruel, about a young man's strength. Surely this could not be her son! And then he threw the towel down on the bench and turned to smile at her with eyes that were as candid as those of the small boy who remained in her memory. This was, indeed, Donald – her youngest son.

But how thin his face was! He must surely be working too hard in those forests that lay somewhere behind the mountains; cutting down kauri trees, hauling them to the river and sending them down to where great ships waited to take them away. And yet he looked well, and happy too, his skin clear, his teeth white. May God look after him and keep him in health, and not let him wander too far from her. Or, if he had to go, may he never forget his home and always come back.

Her son was watching her quizzically. Perhaps the intensity of her thought communicated itself to him; perhaps the unspoken prayer showed in her eyes or in the set of her mouth, for he looked uncomfortable.

'Come on mother, then, your little Donald is starving.' Quickly she stepped to the fire, ladled out a bowl of porridge and set it before him; poured milk from the big jug; added boiling water to the tea leaves in the pot; cut slices of bread from the loaf, baked the previous day, that stood on the table. Then, turning back to the fire, she set two eggs in boiling water and coaxed the crane to where the heat was the greatest.

Donald ate with much enjoyment. He watched his mother moving swiftly about the kitchen, admiring her deftness as she poured more water into the empty black porridge pot, banked the wood fire and prepared to wash the dishes in the basin placed on the bench under the window. This was the scene familiar to him from his earliest memories. And it still pleased him more than he could have imagined. The long hut in the forest that had been his home for nearly a year was separated from him now by more than the barrier of intervening mountains.

He said: 'Where are father and Alex and Ewen?'

'They have gone on ahead. Your father wished to call on Duncan Cameron before the church service.'

'Why? There is no trouble there, I hope.'

Anne McKinnon's eyes clouded. 'I cannot tell you that, Donald. And now we must make ready to go.'

Donald smiled with a puzzled expression, but said no more. He knew that his mother had said all she wished to say.

He climbed the narrow staircase that hung on the kitchen wall, leading to the attic room where he and his brothers had slept as children. A suit of good black cloth, his father's second best, lay on the bed, a clean shirt and socks beside it, and on the floor by the tiny window a newly-polished pair of boots.

Mother never seems to hurry, he thought, but everything is always in order. Would the girl he married some day be as attentive to his needs, serving her husband, and then her children, with such care? He hoped so. He whistled cheerfully at the thought and made ready for the walk to church.

* * *

See Donald McKinnon and his mother, sturdy figures dwarfed by the far-sweeping, scrub-covered, lifeless land, walking sedately along the clay track that led ultimately to the church down by the river. It was three miles away, but they had no need to hurry. Fine powdered dust stirred languidly about their feet, settling on their clean black clothes and drifting also onto the grass that fringed the track. The sun shone brassily upon them and on others like them who were also, on this sacred day, coming from little cabins scattered through the wilderness to join in worship of a Presbyterian God.

'Church will be busy today, mother,' said Donald. 'And I'm sure you'll have no time to listen to the sermon, what with seeing who are come home for the New Year, and how they look. The minister will need to preach strongly to keep minds on his words. Who do you think he will rebuke today?'

Anne McKinnon looked grave, and when she did not even pretend to scold him for his levity, Donald knew that something was crowding her mind. If he had been away in the forest, the small controversies, the petty scandals, the religious arguments that shook Waipu occasionally would have counted for no more than a moment's idle gossip. But now, in spite of himself, he could feel an inward tension rising.

Does it take only so long to get back into the groove? he asked himself. He looked at his mother walking patiently beside him, her handbag, the badge of care and forethought, carried in one gloved hand. Her face was preoccupied but not unhappy. Whatever may be the trouble, he surmised, she is strong enough to bear it. So why should I be worrying?

He broke thoughtlessly into a whistle once more, his spirits rising as he looked about him. Ahead, the track climbed a low pass between two higher hills. It was hot but the birds were still vocal, carrying into high noon the delight with which they had greeted the day.

In the air now, streaming before the easterly that came over the prow of the hill, was the smell of the sea. It was, he thought, noticeable even in the haze that blurred the sky. The humid tang of the salt came to his nostrils, and an accompanying sense of elation. How cramped had been the forest; the confined sky, the cool, damp air, the rotting undergrowth that was the nursery of a strange, parasitic life.

The sun and the sea!

Forgetting his mother he ran to the hilltop and looked down the low incline. There it was, nursing its ragged islands like waifs, murmuring in a subdued voice not so different from what he had heard in his Nova Scotian home on the other side of the world, when he was too young to remember anything else than the soothing touch of his mother's hand, the deep voice of his father.

His mother was smiling as she came up to him. Together they paused for a few minutes, and then walked on sedately.

* * *

Behind and in front of them now were other small groups of men and women in their discreet dark clothes, walking through the soft dust of the road deep in their own thoughts. Sunday morning was no time for idle gossip, for casual greetings. Once again Donald felt the familiar, sober, not unwelcome weight of God's hand upon him. He could not have whistled or sung now if he had tried. The sky remained blue; the sun, the sound of the sea lifted his heart to solemnity and reverence. How puny is man, how wonderful the ways of God! Here we are, my mother and I, going down a dusty road to worship One Who has guided our footsteps through strange places. Was it not a miracle that his mother and father should have been brought safely from Skye to the green wilderness of Cape Breton Island, whose cliffs and deep inlets faced the fog and storms of the Western Atlantic? And, without the help of God, would it have been possible for them, with their family and their friends, to have attempted the long and fearsome voyage across and down the world to this new land, set between the lion-like seas of the Roaring Forties and the blue, immense Pacific?

For many of them, indeed, the journey had called for a stiffening of faith – in themselves and in God. For others, who could always hope for something better over the next hill, it had been embarked upon as a return to Eden. And if Eden did not prove to be the Paradise they dreamed about, God was no doubt right in chastening them. Through danger, adversity and hunger; even when it seemed unlikely that they would be able to settle down in one place together, God had kept one part of His universal mind on them; even though, as some of Donald's friends thought, He had taken an over-long time to decide what was best for His people.

But that was perhaps the greatest miracle of all. Eighty years before, Norman McLeod, their leader, had been born in the parish of Assynt, in Sutherlandshire. His life had been one constant rebellion – against formality in religion, against ease and sloth that corrupted the minds of young and old, against those who would force their will on others; always excepting, of course, McLeod himself, who with God's help would lead his people to a promised land. He had been fisherman, farmer, teacher, magistrate; a dabbler in many doctrines. Now he was old. But, as Donald remembered when he thought back to the last time he had heard him preach, McLeod was still their leader. As the flesh shrunk on his big bones, so did his fervour grow. A remarkable man, thought Donald as dispassionately as he could. One could easily be enslaved by his personality; one could dislike, but never ignore him.

Deep in their own thoughts, they had come by now to the village. Donald looked about him. The little cottages, front doors shut and curtains drawn against the Sunday light; the smithy, the tanner's, the straggle of stores and other buildings that came together at the heart of the settlement. They had not changed since he had last seen them, but the village was subtly different. Unless, he thought, the change was in himself. How the eye can deceive, working with the mind!

He had never before noticed, or else he had completely forgotten, how the minister's tall house stared across the bare fields, dominating the township from a distance. How inoffensive were the houses of his people, simple structures of wood cunningly fitted together, resting lightly, almost apologetically, on the ground they usurped. To his eye, unaccustomed now to what had always been taken for granted, they seemed like timid sheep drawn together hopelessly for their own protection. Against what? The wrath of God? Fear of the unknown land in which they were established?

If Donald had still been out in the hills, he would have laughed at such foolish fantasies. Now, with a wry grin, he took his mother's arm and headed purposefully toward the church, which was part of and yet remote from the rest of the township. Suddenly he was anxious to see the worship begin.

His father and brothers were waiting by the porch. Together, after a murmured greeting and shaking of hands, they went inside, four big men and one small woman. She walked to her seat with a serenity compounded partly of pride. Young Donald, feeling his collars tight about his unaccustomed neck, followed his father and elder brothers; all of them tip-toeing with awkward care, for their weight made the bare boards creak.

A plain building with long narrow windows, forms that were deliberately uncomfortable to sit on. The ghost of a smile showed on Donald's face as he thought of the man who had succeeded – once – in going to sleep during one of Norman McLeod's long sermons. The minister's eagle eye had soon noticed him. The Bible was flung at his head with the promise, 'If you will not hear the word of God, at least you will feel it!' Surely, on such a seat as this, the poor man had deserved what sleep he could get.

The village might have changed, Donald might have grown up, but church was still the same. In the silence, he could hear the breathing of those near him. All the pews were full. Coming together from lonely farms to worship in God's house, they not only strengthened their own faith but fortified their hearts and minds against the loneliness that would come again. They were still one people; and now they waited, tensely but with complete restraint, for the minister to appear.

Those rows of discreetly bowed backs, bare heads and sober bonnets belonged to people whom Donald had known all his life. But now, or so it seemed to him, they had submerged their identity, their individuality. They would speak with one voice, or not at all. Even old Alex Ban, that cheerful tippler and gossip, was looking soberly towards the empty pulpit, his glittering and cynical eye veiled with something like humility. Big men with heavy, patriarchal beards; youngsters wide-eyed with excitement; women who, for a few hours, had forgotten their daily tasks and cares – all awaiting the appearance of the minister.

And suddenly he was there standing in the pulpit, and Donald knew swiftly that the man who had led them to this land was still their master. If he had not been a minister endowed with the authority of God he would have been their temporal chief. His gown swept grandly from his shoulders, and from beneath its folds, strong, well-kept hands gripped the edge of the railing. He stood motionless, his eyes behind steel-framed spectacles looking down on his flock.

Was it his eyes that gave him his power? Donald wondered. He felt as if they were fixed on him, probing into his mind, sifting out base desires that he did not even know he felt. It was the head of an aging lion. The year had left its mark on Norman McLeod. A massive head, still covered thickly with white hair; high cheekbones a little more prominent than he remembered them; a round, full chin with the curving jawbone now clearly defined; a mouth that had fallen away, the lips held firmly together now as if defying the onset of old age.

A strong man physically, thought Donald as those piercing eyes swept across the congregation, holding everyone, whether willing or not, in submission. The precentor, his humble slave, stood below the pulpit, watching with fussy care to make sure that the minister held all their attention. At his signal, the congregation rose to pray.

A strong man physically, but it was something more than physical strength that sounded in that voice, waking echoes of unremembered things in Donald's mind. He seemed to gather all their hearts into his hand as he spoke to his God. His voice was tender as he welcomed back the young men from the forest; sad, as he deplored the need for them to be parted from their homes for so long to earn their living; joyful, when he added that this same absence made their return a time of even greater happiness.

A flash like that from an approaching thunderstorm lit up his eyes as he warned them against their worldliness, the frivolity that beset them in their forest camps. He is not quite right there, thought Donald, as he remembered the bushman's simple, disciplined way of life. But no doubt one can exaggerate in a good cause.

It was good to sit there on a fine summer day and join with his family and his own people in the singing and the prayers. Through one narrow window he could see blue sky and bright sunshine. The errant branches of a tree, a fugitive from the forest, cast a pattern across the glass. A fantail, swooping and darting after insects, came regularly into sight, balancing on the branch with tiny body and widely flirted tail.

A strange peace for the young bushman who had seen dawn break on the high hills. His muscles relaxed, his eyelids drooped, the turbulent drone of the minister's voice began to sound in his ears like waves breaking on a faraway beach.

Donald McKinnon was going to sleep.

Another psalm and a firm nudge from his mother's elbow saved him from disaster. But even that respite could not last for long and, once again, a deadly weight settled on his eyes; his body had no more than a jelly's strength.

Desperately he tried to focus his attention on anything at all. The fantail had abandoned its perch and the branch, stirred by a light breeze, waved hypnotically across the window. He looked down at his mother's gloved hands, clasped restfully in her lap; beyond them at the hands of his father and brothers. Big firm hands, awkwardly holding their books, square wrists jutting brown and firmly muscled from the sleeves of coats. Did his brothers also feel this strange languor, this overwhelming sense of unreality? They had been home for a few days. The damp scent of the bush would be out of their nostrils. A night's sleep at home, and the strangeness would leave him too. Or so he hoped.

His eyes moved further afield. It was not only to the old people that a year had made a difference. Young Jessie McKay was sitting across the aisle with round, glowing cheeks, smooth hair that had in it a touch of fire, and her eyes cast demurely down. It would be pleasant to speak to Jessie again, a shy schoolgirl no longer, but a maid who, even if she spoke idly, would still be worth listening to.

But could that pale ghost of a girl be Christy Cameron? As Donald watched her, she seemed to shrink into her seat, and the minister's voice, suddenly harsh and discordant, rang ominously in his ears.

He had seen it happen before. Girls, and boys too, could be at one time as rosy and as full of life as young Jessie there. Suddenly, like flowers in the hot sun, they would wilt and fade. But the 'sickness' was not in Christy's family. They were robust, strong, and lived to a great age. With a puzzled mind Donald sat watching the girl, who herself was watching the minister with a strange and fearful fascination.

For Donald, too, the drone of his voice suddenly resolved itself into words.

'Not long ago, as many of you will remember – some with tears – a cutter carrying six men overturned and sank in a calm sea not far from the river-mouth. Doubtless in their wisdom these men thought it necessary to sail on a Sunday – as if anything was more important than God's own terrible injunction; to remember the Sabbath and keep it holy.'

His arms stretched out above their heads. His eyes, flashing now like those of a great bird, seemed to burn with an unearthly fire.

'Holy,' he repeated. 'Sacred to Him, to sober thoughts of His mercy and goodness, of His anger and power when the devil struggles for a human soul.

'The cutter sank and the men with it, leaving widows and orphans to grieve for their folly and waywardness.

'The souls of the dead go to meet their Maker like the bubbles from the lips of a drowning man, deep down in the calm sea. They are, indeed, drowning – in the love of God that is as great as any ocean, as strong as any tide; or in the mire of sin that clogs their nostrils, their mouths, their minds.

'And God waits for those souls to come mounting to Him, airy and beautiful bubbles, without stain or blemish. But those that are sinful, unrepentant, incapable of understanding or achieving what God has purposed of them – those ones burst and are as if they had never been.

'Better would it be to lie drowning in the depths of the sea, with the fishes eating your eyes and picking your bones, than to belong to this sad and sinful company. The brightness of heaven, the glory of the saints, the untarnished splendour of the Godhead – these are for the mortals who by their lives become immortal.

'The word of God ordains, and I have repeated to you, what is required of those who will see His face. The body, decked with gaudy apparel, is a cunning lure that Satan uses to take man from God. Spurn it! Loose and lascivious talk that rots the mind; wine and strong drink that open the heart to the temptations of our sensual frame. Reject the devil who so cunningly would destroy us!'

Norman McLeod stood upright in the pulpit. He passed one great hand across his brow. His eyes seemed to burn into Donald's own. He paused for a few moments, while the congregation held its breath. But the thunderclap did not come.

Calmly, almost conversationally, Norman continued: 'When I was a young man I exulted in my strength. From Wick, in faraway Caithness, I took my fishing vessel out to battle with storm and sea. At the universities of Aberdeen and Edinburgh, where so-called wise men were gathered to teach the young, I studied and worked until my brain and body cried out for rest. But I gave them no rest. Rather, I drove them ever harder. From Assynt to Lochalsh and back again, over moor and mountain, I walked and watched the people, broken by their landlords, their faithless chiefs, their false pastors. My heart was sad for them, but I felt pride that I was different. Through winter snow and summer heat my body refused to yield. My pride was in it, in muscles and sinew that had been tortured and tested by years of conflict.

'My body was, I thought, God's instrument. Through me, my friends would be preserved from the devil that had the Highlands in his clutches. The devil who worked through strong drink, through wealth in the hands of powerful and unscrupulous men, through the subtle, sly, insidious temptations of sloth and luxury.

'God made me strong. Men and women followed me. I was no ranting revivalist who sent them frothing and mooing like demented cattle. But through me and my body God spoke to them. They followed me to Nova Scotia, through wild Atlantic storms in a frail and leaky barque. There we carved out homes from the wilderness, until more people, and greater temptations, came there also. They followed me across the world to Australia, a hollow land where the golden calf was worshipped and there was no Moses to curb the fiend's power. And you, my people' – he paused while a smile of singular sweetness transformed his face – 'faithful in your own weak fashion to God, have followed me to this our last home.

'When I was a young man' – his voice was now little more than a whisper – 'I exulted in my strength. But now what does my bodily power avail me?'

He turned in the pulpit, as if inviting his congregation to gaze on his white hair, his hollow, clean-shaven cheeks, his gaunt and shrunken frame.

To his own surprise, Donald felt a sudden rush of pity for the man. Norman is old, he thought, and cannot do anything about it.

'I am weak!' He smashed one hand down on the pulpit rail so that it shivered from the blow. 'I am weak, but God is strong, and He can still speak through this earthly body that He has given me. I have used it for His glory, but soon it will return to the dust from which it came.

'The earthly body? God speaks through me: Put not your trust in things of the flesh. The flesh can corrupt the spirit.

'Look at this maiden, rosy with health; or this young man, straight and proud, walking the world like a conqueror. For them, old age can never come. It is a dream that will never be real. They glory in their youth, their vigour. But the pit lies gaping at their feet. Strength will fail, beauty fade, desire turn to ashes in their mouths.

'Young men and women, look about you. Who have true happiness when youth has gone? The wine-drinkers, the gluttons, the fornicators who made flesh their master? Or those who turned their hearts to God, disciplined and mortified the flesh, whipped the devil whenever he appeared? Young men, your strength, your desire will fail. Put no trust in them! Young women, govern your minds, fear God, live upright lives, stamp out temptation of any kind.'

The voice, vibrant with feeling, urgent with sincerity, went on and on, booming in the brain like a wave breaking in a great sea cave.

Donald's drowsiness had left him, for this was an appeal that forced a response. It was not often that the old man spoke of himself, but now the barriers were down. And Donald, secure in his own youth and strength, felt unexpected emotions rising within him.

How remote and pitiful old age could be! How savage against the youth that had been lost, against those who still possessed it. But surely not everyone felt that way. Old age could be wise, kind and gentle, unless it was tortured with regrets and fears. And usually the old minister gave the impression of inward calmness, however much he might storm against others. One felt that it was not McLeod the man but McLeod the messenger of God who was speaking. Today, indeed, something must have upset him greatly.

Now he was talking of sin, the sins of youth that made God turn his face away. Through many lands, he said, he had sought a place where his people could live uncontaminated by the world, where evil could be stamped out from among them. And everywhere he had failed.

Scotland, where the glory of the early church had been defiled and degraded by worldly, weak-kneed ministers; Nova Scotia, a paradise marred by jealousy and petty hatreds; Australia, where lust for gold brought death and corruption in its train; and even here, in this beautiful land that had been set aside for them by Providence, deadly sin had made its appearance.

There was no doubt now in Donald's mind that the thunderstorm was about to break. The minister was leaning forward from the pulpit. The precentor was gazing down on the congregation with an expression affirming that all secrets were known to him. But where once the minister's gaze had ranged over all his listeners, it was now fixed with a fearful intensity on one person.

Norman McLeod's eyes did not move as he spoke two words, softly now and with an indefinable appeal:

'Christy Cameron.'

The church was suddenly silent, as if no one dared to breathe. Donald felt his mother start, and then her hands clenched on the body of her purse. The girl had risen. Her father, his face bleak and expressionless, allowed her to pass in front of him, and then she walked quietly up the aisle until she stood below the pulpit.

'Christy Cameron,' the minister said, almost tenderly. 'I have noticed your absence from church for many Sundays, and certain rumours have not been allowed to escape my notice. Tell me, in the sight of God and of this congregation, is it true, as has been reported to me, that a child was born to you?'

A feeling of unreality had returned to Donald. It seemed as if he were watching, from a great distance, strangers performing some alien, meaningless routine. These events could not concern people he had known all his life.

His mother had placed a restraining hand on his knee, but he knew that, even if she had not done so, he could have neither moved nor spoken.

The girl stood with bowed head and shoulders.

'Is it true, Christy Cameron?'

She did not move, but a stifled sound that might have been 'No' came from her lips.

The minister stood erect, and once again he looked over the heads of the people.

'Anne McGregor and Katherine McKenzie.'

Two elderly women - kindly capable folk who had helped with the birth of almost every child in the district - rose uncertainly to their feet and came forward.

The minister said: 'Open her bodice and tell me.'

Stout, matronly Mrs McKenzie stood behind the girl as if to screen her from those whose eyes were drawn with an unwilling fascination. Her broad, comfortable frame served well, but Donald could still see Christy standing motionless, her head flung back defiantly. But the minister, as impersonal or remote as God Himself, was no longer looking. He seemed to have withdrawn into a world peopled only by ghosts.

Anne McGregor's brown and comely face still looked cheerful even when puckered with a rare anxiety. Her hands were busy at Christy's breast. Then she turned, raised her eyes to the minister and nodded slowly.

Unconsciously they had formed a strange tableau. The minister looking down from the pulpit, the girl standing forward, the two women slightly behind her on her left and right. It was as if they were awaiting the bridegroom. But there was no man to support Christy Cameron in this hour.

'Where is the child?'

'Dead. It was born dead.'

There was no fear in Christy's voice, and the words sounded clearly in Donald's ears, ringing like a dreadful bell.

'And where is the man?'

Now the silence could be felt throughout the church. The pause lengthened. The minister waited, calm, eternally patient, perhaps even forgiving.

Someone drew a deep breath. It might have been Donald himself. And suddenly he felt that he must leave the church, stand in the sun, and fill his lungs with God's clean air.

It was not pity for the girl; it was not anger against the minister; it was not fear that the name she might be forced to speak would be that of someone he knew and liked. It was a sudden, sharp feeling of elation that he, Donald McKinnon, was free to go where he wished, that he was not tied down by guilt or by petty laws, which forced him from his seat by the aisle and set him striding urgently to the door.

He must get away from this. A fine summer day, the first of his holiday at home, was not to be turned sour in his mind. And as he reached the door he heard the girl's voice, quiet but firm:

'I do not know. I do not care.'

* * *

The trees were motionless in unmoving air. The sun slept on the fields and houses, lifeless this Sunday noon. Walking through the village Donald found himself whistling, and he did not try to check it. How good to be alive, and not to be Christy Cameron, or the man whose name she had not spoken.

Poor Christy. She had been a quiet girl, the only child of parents who worked hard, attended church, served the community and their God with diligence and complete unselfishness. They did not approve of dancing or frivolous music, and so Christy stayed at home, working, reading and thinking. She did not steal out to dances at night, with her mother's connivance, as did many of the girls.

So demure, so busy at her duties in the house and on the farm whenever Donald had been there; so submissive. And this is what happened.

Donald heaved a sigh that combined regret and amazement, and then forgot Christy Cameron completely.

A figure appeared at the end of the road, a short, sturdy man, bareheaded with a long and magnificent beard. He approached swiftly on legs that scarcely seemed to touch the ground; and the speed of his passage, parting his beard, revealed that he had neglected to put on a shirt under his worn, clean coat. While still some yards away he waved a furious greeting, his blue, darting eyes bright with pleasure.

Donald smiled at him. Old Roddy McKenzie's beard had always been considered ornamental. It was, however, the first time he had realised it was useful as well, and a preserver of clean linen.

They shook hands cordially, but even before then Roddy was talking.

'Welcome back, Donald boy. How long have you been over?'

'Just today, Roddy. And how are you?'

'Tired, Donald; tired of doing nothing. Tired of saying the same things to the same people, and tired of hearing them say the same things to me. Come away up to the house, and tell me what you've been doing these twelve months.'

They walked off along the road, across the hump-backed bridge over the river.

'The fish have been biting, Donald. This morning I was sadly tempted to throw in a line, but all I dared do was stand and think what a harvest those Irishmen will be having at the Heads. There are advantages in being a Papist, Donald, even if you might burn in hellfire some day.'

Roddy sighed and reluctantly turned down a well-worn foot-track beside the stream.

'And is that all you have had to do – talk, listen and fish? I should think no man would want more than that!'

'Aye, Donald, life could be worse for an old man home from the sea, nearing the end of a hard but sinless life.'

He squinted suddenly up at his companion, and there was a challenging tilt to his beard.

Donald rose to the bait. 'Old, Roddy? Don't tell me that, now! I should say you have at least five more years before you need to think of your past sins.'

Roddy stopped, shook a rueful head. 'Sins,' he repeated. 'Sins of omission and of commission.'

He produced a pipe from a dark recess inside his coat. Donald watched with unconcealed interest as a tight wad of paper was removed from the bowl, and tucked away in the same mysterious recess. Inspection proved that there was still some charred tobacco in the bowl. Roddy broke a twig from a tea-tree bush, prodded vigorously and emptied it into one broad palm. With his knife he shaved two thin flakes from his plug; and then, by some dexterous sleight of hand, rubbed them to a powder without spilling a crumb of what he was already holding. The new tobacco went first into the pipe, which was then carefully packed with the dottle.

Donald held his breath while the loaded pipe found its way through the labyrinth of whisker, and did not relax until it had been safely lighted and clouds of acrid smoke were tainting the air.

'Sins of omission and commission,' Roddy said, puffing furiously. 'And talking of sin, how is it that you are not at church?'

'I could ask the same question,' Donald replied.

Roddy removed his pipe and spat violently and precisely through his whiskers at a small round stone on the path.

He darted a glance at Donald, and then looked away again. 'I think I'll go to sea again.

'Two Sundays past it would be, I must have smiled at the wrong time and Norman, fire shooting from his eyes, forbade me the pleasure of worship until after the New Year; a punishment that no doubt I can endure. You see how sin creeps into us unawares? But never mind, Donald. Keep a downcast eye and you'll fare well.'

Roddy's pipe was out. Thoughtfully, his mighty beard drooping like the tail of a sheep dog when its master is disturbed, he repacked the bowl with its paper wad and stowed his pipe away in a pocket.

Donald looked at his friend affectionately. In spite of his brave words, and even though the cause of his banishment might have been trivial, there was no doubt that he missed the society of his friends on the most important day of the week.

The gate in the picket fence was open and they walked down a path, neatly dressed with white shell, between edges of whitewashed wood.

'Look at my vegetables, wilting in the blasted heat,' Roddy remarked dispassionately.

Donald always enjoyed Roddy's garden. Neat rows of potatoes, cabbages, peas, beans and carrots in tremendous quantity filled the entire space between fence and house, and not a flower plant was allowed to show its head. The only flower Roddy liked, as he frequently confessed, was that growing on a potato plant.

He worked strenuously in his garden throughout the year, complained bitterly at the tedium of the unending task, and gave most of the produce away.

As befitting an elderly bachelor, it was a small cottage of simple design. A passage extended down the centre and, as they climbed the front steps, Donald could see through two open doors the sun blazing at the end of a cool tunnel. On the left were two bedrooms, on the right a kitchen and parlour.

'Now come right on in,' said Roddy cordially. 'You know your way about.'

They were walking down the passage when Roddy's tremendous voice called. 'Father, are you anywhere about?' He grinned with great enjoyment at Donald's startled face.

From outside the back door an equally loud voice roared testily, 'I'm here, son, enjoying a little peace and quiet. What's all the rumpus about?'

By now they were standing out in the sun, and Roddy quivered with laughter at the expression on Donald's face. Bewildered, he was looking from Roddy to the other man who was rising from a chair against the wall; a short, sturdy man whose magnificent beard, powdered with grey, reached down to his waist; a man, moreover, whose eyes were beginning to sparkle with something like anger.

'Father, I would like you to meet my very good friend Donald McKinnon.' He gestured expressively first at his father and then at himself: 'Old Roddy, young Roddy; and that's how you must call us now. It would never do to be confused!'

Donald's hand was grasped and firmly held.

'But Roddy, I didn't know that you had a father.'

'It's customary, my boy, it's customary. But I must admit that I expected you to be surprised. Now let us all sit down and we can have a good talk.'

Donald stretched out on a long plank of undressed timber attached to the wall of the house. He carefully folded the coat of his father's second-best suit and placed it on the grass beside him. His face wore such an expression of comic bewilderment as he looked from father to son and back again that young Roddy burst out laughing again, his father joining in rather half-heartedly.

'But Roddy, where did you find him so suddenly?'

'Well, Donald, for how many years – ninety, is it? – he's been living in a little place called Applecross, the true home of the McKenzies. Just what he was doing there I am not sure; smuggling, perhaps. But he was far too busy to come with me to Nova Scotia when I decided to leave the Highlands behind me for ever. After thinking it over for a long time, he made up his mind not long since that it was time to travel and see the world. And so, a few weeks ago, there came a letter from Auckland saying that the writer, Captain Roderick McKenzie, would be grateful if his son would arrange for him to be brought by land or sea to Waipu. And that was that.'

Donald was studying the old man, who smiled a trifle complacently and sucked his teeth.

'It was an interesting voyage,' he admitted, 'and the captain a reasonable man who seemed to know his business well enough. He told me that he came from Lochalsh, a Matheson he was, and we got on famously after that. Many's the time we sat in his cabin and sang the old songs. Indeed, I think he was sorry when we reached Auckland. He tried to suggest that I go back with him for another voyage, but I could not do that. However, he promised to look for us if ever he returns to Auckland, and then I might go for a wee sail with him.

'But perhaps it was only the whisky talking. Even a Matheson from Lochalsh can grow sentimental when the bottle's going round.'

They sat amiably in the sun and Donald felt the tension of the morning disappearing as he listened to old and young Roddy dipping into the past. His own father had been born in Skye, across the water from Applecross. The McKinnons had been landsmen but never far from the sea, and his lively imagination, reinforced by their conversation, drew pictures of the land that he had never seen but which he still regarded as home.

The hardship, the injustices were forgotten; but memories of the soft and lovely land remained, and the restlessness was still in the blood of the young transplanted Highlanders.

'You'll stay and eat with us?' Young Roddy had jumped to his feet. 'While we've been talking here the food has been cooking. So come along in.'

They ate in the kitchen. Roddy brought a clean white tablecloth from the dresser. During his bachelor life he had not neglected the virtues of polite society. A potful of steaming potatoes, cooked in their jackets, was emptied into a basin and set in the place of honour in the centre of the table. Sun-dried fish, grilled on the embers of the open fire, were quickly divided into three portions. It was a sight to sharpen the appetite of one accustomed to the monotony of bush-camp fare.

For the first time since he had arrived, the McKenzie household was silent.

* * *

Inevitably, during the afternoon, Christy Cameron came into the conversation. When he described what had happened at church, Donald was unable to say whether the whole story was a complete surprise to Roddy. He nodded thoughtfully but made no comment.

There was a long pause. The older man watched his companion's face, which reflected vividly every thought passing through his mind.

A long, good face young Donald had, with a strong nose, deep-set eyes under a forehead that was now crinkled with thought. A wide, laughter-loving mouth, though now it was as serious as his eyes.

'Roddy,' he said hesitantly. 'This has been at the back of my mind ever since this morning. It's like a cut finger. You think you have forgotten it, and then suddenly you give it a knock and the niggling starts all over again.

'The minister was right. He was harsh and not sparing of her feelings, but he was right. Even I can understand that, to him, evil has always been a force that will allow of no half-measures.

'I find myself wondering, where would we be if there was no Norman McLeod to show us the right path to take, to protect us from evil, to stamp out sin among us?

'Christy suffered, I'm sure. But what is the kinder: to bring her guilt out into the open and let it die in her repentance, or to allow it to stay hidden, feeding on her conscience and whispered about the district?'

Donald looked directly at his friend, and saw to his surprise that his eyes were sparkling and that he was grinning with pleasure.

'You speak like the minister himself, Donald. Pray continue!'

Young Donald refused to be diverted, and indeed Roddy knew he would not be.

'The minister is right but is not Christy herself also right, in a way? The girls of her age are married; she alone is seeing life pass her by.'

A snort from Roddy made him look up quickly, but the man looked innocent enough, and in the vastness of that mighty beard it might easily have been a sneeze.

'Is it possible to be shy and also to want to know life? Perhaps it is. But how could it ever have happened? And who could the man have been?'

'You're growing up, Donald, which means that you are starting to think. And, thank God, you are finding out something that many live and die without understanding. There is good and bad in everyone, but, thank God again, I think we all incline towards goodness. And yet, is it not natural that a strong, pig-headed man like Norman should try to fashion everyone in his own image of God? And is it not natural, too, that a girl like Christy should look for happiness, even though she finds sorrow?

'Donald, it is a great enigma. But I do feel that those who follow the minister are looking back. They are trying to create a state of pure religion that never existed, except in the minds of a few. It might be good if they succeeded, but they have a powerful battle to wage. And wouldn't it be dull if they won? I think even Norman would die of boredom if there were no more devils to whip.

'Perhaps there was, as he believes, a time when good was invincibly triumphant over evil; and perhaps through him and others like him it can be created again. But I don't know…

'It is still true that good must be done to people against their will. Salutary, no doubt, but not calculated to bring love and kindness in its train. There again, Norman would say, what value have love and kindness against an immortal soul?'

In the warmth of the sun, the benevolence of a perfect day, the verbal argument died languidly.

* * *

With the passing of the day Donald began to feel the weight of its long hours press down on his body and spirit. But as he walked home through the gathering dusk he moved quickly enough, his legs, with the long, smooth strides of the bushman, seeming to function without command from his brain. He noted the landmarks as they fell behind him: the black clumps of trees that took a new shape at night; the crest of the mountain range that stood in darker silhouette against the dark blue sky.

No light showed in the McKinnon house. He crept silently into the kitchen and, putting a taper to the banked fire, lit a candle that stood on the table.

The chair creaked under his weight as he sat down and began to eat the girdle scones and honey that his mother had left out for him. The kitchen was warm and friendly, holding into the night the familiar smells of food and cooking. The ticking of the old clock – almost the first sound he had heard as a baby in far-distant Nova Scotia – drew him back in spirit to the days that had gone. The past was comforting and firm. Was it weakness to wish that the strength of the past should continue into the future? Or was it weakness to throw over everything that had proved good and enduring, seeking new gods? He could not see the answer.

And so he sat relaxed in his chair, enjoying the feeling of being home again; watching the candlelight flickering on the walls, hearing the old clock ticking towards the end of yet another year, fortified, perhaps, by the knowledge that his own people were asleep behind these thin walls. He drank heartily of the milk that his mother had left for him, put the jug away in the safe and softly climbed the stairs to his bedroom.

Outside the window, the dark night sky seemed, as it had also done in his boyhood, to be made up of close-packed, moving grains of sand. He focussed his eyes on that hypnotic patch of sky while sleep submerged him. But the last image to flash into his mind was that of a towering Norman McLeod, stern and strangely kind, and Christy Cameron, strong in her weakness and timidity.

* * *

Chapter Two

THAT NIGHT, DONALD MCKINNON DREAMED OF DISASTER. HE WAS back in the forest and he and his cousin, Norman Finlayson, were felling the biggest kauri tree he had ever seen. It hung above them like a sudden precipice in the tangled bush. It was so broad that he did not readily realise that it was a tree, not a cliff.

But the axes did their work with little help from the men, biting deep and sending great chips flying through the air. The scarf was made, and then the long crosscut saw was singing and tearing its way into the heart of the tree. High above them, branches thrust out from the huge trunk, branches that were themselves as great as any normal tree. Donald and his mate paused. Already they could see the branches wavering, they could hear the tree groaning as its death came near.

In his dream, Donald felt an increasing sense of doom. Along with it was pity for the tree, something he had never felt before. And then it all happened with a clarity, a sharp logic that his brain could not accept even though his body trembled.

Slowly the tree began to fall. They moved away and turned to watch it crash to the ground. And, as he watched, one heavy branch casually flicked the top of a tall rimu. Like a cracking whip, the rimu flashed back, throwing toward them a vine, a foot thick, that had been wrenched from its hold in the upper air.

As Donald slept, his muscles tensed and his limbs jerked, for the heavy vine, which now seemed like a great rope used on board ship, was flying toward them; and he knew, with a horrifying nightmare lucidity, that they could not escape it. But he ran, calling a warning to Norman, turning his back on the menace. And as he ran, he heard a cry of love and terror, shrill in the half-light of the bush; and looking, he saw that is was Jessie McKay, her eyes dilated, her arms stretched out imploringly, protectively.

Even in the dream his heart was sad that one so young, so comely, should have to see an accident that would shake the nerve of a grown man.

He stopped and looked back. Norman Finlayson was not in sight. But on the ground was a body, sprawling grotesque and distorted, and round it like a great snake was coiled the rata vine. It looked like his own body but it could have been Norman's.

Donald awoke, damp with sweat, to a new daybreak, the cry of love and anguish still in his ears.

The dream had been shockingly real. He could still smell the sweet scent of decay in the forest; see the trunk of the great kauri, flaking and flecked with moss; feel the terror of that well-ordered nightmare. It stayed with him through the tranquil, lazy day as he walked over the farm with his father and brothers and helped with the household tasks that had to be done, even on New Year's Eve.

But strangely, it was not the terror of the dream that was strongest in his mind. Jessie McKay's face, warm with love, her eyes tender, kept coming before him. He began to look forward impatiently to the dance that was to welcome in the New Year. She must be there; he must discover whether she was merely the creation of a dream.

Am I bewitched? he wondered. Have I been so long in the bush that the thought of a girl I have not seen for a year can make me moon about like a lovesick bull calf? He laughed at himself, but the strange, delightful, intimate feeling persisted through the day.

At times, Anne McKinnon thought as she watched her youngest son, Donald can still seem a little boy, in spite of his long limbs and sturdy frame. At dinner time, in the intervals between talk, his thoughts had been far away; a remote, lost look on his face had made her wish to ask what was troubling him. And yet she knew that it would have been of no use. He might look defenceless, but this was something beyond her care. Donald would have to solve it for himself, as did others when childhood was left behind.

She permitted herself a moment of anxious doubt. The McKinnons were reticent and Christy Cameron's name had not been mentioned, nor had they discussed the events of Sunday. But she knew that Donald had liked the girl, and she had felt many eyes on her as her son had left the church so suddenly. Friendly eyes, curious eyes, quizzical eyes. Surely they could not suspect that Donald had been over-friendly with Christy? No gossip could link their names, she told herself firmly, and put the unworthy thought from her.

* * *

And now it was evening, with a light haze over the sky that softened but did not hide the stars. The father watched imperturbably as his sons made ready to go out. Only Donald planned to attend the dance. The others were going visiting, courting perhaps; but if this was so they did not mention it.

For himself, the New Year could come in unheralded. A comfortable seat in the kitchen, perhaps a drop of whisky at bed-time, even a guarded toast to the future which he would share with the wife he still loved dearly; although passion had been left behind in Nova Scotia, along with his youth. Nor had his affection ever been a matter for conversation.

She had given him three sturdy sons, and it was for them to face the problems of growing up. He suspected that they would manage well enough.

And so, through the warm dusk, the boys went their own ways.

Following the foot-track past the Cameron's farm, Donald noticed that the house was already in darkness. A sad New Year for those good folk, the proud Ewen Cameron and his wife. And what of Christy?

Out onto the road that led down the valley. He walked on the grassy verge, for the summer dust would play havoc with his father's second-best suit. The soft grass muffled his footsteps.

His bush-trained eyes and ears deceived him when a figure materialised out of the darkness in front of him. Instinctively he put out his hand and touched an arm that broke swiftly from his grasp; a slender arm that could belong to no man.

And, possibly because he had been thinking of her, he said: 'Is this you, Christy?'

The white blur of a face turned towards him, and a subdued voice said, 'Yes, Donald.'

For a long moment he did not know what to say. Then, awkwardly, but with a compassion he could not hide, he said: 'It's a long time since I spoke with you, and much has happened since then. You know you have my sympathy, Christy.'

'Thank you, Donald,' she replied steadily, and began to move away.

'Don't go, Christy.' She paused and turned towards him again.

The darkness made it easier to say.

'You're the last girl I would have wished this to happen to. The man – can I help you? Does he know what has happened?'

'I don't want him to know.' To Donald's surprise her voice was almost cheerful. 'I don't want even to see him again.' Again, no bitterness. 'Men are hard creatures. Even you, Donald, could be hard, although kind, too.'

She stopped, and added dreamily, as if she were talking to herself: 'I hope my son…'

She broke off. Donald, bemused, repeated, 'Your son! But the baby died! Christy, he's alive!'

The girl laughed, a sound of pure pleasure such as he had never heard from her before.

'Yes, Donald, he's alive. I've just come from seeing him.

'Oh, Donald, I've lied and deceived until I could burst. I'm glad you know, because I'm sure you will say nothing. Even Norman's spies,' she spoke without emphasis, 'think the baby died. But he's with the O'Connors. They know my secret, and so does kind Mrs McGregor who delivered him, and now you. It will be safe, I'm sure.'

Donald remembered the O'Connors, a childless couple who had drifted in from nowhere and built a crude shack up in the hills. How Christy had found them he did not know, for they kept much to themselves, although the cheerful O'Connor occasionally helped with seasonal work on the valley farms.

'But some day he will come back to me, and I'll bring him up to be not hard like most men, but kind and gentle like you, Donald.'

She had gone before he realised it. He called once, loudly: 'Christy!' But there was no reply.

Instead, out of the darkness, came a talkative group of young men and girls. A voice said, 'Is that you, Donald?' All together, soft-footed and laughing in the night, they went on down the road.

* * *

The fiddler was already hard at it, producing a lively reel that made the new arrivals click their fingers and tap their toes. Donald took in the scene. Two rows of storm lanterns shone like dog's eyes in the dark, shimmering on the stream that ran below. The dance floor was a bridge, its heavy, well-fitting wooden planks, smoothed by the adzes of the builders, having been tried and found adequate in the past.

No house in the district would have held them. And, in any case, Donald was not alone in preferring the outdoor setting. The fiddler, balanced elegantly on the parapet of the bridge, sent his merry music out over the dancers' heads, out to the dark trees that seemed to be listening too. Behind the noise of the music and singing voices there was the cool, unending sound of running water.

Kenny McMillan, master of ceremonies on social occasions by personal choice and popular consent, had been busy. A distraught ewe with a late lamb, awakened from dreams of grass and maternity by the din, had attempted to break through the circle of dancers, and Kenny had just urged her back to pasture. Now, streaming with sweat and oozing goodwill, he was announcing an eightsome reel. Coats were off and trousers were given an extra hitch; and magically, while the fiddler produced a few long, sobbing notes, confusion was replaced by the disciplined order of the dance.

It was an omen, thought Donald, and his heart gave an exultant leap; for there opposite him was Jessie McKay, coppery hair warm in the lantern light, eyes in shadow and a smile on her lips.

Away went the dance, and the sturdy timber drummed beneath their feet, adding rhythm to the maddening lilt of the music. No-one had breath to waste on words, but Donald was still free to think: How light on her feet she was; how slender and pliant her waist; how cool and firm her fingers when he touched them. Jessie, Jessie, if only we could go on dancing for ever!

A whirling climax, a sudden discordant crash of sound from the violin, and someone was passing the music-maker a drink. A grassy clearing lay between the road and the river, and here, sitting decorously on the bank or sprawled in the pale starlight, they recovered their breath and spent it again in talk.

And now Donald found himself strangely inarticulate. He had taken Jessie's arm and walked with her back to her place. She sat on a rug, spreading her white gown about her and looking at him with sparkling eyes and breast still heaving from the dance. Without a word he dropped down by her side.

What could he say? Could he tell her about his dream? She would surely laugh at him. Indeed, the dream which had made her seem so close to him now appeared as a barrier between them, stifling his tongue.

Her eyes studied him, and he felt that her merriment was growing. What must she think of him? She could be no more than seventeen, and yet she made him feel like a raw schoolboy. And what is more, the young devil, she knew it and was enjoying it!

But he could not keep his eyes away. His fingers were fumbling in the short, midsummer grass while his mind fumbled for something to say. Finally, in a voice that seemed to grate on his own ears, he said: 'You've grown up since I saw you, Jessie.'

She gave the remark due attention.

'I mean,' he went floundering on, 'only last year you were more like a schoolgirl.'

'Was I?' she inquired artlessly.

'Yes,' he said, becoming suddenly fluent but knowing even as he spoke that this was not what he wanted to tell her. 'You had pigtails, and your hair was a brighter red than it is now, and you were fat – chubby, I mean. While now you're…'

A chill froze his tongue and he paused hopelessly, knowing that the more he talked the worse it would become. He might have been describing John McKay's horse, not his daughter.

Jessie McKay looked at the boy she had known all her life, and who, she suddenly realised, had grown to be a man – and a stranger. His hair, his strong eyebrows were as black as ink in the soft light; his teeth were white as he talked. And what nonsense he was talking! Donald McKinnon, who had always been so clever with his tongue!

And then, to her delight, his eyebrows were grim and formidable, his mouth clamped in a firm line. He lay beside her in a stubborn silence, tantalised by her unforced ease, by the way the moonlight gave shape to her curving lips and magic to her eyes.

I'll leave her after the music starts, he decided. There will be other days, other nights when my tongue may not betray me; and then, for another year, there will be the bush camp with no girl to trouble my waking hours.

The fiddler was deep in conversation over a bottle. It was a charmed night, soft and warm, and for a few minutes yet no one was tempted to disturb it. Voices were low, and from the forest trees there came the never-changing, muffled hooting of native owl, as insistent as the beating of a drum.

'Do you mean to work in the forest all your life, Donald?' Jessie, though not reluctant to test her feminine power, had decided that the silence had lasted long enough. Now, with one simple question, she had Donald talking easily, with no trace of self-consciousness. And the range of his ideas surprised even him as they found an outlet. There seemed no limit to the plans he had been nursing, and which had taken form in a moment.

Then he stopped and laughed; a man's laugh full of delight and amusement at himself. Donald did not know, but with that laugh he had made himself a part of young Jessie McKay, a part that she would never completely or willingly give up. He leaned towards her, and her youth and beauty added to the joy that for no conscious reason had overwhelmed him.

'Jessie,' he said, 'it's time I stopped to listen to myself. And do you know? This is not me talking. Plans? I've never made a plan in my life. I enjoy working in the bush, the companionship of other men, the cheerful weariness at night, the feeling that the timber we send down the river will be turned into houses in busy cities, bridges across great rivers, ships to sail the seas, and wharves against which they can tie up in port. A farm with cattle and sheep and a house of my own? That may be very good, but it lies in the future.

'All I know, Jessie, is that I'm restless. Perhaps I could go out and build the houses, the bridges, the wharves, or even sail to other lands? I don't know.

'Jessie, sometimes I feel life boiling up inside me. It's a strange, strange feeling; as if all God's creatures, men and women, trees, birds, the sea and the sky, were a great feast to be enjoyed before it disappeared forever. Should we be solemn and frugal and let life go by, or should we seize it with both hands? But you wouldn't know, Jessie. Women need make no such decision.'

'You might be right, Donald,' she said softly. 'But might that not be how Christy felt?'

Donald looked at her sober face. Their eyes met, and a current of understanding passed between them that was deep and satisfying.

'Yes,' he said thoughtfully. 'That could be the answer.'

They sat quietly then. The owls were hooting still, a monotonous, strangely compulsive sound. The stream ran coolly, and the dry, warm scent of summer was heavy in the night.

'I've been wondering, and so have others, what made you leave the church yesterday.'

But Donald, for the present, had talked enough of Christy and her problems. This night was too good for anything but sheer enjoyment.

'I didn't want to stay,' he said shortly.

The music had started again, and the New Year was whirling nearer. He helped Jessie to her feet and they went back to the dance.

Afterwards, when the fiddler had given up, they walked in a group down the dusty road.

'You'll be at the sports, Jessie. I'll see you then. It's been a lovely evening.'

'No, Donald. I'm to look after mother and the baby. I made that bargain so that I could come tonight – and I have enjoyed it.' She reached out impulsively and squeezed his arm. Then Donald was alone, facing towards home, weary now but cheerful in the quiet night.

* * *

Chapter Three

DONALD'S BREATH CAME PAINFULLY FROM HIS LABOURING CHEST, his legs seemed to move mechanically, but he still found time to admire Archie McMillan's untroubled back and effortless action. A little, dark man, all sinew and gristle, he ran with short, swift strides, his arms pumping at his sides. Without breaking his rhythm he looked over his shoulder at those, including Donald, who were toiling in his wake. He waved to a friend beside the track and then, putting his head down, fled away like a sprinter.

Hopelessly, Donald tried to increase his own pace. Four times round the track was a mile. Three laps had gone and Archie, who had been dancing spryly last night when the old year passed away, was just as light on his feet now. He playfully jumped a fence to show his contempt for those who were still struggling to the finish.

Donald walked with him over to the tub of water in which they were glad to douse their heads and arms. The heat was ferocious.

'If it had been ten miles, I might have beaten you, Archie,' he said. 'But you made the pace too fast for a start.'

Archie smiled. 'That's something you will learn, Donald, as you grow older. Study your opponents. I must admit I've been preparing for this race. I ran home from the bush camp a couple of days ago.'

'What, without stopping?' asked Donald.

'Oh, no, Donald. I stopped for lunch – a man must eat, for sure!'

In a friendly group, with a chorus of congratulations, real and ironic, the runners moved back through the crowd. Donald looked about him, breathing normally now as he put on his shirt and boots. His mother was smiling.

'You lost again, Donald. You are too big to run fast, I think. Perhaps you should start playing the pipes. Or there's the standing jump, or lifting the anvil, or throwing that great tree. The things that grown men will do!'

Donald regarded her solemnly. 'Mother, who have you been talking to? I think you know more about these sports than anyone else. There is one thing they forgot – a race for married women, twenty yards with a pot of porridge in their hands. And then you could have saved the family name!'

It was a sociable day, full of talking and eating and greeting friends and baiting enemies in the politest possible manner. And for those who were momentarily tired of these pursuits, there were always the sports to watch.

Jessie McKay's absence cast a small shadow on Donald's day, but in spite of it he felt the warmth that came from pleasant society.

And so, even when Roddy McKenzie looked at him thoughtfully and spoke in his most casual manner, the words did not register at once.

'They are talking about you, Donald, lad,' said Roddy. 'You've certainly given them something to keep their tongues clacking!'

For a moment Donald felt that he was once more a small boy, brought out to the front of the schoolroom while a sarcastic teacher made fun of the way in which he spoke English.

He felt the warm skin on his face tighten and grow cold. His voice was remote even in his own ears.

'What do you mean, Roddy?' A harsh note made his friend reach out a soothing hand.

'Not anything important,' Roddy said. 'But you know your people. They have not much to think about in this quiet backwater of the world, and have always been great ones for sharpening their wits with a bit of deduction at their friends' expense. And you have provided them with something that challenges their powers.'

It was still unreal for Donald, and he said nothing while Roddy paused to marshal his facts. His ironic eyes were on his young friend's face.

'First, there is the point that you've always been friendly with Christy Cameron; then, as was quickly reported to those who did not see it for themselves, you walked out of church just before Christy might have mentioned the name of the young man responsible for her appearance before the minister. And thirdly, it seems, you had a meeting with her last night, a meeting that ended with her running away just before another party arrived to surprise her.'

Roddy's light blue eyes flickered sardonically. 'And that, my young friend, is quite enough.

'Of course, no one really believes it, but can you blame them for enjoying a good bout of conjecture? Very stimulating to the mind and brain.'

Donald was aware of the groups that had formed and dispersed all about him. People he had known all his life. People who, as they had proved time and time again, were capable of sacrifices and unselfishness far beyond what was necessary when a neighbour was in trouble. He looked at them objectively. Was it only kindness and goodwill that showed in their faces, or was there also an insatiable curiosity, a greed for gossip? He watched two women who came together and began to talk immediately. He knew them well, but how well did he really know them? Their faces were thrust together, alert, intent, hungry for each other's words. They laughed, nodded a casual farewell and went their own ways.

The conversation, he knew, might have been on anything from knitting socks to the baby's appetite; but now he wondered. Were they talking about Christy and me too?

Johnny Beck approached. 'Good day to you, Donald,' he said, and went by.

Why didn't he stop to talk, as he would usually have done? He must have heard the tale, also.

A sudden distaste overtook him. He wanted to speak to no one, least of all to his friend Roddy, who still stood watching him with his shrewd and reckless eyes. Abruptly he turned and walked quickly away from the sports ground, down the road across the bridge. Now he was running, as if by the speed of his legs he could leave his shame and disappointment behind him.

The east wind blew steadily in his face; warm, humid but infinitely refreshing. With it came the crashing of the waves beyond the low sand-dunes. He left the road and picked his way through the tangle of spiny growth.

And now he was on the beach; a stretch of glistening, smooth sand that extended in a long curve to left and right. The breakers raced up the sand, chasing the small bubbles of foam almost to his feet. The gulls were fishing far out to sea, and the world might have been empty of human life.

Already he had recovered from the shock of Roddy's words. Let them talk if it pleased them, but the sea breeze could blow them over the horizon for all he cared. The settlement, he realised, drew its strength from many things; some of them wise, unselfish and rich in value, others petty and to him at this time, distasteful. He would possibly do something about it, but for the present he planned to cast such worries from his mind.

He looked around again. Not a soul in sight; only the sea sweeping grandly in and the haze that rose from the breaking waves. The sultry sun seemed to gather new strength from the bright sea and sand. How good to be alone again, away from the curious eyes and tortuous minds. A swim would clear away the last traces of his discontent.

He folded his clothes carefully under one arm, tied the laces of his boots together and slung them over his shoulder. Sometimes knee-deep in the water, sometimes in the soft and streaming sand, he ran steadily along the beach, the air cool on his body. Where a solitary, wide-spreading tree grew in the sandhills not far above high-water mark he dropped his clothes. The shock of the first breaker as it roared over his head, cool from the ocean depths, caught his breath and then sent his blood leaping. The surf was strong, a challenge to his own strength. The undertow dragged at him, and suddenly he was rising and falling with the crest of each wave as it raced past him to break with the noise of drums.

He floated easily on his back, studying the sky that had been swept bare by the droning wind, watching the lacy patterns that streaked the green mane of each long wave, at peace with himself and the not too imperfect world.

He stayed out there for a long time, swimming fast in a brief burst, then floating idly, enjoying his mastery of this strange element; then rolling and diving like the porpoises that often played in the bay. He thought of what Roddy had told him about the islands in the Pacific, a few day's sail away; the seas that, it seemed, were always blue; the simple, easy-going islanders. There a man could surely live his own life. Someday, perhaps, he would go there.

And what would Jessie think when the gossip reached her ears, as it surely would? As he swam slowly landwards again, he lifted himself on the crest of a wave in an attempt to see her house, but the sand-dunes hid it from view. She probably had not even thought of him today. He could picture her as she moved busily about the house, enjoying the rare occasion on which she was 'in charge'; scolding her mother if she did not eat her lunch and rest; finding an excuse for handling the baby brother so much younger than herself.

The exotic islands of the Pacific had faded from his mind, and he was still thinking of Jessie as he ran up the beach. Once again cheerfulness took command.

In a sheltered bay of the sandhills the sun dried him quickly. Salt encrusted his arms and chest. He rubbed it with a sadly-crumpled shirt and dressed reluctantly. He stretched out under the tree. Through its branches he could see a moving pattern of sky and greenery. It was cool and comfortable, and within a few minutes he was asleep.

It was there that Jessie McKay, coming down across the sand from her home, found him not so very much later.

As if he had felt her eyes upon him, Donald awoke and looked at her without surprise.

'Miles of empty beach,' he said, 'and you must come here to disturb a man making up for the sleep he lost last night.'

'I thought you would be at the sports today, Donald.'

'And were you not looking after your mother?'

They laughed together while she wrapped her towel about her waist and looked from Donald to the sea.

'And surely, if I did decide to come for a bathe, is it not surprising that I should come here? Have you forgotten that our house is just across the river, and that our boat is moored at the end of this track, beyond the sandhills? And that this tree has the most pleasant shade of any on the beach?'

'I do remember, now that you've told me,' and he grinned at her challengingly.

He whistled a snatch of the music to which they had been dancing not so many hours before, as if to deliberately remind her of it. He was teasing her, but she did not mind.

She looked down at him, spread at ease on the sand. Where was that self-consciousness that had made him falter last night, causing her to feel that he was young and uncertain? Truly, men were unpredictable creatures. 'But now I must have my swim. I'll come back here, if you wish to wait.'

Donald watched her run lightly through the loose sand. The breeze caught at her thin summer frock, and her hair danced in the brilliant afternoon sun. She was beautiful, he thought, and she was good, too. Then she vanished from sight.

For what seemed a long time he lay back on the sand, but when he turned his head he could see her far along the beach, a small figure in the surf. Then she ran swiftly up the beach, dwarfed by the immense sky, the lonely and seemingly limitless stretch of sand.

He waited lazily for her return.

* * *

Her hair, he noted, had been wet at the nape of her neck. She had pinned it up for the swim, but the wet curl had escaped the pins and lay on the warm, golden skin above her frock. The sun's heat was now a caress rather than a torment, and they moved out from the tree's broad shade. She rested on one elbow, her body half-turned towards him, her face towards the sea.

And now he felt that he could talk without being choked by a mingling of anger and shame. Quietly, as if he was speaking about someone else, he told her of his conversation with Roddy McKenzie.

She looked at him inscrutably when he had ended and then, to his surprise and momentary annoyance, she began to laugh.

'Poor Donald. It is indeed a pity. So serious, so well-meaning, so sorry for himself!'

Her eyes were on him, tender yet mocking, and he had to laugh himself, although he was now on the defensive.

'I'm not sorry for myself,' he blustered, feeling a red wave creep up his face. 'I'm sorry for that poor girl and her baby, and I despise those sharp-tongued, prying gossips who try to create more scandal when they already have enough to fill their plates. Is that their religion? Is that the way Norman McLeod hopes to make a new world? They may fear God, but what of God's love for those who are unfortunate?

'I'm tired of it all, I'm tired of Waipu, and I'm going up tomorrow to tell the minister what I think of him and his spies!'

He had been talking rapidly, not measuring his words. But now he stopped, conscious of Jessie's sudden soberness.

'Don't talk like that, Donald. They are our people, and Norman is our leader. There is nothing evil in their talk, Donald. You know yourself how kind they are. But they feel, and I feel too, that Christy has cut herself off from them. It's sad, but even her parents feel that way, I think. It's sad, but it's true. They are not judging her, but they cannot accept her now.'

Donald was listening intently.

'Jessie,' he said at length. 'Where did you learn all this? Do girls wonder about such things? I'm sure when I was seventeen such thoughts never entered my head.'

'I've been thinking about Christy all day. It's all been so wasteful, and her life now is emptier than it was before. No husband, but just a fierce and ugly moment that she must regret.

'Love should be something different from that. When you said you were sorry for Christy and her baby, I could have wished that it was still alive. She would have had something to love, someone to love her.'

She did not ask the question; indeed, the question would have been too fantastic to ever enter her mind. And Donald was relieved, for he remembered his promise to Christy. And yet, if Jessie had asked him, he would have felt bound to tell her the truth.

Somewhere, Donald thought, something was wrong. He remembered Christy as he had seen her last night. She had not been thinking of the shame of the morning exposure. Perhaps, if indeed her baby had died, the shame would have beaten her down. But she had been fortified by a strength that came from something beyond religion, something that was, perhaps, the first religion of all.

But would he want to see Jessie in her place? Even the thought brought a coldness to his heart. Norman's way, indeed, was the only right way. It was rigid, but there was room in it for love, unselfishness and a life that was disciplined but none the less free.

He sighed. Jessie's eyes, so near his own, were fixed on him with an intensity that drained all expression from the rest of her face. Involuntarily his arm reached out and gathered her to him. They kissed; the booming of the surf seemed to blend with the thudding of their heartbeats, and the warm sun shone on them alone. Swift, disconnected images formed and dissolved before his closed eyes: the stern, omniscient face of the minister; Jessie's body, slim and smooth, against a background of blue sea and white foam; Christy Cameron at her dark and secret meeting with a man whose name he did not know.

His strength was melting in a delicious languor. Jessie lay soft and quiescent in his arms. But the fever passed. Their eyes opened and they smiled gravely at each other.

'Jessie, Jessie, what a day! Shall I come home with you?'

'No, Donald. Let us stay here just a few minutes, and then I must be off to prepare tea. And your mother will be expecting you, too.'

They kissed again, briefly, like lovers who will part to meet again soon. And still they sat there, ignoring the sun that slid so swiftly down the sky.

'And what are your plans, Donald? Are you going back to the forest, or will you stay in Waipu?'

'There's no place for me here, Jessie, the way I feel now.'

His eyes sparkled suddenly. 'Do you know what I'll do? Among all those at the bush camp there will surely be some talk of Christy. I'm going to discover who the man was. I'm certain he doesn't know what has happened, and wherever he is I'll find him and bring him back to her. She may say that she does not want to see him again, but that is only her pride speaking.'

He helped Jessie to her feet, his long arm rested lightly on her shoulders.

'I know now,' he said, 'that they should be together.'

* * *

Walking back along the beach alone, he found that there was an excitement in the decision that he had suddenly made. What kind of a man would Christy's lover be? And what strange coincidence had brought them together? Would he be ashamed, or sorry, or elated, when the news reached him? Would he come back to Christy?

The township was quiet now, for all the sportsmen and spectators had gone home. Tongues would still be wagging, no doubt, but the long day of concerted interrogation would have dulled their edge. Curiosity would have been almost satisfied, a store of knowledge gathered that would not lose its staleness until another New Year's Day.

But was he any better himself? Donald halted suddenly as this disturbing thought struck home. Was it curiosity that had made him decide to seek out Christy's lover? Was he honest with himself when he told Jessie that he wanted to see Christy happy, or was it an excuse for him to enjoy his restless desire for change? Did he feel that he could end that restlessness by going away from Waipu for such a flimsy reason? Was he himself running away from the realities of life, afraid to face it as it was?

Donald shook his head, and suddenly found he was staring at a cow that watched him with placid gaze from the security of a well-fenced paddock. That could be me, Donald thought. My horizon limited by a fence; food and shelter to be gained without effort or thought; a mind undisturbed by problems of any kind. But all he knew was that he could not stand still. He could not quietly marry Jessie McKay and make himself a home, knowing that Christy Cameron was living a half-life a few miles away. And he could not, now, throw off the disciplined code of Norman McLeod, any more than he could, at present, accept it.

And while these thoughts chased one another through his head and his feet carried him along the dusty road home, he felt his mind and body tingle with a strange excitement. Just to live was enough. What magic there was in the joy and sorrow of life! Wherever the road might lead, it certainly passed through some memorable country.

The air was cooler now, and his sunburnt back was hot against his shirt. His skin was dry and salty from the sea and air. He hoped that his mother would have water boiling on the fire for a bath in the familiar wooden tub. He was sure that she would.

* * *

Chapter Four

THE MINISTER HAD NOT DONE IT DELIBERATELY. DONALD HAD intended to reason with him, to argue Christy's case, to move from a lofty spiritual plane to the more humble one of practical life; to show, without fear or anger, that it was not kind to place a timid, unhappy girl in a position so brutally public. Donald should have known better.

The house itself was formidable, a large, square, unadorned building with no trees about it. Its windows glared at him fiercely, like the eyes of the minister himself. He followed the servant girl down a dark, central passage. She knocked at the door and, as Norman McLeod answered, Donald's courage melted away.

There was no doubt of it; Norman was old. He sat in a sturdy rocking chair by the window, a long dark robe wrapped about him, a book on his knee. There was genuine pleasure in his smile as he greeted Donald and gestured towards a chair.

'Donald McKinnon,' he said thoughtfully when his visitor was seated. 'I knew your grandfather. He was Donald too. That was at Ullapool, where he had gone to try the herring fishing. But he was a landsman first and last, and he soon went back to the Big Glen on the island of Skye, to his cattle and his sheep and his crops.

'They say, you know, that it was a man from the Big Glen who was taken out into the Minch by a fisherman friend and did not seem to be enjoying the experience greatly. His friend said, "Is the sea too rough for you?" He answered, "I don't mind the sea being rough, but could you not keep your boat in the valleys, instead of climbing all those mountains?"

'Up to the Summer Isles or down from Assynt to Rhu Rea and across to Hesinish on Lewis; Scalpay, Loch Maddy on the watery island of Uist; down past Ronay and Floddaymore and through the racing tides to Barra and the Western Ocean.

'No more than names to you, Donald, but your grandfather knew them, and he a landsman.

'And have you heard tell of the great whirlpool of Corrievrechan, and the close channels where the mad tides struggle and heave and jump like breakers on a cliff? But the water is deep, and the fishing best where the sea is roughest.

'You've never been a fisherman, Donald, and you've never seen Scotland. Where, I wonder, will your road take you?'

He went on and on, his voice following his thoughts. The names came magnificently from his tongue, names that carried with them the magic of the old speech that Donald had learned before he was taught English.

'A hard and a senseless life, and I gave it up. But it was better than starving in a croft, blessing the tacksman for the sticks of firing he allowed you to gather in the woods; better than yielding to the fat and drunken parish priest who forgot God in the dazzle of his own petty authority.

'And yet I sometimes think I should never have left Scotland.'

He is not rambling, Donald thought, although he does not expect me to answer. Norman McLeod's eyes were fixed on him, and they were alert and shrewd, not withdrawn in an old man's dream.

'I should have stayed in Scotland. A cold, harsh place was the Highlands, but the poverty, the injustice, the barren rocks on which they lived put strength into the people's hearts and bodies. They were the ones to fight the devil, whether he was dressed as a soft parish priest or appeared in his own raiment – tempting them with strong drink or bodily lust. They could be roused, and when they turned to God, the devil went out like a whipped cur.

'But this mild, unvarying climate is different.' He looked with no pleasure through the window at the serene blue sky and the green fields. 'It breeds a softness, a love of ease, an indifference to God and to anything that might disturb the search for comfort and wealth.

'No words of mine can stir the young men's hearts. Life is too easy. They are soft, and do not care.'

His great hands turned the book over and over on his knee.

' "In stripes, in imprisonments, in tumults, in labours, in watchings, in fastings… by honour and dishonour, by evil report and good report, as deceivers, and yet true." '

He paused, and looked at Donald with a measure of kindness in his eyes.

'I noted, Donald, how you left the church on Sunday morning. And I have thought about it since then. How strong are you, Donald? Has the softness entered your spirit, too? Do you not know that God must not be mocked? His demands are great, but so are the rewards. A heart that will not flinch from the blows of the unbelieving world; a body that will stand firm and a tongue that will blast the evil that waits for the unwary.'

He was speaking softly, with great feeling. This is the other Norman, Donald realised; not the ranting roarer who frightens his flock into submission, but the zealous teacher who can persuade you against your will. But is it against my will? he wondered, as he watched concentration settle on Norman McLeod's face, his audience almost forgotten.

'At Ullapool when I spoke to them of good and ill, they listened and gave up evil ways. But now, at times, I feel the devil shaking his fist in my face. There are people among us, Donald, who sympathise with the sinner. Donald: Where do you stand?'

Donald had spoken no more than a formal greeting since he had arrived. And, for what seemed to him a long time, he did not speak now. A host of fleeting impressions passed through his mind. They came chiefly from the seemingly idle talk that had preceded Norman McLeod's question, but they were coloured also by the tales he had been told, the conversations he had heard during the earlier years of his life.

The young McLeod, high-spirited and pugnacious, enjoying his defiance of those who oppressed and sought to mislead him and his friends, defying also the stormy Minch to gain food for his wife and children; the McLeod who, voyaging in an ill-found barque to America, forced the captain to sail on and not turn back when a great gale struck them; the McLeod who saw visions that were firmly based on his own sane practicality, and in his old age had led his people once more across the world to an unknown land.

This was the man who now asked him the question. And Donald, at this moment and under these circumstances, could give only one answer; the answer that any clansman would have made to his chief.

Norman McLeod was no longer an old, tired man. If there had been wars to fight, Donald would have followed him to the end. He was the rock on which they had leaned in the past, the strong right arm that gave vigour to their bodies.

'I am with you, Norman,' he said; but even as he spoke he felt a flicker of doubt that he resolutely rejected. Was he betraying himself and Christy, and all those who wanted to think and act for themselves? That could not be so. His loyalty lay with Norman McLeod and the laws he had set down for his people.

Yet it was in a subdued frame of mind that he walked through the township and down to Roddy's house.

'And how was Norman?' Roddy asked him, as he put an extra knife, fork and spoon on the table and urged him towards a chair.

'You can guess,' Donald answered ruefully. 'I've sworn allegiance to him, renounced all who would go against his will and become his slave for ever. And all in about five words.'

Roddy's beard wagged thoughtfully while his father, who today more than ever seemed a silent echo of his son, watched with remote but knowing eyes.

'Yes, that is how I thought it would be,' young Roddy continued. 'And you feel relieved that any more making of decisions has been taken from you, and elated that the road ahead is now firm and clear?

'You know, Donald, you are too romantic and a mite over-concerned with religion. You wouldn't believe that there could be good heathens, would you?

'Do you remember, father, the young man from Iceland who sailed after the herring with us for the best part of a season?'

'I do remember, Roddy, because indeed I told you the story. And the only time you sailed after herring was in your very good imagination.'

'Well,' said Roddy, ignoring the interruption, 'he was a very likeable fellow, but with one strange habit. When the nets fouled or he dropped something on his foot, he did not talk to God about it but to someone named Thor. He had a regular gallery of gods, including one by the name of Odin, who was very powerful, and Woden, and scores that I forget. And then there were the valkyries, strange birds that appeared during storm or wreck and took the souls of brave men. Rather like those seagulls out there, I imagine, but built on a larger scale.

'He almost converted us, but then he fell off the mast one day when talking to the valkyries, and that was the last we saw of him. A fine man, though, wasn't he, father; or don't you remember him?'

Old Roddy growled in his beard, and his eyes were almost malevolent as they rested on his son.

'If you were a few years younger, I would take a stick to your shoulders,' he said. 'You were always an undisciplined, irreverent lad, and

I take some of the blame for it. You should have been married, Roddy. A wife would have brought you down to proper size.'

'I'm married to the sea, father and – this will be a surprise to you, Donald boy – only yesterday I decided to return to her.'

He grinned in a friendly fashion at his father. 'We're one too many for a little house like this. Sometimes, indeed, I think we are too much alike. But in two week's time the MacGregors will have the *Fiona* ready for the sea. And then it's off to Auckland for me with a cargo of butter, firewood, home-knitted socks and kauri gum – all the wealth of Waipu!'

'Roddy,' Donald said, 'I thought you were here for the rest of your life.'

'And so did I. When I begin to feel like an old man, Donald, I'll come back and be happy. But now I can feel senility creeping up on me like a long night's sleep. And what is worse, there are times when I do not seem to mind. Old age is a grand thing, no doubt, but there's no need to welcome it before its due time.'

He tied his beard dexterously behind his back, out of harm's way, and gathered the dirty dishes into a bowl.

'She's a cutter, the *Fiona*,' he explained. 'Not that that will mean anything to a landsman like you, Donald. But she's a clean little craft; not as big as some I've sailed in, mind you, but at the thought of her I feel the years dropping away from my shoulders.' He cocked a speculative eye on Donald. 'And what's more, she can be handled easily enough by two men, only one of whom needs to be a good seaman.'

'Where will you go from Auckland?'

'That depends on several things. There is room for a fast-sailing craft in the north, from what I hear; and I don't think cargo will be lacking. But enough about that. Let us forget the sea and talk about the land.'

Roddy's face was so solemn that Donald knew he was laughing at him.

'You'll be away back to the forest, Donald. When? Tomorrow? The next day, with your axe newly sharpened, a bundle of woollen shirts to keep out the rain and keep in the sweat, and big boots to puddle through the mud?'

'Tomorrow I am going,' said Donald shortly. 'And now I must be on my way. The best of luck, Roddy, and I'll see you back here one day.'

'He'll be back, and sooner possibly than he thinks,' said old Roddy, looking at his son with no great favour. 'And now, Donald, I must say this to you.

'Young Roddy here is my son, and he has been a good son, too. But I have to warn you that he can twist a thing into any shape to suit himself.

'He is going away, and for that reason he would not wish anyone to resign himself to happiness in the place he is leaving. He sits here with me of an evening, talking of Noumea, the Solomon Islands, the Fijis, of birds of paradise, sea slugs and sandalwood to steal from the black heathens and sell to the yellow Chinese. He can't bear to see a man settled. He knows I cannot come with him; but what he doesn't know is that I wouldn't go for all the pearls in the Pacific.

'And now, I can see, he is turning on you. Don't listen to him, Donald. Keep at your woodcutting, and someday you will be able to buy land, and marry a good girl, and be happier than young Roddy here has ever been.

'Let him go on his way; let him find some other shiftless body to take tramping round the Pacific.'

The old man inflated his cheeks and puffed explosively at his son, who had been busy at the dishes through this long tirade. 'And yet,' he sighed, 'if only I were a few years younger!'

'Father, you are right. Don't listen to me, Donald. The heart of the universe; the riddle that no man can solve, but to which God, in any one of his manifestations, may be the answer; the glory of the world, the mystery of the stars, the grain of sand, the uncurling of a leaf: All this, Donald, you can wonder about as comfortably here in Waipu as in any other part of the world. Much better, indeed, because there is less to distract you.

'But don't worry too much, Donald. Think less, act more, and it is surprising how your problems solve themselves.'

The dishes were done and stacked neatly away. Young Roddy wiped the table down and, unhitching his beard again, combed it out with his fingers. He spoke to Donald with great affection and a perverse glimmer of amusement. 'Look after yourself, Donald. And now, goodbye!'

* * *

Chapter Five

DONALD'S AXE HAD, INDEED, BEEN NEWLY SHARPENED AND wrapped carefully in cloth to preserve its edge. He carried on his back a bag with heavy shirts and socks that his mother had knitted, as she did every year for her husband and sons, and on his feet were new boots that would be more comfortable when they had been greased a few times and worn through a winter's rains.

And now, with a strange, unaccustomed pang, he stood watching Jessie McKay as she walked back down the track up which she had accompanied him for the first mile of his journey. The sound of her voice was still fresh in his ears, a warm, lilting voice that accorded well with her candid eyes, her bright hair.

So small and lonely she looked; he wished that he would see her again soon.

Where the track curved out of sight she turned and waved to him. He waved again and even when she had disappeared, stood there thoughtfully as if she might return.

Was it natural that one should, at the same time, like and dislike a place so ardently? In Waipu was everything he loved, and everything he hated – although he doubted whether his feelings were as strong as that last word implied; whether, indeed, his love did not outweigh his irritation and dislike of the pettiness, the harshness that at times broke through the placid life of the settlement.

He would know better when he had fallen once again into the routine of the bush camp. Work was the solution. 'Don't think so much,' Roddy had told him. Good advice, no doubt, but could a man control his thoughts? Or should he empty his mind and let aching muscles bring him an animal-like peace? Was it right to do so? Was it not a denial of the intellect and conscience with which God endowed every man?

Right and wrong. The stern old religion, the soft message of goodwill; love that broke down barriers that were blessed by God, love that transmitted desire into something less selfish and possibly, to a young man, less exciting; restlessness that could be the craving for knowledge, or an attempt to escape from truth and reality.

Down there, in that quiet valley running down to the sea, under a sky swept clean by the relentless easterly wind, men and women faced this same problem. The land had been barely touched by man, and yet those struggling to master it could not evade these other issues. Nor would they want to do so. For they were men and women, born to take sides in the war between good and evil. And, Donald reflected, you could spend all your life trying to decide what those two words really implied.

Old Norman was sure he knew, in much the same way as a smith could tell the temper of metal struck by his hammer. Young Jessie certainly knew, by a divine instinct that seemed to pass from some mothers to their daughters. His friend Roddy had more than a glimpse of the truth, sufficient to make him feel confident that he could leave judgement in the lap of God. And Christy Cameron? There was a riddle that he would not dare to solve.

Through all his abstraction he had been watching for Jessie. And now he could see her where the track sidled round the last spur that jutted into the valley. He knew she could not see him, but nevertheless he waved again. She paused, turned momentarily to look back at the hills, then passed out of sight.

And now there was only one thing to do before he began the long climb to the top of the range. He looked at the sun, and then northward over the jumble of foothills among which lay O'Connor's shack. The day was past its peak. He would have to hurry.

Even that morning as he walked with Jessie he had wondered whether he should tell her what was in his mind. But he had promised Christy to keep her secret, and he was not inclined to break that promise. And even if Jessie had known the full story, she would surely have dismissed as a harebrained notion his plan to look at the baby in the hope that it might give some clue to the father. It was easy to say, when studying any child, 'How like, or unlike, his father, or mother, or grandfather, or cousin!' But he was inclined to agree that his plan was likely to fail; and behind his decision, he realised, was the desire to see how the child was faring in its lonely home.

* * *

O'Connor's place, crude walls of split timber, thatched roof, huge wooden chimney, lay pleasantly enough in a fold in the hills, near a spring that provided water for the man and his wife, fowls, and cattle that could pull a plough as well as give a mite of milk. Donald was welcomed heartily. They urged him to share their meal, and were full of questions about the valley below them, which they so rarely visited.

O'Connor was hoping that his crop of oats, sown in the ashes of the bracken on his hills, would be well worth the harvesting. His wife looked as if she worked too hard. Her fingers were restless and her eyes strained. She was hungry for gossip from the outside world.

Donald scanned the room in which they lived: the fire in the chimney; the rough table and chairs on a packed earth floor; the beds made up in the corner away from the door.

There had been no talk of a baby. There was no baby.

O'Connor walked back with him to the spring, still chattering about the small things that made up his life, obviously grateful for the casual visit. He filled two large pails and returned to the house while Donald went on his way.

And what to do now? he asked himself.

Christy must be mad. The ordeal had been too much for her mind. The baby had died, but in her poor, deluded imagination he still lived. Where had she been that night when Donald had met her? Wandering in the darkness, comforting herself with the thought that her son was safe, believing even that she had been to see him.

The pity of it made Donald's young face grin savagely. All the more reason for finding the man responsible. Who knows; he might be able to heal the wound he had inflicted.

Over the crest of the hills by the track that led between two peaks, clothed with silent green forest to their summits. Below him now the westering sun cast long shadows across a wilderness of trees; land that was generally low-lying but ridged and twisted with miniature ranges, intersected by tortuous inlets from the western harbour. In this land, the sea was never far away. Its tides would wash up muddy streams far from the smell of salt, but once down in the forest it was hard to remember the beaches, the clean air, the crying gulls of the coast.

This was, indeed, a different world. To him, the east side of the ranges always seemed to have the brightness of morning, a gaiety and warmth; the west was sombre as an autumn evening, often heavy with clouds, melancholy with the colours of the sunset. And yet he loved this other world, too.

A strange land, unmarked by man, forgotten by its creator; or perhaps left to work out its own troubled destiny. His eyes moved over the wrinkled landscape, seeking for the signs that he knew were there of man's activity. A faint wisp of smoke where slabs were burning at some bush camp. A scar on a distant hill-face, where logs had been sent shooting down to the stream. Try as he would, this was all he could see; and yet timber had been going out of the Wairoa for years.

Near him, a grove of kauri trees stood on the hillside, their grey-blue trunks superbly matched and free from vines or other parasites, rising fifty feet before they broke into jutting branches that gave them a ragged crown of green. Even they might fall some day, although it would be a tremendous task to drag those logs down to the water. Mentally, he went over the different stages that would be needed. On the steep grades, the squared logs could be let down without much effort, except to keep them from running away. Then three or four miles on a skidded road, carefully built to take advantage of the fall in their height; each log, for they were six feet through, jacked onto the catamaran – a sledge made from long saplings fastened together – and hauled out by bullock team. There was a driving creek about four miles away. But the water it normally carried would not be sufficient to take such timber down to the river. A dam would be needed to hold the late autumn rains or, if those failed, the deluge of winter. The logs would lie in the creek, piled grotesquely bank to bank, until the dam was tripped and a man-made flood sent them hurtling down toward the sea.

How much time and money would all that take? More than he – or any other man for that matter – was willing to spend at present. The bush contractors were still nibbling, like mice at a huge cheese, at the forest filling the land below him. Hundreds of years might pass before they would have to think of the kauri stands on the high ranges. The forest was inexhaustible.

How many millions of trees were there? Most of the land that he could see now lay under a screen of inferior growth, a green carpet that might be fifty feet deep. It was not too fanciful to see these trees as grass, with the colonnaded kauris rising above them. Sometimes magnificent single trees broke the surface, but more often they were in clumps that might cover several square miles. They were proud trees, leaving the soft, fertile land beside the rivers to the lesser pines that fought their way up through the tangle of vines and scrub. They drew up their own ranks,

The Reverend Norman McLeod in the mid-1860s. — Waipu Heritage Centre. "We've had our time, Roddy, and we've done what we can with it. And we can only hope that they will not forget us when we're gone."

A pioneering farm. The first cabin built, the milking shed and the fences up, and the memory of the forest still fresh in the ground.
— The Kauri Museum

The side scarfs are cut to give the big saw sufficient movement. A magnificent tree in its final hours. — Tudor Collins Collection; The Kauri Museum.

A log from the big Omahuta tree: a thousand feet of timber to each foot of log. The bushmen are using timberjacks to roll it. On the edge of the saw-face are three marks where wedges were driven in to keep the cut open and topple the tree once the saw's work was done. — The Kauri Museum.

6am. The cook blows his horn and the boys have fifteen minutes to get to the table for breakfast. — Northwood; The Kauri Museum.

After the evening meal, a game of cards. The general rule was lights out by 9pm. The old-time bushmen worked a 10-hour day. — Tudor Collins Collection; The Kauri Museum.

With the dam full and spilling over, the kauri upstream will be felled and rolled into the water, ready to pass through the gate when the dam is tripped. — Tudor Collins Collection; The Kauri Museum.

A large, squared log being moved by bullock team. Very wasteful of timber, squaring was done for ease of moving the logs through the bush and for shipping on sailing vessels. The logs could be close-packed and did not roll in rough weather. — The Kauri Museum.

A log of 33-foot girth sits on skids while the bullock team waits patiently. Timberjacks are at the ready to keep the log moving. Note the bushman coolly standing on his axe, its head driven deep into the end grain of the log. — The Kauri Museum.

On the upstream side of a kauri dam, the gates recently closed. — Tudor Collins Collection; The Kauri Museum.

The rush of water from a tripped dam descends on the heap of logs and will carry them downstream, eventually to the sea. — Tudor Collins Collection; The Kauri Museum.

marshalled on the higher ground, allowing no others to grow in their shade. Proud, powerful, and doomed.

He must learn all he could, Donald decided. Perhaps next year he could take up a contract himself. The line of advance for an ambitious bushman was well defined. The contractor undertook the main financial responsibility and allocated the work to his sub-contractors. They in turn hired men for felling the trees, for pitsawing the timber, for dam-building, for the humbler but necessary work of road-making. Men with trained bullock teams were still scarce, but that was the way of the future.

Donald walked easily down the track while he thought of his first year in the bush when he was eighteen; the rolling road, painfully cut by hand to a width of thirty feet, along which a fleet of logs was manoeuvred to the mill. Downhill, the great logs needed no urging, but it was a different matter on the flat. Parbuckling: The word was out of date now, but it brought back to his mind the weary hours when ropes were hitched to the trees standing by the road, led around the logs, and hauled on by a gang of men until the logs rolled slowly forward. That was all past now. The bullockteam, the timberjack, the catamaran had made skill as important as brawn, although both qualities were still necessary.

* * *

The pale moon threw black shadows across the clearing where the huts stood silent and dark, except for a lantern that glimmered in the storehouse. The cook, himself just back from the holiday, was morosely checking his supplies, but paused long enough to cut Donald a few slices of beef which he ate with cold potatoes, baked in their jackets.

The backlog was crumbling softly in the great chimney at the end of the hut where the men ate and slept. By its erratic light Donald made his way past the long table to his bunk. The air was warm, and he could hear the breathing of the men deep in sleep. Some others were back early too, he reflected. He took off his boots, spread his blankets; and suddenly this seemed the world he knew best. With a feeling of guilt, tempered by a strange relief, he realised that he had not thought of Christy Cameron since he had come over the hills from the O'Connors. Nor, indeed, had he thought of Jessie. He twisted into his blankets and tried to bring before his mind's eye the image of Jessie as he had seen her that morning, which now seemed ages away. But his mind and muscles seemed to relax together, and within seconds Donald, too, was asleep.

* * *

It was axes, timberjacks and the great crosscut saw next morning. A blast from the cook's horn, a splash in cold water, fingers run over whiskers that would itch before they became beards; a hasty breakfast, and time for no more than a few words with friends who had not been seen since the old year had passed.

Then orders from the subber, Jack Foster; a chunky Englishman with black, snapping eyes, an impatient lock of hair across his forehead, and a great desire to make his first big contract a success. He was young – younger even than Donald – but in the few years since he had left his ship in Auckland he had proved his ability to bring out the timber and to look after his men. Even the older ones stood quietly and listened with respect.

The pressure was on. Ten million feet of kauri to be taken down to the big booms in the river. Trees that had grown by precipitous bluffs, on rounded knolls far from the stream, deep in recesses hemmed in by a tangled screen of other forest. But ever since the previous winter the great trees had been toppling; each huge cylindrical trunk cut into two or three sections, squared down to the heart-wood with broad-headed axes. Dragged to the creek-bed by bullock teams or coaxed by timberjacks along awkward grades until they could be sent sliding down the chute to water.

Most of the timber was on its way, but this was the testing time for the subber's temper, as well as for his purse. The dam was ready, and its builders, members of a skilled and mysterious craft who knew as if by instinct the weight of wood needed to confine the water, had gone away to another job. Behind the dam, logs already choked the steady trickle of the stream; in front of it, many more lay waiting the thrust of the water that would come when the dam had been filled and tripped. None of the men, from Foster to the boy who greased the skids on which the timber rode, would be fully happy until he saw the dam gate open and the logs leaping downstream on the flood.

Foster spoke to Donald and his cousin Norman Finlayson.

'I've been taking a look at the driving creek further down,' he said, 'and I'm not over-satisfied with it. Bad corners where the sticks could jam. Standing trees that could splinter the heads off our logs. Start from the Half-mile Bend and work down to where the Red Creek comes in. A good two weeks work, I should say. Finish it in three days and I'll be proud of you.'

He grinned at them, while his eyes seemed to be sizing them up: two men who might easily have been brothers; above average height, big in bone with room for the flesh and muscle that would come in a few years' time. Dependable men, who used their brains as well as their bodies, who asked few questions and did not take kindly to fussy control.

'I've another book for you, little Donald,' he said, using the nickname that had clung since Donald first worked with his fellow-Scots in the bush. 'It's by Mr Thackeray, and all about Virginia, which isn't so far from Nova Scotia, is it?' He drawled the name in a cheerful parody and added: 'The cook will fix lunches. Take them with you each day. There's no need to camp out at night.'

And then he was away to where the bullock-drivers were yoking their soft-eyed, ponderous beasts for the day's work.

* * *

Axes, timberjacks and crosscut saw. It was work that pleased both Donald and Norman, although it lacked the excitement they still felt when the big kauri shivered and fell before them. The driving creek was in good enough condition, but Foster was not the man to leave anything to chance.

They worked steadily. The creek had been used in the previous winter, and had scoured out severely. But here and there the bushmen could still see signs of trouble that might bring more losses in the future. Carried on the crest of the flood, a log had jammed between two other trees and had been left by the falling waters.

'What shall we do?' said Donald. 'Fell the lower tree, screw it up out of the way and roll the log down to the stream?'

Norman was silent for a moment. 'No. We'll take the other tree and see if we can drop it uphill. It will be out of the way there; and we'll leave the other one standing. A good buffet from a kauri log will knock the daylights out of it, if the water comes high enough.'

Two axes, falling in turn on the scarf that widened on the tree's upper flank; great chips flying from the rain of blows; the crosscut saw singing and biting. Down it came. Timberjacks set firmly against the side of the derelict log. One holding, jammed between good timber and solid earth, the other screwing steadily until the log groaned and moved a few inches. The second jack spinning down while the first one took the weight; into another position, forcing the log away until it slid a few more feet. And so, men and jacks working together, the great squared log came to a clear space by the stream.

By now Donald was sweating, for the sun had crept down into the narrow valley, and there was no movement in the air. But it was good to be active again, to see before him a task that had to be done, to feel the sun burning his body while hands and brain worked together. There was time for talk, too, as they made their way steadily downstream. But it was idle talk that did not tax the mind.

Their homes were many miles apart, but their parents had not lost contact in the years since they had come from Nova Scotia in the same ship. There was an easiness in the relationship between the two men that communicated itself to their work.

They were late back to camp that night. The other men had eaten and were talking or playing cards outside the hut in the last of the daylight. Others, for whom the first day's work had been a penance, were already in bed as Donald and Norman took their plates to the long table. Half an hour after darkness came the camp was asleep.

* * *

On the twelfth day, the Red Creek and the end of the task were in sight. Here the stream narrowed between walls of volcanic rock, and there was not much they could do to improve it.

'A few charges of blasting powder would bring those banks down,' said Norman.

'And probably dam the stream forever,' Donald added. 'I think we'll leave it alone.'

And then, slipping and jumping through the shallow water in the gorge, Donald saw the big kauri.

It stood on a terrace above the steep bank of the Red Creek and, at first glance, it hung above them like a sudden precipice in the tangled bush. It was so broad that one did not readily realise that its face curved in a great circle. It was the biggest kauri he had ever seen.

Donald stood still; and the sun, though blazing down fiercely, seemed for a long moment to have lost its heat. It was indeed the kauri he had dreamed about that night in Waipu.

He looked at it steadily, but his eyes were inevitably drawn to Norman Finlayson, standing there beside him, cheerfully studying the tree, his face free from any foreboding. And why should he fear anything? Donald asked himself. A dream was nothing. And yet once again he heard the echoes of Jessie's voice in his ears, and saw a figure lying still on the ground.

He stared again at the monstrous kauri. The great branches, some of them four feet through, stood out from the trunk as he remembered them. And there was the tall rimu, instrument of death, just where the kauri might flick it as it fell.

'A good tree, Donald,' Norman said, 'although I've seen bigger. I wonder why they left it here? Too big for their saws, I imagine, although our ten-foot blade could handle it, with plenty of wedges and a two-foot scarf on each side.'

'No, Norman. Let us not think of touching it.'

Norman looked at Donald with surprise, for his voice had been unusually serious.

'I wasn't intending that we do it now,' he added, 'but what good timber is going to waste there! And besides, it is a danger to the drive. I'm sure Jack would want it taken down.'

The tree was immeasurably calm. To Donald with the nightmare still upon him, it seemed to hold a threat that was all the greater because of the deathly silence. But he followed Norman as he splashed through the stream and climbed on to the terrace.

It seemed impossible that any axe or saw could bring it down. Great slabs of flaking bark broke the smoothness of the trunk, themselves only minor blemishes on its perfect symmetry. Debris, the accumulation of centuries, lay at its foot, a massive pile six feet high.

Norman pointed to scars that showed high on the trunk.

'You see, they have been at it for the gum. If the tree is left, it will die soon in any case.'

'We'll leave it alone,' said Donald grimly and unsteadily. 'It – it's too big for us.'

Norman could not hide his puzzlement. 'We'll see what Foster says.' And they went back to finish their work.

* * *

Donald's mood had changed. For the rest of the day his tongue was silent, and his eyes were drawn to where the great green crown of the kauri showed above the lip of the gorge. It may have been only his fancy, but even the birds seemed more quiet, and the heat had an oppressive, leaden quality that he had not known before.

They worked hard, but for Norman, too, the pleasure had gone from their assignment. He had thought to know all Donald's moods, which could change so quickly but, in spite of that, were usually comprehensible. But he could not fathom his friend now.

They were walking back to camp, earlier than usual, when Jack Foster met them.

'A good job finished,' he said. 'I suppose you are sorry.'

'It's been a good job,' Norman agreed.

'Well, let's go back and have a look at it,' Foster replied. The two men dropped their timberjacks and followed him down the stream. Occasionally they stopped to discuss the effectiveness of some of the work, but on the whole Foster was satisfied.

Norman asked: 'Is the contract working out well?'

'Well enough,' Jack replied. 'I'll know better after the rain has come. But we have moved a few more logs this week. And we'll move more before the end of the month. Those who decided on an Auckland holiday should be back soon.' He grinned cheerfully. 'But they will be worth little for a few days.'

They followed him until, once again, they stood at the junction of the Red Creek. Jack Foster stretched out easily on the bank, and the others dropped beside him.

'That should serve well enough,' he said. 'The logs will run. But that big kauri... It's not strictly in my area, of course, but I would like to see it out of the road.' His eyes twinkled. 'Much safer down than up, I should think. What do you say?'

Donald knew that, when Foster spoke in this way, his mind was already made up. And perhaps, he thought, this tree had been his chief purpose in setting the men to clearing the driving creek. For no other valid reason could he have brought them this far from the camp.

He realised that Jack Foster, and Norman too, were waiting for him to speak. And suddenly he decided that he must tell them.

'I would not want that tree to come down,' he said. 'You see, I dreamed about it one night in Waipu.'

He could feel the blood rising in his face. In the broad light of day how fantastic it must sound, but he had to go on.

'I saw this tree. Every branch was the same, and I can remember every mark on the trunk; and that rimu was standing there, too. Norman and I were felling it. The tree came down, we moved back, and there should have been no danger. But it crashed into the top of the rimu, a big vine was flung towards us, and – one of us was struck to the ground.'

As he spoke he had seen it all happening again, and there was a tension in his voice that the others could not ignore. Foster spoke cheerfully.

'Anyway, Donald, you survived!'

'I'm not worrying about myself, Jack. I cannot be certain, but I think it was Norman. And I'm sure it was this tree. I knew it as soon as we came down here this morning.'

Jack Foster's active body was still relaxed on the bank. His eyes turned to Norman. 'Well, that's serious. What do you think of it, Norman?'

Norman hesitated, seemed as if he would pass it off as a joke, and then, seeing how disturbed Donald still was, he said slowly: 'Well, Jack, I don't know what to think. A dream is a dream, and there are some who say they can't be believed; but there are others with a gift of second sight, and I should not want to be dreamed about by any of them. I didn't know you had the gift, or the curse, Donald.'

Donald grew stubborn. 'And neither did I, Norman. But this is how it happened. I didn't enjoy the dream then, and I'm not liking it now. It is possible we could cut the tree down, and perhaps nothing would happen. But I would not be happy until it was all over.'

Norman sought for his next words, more concerned that he should not offend his friend than about anything else. 'And as far as that goes, what would happen if two other men had the job? Should we warn them? Would the same fate threaten them as Donald feels threatens us? Mind you, I am not afraid, Jack, and if you want it done, I'll go ahead. But thanks to Donald, here, I would be very careful.'

One broad hand flexed and unflexed on his knee. His face was worried, almost apologetic, as he looked at Donald again. It is as though he is sorry to be causing so much trouble, Donald thought; and he realised how well he liked this cousin of his whom he had known all his life.

Suddenly Norman's brown, good-humoured face became cheerful again. 'It is an interesting speculation, Donald. We are warned, and do not cut the tree down. Does it wait there, year after year, until some other innocent men decide to fell it? And does it injure them? Or does one of them also have a warning dream, and the tree stay there forever? But perhaps it is dangerous only to us, and anyone else – Jack here for example – could swing his axe at it without hurt.'

Jack Foster sat listening, amused at the deliberate, careful reasoning with which Norman was attempting to turn Donald's fears and forebodings into something less personal.

'You've said nothing yet, Jack. What do you think?'

'Well, I am only an Englishman, and as far as I'm concerned a dream usually means too much to eat the night before.' A hint of impatience showed on his face. 'Which reminds me that the cook will be sounding for dinner – and, in any case, this won't bring any logs down the river!'

He rose to his feet, adjusting the broad leather belt at his waist; an energetic man who was most happy when his mind and body were both active. His sturdy, thrusting figure moved off, and they had to hurry to catch up with him.

'There is one thing worrying me. This creek is too tidy. Not enough brush and light timber in it for my liking.'

'How do you mean, Jack?' Norman was frankly puzzled.

'It's a theory I mean to try out, Norman; and this might be the proper time and place. I will be interested in what you think.

'You must have noticed that the first drive in a creek is nearly always the best. Have you wondered why?'

His eyes took each man in turn.

'Here is what I think, anyway, and it may be right. What happens when you start operating a new driving creek? All the rubbish is cut and left for the water to take away when it takes the logs. There must be tons of it: trees that are not worth the milling but which would snag and foul the logs if they were left to stand; tough shrubs, vines, and even fern. And it is all piled deep in the stream.

'Trip the dam in a creek like this we're working now, and the water's gone down the valley as fast as a dog on a good scent, as violent as a tidal wave. It takes plenty of logs with it, but there are plenty left stranded, too.

'But think what it is like on the first drive in a creek. The water's out of the dam quickly enough, but soon it is moving more slowly. Why? Because it comes up against the mass of rubbish choking the watercourse, and is checked for a while. The water banks up behind the cut stuff as it tries to find a way through; and it does get away sooner or later, taking the debris with it. But the water held back is deep enough and slow-moving enough to float the logs quietly down.

'I cannot afford to have half my logs left stranded by a poor drive, Norman. Not this year. Though there are some not so far away who wouldn't mind seeing my contract break.

'When the dam is tripped we must get every log down to the harbour. I'm going to choke the stream-bed with rubbish down there by the Red Creek – make a floating dam to back the water up – and that's why I want the big kauri down. It's a menace left standing, and there should be four good logs in it. But those branches might be the most valuable part of the whole tree. Dumped into the stream they would break the force of the water better than anything else. Don't you agree, Norman? Donald?'

* * *

To Donald, even the river seemed to be awaiting his answer. A tiny trickle of water swirled past stones now baking in sun, stones that the fury of the same stream would soon be pounding toward the sea. And with them would go the logs that now lay like tranquil monsters waiting to be roused from their slumber.

He looked back down the stream. The talk had dimmed the vividness of the remembered nightmare. Norman had taken it calmly, and Jack was obviously humouring him; but there was no doubt his original intention still remained.

Had he let his imagination carry him away? It had happened in the past, and there was no reason why it should not happen again. It was not good to feel intensely, or at least to show others that you did.

He smiled sheepishly at Norman, who slapped him on the back cheerfully.

'You need worry no more, Jack,' Norman said, with a swift understanding of Donald's wavering mood. 'We'll do it. Any time you say.'

Foster did not answer. He was already moving away, his mind busy with another problem.

* * *

Chapter Six

DONALD HAD A RESTLESS NIGHT. HIS MIND AND BODY WERE OVER-tired. Sleep did not come readily, and when he did sleep, tortured images, nightmarish and fantastic, haunted his dreams. At intervals he lay awake, listening to the even breathing of Norman and the other men in nearby bunks; a reassuring sound in the long hut where flickering shadows cast by the fire still danced on the walls.

He would be glad when the accursed tree was down. If Jack agreed, they would do the job on the following day.

He let his mind drift away from the bush camp, back to Waipu and the sound of the fiddler playing on another summer night and the bright face of Jessie McKay as she danced opposite him.

How pleasant it all seemed, looking back, but he remembered that he had been happy to get away from it all. It seemed that true content was an elusive thing.

Christy Cameron. How was she faring? He had heard nothing about her in the men's talk that could give a clue to her secret. Nor had he thought much about her. The men had been reticent. Like him, they seemed now to be separated from the people at home, not only physically but by a wall of indifference. In the bush, their work and the talk of their companions filled most of the waking time.

Jessie McKay. He hoped she was happy, and was sure she would be. And Roddy McKenzie. He would be somewhere at sea now, or perhaps even in Auckland, with old Roddy moodily tending the garden and wishing that he was fifty years younger.

And Norman McLeod, who had warned him against easy living and soft thinking. Strangely enough, he found himself wishing that the old minister was near at hand so that he could confront him with his problem. There was nothing more sure than that Norman McLeod would resolve it for him, one way or another. Would he laugh at him for fearing a dream, and tell him to guard against the evils of superstition? Or did there linger in him a memory of the days when even God could speak through dreams?

And at that moment, with his body relaxed and his eyes closing in sleep, Donald saw once again the giddy plunge of the great kauri; and every overburdened nerve was tense again.

He decided that it was impossible to hope for sleep and settled down to endure the hours that must pass before dawn. And the next thing he knew was the blaring of the cook's horn, and the stirring of men in the half-light of the coming day.

Norman spoke to him as they made ready for breakfast: 'Did you sleep well? No more dreams and omens, Donald?'

'No. And what about yourself?'

'Never slept better in my life. In fact, Donald, there is nothing I would like to do better than drop that old kauri and leave the worry of it behind!'

'We'll see Jack about it,' Donald replied.

Foster was eating his breakfast. 'You'll need help,' he said doubtfully, 'and there's no one I can spare just now.' He glanced at the burning sky. 'No smell of rain yet, but I think we'll have some soon. This drought can't last much longer.

'We'll leave it for a while, and I'll think it over.'

Day followed day with a royal sun marching overhead and sinking down away from the parched land. Sometimes there were clouds, but they carried no rain and seemed to melt away in the calm air. On Sunday few of the men stirred far from camp. They closed the gate of the dam temporarily, backing up enough water for swimming. But most of the men lay on their bunks, talking idly or reading the battered camp books.

Then, on the Monday, Foster signalled to Donald and Norman. 'That tree: We can start this morning. Now it is for you to say. I can easily put some of the others on to it, so speak up.'

'We're going to do it, Jack. Don't worry,' said Norman.

'I'm not worrying. Sailor and Bill Cowan will help you.'

* * *

Less than an hour later with the other two men they were on their way down the stream. The moss was dying off the banks in sheltered places that normally remained moist enough through the fiercest summer. If there was not rain soon there would be fire; but the sky was still clear, with heat creeping up on them even at this hour.

With the decision made, Donald felt his anxiety dying. Norman had never seemed more cheerful or full of life. It was absurd to think that a tree could kill him.

They set down their axes, wedges and the long crosscut saw and studied the tree.

Now, to their trained eyes, it seemed to have a slight lean out of the perpendicular. The weight of its great crown was not evenly balanced. One huge branch reached downstream along the terrace.

'Should we send the Sailor here up to take that branch off, Norman?' said Donald.

'No. The weight lies in the direction that we want the tree to fall. Take it off, and the tree might sit on the stump when the cut is through. I do not like the idea of moving it off with wedges. Let the weight of the tree do its own work.'

Norman spat on his hands, and his axe, swung shoulder high, sank deep into the bark. Donald felt a pang. The tree would never be the same again, even if they went away now. This was the end of the thousand years or more during which it had drawn life from the soil, moulding the landscape to its own pattern. But there was excitement too in the thought, a challenge to skill and strength that keyed up the muscles and sharpened the senses. In the manner of its death, the tree would still be great.

* * *

In the shade of the huge branches, the air seemed different; cool and damp, as if the kauri was breathing. Norman's axe still hung in the bark, a symbol of destruction. They trimmed sturdy battens for driving into the tree, a platform from which they would be able to work. For the cut would be made about six feet above the ground.

A careful measuring with the eye to determine the size and shape of the scarf. Donald and Norman braced themselves on the platform, their nailed boots holding to the slippery wood, with the massive curve of the trunk between them; and then, in smooth flowing succession, the axes began to bite. After an hour the pile of chips, raw fragments of sapwood, was spreading around and below them, and the scarf had been cut a foot deep. But it was still no more than a minor blemish on the flank of the great tree, and its branches dreamed in the sun, regardless of what was happening below.

They watched critically while the Sailor and Bill Cowan continued the attack. The axes were biting deep, and the clean, straight-grained fillets of timber jumped sharply away from the tree with each blow, as if they had wings. The big scarf was taking shape. By noon it would be deep enough to shelter a man, the upper plane sloping into the heart of the tree, the lower plane smooth and flat. Then the side scarfs, child's play compared with this, and soon the long saw would be snarling through. A tremor in the tree's high crown, a subdued groaning as fibres stretched and snapped, would show that the end was coming.

Norman's face was eager and intent. Donald, the sweat drying under his woollen shirt, now felt no faint echo of his earlier fears. This was the work they knew and enjoyed. They lay back lazily, waiting to relieve the other men when they showed signs of flagging. And Donald, the dark cloud lifting from his mind, felt a sudden, surprising desire to talk.

'How strangely we are made, Norman,' he said. 'I didn't tell you all my dream, but what shocks me now is that, until I saw this tree growing here, you had taken second place in it. Jessie McKay was there, too, though why that should be I do not know. But when I awoke, it was her voice that I heard in my ears, and there was such fear and love and anguish in it that my heart seemed to stop beating. And all that day I thought about her, although why that should be I cannot imagine either. And then that night she was at the dance, as I felt sure she would be, and it was as if we knew everything in each other's hearts.

'I hope to marry her,' he added, 'if she will have me, which I think she will.'

'Donald!' said Norman with honest delight in his eyes. 'So it has happened at last! I see I should have been at Waipu this New Year, to help with the courting. And perhaps I could have found someone for myself. Little Jessie McKay – it's a long time since I saw her – all red hair and eyes and freckles. We are away from our people too long, Donald.'

There was a sadness in his voice, partly genuine, partly compounded of cheerful self-mockery, as he added: 'It's a lonely road I'll be treading when you leave me and the bush for Jessie and a comfortable, easy farm, Donald.'

He sighed, and gave Donald a sudden push that sent him tumbling down the bank; and in an instant they were scuffling in the fern, boots and arms flying as their bodies strained in battle. Bill and the Sailor stopped to watch and Norman twisted from Donald's grip to call at them: 'Come on down. It's time we did some work!'

And once again the axes were at their unending task.

* * *

Jack Foster arrived when the afternoon was half gone. The tree still stood motionless in the calm air; but the saw, a deadly destroyer, was working in towards its heart. It was a long, slow drag, two men at each end, the teeth of the saw at each stroke gouging out a strip of wood that broke into heavy sawdust.

The wedges were in, tapped ever deeper to keep the saw from sticking, but Foster soon noted that they were hardly necessary. There may have been no perceptible movement in the tree, but the weight of its branches, the deep frontal scarf and now the saw-cut had caused it to lean a fraction more in the direction in which it would ultimately fall.

The men had worked so long that they were no longer sweating. The sun that reddened their faces had dried up their skin, and there was a weariness about them as they straightened to hear what Jack Foster had to say.

'A good, tractable tree, it would seem,' he remarked. 'You should have her down soon. Are those side scarfs deep enough?'

Norman rubbed one hand along the bristly line of his jaw.

'We've given some thought to that, Jack, and they seem to be all right. We don't want them too deep, or she might twist.'

Foster nodded slowly, though his mind was still busy with the calculation of factors that did not concern the others. 'You are probably right. And now, who needs a rest? I'll give him a spell.'

The rasping of the saw began again, a sound not altogether unmusical for there was in it, too, the high, singing note of true, well-tempered steel. Jack relieved each man in turn; and now, as Donald stood aside and watched, it seemed that the final moment could not be far away. Tension mounted in him again. He looked anxiously at the towering column of the trunk, beyond it to the tall rimu, and then back to Norman. Just then Norman caught his eye and, while the saw blade swung through the tree away from him, called out: 'Time for me to take cover, Donald?'

Donald shook his head, and forced a smile through lips that had suddenly become even more dry. 'Not yet, Norman, but we'll be away out of it soon.'

The saw stopped and they all listened, interpreting the disjointed creakings, the spasmodic groans that came from its tortured heart – the voices of a tree in its death throes.

Jack Foster said: 'We'll try those heavy wedges now. Tap them gently, Sailor, and they should start her moving.'

'A few more cuts would be better, Jack,' said Norman; but Foster had already thrown the wedges up to the man on the platform.

'We'll leave her now,' Jack added. The noise from the tree was growing louder, and to Donald there seemed something frantic in the causeless motion that had come to some of the branches visible above their heads.

'Leave her, Sailor!' Foster spoke crisply, his face turned upward, one hand moving impatiently. 'She'll go now, so out of the way.'

He paused while the others walked, in no great haste, down the terrace, and Donald saw that he was worried. For this was now a contest between the tree's weight and the strength of the timber yet uncut. And the balance could be so delicate that one small tap on a wedge might send it tumbling.

Norman, deliberately casual, had sprawled on the bank while Donald and the others watched Foster walk toward them, glancing back as he came.

* * *

From where he was he could see the whole tree shiver as if caught by a sudden flurry of wind. There was a single report as sharp as a pistol shot, loud as a nearby clap of thunder, as fearful as a lightning flash. A rending and tearing as if a ship had driven on to a reef, and the whole great mass began to slide downward.

They yelled in triumph, and then it happened so quickly, so unexpectedly that all was over before Jack Foster's warning call had fully registered in Donald's mind.

The tree seemed to cry in agony. Suddenly the butt end of the falling log reared into the air and came plunging towards him like a giant battering ram. His brain was saying: The cut was not deep enough; the tree has split and thrown back.

His eyes had caught a glimpse of the white heart of the tree, suddenly and frighteningly revealed right up to the first branches. But his body had already acted. In one swift movement he had grabbed Norman by the hair and one arm, flung him down to the creek bed, and jumped after him.

Behind them, unseen, the butt of the log crashed to the ground. Silence that might never have been broken, so profound it was, so swift had the accident been in its onset.

Donald was on his feet again, scrambling up the bank after one quick glance to assure himself that Norman was safe. Sailor and Bill were there, bewildered but unhurt. And Jack Foster was running towards them crying: 'Where's Norman? Where's Norman?'

'Here – and in one piece. Though I am thinking that the tree would have treated me more tenderly than did Donald!'

The giant was prostrate now where it had once stood so proudly; a monster that brought even into its death something of its strength. They approached it cautiously, as they would a stricken animal that could still kill with one last flick of its paw.

The log had carved a deep furrow, as wide as a wagon track. Its crown was a welter of torn and broken branches, strewn over the stump where they had been working only a few minutes before.

Foster shook his head. 'A sad waste of timber,' he said; and looked up in surprise as Donald and Norman suddenly began to laugh as if they would never stop. 'You and your dreams, Donald! For God's sake don't do it again!'

Norman wiped his streaming eyes, and the laughter left his face.

'Yes, Donald. That dream. It misfired a little but it was a warning. Without your quickness, Donald, I would be dead.' He pointed towards the splintered underside of the log. 'That's where I was lying, tempting fate it would seem, and that is where you would be looking for me now!'

'And after that we'll boil up some tea,' said Foster. 'You look as if you could do with something stronger, Donald.'

Donald's mind was indeed in turmoil. He looked at the fallen tree. The nightmare should have gone with it. But he found himself thinking: We have beaten you once. Can we do it again?

He drank his tea, oblivious to Norman's high-spirited chatter born from his relief; his mind revolving endlessly on dreams and portents.

'Can anyone tell me this?' he said. 'Did my dream cause this accident? If I had not dreamed, would it still have happened?'

Sailor and Bill Cowan considered this startling question phlegmatically. For a moment it seemed as if they might speak, but they compromised by dipping deep into their mugs of tea.

'No,' said Foster firmly. 'I caused it by being too hasty. Five minutes more sawing, or even less, and she would have gone down as sweetly as you could want; and all this timber would not have been wasted. You must have made me anxious in spite of myself, Donald, and I was too impatient to prove you wrong.'

'Don't say any more, Jack,' Norman intervened, 'or he'll be deciding that he was responsible for your impatience, too.'

* * *

One of the men, coming back from his holiday, had shot a wild pig, a monstrous brute that the cook had nevertheless roasted until the flesh was almost tender. And the camp fed well that night.

Afterwards the men gathered round the fire in the great chimney, where socks and clothing were hung to dry, giving the hut a strangely domestic air. They sprawled on the floor, enjoying the warmth, for a chill wind from the west had sprung up in the dusk and the sunset had been a murky one.

Norman's high spirits had not deserted him. Dramatically, with poetic exaggeration, he had reconstructed the story of the afternoon. They were impressed, for even a near accident was rare enough in the bush. And Donald's part was not allowed to go unnoticed.

'It was amazing,' said Sailor. 'He must have been expecting something for, as soon as the tree threw back and before I could guess what was happening, he jumped onto Norman and tossed him out of the way as quick as an Irishman stealing a pig.'

'This second sight is a strange and marvellous thing,' Bill Cowan agreed, 'and you can't persuade me to believe otherwise, even though Donald here didn't get it quite right. You must be more observant, Donald, and next time make sure you remember all the facts proper.'

'But he has an excuse, Bill,' Norman interrupted. 'His mind was not properly on the job, for he dreamed about a girl, too, and the next day he met her!'

'That's enough now, Norman,' said Donald, and Norman could see that he meant it. But it was too late. While the others sat there grinning, the men from Waipu and its sister settlements quietly and remorselessly set to work on the hapless Donald.

'Now, let me think,' said Alex Fraser, his voice oozing goodwill and mock curiosity. 'Would it be Katie Campbell?'

A roar of laughter went up, for Katie, voluble and stout, would never see fifty again. She had defied custom by refusing to remain a widow after burying each of three successive husbands, and it was reported that she would not say no to another.

'Or could it be Mother Caffin over at the bay? They tell me she is building another room onto her accommodation house, and that she has the seeking look in her eye again.'

'No, Alex, it's not her either,' Donald replied. 'But I did hear she was inquiring very tenderly after you, especially when she found three bottles of whisky missing from the cupboard after you went off last year.'

The laughter was now on Alex for they all knew that when he was thirsty and short of money on holiday, nothing could stop him laying his hands on any available drink.

'One blessing, we haven't had to carry Alex out of the bush again yet,' added Norman.

'He'll walk next time, even if he has to crawl on his hands and knees,' growled another man.

Donald smiled as he remembered the tale that in less than a year had become something of a legend among the bushmen. Alex, his back wrenched in an accident, was placed in a litter and carried by his mates on the long road to a doctor. A blazing hot day, and after ten miles of rough going they were only half way there. They reached Murphy's store and, after consultation, set the litter down carefully and went in for refreshment, assuring the victim that they would not be long. The first drink was followed by a second, and the third was being poured when a voice from behind them said: 'What about me?' Alex Fraser's thirst had overcome his injuries. But he walked the rest of the way.

* * *

Donald was hoping the subject would change, and it did, though for a different reason from what he expected.

Stan Phelps, just in from a month at Auckland, had been dozing in a corner, and it was not until he spoke that Donald noticed the red eyes, the dishevelled clothing that showed his year's wages had been well and truly spent.

'You're talking of whisky, but none of you blue-nosed bastards would give any to a man who is dying of thirst!'

'I'm sorry, Stan, but we haven't any. You know it's not allowed in the camp.' One of the older men spoke. 'Anyway, you'll feel better in the morning.'

He was right. Stan Phelps would feel better in the morning. But that was not helping him tonight, with the liquor sweating out of him the hard way and the thought of his weeks in Auckland prickling in his mind. He sneered, and the deep lines of his face seemed in the dim light to be smudged in soot.

'You've got some stowed away, somewhere, along with your bibles and psalm books, you bible-banging, psalm-singing Nova Scotian...' He searched for a suitable word and, when he could not find it, spat towards the fire.

His desperate eyes challenged them, but there was no response. They knew Stan, and liked him; and in a day or two he would be quiet and cheerful again. But tonight was different. Their good humour, their indifference, maddened him.

'Good boys,' he sneered. 'Foster says no drink, so you leave it at home, along with your wives and your girls, until you creep down again to your church-going and your caleys – or whatever you call them in your whining talk.'

'That's enough, Stan. Go to bed.'

'It's not enough, and you can go to hell.' He stood up, a stocky, angry figure of a man, burned black with the sun and hairy of arm and chest. He wanted a fight, but even his belligerent eye could not bring any of these passive men to their feet. He could only try to hurt them with his tongue.

'Caleys and whining songs and howling pigs' bladders that you call music. I've seen it all, and the men trying to get themselves a girl in the corner.

'But thank God you're not all the same.' He grinned maliciously. 'Johnny Bain not back yet, is he? And I don't think he'll be coming back either. At least that wasn't his idea when I saw him last in the front room of Madame Rosay's house in Albert Street. Said he had had enough of you all and of Waipu, too. Cold-blooded lot, he said. Seems he had been chasing a girl and getting on well till one day she told him to go back to the bush. Just as sudden as that, it was. No reason except that she didn't want to see him again. A meek and mild one, too, he said, though he found her no different from most of the others.'

Alex Fraser rose slowly to his feet and walked across the front of the fire among silent and waiting men who were not sure just what they were waiting for.

He reached out with one hand and touched Stan Phelps on the shoulder.

'Come on Stan,' he spoke quietly. 'You've said enough, and we have heard enough. You'll be sorry about it in the morning.'

Phelps quivered under his hand, and his eyes did not move from Alex's face.

'I know how you feel, and if I had anything to help you I would gladly give it to you. You should have saved a bit of your own medicine for tonight – that's what I find best for myself!' And the other men grinned with him.

The fire seemed suddenly to go out of Stan Phelps. He was now no more than a tired, aging man, with slumped shoulders and dull eyes, who allowed himself to be led away from the fire to his bunk.

Alex sat talking to him for a while, and then came back to the rest. 'I don't suppose anyone would happen to have just one wee dram?' he asked plaintively. 'I've worked up a thirst that a pail of water wouldn't cure!'

* * *

So that's where Johnny Bain has gone, Donald thought, while the copy of Mr Thackeray's novel lay unregarded in his hands. Johnny had been with them for a few months until not long before Christmas. Young, dark, restless, never content to stay long in one place; a hard worker who would quickly lose his enthusiasm, turn moody and unpredictable and then disappear. Friendly, agreeable, good company when he wanted to be. But not a man to make close friends.

* * *

Nine o'clock, and the group about the fire began to break up. The wind, heard all evening in the trees, hit the roof of the hut with a sudden force and following hard on the gust came a scatter of rain. The door opened and Foster entered.

'It smells like rain out there, men. The cloud's down low and I think the storm's already broken up in the hills. We'll get some water in behind the dam tonight, I'm thinking.'

Jack Foster was tense, but cheerful. The climax to his year's work was approaching. All was in order: The moment could not come quickly enough.

'We'll have to watch the dam.' His eyes fastened on a lad who was starting his first term in the bush. 'Jimmy boy, get yourself a lantern and coat, and down you go. Sleep when you can, but don't let the water fill the dam without bringing a message to me. I'll be down to see how you're faring during the night. And men, be ready for a quick call!'

He was away again, but he had left in the hut something of his own excitement. The men went out to look at the dim sky, the ragged clouds that had closed down on the top of the forest. They shivered in the wind, drawing their coats close and arguing amiably about whether the rain would come. Late summer was the time when tropical storms could blow up with little warning, roaring across the mountains and leaving in their wake flooded streams and eroded hillsides.

'It would be Foster's luck to get a full dam and a good drive now, just when he wants it,' said one of the men. Foster, like many of those who leave as little as possible to chance, had already won a reputation for being lucky.

* * *

Donald and Norman found they could not settle to sleep. They walked down the track to the dam. The light of their lantern picked up the shadowy, slowly moving logs that the water had brought down to the pool.

Young Jimmy was busy. The gate of the dam had been closed earlier that day. As the water mounted it found weak spots between the heavy planks, spurting into the dying stream below. The boy was out on the top beam, his lantern jerking spasmodically as he dropped armfuls of matted undergrowth down the angled face of the dam. Drawn against the planking, it sealed off the leaks.

Their spiked boots grating on rock, they scrambled down to the empty riverbed. And now the dam loomed high above them, sloping away into caverns of darkness. They examined the gate; solid, horizontal planks firmly based behind the great vertical rafter, itself locked against the bottom sill and secured by rounds of wire rope to the top stringer. They could feel already the threat of the water banking up behind the timber. A sudden jerk at the trigger rope and the rafter would swing high above the rioting water. But the trigger was secure and the gate looked massive and immovable in the flickering light.

They climbed out along the broad top beam and sat with legs dangling. The stream was still quiet. If the storm was to hit hard, the rise would be rapid and the dam would fill like a bucket held under a tap. It was strange to think that above them in the clouds was the power that could send great logs spinning like twigs down to the harbour.

They sat in silence, with the moving, restless darkness of the storm out beyond the lantern's range, listening to the wind and the stream. After the long weeks of hot, dry summer it was good to feel the cool breath of air in motion.

'It's surely been an eventful day, Donald.'

'Yes, it has, Norman.'

And the night seemed to press closely upon him, bearing an indefinable threat.

'A long road we have covered, you and I,' Norman's soft, quiet voice went on. 'How strange it would have seemed, when we were boys playing on the headland at St Ann's, on far Cape Breton Island, if we had been given a vision of, perhaps, this night: Deep in a strange forest, waiting for the rain to bring a summer flood down a river. And yet, how little we have learned with all our travelling. Where do we come from; where do we go? We could have stayed all our lives at St Ann's and have been no less wise.

'There was a song our uncle Alex had from the Red Indians in Nova Scotia: The river of no return, down which every man went in his canoe. A river with long calm reaches where he could float lazily, with fierce rapids in which he could drown. And the country through which the river flowed he never saw again.

'The river of no return.' And as Norman's voice spoke them, the words had a music that roused Donald's blood and set a chill about his heart.

'Don't speak like that, Norman,' he said. For it was in his mind that he had heard men who were old, and ready to die, talk in the same way.

There was movement now in the stream behind the dam, a stirring of logs as they felt the gradual rise of the water.

Norman shook himself as if breaking from an uneasy dream.

'I must tell you, Donald, that I had not taken your forebodings very seriously; and yet this afternoon, if you had not been so ruthless in saving me, I am not sure what would have happened. A strange, listless feeling held me and I couldn't make up my mind whether I was tempting fate by lying there, or whether it might not be a little presumptuous to struggle against whatever is ordained. If God wanted me to live, the tree would fall elsewhere.

'I thought of Abram who was commanded to offer up his son as a sacrifice, and went on, hoping no doubt that God would give some sign. Do we not all, in one way or another, hope for some divine intervention in our lives? For if it comes, it means that we too are immortal, and need not be earthbound like trees or animals.'

Norman laughed. 'Abram heard a voice from heaven, but all I got was your hand in my hair!'

The clouds still moved above them, driven by a westerly wind that was moist in their faces, hinting of the sea. The trees, dark ghosts beyond the patch of light, seemed to lean together in the wind talking of unknown things. It was a time and a place for men to speak of their secret thoughts; and it was without surprise that Donald found himself putting into words his own inarticulate ponderings.

'For Norman McLeod, the hand of God can be seen in everything we have done: the journey our fathers made from Scotland to Nova Scotia; the search for another land to the south; our arrival. He would have none of your doubts, Norman. And he feels that it is God's purpose to make a community here that rejects the world.

'When I listened to him at the New Year, it all seemed simple and right. But still I am not sure. Cannot the world be enjoyed in moderation without endangering our souls? Cannot a man and a woman have pleasure in their love without feeling that they are destroying themselves? And is Christy Cameron to find hell on earth, as well as in the hereafter, because she had a fatherless child?'

Donald kicked with one booted heel at the beam on which they were sitting.

'Poor Christy. She told me, Norman, that the baby was still alive, and I decided to poke and pry and try to find out, from the talk of the men up here perhaps, who the father might be; and make him come back to her. But now I think she was just deluding herself, and that the baby did not live. And so I cannot act the part of God after all.

'Tell me, Norman: Where was Johnny Bain before he came to us last year?'

Norman thought for a moment. 'He was working with Bill McKenzie on the North River, pit-sawing timber for bridge-building. But just how long he stayed there I don't know.'

'He could be the one,' said Donald, 'but he'll be well out of reach now, even if I wanted to find him.'

Heavy raindrops splashed down, but stopped almost at once.

'It's time we were away to bed, Norman. Jack will get his drive, but not before dawn, I hope.'

Donald laid one arm across his friend's shoulders.

'I had a thought of leaving the bush. Getting married and taking up a farm, or chasing around the country after Christy's intended husband, or even going to sea with Roddy McKenzie. At New Year I might have done any of these things. I'm restless, Jessie tells me, because I can't make up my mind which way to go – backward, I suppose she means, with Norman McLeod, or else into the undisciplined, less rigid world that lies ahead. But now that we have survived the tree, I'll stay in the bush for as long as we work together. You're good for me, Norman. Hit me with your axe if I start dreaming, or thinking too much again.'

Young Jimmy, wrapped in his coat, called them a goodnight as they went along the track back to the camp. The warm smell of sleep filled the hut. But Norman lay awake for a long time, a strange uneasiness in his mind, while he listened to Donald's deep, regular breathing in the next bunk.

* * *

Chapter Seven

DONALD AWOKE TO A PALE DAWN, THE WIND BELLOWING OUTSIDE and rain like a great roll of drums. Jack Foster came in, but the men did not need any calling. Clothes thrown on quickly, a hot drink hastily served by the cook, who had discarded his usual Olympian calm.

'Why is it always raining when a drive starts?' a plaintive voice asked.

'It might be because it takes rain to fill the dam,' Norman said dryly.

Flaring light from the fire, dampness that seeped in everywhere, faces that in the uncertain light seemed withdrawn and introspective. Spiked boots carefully tied, long poles, axes and timberjacks in case there was a jam.

The rain was cold now and a small stream was running in the hollow track that has been dusty and dry for the months of summer. The men walked quietly, in a world of wind and storm.

Jack Foster was already at the dam when Donald and Norman arrived. He was restless, and the water ran unnoticed from his hair.

'I want four of you here,' he said. 'Alex, take the others down the creek and keep the logs moving when they come to you.'

The men sorted themselves out, Norman and Donald with the Sailor and Bill Cowan, as they had been the previous day. They stood with Jack Foster, their eyes on the water that was now lapping the dam within five feet of the top. A long, narrow lake, an impressive bulk of water, filled the straight reach of the stream. On it, moving slowly as they were caught in eddies of the current, were the kauri logs, floating high like empty ships.

Automatically, Donald counted them and estimated the timber and looked at the rain-filled sky and the grey, ragged clouds that blanketed the hills. There was still plenty of rain to come, he felt sure.

Jack Foster's voice broke into his slow, early-morning thoughts.

'We'll pass some of those logs through,' he said, and walked out along the dam.

* * *

They worked quickly. The top planks were unfastened from the gate and carried to the bank. Heavy work, with spiked boots biting into the rain-soaked timber. The water began to spill through the gap. They poled one log from where it was lying hard against the wing of the dam. The water caught it and carried it over the top, a giant's toy now in a giant's grip. Others followed, drifting downstream until they grounded to await the full power of the drive that would come when the gate was opened.

It was breathless work as the daylight gradually broke through and the water, in growing volume, roared over the spillway. The logs were moving more quickly now, in a strangely patterned, eccentric dance; grotesque monsters caught in a power greater than their own. Donald's eye kept going back to three great logs that had run together out in the lake. Sometimes they moved, but awkwardly across the flow of the stream. At any moment they might separate, but perversely they could lie together in a crude raft that would block the gate.

Norman was watching them too, his eyes keen in his lean, brown, rain-wet face. He signalled to Donald: 'Shall we push them down?'

Donald nodded. They walked off the dam and along the bank to where one log was precariously moored. Out along it, a leap on to the high crest of another and then a thrusting with their poles at the outer log. The log clung stubbornly. Norman jumped on to it. Both men pushed against each other with all their strength until the logs began to move apart and – slowly – down towards the dam.

'Come back with me here,' Donald called.

Norman looked around and shook his head. He pointed with the iron-shod pole at the wing of the dam. 'That's where I come ashore,' he called.

* * *

The logs on which the two men were riding seemed scarcely to move, but now the dam was near, and Donald ran down to one end of the log so that he could leap to safety when the full current caught it. Foster and the others were free for a moment, waiting on the walking plank for Donald and Norman to join them. Norman, his twenty-foot pike pole balanced in two hands, crouched like a Maori warrior ready for battle. His eye was calculating the distance and time before he should jump.

But suddenly the nose of the great log swung giddily, inexplicably, and the world was full of the thunder of water. The lake seemed to open beneath Donald's feet. The log on which Norman was riding stood crazily on end and buried itself in the cataract. While yet he was not sure that he himself would live, Donald knew not even a miracle could save Norman this time. For the dam had tripped itself. The drive was on and no man could stop it.

His own log, yards behind the other, was rocking madly, dipping down the steep wall of sliding water that burst in spray at the base of the dam. But he seized his only chance precisely and with a strange deliberation. The sharp-tipped pole in both hands, spiked boots holding firmly, he stabbed with all his power at the heavy planks on the wing of the dam. His mind was overwhelmed with sadness for Norman, but part of his brain was working with coolness and an objective efficiency. The point sank deep and, before the pole could be wrenched from his hands, he leapt high in the air and then slid down to the comparatively calm water against the face of the dam.

The others had come running. He looked up, and there was Foster leaning down and prodding towards him with a pole. He seized it, and was hauled to safety.

* * *

They stood aghast as the water thundered through. The spray rose in clouds, joining with the rain in a murky haze. And through it they could see the logs flung like small sticks, turning over and over, jarring, grinding, with the sound of wounded animals. And somewhere down there was Norman.

Donald shook himself, as if by doing so he might awaken and find it was no more than a dream.

'What can we do, Jack?' His brain was numb, and the skin tight around his lips.

Foster's face was grim. But was he not at the same time, in one small corner of his mind, counting the logs as they went through so swiftly, finding some grain of comfort in the fact that the drive was a success?

'Downstream quickly, Donald. He may have been thrown out on a bank. Stranger things have happened.'

They moved away off the dam, along the swollen river, forcing a way past trees and through bushes that dripped a cold dew. The roar of the water was in their ears, in their minds even, although less savage now. The logs rode swiftly and smoothly. The banks had been scoured, turning the stream a tawny brown, and there were few places where a body could rest.

For a while Donald plodded numbly after the other men, unable to think, his body cold and wet and a huge wave of depression suffocating him. Then the agony, the reality of it struck at him sharply. Norman. Dead. Drowned in the river. Echoes of the familiar voice sounded in his mind. No more. No more. No more. A lonely road I'll be following when you leave the bush. A laugh that was ironic, warm, friendly. The river of no return. The river of no return.

And as the cold fastened more firmly on his body, his mind came suddenly alive. Pushing past the other men, he ran. Stumbling, slipping on greasy tree roots and banks of heavy clay but recovering and stubbornly forcing his pace. Drowned Norman. Dead Norman.

He did not look at the river now, although its horrifying, animal breathing filled his ears. He lunged through a tangle of vines, slid down a steep bank into the shallows. Through the gorge, picking his way along a rocky face just above the swirling water. Down to the Red Creek, deeper now but calm enough. And up onto the terrace.

The water had been there, the first wild surge from the opened dam, but it had gone now, leaving a mass of debris cast up against the great kauri log which the river had broken against but had been unable to move. In the sombre, rain-darkened morning light it was like a dismembered giant; something killed from fear or hatred rather than because it could be profitably used. And there, lying in a water-washed swirl of silt, was Norman.

He lay partly on one side, his legs curled up as if he was sleeping. There was river dirt in his young beard, a dark red bruise at the hairline beside his ear. One boot had been torn off completely, but the leg was not even scratched.

* * *

Donald bent down and touched one hand. There was pathos in the long, strong, lifeless fingers, in the minute cracks along the palm, the calluses caused by work, now softened by the water.

But death had made so great a change that Donald found himself looking with a curiosity, a sense of unreality that dulled the edge of pain and bereavement. This was not Norman. Alone for the first time in the presence of death, he could not accept it as a final dissolution. Norman had gone away.

He lifted the body carefully from its muddy bed and laid it down on the grass higher up the terrace. The rain fell steadily on Norman's upturned face. I must take it away from here, Donald thought. He turned one last look of hatred and of fear on the giant kauri that, in his mind, would always be a part of Norman's death. Then he lifted the body over one shoulder and began to walk back up the stream.

And that was how the others met him.

* * *

Chapter Eight

ANNE MCKINNON WALKED DOWN THE VALLEY A LITTLE WAY WITH Jessie, and then stood watching the girl until she was out of sight. After the storm, summer had come back with a new strength. Heavy clouds, grey and white in the sunshine, rolled over the eastern horizon. But there was a weariness about the year now. The grass sparkled with no springtime zest. Summer had killed its earlier vigour; nor would it revive until autumn, and winter, too, had gone. She half decided to call in on the Camerons, but then, thinking of the work that needed doing, turned back towards her house.

Jessie was cheerful as she went quickly down the valley. There had been no real reason for visiting the McKinnons, but she had jumped at the slender excuse her mother offered. She had sat talking for an hour or two before helping Donald's mother prepare lunch. Idle, pleasant talk, with Donald's name coming up only occasionally. There had been no news from the forest, but her heart had been warmed by the slight contact.

Donald would be back sometime, she knew; and her thoughts were mildly rebellious while they still accepted the situation that made it necessary for young men to go so far away for such long periods. She wondered if Donald would ever be able to leave the bush. Her mind centred on the thought of a little farm, much like that of the McKinnons which she had just left, where it would be possible for husband and wife to be together most of the time.

The track she followed was joined by another, and down it she saw a figure approaching. She recognised him with a jolt of surprise: The talkative Danny McMillan. Why was he back from the bush? He too, she knew, was working with Jack Foster.

Danny was strangely silent. 'Jessie,' he said formally, and shook hands.

'What has brought you out, Danny?' she asked.

'A message for the minister,' he said. 'There's been a drowning. Norman Finlayson. They are wanting the minister to speak over him.'

Jessie had suddenly gone pale to the lips. She couldn't speak, and Danny continued stolidly.

'He went through the dam. A branch caught the tripper rope and tripped it. Donald McKinnon found him on the bank down the stream. Scarcely a mark on him, but the water killed him as surely as the logs would have done. And Donald nearly went too. A miracle that he wasn't carried through the dam.'

'Poor, poor Norman. And Donald – is he safe and well?'

'Yes, Jessie. But feeling it badly. It's a shock losing your best friend like that. And he and Norman were very close.

'Jessie, I would walk down with you, but there's no time to waste. We took Norman home, and they want the burying done tomorrow, and it's a long road for the old minister. He'll have to ride his horse.'

'Thank you, Danny. I'll go back and tell Donald's mother.'

Danny went striding off, his immobile face breaking into a brief smile. Jessie turned back the way she had come. Thank God Donald was safe; but Norman's mother – how bitter it would be for her!

Down the track someone else was approaching her; a woman. Christy Cameron.

Christy's eyes were lowered, and she would have passed without seeing or acknowledging Jessie. But Jessie spoke, and she looked up.

'Hello, Christy.'

Her face held neither pleasure nor distaste at this breaking into her thoughts.

'I have a message that you should pass on to your mother. There's been an accident in the bush. Norman Finlayson drowned, and his funeral is tomorrow. They have just come for the minister.'

'How did it happen?' Christy asked.

Jessie told her, and she smiled strangely. 'So Donald is safe. I'm glad of that. He is a good man.'

'And so was Norman,' said Jessie passionately.

'Was he?' Christy replied casually. 'I did not know him well.'

Jessie found that she was speaking quickly: 'Christy, you must be less… Less harsh. We know that you have been unhappy, but that is all past now. There are many good, honourable men, and you must not allow yourself to become bitter. People will forget, if only you let them.'

Christy, she noticed, was smiling, her mouth curved as if in triumph. And her eyes were no longer humble.

'Cannot you see, Jessie, that I'm not interested? They begin as children, and then one can love them. But they change. Pride, greed, envy, desire – all these things twist their minds. And then when they are old they are just the empty shells of what life made them; talking endlessly of what they have done or what they wished to do. It is as well for your Norman that he died young, before life ruined him.'

'Christy, you must be mad!' But there was no trace of madness in Christy's face; nor did she raise her voice from its soft, persuasive tone.

'I don't think so, Jessie. And even Donald: I put him to the test at the New Year. He kept my confidence, I think, but he was prying about with a curiosity that he should not have tried to satisfy.'

'What do you mean, Christy?'

'Nothing that is not still between Donald and myself.'

'But is it important?'

Christy looked at her with level, intelligent eyes. And suddenly she smiled, with a tenderness that was strange and unexpected.

'You love him, Jessie. I wish you well. Ask him if you like, but I don't think he will tell you. And it is not important to you, in any case.

'Does he love you, Jessie?'

Jessie did not answer. She felt anger, pity, fear, and above all, the desire to be away from Christy. Perhaps then she would be able to think without feeling that all her thoughts were being explored.

'Goodbye, Christy,' she said desperately. Christy stood watching her. 'I don't know what is ailing you, but I pray God that He gives you happiness and peace.'

There was courage, and an appealing dignity in her attitude as she added: 'Yes, Christy, I do love Donald. And I will always trust him because I know he could not deceive me.'

She walked away, but Christy stood still for several minutes, not watching her, nor watching anything, her eyes remote and a slight smile on her lips.

* * *

Chapter Nine

THE FIREPLACE WAS EMPTY, BUT IT WAS STILL THE CENTRE OF THE great room; and the chairs were grouped as if at any moment the warmth of burning wood might come from the hearth. Donald sat with his father and brothers. In the dim light of dusk he watched Norman's father greet the slow-moving men who came to the door, shake hands with rarely a word, and then find themselves a place to sit.

Norman, are you too watching from some strange, high heaven, with sadness in your mind that these should mourn? Is the truth something that we can bear? Does what we have been thinking matter at all in the face of the mystery that is creation – and death?

The minister led them to the grave-side on the hill not far from the house. Old, weary, immaculate with his white stock and formal black coat, his striped trousers and heavy boots. For Donald, there was no feeling of pain or sorrow. In his mind's eye he held the picture of Norman working, talking, laughing. The raw wood of the coffin lay beside the raw upturned earth. This was formality; the other was reality.

But now the voices were joining in a psalm. The minister standing motionless, his caverned eyes closed, while the deep voices of the men and the clear, sweet music of women's voices blended in a harmony that rose and fell and then rang to a triumphant ending. They are not lamenting Norman's death, Donald was thinking. They are saying farewell to one who has gone away.

The service ended. Norman McLeod raised one arm and held them at the grave-side. There were lines of fatigue on his face, but he was serene. A waxen skin, with the strong bones behind it, and all his spirit in his eyes.

'You are my people,' he said in a soft voice that carried through the quiet air. 'Do not think that this young man has been lost. And do not grieve for him.' His face changed in some indefinable way. 'He was young, and he has gone from us. Where? To a heaven whose residents know no care, who live pampered lives under the benevolent eye of God? I do not think so. In God's house there are many mansions; and we who have fought and suffered and sometimes won, but who have never considered softness and luxury the crown to our ambitions, would never be happy if that was all God had to offer us.

'But think of this. Who knows what glorious work may not be awaiting those of God's servants who have proved their strength and courage? In what far corner of limitless space may there not be other battles against evil, sloth and arrogance? Would not that be the fate we crave, to fight God's enemies wherever they may be found, with whatever arms God gives us? And who could do His work better than the young and the old and the valiant who have served Him in their earthly lives? That is what I think, and that is what we should hope.'

* * *

In the room now they were talking about the minister, about the young man who would never go away again, looking with keen, solicitous eyes at the father who walked mechanically from one group to another. They were themselves restless, for constraint was not natural to them. Donald stood up and joined Alex Fraser and two other men by the window.

The door opened, and a woman brought in two lighted lamps. Through the door came the busy hum of women's voices from the kitchen. The tension eased as food was carried in by girls who smiled shyly and quickly disappeared.

'You will all have something to drink,' said Norman's father courteously. Bottles and small glasses circulated.

Alex Fraser took a slow swallow. 'It's been thirsty work,' he remarked cheerfully, and then lapsed into an uncomfortable silence.

Big, bearded Hector Macdonald spoke: 'That was an inspiring message the minister gave us,' he said. 'It's all a mystery, and maybe he can see deeper than most. But I'm not so sure that is what I want. A little comfort in heaven would be very pleasant, and the prospect of more struggle, battles with fiends and devils in some far corner of space, does not excite me at all.'

'Indeed, Hector, that is so. But perhaps the minister is wise. It is best not to expect too much, even from heaven, and it may not be as bad as he paints it.' Alex sipped appreciatively at his whisky. 'And doubtless that nectar they are always talking about will be almost as good as this.'

'You know,' said Hector, 'men can go in strange ways. A flick of God's little finger, and someone is called away. A shake of His head, and death draws back again. There's no rhyme or reason to it. I sometimes think that, because there are no wild animals in this land, God is hard put to find ways of doing it. But fire, forest and water are still our enemies.'

'Especially water,' said Alex. He carefully refilled his glass and offered the bottle to the others.

A piper had started to make music in the far corner of the room, pacing slowly up and down as he played. There was an ineffable sadness in the lament, but there was also the spirit, the vivacity, the strength of youth that could never perish but was always renewed.

'That is more like it,' said Alex comfortably. 'If only Norman could hear that, he would be proud. May God have a warm place near His heart for the good lad. We'll miss him.'

They stood silent again, their minds on mortality, the inexplicable workings of fate.

'And talking of wild animals,' Hector resumed, 'not even the most ferocious of them could always be sure of their victims. Remember the bears in the old country? We had some merry sport hunting them out at times.

'You all know, of course, the story of big McLeod, whose children are still called "Bear" in honour of his exploit?' He didn't wait for an answer.

'Winter was ending in the Middle River and, with the snow gone, big McLeod went out to his farm. He took with him his long iron crowbar for digging out boulders and rolling the logs away, for you see he was minded to do a bit of ploughing. And he took with him too his young heifer, and every now and again he would pick her handfuls of wild turnips and anything else that would tempt her appetite.

'The fine spring day went on, and the sun became hot, and at noon he led his heifer away to the shelter of the woods, where she could rest and, perhaps, sleep. He himself had his bite of lunch, and then began to work again.

'Now you must know that, during the winter, the great brown bears seek out for themselves a place to rest; nor do they stir again until the warmth of the returning sun awakens them. And then they go foraging fiercely, for their hunger is great. But as big McLeod worked, the bears were far from his mind. He heaped up the big red boulders, and gathered together the timber that would hinder his plough, and he listened to the bell jingling on his heifer's neck.

'Then suddenly he thought: she should be resting. What can be disturbing her? Is it perhaps flies, or other insects? So he took up his long iron bar and went to see.

'Now it seems that, if a bear encounters another animal that is big and strong, it will kill with one great sweep of its paw. But if the animal is young and tender, the bear will not maul it, but will carefully seek for the nerve at the back of its neck and paralyse it. And that is what big McLeod found when he reached the shade of the trees. His little heifer looked up sadly and hopelessly into the face of the biggest bear he had ever seen.

'McLeod let out a roar, and the bear jumped to his hind legs and stood up, fully nine feet high. He backed quickly against a tree and looked at McLeod who, his heart full of anger, looked back. McLeod grasped the crowbar firmly and began to circle slowly around the tree, and the bear backed around it too. Round and round they went, but with each circuit of the tree, McLeod gradually came nearer, until he measured the distance and knew he was close enough. Before the bear could guess what was happening, he swung the great iron bar hard against the side of its head.

'The one blow was enough,' Hector said emphatically, 'and the bear did not move again until they cut it up for steaks and a skin that kept the children warm for many a winter's night.

'A great man was the Bear, and there were many more like him in those days. A powerful man with a broad axe; a boat-builder, fisherman and farmer.'

* * *

They all thought about the Bear for a while, and around them the music surged and sang: its undertone of sadness; its high notes of splendour and courage.

'I did not meet the Bear, but the story I heard was different,' said Alex. He looked around at those who were listening. 'And I think I can tell it in this company.

'It was springtime, and young McLeod and a companion had gone for a ramble in the hills, seeking no doubt some blueberries for a pie. They came across a little cave, which they entered, to find that it held a pair of bear cubs. "McLeod," said the other, "you watch at the cave entrance while I pick the little ones up. They will make good pets to take home with us." So McLeod went outside the cave.

'Suddenly he saw something stirring down the valley, and he moved away a few paces to watch. And when he looked back the blood froze in his veins for there, completely blocking the entrance to the cave, were the hindquarters of a huge bear.'

Alex paused. 'What could he do? Desperate measures were called for. He did not give the bear time to enter any further. With a tremendous leap he landed behind her, seized her tail firmly in both hands, planted one foot hard against each side of the cave, and held on grimly and silently.

'A plaintive voice drifted out to him: "Are you there, McLeod? Are you there? Tell me, McLeod, what's darkening the hole? Is the bear coming?"

'McLeod tightened his grip, and found breath to answer: "She surely will be, and quickly too, if her bluidy tail breaks before I can drag her out!"

'And ever since then,' Alex added, 'if you chance to meet one of the Bear's kin and call out, "What's darkening the hole?", you will have a quick answer.'

Alex laughed with the others, then coughed self-consciously and stood deep in thought. Old Hector shook his head. 'There's something wrong with that story, and I'm not believing it. You don't gather blueberries in the spring.'

Donald went over to his father. The piper was standing still now, tapping with one foot to a steadily quickening rhythm, his ruddy cheeks swelling and deflating, his eyes staring with honest effort. Men could still laugh and enjoy one another's society, as was only right and proper. Norman's father came up and stood beside his friends and cousins, the McKinnons.

'I feel that I should have saved him,' Donald said. 'The thought has been eating me ever since we found him. I should never have let him do it, knowing the danger.'

Then, for the first time, he was able to speak freely; and as he told of his dream, and of how the kauri tree nearly trapped them, of the foreboding that had oppressed his mind, the story no longer seemed strange or fantastic. This was the way things happened in the world, with mystery colouring the most commonplace events.

Norman's father listened, nodding his head slowly at intervals. He reached out and shook Donald's hand; a sober man, bruised but not defeated.

'Do not let your heart be vexed, Donald. This was the way he had to go. And now he has set foot to that strange road, there is nothing we can do to bring him back. It would be wrong to wish for it.

'Norman was a fortunate man,' the father said slowly. He looked around the well-filled room. 'He had many good friends, and no enemies.'

They stood thoughtfully for a while, until the elder McKinnon spoke to his son. 'Come home for a bit. Your mother would like to see you, I am sure. Most of Foster's work should be finished, I suppose.'

'Thank you, father. I've brought my gear out with me. Jack Foster had a talk with me and knows I'll not be back with him again. It was a good life, but I couldn't enjoy it now any more.'

* * *

Chapter Ten

WHENEVER HE HAD COME HOME BEFORE, THERE HAD ALWAYS BEEN the thought that, in a few days, he would be going back again. Now it was different.

What should he do? The farm needed looking after. From what he had been told, there was a good market in Auckland for beef and mutton – as much as the farmers could produce. The war with the Maoris might be a slow, spasmodic affair, but the hoards of soldiers still required feeding, and little food could now be raised in the troubled area south of Auckland. It was to the north that they had to look for their rations.

The idea appealed to him – at first. He worked hard, clearing light scrub from the low hills near the house. Too late for a good burn that year; and perhaps that was why he found it hard to raise any continued enthusiasm for the task.

On his second evening home he had gone down to see Jessie. Her small brother was demanding much attention, and Jessie talked to him over a mass of freshly washed clothes that were being folded and ironed. It was good to see her again. But the magic of the New Year meeting had waned. He felt vaguely depressed by the thought that this was his life for the next few years: work on the farm; talks with Jessie and his other friends; marriage; more work.

He went to church, but even Norman McLeod was staid and undramatic that day. The faces of his congregation were placid and undisturbed. Donald could raise no flicker of the excitement that had stirred him when he had heard the old man's words before. Religion: Did it matter very much whether McLeod did see destruction threatening the people if they ignored the old ways? And could the doubts in his own mind be of any importance? The formidable simplicity of what McLeod preached; the softer, kinder way of life that was, perhaps, more closely attuned to Christ's teachings and example. As he sat in church that sleepy Sunday, the choice did not seem of great urgency.

Christy Cameron did not appear at church. He had not seen her, but it seemed that she had now been accepted as part of the community – one of the crosses that the people were willing to bear, although they preferred not to discuss it. According to Donald's mother, she had lived quietly on the farm, keeping well out of her father's way at meal-times and going early to her own room at night. For he too did not like to be reminded more than was necessary of his daughter's error, or of her actual existence.

He wished to see Christy, and yet he hoped that the meeting would not take place too soon. In his mind, he realised, her misfortune was linked with the other tragedy that was still too close to be thought about. He remembered his last conversation with Norman Finlayson, the strangely brooding atmosphere of the forest as they sat on the dam that night. To forget that, he had to forget Christy, whom they had talked about together.

And yet, as he worked on his solitary tasks about the farm, his mind went back to the girl. Could the baby still be alive? Had she misled him deliberately when she said the O'Connors were caring for it? Who could really tell what was going on in her secret mind?

* * *

On the second Sunday Jessie invited him to have dinner at her home after church. She was preoccupied as they walked to the house, and gave only short answers to his attempts at conversation.

Finally he said: 'What is it, Jessie?'

Her eyes were troubled, and he could see that she was finding it difficult to frame the words.

'Donald, have you seen Christy Cameron since you came back?'

'No, Jessie. I've been wondering about her. Remember, I thought at one time I would try to find the man? I have an idea who he might be; but if I am right, I think she would be better without him. In any case, I do not believe the baby is alive; and the sooner it is all forgotten, the happier for everyone.'

'The baby?' said Jessie. 'But surely there was never any chance that it was still alive? What have you been hearing, Donald?'

'It was a confidence that I felt I could not break. For some reason, Christy told me that her baby was with the O'Connors. But when I called there, on my way back to the bush, I felt sure they were caring for no child; their own or Christy's. It was a dream, I felt; something that she had made herself believe in to soften the shock.'

Jessie's face brightened, and she told Donald of her meeting with Christy.

'Could she have told you half the truth?' Jessie asked. 'I have been trying to fathom the expression on her face when she was speaking to me. She seemed to be gloating over something – unless, of course, she has deluded herself. But if the baby is alive and is being looked after by someone else, where could it be?'

'Ask old Mother McGregor the midwife. If anyone knows, she will; although she too might keep it to herself.'

They walked on slowly. Then Jessie spoke excitedly: 'What a slow one I am! That might be the answer! She was down two weeks ago to see how young Johnny was faring, and I heard her tell mother that she was caring for a baby left as an orphan. Not one of our people, she said. And then she spoke of a party of kauri gum diggers who had brought the baby to her.

'What a sly old one she is, if that is true! And yet, can you blame her, if Christy had begged her to do it?'

'You may be right. In any case, it seems that Christy can look after herself very well.'

* * *

Jessie's father sat in his comfortable chair, picked up his pipe and polished it on the palm of one big hand. Then, remembering it was Sunday, he put it down regretfully. 'And how does a farmer's life suit you, Donald?' he asked.

'It has one virtue,' Donald replied. 'I look forward to doing nothing on Sunday more than I ever did in the bush. There's something back-breaking and heart-humbling about farming that I had not fully appreciated.'

McKay nodded his head slowly. 'You must not let it worry you too much,' he said. He lowered his voice. 'Would you be interested in this? They say the fish are running in the bay, and it is time we laid in supplies for the winter. I know we should not discuss this today, but I might not see you tomorrow and I should be grateful if you would come with us on Tuesday. Say no more now; just yes or no.'

Donald agreed readily.

'It will be an early start. We'll be meeting at the boatshed below our house here. Don't worry about bait or food – your task will be to catch the fish!'

After the quiet Sunday afternoon, Donald found that he was more relaxed and content than he had been for a long time. As he walked home, his thoughts went back over the events of the last few months. It was strange how, in his mind, Christy Cameron, Norman McLeod, Jessie and Norman Finlayson were linked. Was it purely by chance that his quiet life had been so suddenly disrupted? And in so many different ways. It began, he could see, that morning when Christy was brought before the minister in church. Since then he had fallen in love, lost his closest friend, had vowed to find Christy's lover – and had not done so – and had pledged himself to follow Norman McLeod – and had straightway jibbed at the promise.

Donald considered himself with no great favour. That was his trouble: he was weak as well as restless. He would have to do better in the future. In the past he had often laid that injunction on himself, and promptly forgotten it. But now he felt the weight of all those recent events on his shoulders. He really must do better.

* * *

From where he sat near the bow, the graceful, flared bow of the boat seemed to leap half-heartedly and cut deep into the curving, breaking wave. But magically, under the drive of the oars, the wave slid under them, caught and tamed by the cunning lines of the boat. The rowers bent vigorously to their task while more waves rolled past; and then they were out in the smooth bay.

The tide-marks showed in light streaks on the dark water, and a newly risen sun was dissolving, in a golden mist, the bank of black cloud that lay on the horizon. The day was calm, but not too clear. The sun winked an eye, then disappeared behind light cloud.

Donald sniffed the cool, crisp air. Two of Jessie's brothers, strong-armed and strong-backed, were at the oars. The eighteen-foot boat slid smoothly forward, the water bubbling at its bow and rippling in its wake. McKay himself was busy with the lines, and Donald went back to join him.

'How far do we go?' he asked.

McKay pointed with one brown arm. 'See Sail Rock out there? See that notch in the hills to the west? We row until we're between them. Now, see the tip of Bream Head? And that scar on the hills behind us? Just where those two lines cross, we stop. And that is where we'll get a boatload of fish, or my name's not John McKay.'

'Have you been there before?' Donald said innocently.

'Every year,' McKay declared. 'And if the fish are not ready, there are plenty of other places we can try.

'To tell you the truth, Donald,' he added softly, 'I suspect we could fill the boat anywhere in this wonderful bay, but the boys need to work for their keep, and that's just a good, steady row.'

The boys grinned cheerfully as he called: 'Come on lads. We must be there while the tide is running!' The boat surged forward and, with the lines baited and ready coiled, Donald and the older man settled down in the stern.

'We have beaten the others out,' McKay observed complacently. Only then, glancing round towards the river mouth, did Donald see three other small boats in line abreast.

'Do you always come out together?' he asked.

'Not necessarily,' McKay replied. 'But when one of us decides it is time, some of the others usually come too. It makes for friendly competition. I like to be first – and so do they, I suspect.'

Donald watched for the points and was ready to suggest that they should anchor when McKay, who had been brooding with his eyes half closed, told the boys to ship their oars and start work.

They were on to fish at once. It was as if John McKay was among old friends. His line went down with the heavy sinker, playing over his sensitive first finger. Silence for a moment. Then he began to talk gently, encouragingly: 'Come on now, that's right; take a good bite – now, don't play with it. There you are!' A quick jerk on the line, a pause, then a steady pull. 'Don't worry, little fellow; you're caught' – until Donald could see the gleaming, swirling fish coming to the surface.

Two on together! The low freeboard of the boat made it easy to lift them in. 'You beautiful fish!' A firm blow on the back of the head, hooks out, bait on, and over the side again.

'No time to waste, boys. Take them while they're feeding!'

It was a long time since Donald had been fishing, but when the line running through his own fingers trembled nervously and then tensed, he felt the old thrill return. By the time the others arrived, they had taken three dozen fish, and the bottom of the boat was well covered.

'How are they, John?' A voice drifted over the water.

'Could be worse and could be better. But doubtless there will be enough for you as well as for us.'

A signal came through his line, and his voice grew soft and hypnotic. 'Come on…that's right. But don't be alarmed; you're quite safe now!' And the fish piled higher and higher.

However keenly he tried, Donald could not take as many as McKay. And then, after about an hour, the run eased. Whatever fish were about, it seemed, John McKay talked off the others' baits on to his own. The catch was still mounting, but more slowly now.

There was time for Donald to look about him. The other boats were not far away, but apart from them the great bay was almost empty of life. No wind, a low, unmoving screen of cloud, a few idly circling gulls. The boat swayed gently against the lapping water.

'How many have you now, John?' came the voice from the nearby boat.

McKay cast an experienced eye over the catch, and halved the tally. 'At least fifty I should say.'

'Och, that's better than we have done, I think!'

'He can tell a short, tall story, too,' McKay muttered to his crew, and bent to his task with new energy.

Soon the boats lay completely motionless, and many minutes passed without a bite. 'The tide has stopped; there'll be no more fish for a while now, until it starts running again. Shall we have some lunch?'

McKay stared thoughtfully at the red-rocked cliff about half a mile away. 'You know, even now I think we might find some crayfish over there. Your father and mother would like a nice crayfish for their tea, wouldn't they, Donald?'

The boys were already shipping the oars. Donald slid through to the bow and hauled up the anchor and they were quickly away.

'Giving up already, John?' said a slightly mocking, but very polite voice from the other boat. McKay did not bother to reply.

* * *

The crayfish were not easy to find, but find them they did, tempting them from weed-festooned caverns in the rocks. The crayfish grasped the baits. Their heavily armoured, fantastic bodies came sliding up through the blue water, pincers waving helplessly. They whipped their great tails in frustration, poor paddles in air, when they were thrown on top of the other fish.

The boat was taken in gently between the rocks to a patch of unbroken sand. They jumped out, pleased to stretch their legs. The sun shone briefly. They ate a lunch that included no fish.

But John McKay was inexorable. This was a day set aside for fishing, and more must be caught. With a groan the boys again took up the oars. Back to the same place, down to work with renewed vigour.

* * *

After a while, Donald found, it became almost automatic. There was a growing weariness, but there was pleasure too; pleasure in the knowledge that this would be food for the bare winter months. The same thought must have been passing through John McKay's mind for he said: 'Sun-dried fish, grilled over the fire, eaten with scones that have been lightly burnt on the griddle! What could be better, Donald? Can't you taste them now?'

Donald's mouth was dry and his lips chafed with the sea air, but he smiled and nodded his head.

'It's been a good day, Donald. You have enjoyed it?' John McKay hauled in his line, dropped it in careful loops, and removed the baits. The other followed suit. 'We must do this again. And then in the winter we can go after the pigs, or across to the Heads where the wild cattle are still running. Life does not need to be dull on a farm, Donald.'

He was leaning forward, his eyes on Donald's face, waiting for him to agree. But Donald had relaxed in the stern sheets, listening with no great attention, his mind far away.

The soft insistent voice went on. 'And then in the spring, when you get your crops in and the cows drop their calves, and the beef cattle come fat out of the bush… It is a good life, Donald, and you will never regret that you have given up wandering.'

And now, while the oars dipped steadily and the boat moved back to the thin line of beach, Donald started and looked at his friend.

'But I'm not sure that I have given up wandering. I'm not sure of anything, except that this has been a grand day, and that I'm grateful to you for bringing me with you.'

He caressed with one hand the sturdy, worn timbers of the boat, so like – and yet unlike – those that had made the dam at Foster's camp. Of course, they both came from the kauri trees, the best timber known for boats and for dams. The kauri tree! And a pang that was almost physical shot through him. This, too, Norman will never know again: the delight of a day or two on the sea, the feel of salt air, the lonely circling of gulls above the bay.

Donald's face was, in a moment, so sad that John McKay stopped talking. He reached across and patted Donald's arm. 'Work it out for yourself, lad. That's all any of us can do. But don't you forget, wherever you are, that you have some good friends thinking of you.'

* * *

With the passing of afternoon the day had mended, and now the sun shone. The breeze had freshened from the east.

The mystery of men and women, thought Donald sombrely. A community has its own invisible strength. Its members can tie you with cords of unselfishness, responsibility and love until you become a willing prisoner; until you reject as unimportant the defects that show on the surface. But, he thought desperately, he did not want to become a prisoner, however cheerful. He tried to remember his feeling on the day when Roddy McKenzie told him how his name and Christy's were being mentioned together. But he could not feel the same resentment over what now appeared a trivial incident.

At intervals during the day he had been thinking about Roddy the seafarer, wondering idly how his voyages were going. He had not been home for several weeks, and no one had seemed to know when he would return. It came as no great surprise to Donald, therefore, when one of the boys stopped rowing long enough to point out to sea and say: 'That sail creeping up on us might be the *Fiona*. We will soon know, for she has changed direction and is coming in towards Waipu.'

Donald stood up to watch the cutter. She was under full sail, moving smoothly and swiftly in the easy sea. She rapidly overhauled them, changed course a few points to come flying past the stern of their boat.

Donald stood up, bracing himself to the heave of its wake, and roared: 'Hullo there, Roddy!'

Roddy pointed in comic surprise and his voice came clearly: 'Little Donald! We'll see you in the river!' Grandly the cutter swept on, her tall sails drawing, leaving a creamy wake that bubbled until the waves destroyed it.

They rowed on vigorously now, riding the waves where they curved and broke at the river bar. Then it was a steady pull up stream to the landing near the McKay home.

The *Fiona*, her sails neatly stowed, had anchored there too. Roddy, with three other men, was on the deck. 'Some visitors for the McKays,' he called. 'We're coming ashore now.'

They met by the landing. John McKay took charge of a situation that might easily have got out of hand. 'Jessie, up to the house with our guests; and bring some food back with you. And as many workers as you can find. The fish will not wait.'

The monstrous catch was unloaded, the fish opened, gutted, turned inside out and hung on wires to dry in the sun. But not before the fishermen, and Roddy, had eaten and drunk.

'You've come back already from the bush, Donald,' said Roddy, leaning his short, sturdy body against a fence post and watching the younger man while he worked.

'I've been back a few days,' Donald replied slowly. 'You will not have heard the news yet. Norman was drowned.'

'Now how could that have happened?' Roddy asked. Donald noticed that he was surprised but not shocked. Never yet had he seen anything that could come close enough to Roddy to startle him very profoundly. His eyes were sympathetic, but he reached for his pipe and began to pack it calmly while Donald told him the story.

'Well, well,' Roddy remarked. 'But no doubt the lad's been saved a lot of grief. And when do you go back to the bush?'

'I've finished there for a while.' And then the words came without rehearsal: 'Roddy, would you have room for a working passenger for a voyage or two?'

Roddy did not answer directly. He combed his beard with one hand while his eyes rested thoughtfully on Donald. Along the rough table, John McKay's family was busy with knives and fish and cheerful talk. The new arrivals, cousins who now lived in Auckland but who were familiar with Waipu ways, had changed into old clothes and were also hard at work.

'You wouldn't be running away from something, Donald?' His chuckle made the remark an idle joke. 'But why should you want to come sailing?'

'I don't know – in fact, I haven't even asked myself why. But perhaps it's because I don't want to go back to the bush; nor do I fancy becoming a farmer; and it might be that I would just like to see something new and strange. The voyage from Nova Scotia seems so long ago, now.'

Donald seized another fish, and the knife in his big hands sent the scales flying in clouds. One cut and the head was off, a slice in the soft belly and the guts spilled, to be thrown into a box.

'I'll think about it, Donald, and you will know tomorrow, after we've unloaded our cargo. It's an interesting and adventurous life you'll be taking up. Just let me show you.' A laugh came from deep in his beard as he reached into a tight pocket and produced a folded length of paper. 'Here it is: cargo for the good people of Waipu, all the way from the thriving town of Auckland. It's a fine list, Donald. Let me read it to you.'

Roddy frowned with concentration. 'One ton of flour, two chests of tea, ten hundredweight of salt, one box of candles, a dozen of buckets, four bags of sugar, two kegs of nails, three casks of beef – that would be for the gum-diggers, not for themselves – one keg of paint, one case of porter, similar of wine' – he shuddered – 'two tins of confectionery, another bag of sugar, a parcel of drapery and one box of lead. That's it, apart from a few miscellaneous items, which would only weary you if I mentioned them.

'Passengers, too. They are useful at times, especially if they know a little about working the sails. Usually, indeed, they save me the expense of engaging a regular crew. And that's why I think I might let you come. I've already persuaded most of the willing ones to take a trip with me!'

John McKay called: 'Roddy, come on up to the house and clean yourself. And you too, Donald. We can safely leave the rest to these young ones.'

Donald wiped his knife on a handful of grass and they walked up to the house together. Jessie was there already. He saw her in the kitchen where she was helping her mother prepare tea. She gave him a quick smile and went on with her work. They washed themselves well in the sunny yard at the back of the house, and then went inside.

John McKay showed them all to seats with slow ceremony, and passed a bottle and glasses around.

'Your father is well, you'll be glad to know,' he told Roddy. He thought you might be back today, or so he said when I saw him last. Doubtless he'll be watching, and will have meat and potatoes ready for you!'

'And I mustn't keep him waiting,' said Roddy, rising briskly to his feet. 'Are you coming along with me, Donald?'

'I'll call on you tomorrow in the evening, Roddy, and we'll see what we are to do.' Donald grinned at his friend, who clapped him on the shoulder and went striding down to the river.

* * *

Jessie walked with him towards the village when Donald left after an early tea. High summer might have gone, but the air was warm in the quiet lane, and the evening light was clear. A great stillness had settled on the world, for the wind had dropped with the approach of night.

'Was it a good day, Donald?'

'I have had few better that I can remember, Jessie.'

'Now that he has started, father will be away after the fish again. You must go too, if you would like to.'

'Yes,' Donald agreed uncomfortably. Then he turned and spoke to her directly. 'Jessie, now I am here with you I don't know why I have done it. But I've asked Roddy to take me with him on the *Fiona* for a voyage or two. If he agrees, I'll be away in a few days.'

'To Auckland is it, Donald?'

'I didn't ask him, but that's what I expect,' Donald replied. 'I don't see the *Fiona*, or Roddy either, sailing much further afield.'

'Well, that will not be long,' Jessie said cheerfully. 'You're a strange lad, Donald. I might think you were running away from something if I didn't know you were the kind who would never do that.'

Donald walked on in silence. The thought passed through his mind: That is what Roddy said, too.

'And while you're in Auckland, Donald, you may be able to discover something to help poor Christy.'

Donald looked at her again in a puzzled way.

'What do you mean, Jessie? I remember you telling me once that Christy had offended against the community, and that she could not expect anything to be the same for her again. And that I should let matters take their own course.'

'That is so, Donald, and it was you yourself that made me change my mind. Before you went away to the bush, you told me that Christy's life was only half complete without a man to share it.

'Yesterday I saw Christy. There is something strange about her, Donald, but it is nothing that could not be cured if her life became whole again.'

'Did she mention the baby?'

'No. And I still cannot make up my mind whether it is alive or not. But it is Christy, not the baby, that I have been thinking about. It is Christy who we must try to help.'

Donald looked at her with puzzled eyes. He felt anger rising within him; not with Jessie, but with circumstances that seemed to conspire to baffle him.

'What should I do?' he asked. He was holding a crayfish in one hand, carrying it by the two long feelers that advanced horn-like from its head. Forgetting what he was carrying, he shook his arm with too much vigour, and the crayfish went flying onto the grass.

'Now see what's happened!' he exploded.

'Oh, Donald, you are funny when you're cross!' Jessie was laughing helplessly; and when he joined in, as he had to, the tension of the moment passed.

'Do you mean that you, too, have changed your mind?' Jessie asked.

'I've changed my mind about many things, Jessie. The minister is right; he must be right, and I must follow him. If I see Christy, I'll tell her that she must do the same.'

'You'll not be starting to lecture me, Donald?' Jessie was smiling again.

'I'm serious, Jessie. Why must you make fun of me now?'

'I wouldn't do that, Donald, but it does not seem so important to me as you would make it. Just tell me this, Donald: When you grow stern, and fierce, and begin to hate music and singing and dancing, will you still like me?'

'Of course I will, Jessie. Nothing could change that!' He looked at her sharply. 'You're laughing at me again, you rogue!'

Jessie continued to smile, for the Gaelic word he had used was a lilting endearment more than anything else. 'But you will not change too much, Donald?' she repeated.

He looked at her again. 'I do think I have made the proper decision.' He was very close to her there on the quiet country road. Her eyes were regarding him with a serene amusement, as if all his problems were of very little moment. 'Jessie, I know I'm a wee bit fishy, although I've washed as much of it away as I could; but would you mind if I kissed you?'

Her eyes were still smiling. 'Donald, my dear, you are a great worrier.'

Unregarded and unlamented, the crayfish fell to the ground once again.

* * *

'And now we must hurry,' said Donald. His arm was around Jessie's shoulders and her hair against his mouth. Her warm soft body, pliant but firm, made all his thoughts seem folly.

He spoke to the hidden face. 'It's a sad thing to say, Jessie dear, but bed has been for me somewhere to sleep. But I am thinking that, with you beside me, it would be a place of many delights.'

And now she did look up with warm, bright eyes and cheeks that were rosy in the fading light.

'Donald, Donald my dear one, you should not talk like that.'

Her hands were linked behind him, and her body firm against his. He felt her sigh before he heard it.

'Now we must go our ways. Auckland is not very far, is it Donald? You'll soon be home again.'

She stepped back, smoothing her dress with hands that, as they moved, for him held all poetry in their motion. One arm came softly forward and rested on the sleeve of his coat.

'It's hopeless, you see, Jessie.' He shook his head sadly. 'I begin to tell you, seriously, how I plan to mend my ways, to take the straight road that the minister has surveyed for me, and what happens? In a moment I've forgotten all about it and am kissing the most beautiful girl in

Waipu! What is wrong with me?' He laughed, but Jessie could see that he was perplexed.

'That is what has been troubling me the most. I think of poor Norman, and my heart is sad, but then my mind goes skipping off on other thoughts, and I forget him and my grief. I'm weak as water, Jessie.'

He would have gone on, but Jessie's voice stopped him. She was as near anger as he had ever seen her. 'That's not so, Donald, and I'm tired of hearing you say it. Stop thinking about yourself – it can become a habit that cripples you. Norman is dead, but he would not want to see you lamenting him all your days. He would say that you have your own life to live.

'And is it necessary to make excuses for kissing me?'

Donald looked at her in bewilderment.

'There are men, and women, who become stern in their religion because they dare not accept the pleasures of life as it comes to them. You yourself know some who are like that. They build a wall behind which, poor frightened creatures, they skulk and cower like animals. I hope you will not become one of them!

'It is surely no crime to avoid anything ugly, when you can. But it is wicked to pity yourself for something that lives only in your imagination.'

Jessie drew breath. Donald said quietly: 'But what about Norman? It troubles me that he, my closest friend, should be dead; and that I should forget him so easily.'

'You have mourned him, Donald, already, and do not need to wear your sorrow like a black cloak.'

'I won't do that, Jessie.' He gave her a slow smile. 'But I can't stop thinking this: The night before Norman was drowned, I could feel that something evil was abroad. Could it have been the devil who, the minister says, is always ready to enslave us? And was he also at hand when Christy fell into the darkness of temptation? Sometimes I think he must have been; sometimes not. But this I do feel. Ever since I spoke with the minister, and then forgot my promise to him, something evil has been dogging my footsteps. To put it to flight I will gladly follow what the minister commands. And that includes having no part in Christy's affairs.'

'This has gone beyond my understanding, and I suspect beyond yours,' said Jessie. Her hand touched his arm again. 'But do you have to worry about it so much? The worst devil, my father has said, is the one that lies in wait inside a man, seeking for a chance to twist his nature. And there is no devil within you, Donald; or else he is a very weak and timid one!'

Donald shrugged his shoulders. 'If that is so,' he said, 'he grows stronger when I think about him. I'll let him lie. But I will also let Christy go the road that has been chosen for her. And I must be firmer with myself, Jessie.'

Jessie shook her head hopelessly. 'Oh, Donald, Donald!' She looked at his serious, withdrawn face, her love showing in her eyes, and said: 'Goodbye, Donald. We'll see each other before you go. And don't forget your crayfish!'

Belatedly, Donald roused himself, but Jessie was already hurrying back down the road.

* * *

Chapter Eleven

THE MINISTER'S HOUSE, WINDOWS PALELY LIGHTED IN THE DIM dusk, loomed up on the open fields to his left side. Donald hesitated, and then walked firmly through the open picket gate to the front door. It opened to his first knock. The minister was in his study, the girl told him. He suddenly realised that he was still clutching the crayfish and, before following her along the hall, cast about for somewhere to leave it. There was a small table, in the centre of which stood the minister's tall beaver hat. He placed the crayfish carefully beside it and hurried along to where the girl was waiting.

The room was quiet, and he was startled to discover that the minister was not alone. He sat in his deep chair by the fireplace. Facing him, half concealed in the shadows, was Alex Grant, relaxed with his hands on his knees; a big-boned giant of a man with the calm, silent, monumental dignity that sometimes comes with old age. Lamplight glittered on the minister's steel-rimmed spectacles, making his face a mask. He did not seem surprised to see Donald.

'Sit down by the table,' he said. 'You know Alex, of course. We have been talking about the old days.'

Old Alex nodded ponderously. He cleared his throat, clasped his hands firmly across his body, let his eyes move between the minister and Donald, but did not add to the conversation.

'Your mother is well? A good woman. And I hear that you have been fishing today with John McKay. And how is young Jessie now? A well-mannered lassie she is, Alex, brought up to the old ways and likely to make some man a good wife.'

Alex Grant inclined his head. 'I know the girl. She was my sister Annie's grandchild.'

But Donald scarcely heard him. He was watching the minister's face in surprise. The glinting spectacles could not hide the smile that came so suddenly but did not disappear.

The minister laughed out loud, and there was nothing harsh in the sound. 'I hear, but not from the McKay household, mind you, that you have been seeing something of the girl since you came home, Donald. She would be a better choice than many a young man makes. Comely, but obedient, with a good strain in her. And she's one of our own people, Donald; and so are you!'

The mask was now being lifted to reveal goodwill and a masterful benevolence. Alex Grant eased his big body in the chair, cleared his throat, and did not speak. His eyes, behind shaggy brows, were studying the young man casually.

Donald could find nothing to say, and the minister gave him little enough time. 'We must hold together,' he said impressively. 'Our young people are falling away. Off to the forests, away to sea, to the towns and the goldfields. And few of them come back. They are enfeebled by their contacts. Their true blood runs thin, and when they marry they bring into the world children who never learn what their heritage might have been. But I must not think of such things.

'Keep close to the soil, Donald. Take up your piece of land. Marry and raise a brood of sturdy, God-fearing children. Our congregation will need them in the years to come, if our ideals are to survive.'

He paused, and Donald was about to speak when Alex Grant said: 'I do not hold with many of these young people, gadding about here and yon, as you have said, Minister. As I felt obligated to tell you only last Sunday, I saw two of them smiling as they came out of church after the service. They are worldly, and light-minded and frivolous at the same time.'

Donald looked at him directly. 'And not the young people only, Alex. Others may fail, too. What about the man who, while saying grace before the family dinner, glanced up and saw one of his grandchildren crawling over the window sill. "Bless this food we are about to eat," he is reported to have said, "and come down from there Johnny before you get your bloody head knocked off. For Jesus Christ's sake, Amen."'

'The circumstances were different when I said that, Donald,' Alex replied comfortably. 'And I'm sure that the minister does not want to hear such pointless anecdotes and bushman's language. Furthermore, I'm quite sure that my grandchild would have fallen and hurt himself had I not called to warn him in that way.'

'You were in error, Alex, even though you may have been sadly provoked,' said the minister. 'The Lord would have kept the lad safe, if He so willed, without your worldly intervention at such a solemn time.

'But what are your plans, Donald, now that you are home again?'

'I intend to make a voyage or two with Roddy McKenzie to Auckland,' Donald said.

The minister frowned. 'With Roddy? Why? I do not care for the man. You should not go with him.'

'But surely there is no harm in Roddy? I know he was forbidden church for several Sundays not so long ago, but his fault was not overgreat.'

'Do not stand against me, Donald, or argue on matters outside your knowledge,' the minister said harshly. 'I have watched the man for long enough. A disputer, a mocker, lacking in reverence. He believes in nothing, Donald, and he would make others be like himself. A difficult man to catch, mark you, for the devil is cunning and gives his followers keen weapons. And the devil has Roddy McKenzie, for sure!'

'But I've always found him kind and friendly,' Donald protested, though softly.

'You know, Minister, it would be better for these young people if they would listen to and obey their elders,' Alex said. 'To smile on the way out of church shows a sad frivolity. Their minds are away from God's word. What will you do about them?

'That sermon you gave on human vanity, which confronted the Boularderie people before we left Nova Scotia, would be timely if repeated now. It was very powerful,' Alex added, shaking his head: 'Very powerful.'

'Be quiet now, Alex. We are discussing no young fool, but Roddy McKenzie; a hardened and confirmed sinner; a sceptic. I see that he has already misled you, Donald, when you act as his advocate with me. Now, be warned. None is more dangerous than the man of goodwill. He can see harm and evil nowhere. Boneless benevolence is the partner of a dying soul. I hope you see the danger that is near you, and withdraw from this project. Afterwards it might be too late.'

'As you have often said, Minister,' Alex continued, 'these young people are our greatest worry. But they are also out greatest hope, and I must admit that, on the whole, I like them.'

The minister's anger had blown itself out. He looked at Alex good-humouredly. 'Alex, my friend, you are a loyal and single-minded man; but I sometimes think, too, that you are an old fool!'

Alex Grant smiled, then sank back into his own private thoughts.

Donald stood up. 'That is what I plan to do, Minister: One or two voyages with Roddy, who I still think is my friend, and no greater sinner than the rest of us.'

'There can be too much talk of sin,' said the minister moderately, 'and not enough done to counter it. Perhaps – who knows? – you may be God's agent in this case.' He stood up also. 'Alex is going, too. Perhaps you will walk with him to his house.'

They followed the minister down the passage. 'Bring a light, girl,' he called. There was a flurry of footsteps from the kitchen, and the little servant girl was there with a lantern.

The minister's keen eyes swept the hall. 'You have brought me a crayfish, Donald. That was a kindly thought. The land and the sea – they can supply us easily with our simple material needs. And now, goodnight to you both.'

* * *

As he walked home, Donald pondered the fact that, once again, he had failed to ask the minister what was foremost in his mind - whether he should have taken more notice of his dream before Norman's death. But somehow, after his interview, he knew now what the minister would have told him.

The land lay quiet as a calm sea, landmarks sensed but not seen. A sleeping land, but it held in small compass, behind that deceptive mask, all the hopes and fears of mankind everywhere. God's agent or devil's advocate? A man could be either and not show it on his face. But surely the issue need not be as sharply defined as that. The minister himself had seemed less adamant tonight. If he could change, then there was room for change in others, too. Christy Cameron could become a woman accepted by her community, with a full life ahead of her. The inscrutable Roddy McKenzie might show where he stood. And others, like himself perhaps, could steer a middle course and find happiness, and stability, at the end of it.

He thought of Jessie again. He would be missing her while he was away. And yet, he felt, the warmth of her body, the touch of her hands and lips, could stay with him and satisfy him well enough, if he loved her. When his restlessness had gone, if it ever did go; when he could see before him the road that a man should follow, he would be able to come back and take Jessie as his wife. A farm like these he was passing now. Cattle and crops thriving in the sun and the rain, a warm house, children, and a friendly dog to watch him as he worked. The thought of it pleased him, but he knew he was not ready to accept it.

A medley of impressions chased through his mind on that calm, dark night as he walked the familiar road, and the sky, empty of stars and moon, pressed down on him like a dark, smothering blanket. He smiled at the memory of the crayfish, which the minister would soon be enjoying. With the thought came a picture of the *Fiona*, storming past them on a lively sea, and of Roddy McKenzie, his beard streaming in the breeze; an uninhibited Roddy, living a life that was governed by his mistress, the sea itself, and her insatiable demands. A free, unfettered life, with no shore-bound problems attached.

Or were there? He would, he hoped, soon find out.

Now, through his body, there ran a ripple of excitement. Young Donald McKinnon began to whistle. His feet moved faster on the dusty road and then, rather to his surprise, he was singing.

It was a song that he had forgotten he had ever known; a song that they had sung when the ship had eased herself out of St Ann's Harbour in faraway Nova Scotia, at the start of a voyage across the world; a cheerful, spirited song with a touch of sadness to it, but with more of a reckless zest for what the future could bring. His own voyage might not be so long, but with Roddy McKenzie as comrade it would surely be lively.

* * *

Part Two: The Sea

Chapter Twelve

THEY WERE, FOR DONALD, STRANGE BUT EXHILARATING SENSATIONS: The creak of the cordage, the whistle of wind through the rigging and the hiss of water against the *Fiona's* smooth sides; a buoyant lift to the deck beneath his feet that seemed to come from wind's urging more than from movement of water. For they were still in the river, going strongly down the stream with a fair west wind.

On each side now Donald could see the sand of the beach, gouged by the river into two banks on which surf broke sluggishly. But the channel was clear, the tide full and the open sea ahead of them. The bar should not be hard today.

The *Fiona* lifted her long bowsprit to the first of the mild sea rollers, and left a creaming wake down its long green back. And then, although Donald did not notice it for a few seconds, the wind dropped to a faint breeze. A bellow from the tiller made him jump. 'Up with the mainsail,' Roddy roared. 'Quick, lest we be wrecked on our own front doorstep!'

Donald began to fumble with unaccustomed ropes, desperately, while the breaking surf seemed to growl as fiercely as Roddy McKenzie. The sail climbed into position while the cutter gradually lost way. Donald's heart was in his mouth, not for himself for he was a strong swimmer, but for Roddy's fine new boat. There was regret, too, that his adventure might end so soon. He had no time to look at Roddy. His eyes were on the slack sails. But then he felt the wind freshen on his back again, the sails filled, and the *Fiona* was driving on her way.

He went back to Roddy, imperturbable at the tiller. 'We'll set the gaff tops'l soon,' Roddy observed blandly. 'That's the one that sits so neatly against the topmast above the main. You have a good head for heights, Donald, I hope.'

'At present, Roddy, I've no head for anything. What would have happened if the wind had not come again so providentially? Would we have been wrecked?'

'I don't think so, Donald. Not this time. But you've learned your first lesson as a seaman. If you want to stand and dream, do it with your eyes and ears open. Be the sea never so peaceful, she is always like a hungry animal waiting to seize a victim. Do not trust her for a moment, Donald. Watch her as you would a shrew with her eye on your purse.'

Donald grinned. 'That's one to you, Roddy. But remember the old story about crying wolf!'

'I'll never cry wolf, Donald, unless the animal is there – at least, not often. And I'm sure you'll always jump to it as quickly.'

Donald found that there was enough to learn to keep his mind occupied. And it was with something of a shock that he glanced back to see that the shoreline had disappeared, and the mountains, strangely diminished, seemed to rise directly from the water. They had cleared Bream Tail, jutting out from the southern tip of the bay, and a new panorama opened before them. Unknown islands, a tortuous, hilly coast, its tree-clad slopes blue in the haze. And far to the east, a limitless sea. Not until you reached South America would there be a landfall in that direction.

He studied the sails with an anxious eye. They were all drawing well, the main sheet eased out and the white canvas firm and sharp and beautiful against the blue sky.

'She's a good sailer,' Roddy observed. 'Times like these we could do with a square sail. It would push us along, going directly before the wind as we are. But I don't like them. Not enough give – as they found out on the *Lapwing* a few months ago,' he added gloomily.

'What happened to her, Roddy?'

'Coming out of Whangarei, sailing a course much the same as our own. Stays'l down, square sail set, single-reefed main. Wind steady from the north-west, heavy cross sea from the north-east. Making six knots. Sudden wind from nor-east; captain came up to find her on her beam ends. No rudder; soon, no ship.'

'And what about the men?'

Roddy blew gustily through his whiskers and spared a moment to look at the tops'l. 'They saved themselves in a small boat they carried; all except two who couldn't be found – then or afterwards.

'And that's why I say, carry no more sail than you know you can manage. You may not get there so fast, but you get there – barring calm or calamity, storm or waterspout. And that, Donald my friend, is the most important thing of all.'

He cast a glance at the sun. 'Now, Donald, if you have no more questions for the moment, it's time we had a bite to eat and a drink to sip. You're the cook.'

The cutter was surprisingly roomy. Forward from the tiller was a cabin with space for several bunks and a small table. From it opened another door. 'Ladies' cabin,' Roddy had explained, 'to be used if ever we are so favoured.' Then the long clean sweep of the deck; white planking as smooth as fine silk, broken only by the hatch covers.

* * *

By mid-afternoon the craggy, tortured heights of Whangarei Heads were veiled in the distance. A green land, fringed with shining beaches, lay on their starboard flank. An empty land untouched by man, or so it seemed to Donald scanning it from the sea. He had had a spell at the tiller, learning to balance the weight of it against the strength of the rudder and the ship's drive. He did not allow his mind to wander from the task until Roddy, with a satisfied nod, came back to relieve him.

Donald sat for a while watching his friend. A sturdy and stocky man, comfortable in his self-assurance, quick of hand and alert of eye. A man who was doing something that had meaning for him. A far, far different man from the one he had known at Waipu, frittering away his energies and talents and not enjoying it.

Roddy was scanning the coast. They were passing a high point, buttressed with red rock, and before them was a tangle of scrub-covered islands between which the water moved languidly.

'We're making in to Omaha,' Roddy announced. 'Give a haul on the mainsheet, Donald.'

The *Fiona* came round on the wind and settled diligently to her new course. The deck leaned until the water seethed along the port rail. A narrow entrance opened up before them; so narrow that Donald found himself growing tense and measuring distances with his bushman's calculating eye.

‘Have you been in here before, Roddy?’ he asked, keeping his voice quite casual.

Roddy looked at him. ‘This, as you will soon learn, is the anchorage of my friend Kenneth Mackenzie, better known as Kenny Omaha – a name to be reckoned with wherever ships sail. In the Western Ocean, from Sydney, Nova Scotia to the Bermudas; from Auckland to the far islands of the Pacific and Australia.

‘Yes, I have called in here before,’ he added. ‘Let us hope that he is in residence this time. It’s important that we see him.’

The tall cliffs had weakened the wind and they glided easily into the little harbour.

‘They are good seamen here, Donald, and don’t be forgetting that.’ Roddy grunted with satisfaction. A schooner lay at anchor, tucked in behind the point; a rakish craft with lines that showed strength and speed, stained in her paintwork by long months of sailing.

‘That’s Kenny’s!’ Roddy cried. His shout echoed across the bay as the *Fiona* shed her sails and came gently to rest.

* * *

These too are our people, but how differently life has fashioned them, thought Donald as they drew chairs to the table and began to eat. Kenny Omaha; a great talker, with a courtly manner and expressive hands; with eyes that were knowing and, at times, reckless. A lean man, dark and tall, with a long black beard and skin burned brown by sun and wind. He had greeted them warmly enough, with a clap on the back for Roddy and a keen, probing glance at Donald, quickly followed by his ready smile.

Donald spoke little during the meal. This was unknown territory for him, and he was content to listen while the two men talked of strange ports they had seen together when New Zealand was for them no more than an unread name on a chart.

‘And now,’ Kenny announced, ‘Roddy and I must away to talk business. Look after your visitor well, my children.’

The brood of young Mackenzies stood shyly and solemnly about Donald. ‘Would you like to see father’s collection?’ one of them said, and they escorted Donald to a door that opened off the big room.

'This is where I had my bed,' one lad told him, 'but since father came home from his last voyage I've had to move in with Johnnie. There's no room for me here now.'

The small boy carrying the lamp moved forward. Donald followed, and felt his heart jump inside him at what the light half revealed. The solemn children burst into peals of laughter.

A face with glaring eyes and twisted, pain-wreaked features leered at him from the shadows. It was a devil's mask such as no mortal could contrive: inky black with fierce splashes of red; cruel beak-like nose and chin; eyes fashioned from pearl shell. A shrivelled head, the death agony caught in its writhing lips and dilated nostrils, its skin like highly polished black leather, watched him stonily from a shelf near the door. Spears festooned with feathers, cruelly barbed; axes with carved and pointed handles; ball-headed clubs bristling like sea urchins with needles that would maim the victim before he was crushed or battered to death; necklaces of shark's teeth and human bones.

A gruesome collection, even when your heart could beat normally and you could realise that there were no enemies here; only the trophies of a violent age. But an age that still existed, if reports were true, a few days' journey across the Pacific Ocean.

The children had been watching him with keen enjoyment.

'This is my favourite,' Kenny's daughter remarked. She selected a tiny arrow, beautifully carved from ivory – or was it from a human bone? 'One touch of this sharp tip, father says, and a man would die. Poison. But it is clean now. We boiled it as soon as father brought it home. It comes from the far Indian islands, he says.'

'Did he collect them all himself?' Donald asked.

'He did indeed,' young Johnnie told him proudly. 'And it was difficult to get some of them from all accounts.' An old-fashioned boy, Donald thought, precise in his speech beyond his years. And knowing of much that could never be learned in the bush, or on a quiet Waipu farm.

Johnnie chuckled and the rest crowded in, as if to hear a favourite bedtime story repeated once again. 'The kanakas did not always want to give them to him. That mask belonged to a witchdoctor. Father had to shoot him.'

The girls shivered with excitement, and stared expectantly at their brother. 'The witchdoctor came down the beach to where father and his men were standing. He shook his spear in the air and began to cry out, bones rattling around his neck, and his ankles and his arms. Then he stopped calling and pointed his spear at our father. And none of them said anything. Father was ready because he had seen this happen before. He did not move, and then suddenly the kanakas threw their spear at father, but they missed. This spear here was the one that went into his boat, and was still sticking in the wood when they rowed away.

'Father fired and the witchdoctor fell down dead and the other men shrieked loudly and ran off as fast as they could. Father was angry because he had hoped to load many kanakas there, but the village was empty when he reached it. They had all gone to the bush. So to teach them a lesson, he burned their houses down.'

'But why did he want the kanakas?' Donald asked.

'Oh, they are needed to work in the Fijis, and in Queensland, and in New Caledonia. Father takes them there, and after they have worked for a while he takes them back to their homes. He told us that, when he takes them home again, they have smart clothes to wear, and umbrellas, and new boots and hats. But the trouble is that they sometimes don't want to go in the first place because they cannot speak the Gaelic, or even English, and don't know where they are being taken to, or even if they will ever come home again. And that is why father sometimes has to make them go with him.'

Answering their mother's call, the younger children ran off to bed. But Johnnie stayed with Donald, and told him the rest of the story about Kenny's collection.

Donald listened and wondered: What kind of folk are these kanakas? Are they like the Maoris, or are they scarcely human, like those who had lived in Tasmania and had been hunted as if they were kangaroos by the white settlers until none of them remained? Did God look down upon them with compassion, heathens though they might be and drenched in blood and superstition? Or had He created them and then put them out of His mind, forgetting that they existed?

He walked slowly back to where the light burned on the table, and sat down to wait for Roddy's return.

Someday, perhaps, he might go sailing to the Islands and see for himself.

* * *

They slept that night in Kenny's house. A wind had sprung up during the evening. They did not feel it down in the sheltered bay, but Donald could hear it surging through the trees near the top of the ridge, and the sea was noisy behind the point. It roared like an angry black man trying to keep the white invaders from his village.

Donald was tired, but his brain was nervously alive. As he lay in his bed, his mind was grappling with the problems of seamanship. All that he had done during the day, all that he had seen and that Roddy had told him, came back to be lived again. In his mind's eye, too, he saw Kenny confronting the savages on an island beach, heard the report from his gun, and saw the witchdoctor drop down. His last memory before falling asleep was of the painted mask, huge, cruel and fierce, its pearl eyes expanding as they stared through him, into his very heart.

The wind was still high in the morning. Donald stood on the verandah watching the low cloud scud across the hills. There was no rain, but the sea was dark and threatening.

Kenny and Roddy came out to join him.

'A northerly,' said Kenny. 'It should hold as it is, but it may back around to the west before it drops – though at this time of the year, it shouldn't be too bad. Will you be going on today, Roddy? You're welcome to stay, and I'll enjoy your company.'

Roddy shook his head firmly. 'Thank you, Kenny, but I've perishable goods on board; butter and eggs from the good Waipu housewives. They must reach the market today, or my reputation will be lost and my character gone forever.'

'We'll meet again, Roddy, and perhaps sooner rather than later,' Kenny said, and they went through to breakfast.

* * *

For Donald, the *Fiona* already seemed a familiar friend. Yet, just one day ago, he had not known her. He looked at Roddy for instructions.

'Double-reefed main, I think, Donald; stays'l and jib, but we'll see how long to keep that canvas on when we get outside.' The *Fiona* slipped slowly away, her running gear neatly stowed, her small boat lashed to the deck. They turned and waved to Kenny and his family, small figures on the verandah of the wooden slab house.

For many, perhaps, this could be a life that was dull and tedious; but not for me, yet, thought Donald as he watched the close shoreline slide past. Flurries of wind filled the sails and then died, making the canvas and rigging rattle and slap. But the *Fiona* kept moving, a living creature it would seem, at home in her native element.

Now, through the narrow entrance, they could see the water oddly stirred. The waves were not high, but they were jumbled and heaving restlessly, with flecks of white spray breaking their crests. Donald felt himself grow tense, but with elation, not fear. The *Fiona* trembled under the impact of a heavier gust, and shook her bowsprit nervously as the swell from the open water funnelled into the entrance.

Roddy leaned forward from the tiller, his nose and eyes testing the weather like a dog scenting its prey. 'We'll take in the jib, Donald,' he said. 'I'm in a cautious mood today. We will accustom you gently to this seafaring life. Down with her quickly, and stow her well. We'll not be needing her again for a while. And when you've finished that, a good bushman's lashing around the small boat will not go amiss.

'We'll make a good run now,' said Roddy, turning a critical eye on the sails and bracing himself easily against the tiller. The wind was on their port quarter, the main sheet eased and the sail as stiff as a board. 'Have to watch those waves if they grow any bigger. But she's a grand little ship before the wind. Plenty of beam, Donald; that is the secret of MacGregor's work. Not like some of those others that you see in Auckland; as thin as a match, wandering up one side of a big sea and turning broadside on in a trough. And before they know what has happened the mast is shaken out of her and she's upside down.'

Donald watched the following seas with a fascinated eye. They came towering behind the little ship and hung for one long moment above her. Then, somehow, the *Fiona* was riding the giddy crest, and the wave was surging ahead of them. The rigging hummed in the wind.

'Your stomach feel all right, Donald?' Roddy gave him a shrewd look. And Donald was pleased to realise that his breakfast was still sitting comfortably enough. 'I'll show you what we'll be doing – wind, sea, and the Good Lord willing. Bring me the chart, Donald.'

A brown finger with a badly broken nail indicated their position on the small chart. Donald's eyes ranged over the pattern of islands and projecting headlands that seemed to hem them in. 'Don't worry. There's plenty of room to work. The Great Barrier there is thirty miles away, and the others will concern us little. But we'll not hug the coast. Seas are choppier in shallow waters, as you can see! And apart from that, the wind could veer to the east, which might not be pleasant.

'But this is how it seems to me. A long run up the channel here, then round North Head and into the harbour. With any luck, we should eat ashore tonight. But you can forget those fancy town lodgings and expensive hotels, Donald: We'll sleep on board!'

And so, for a while, it seemed that the day would work out as Roddy so cheerfully forecast. Rain came in heavy squalls that flattened the waves. The *Fiona* ran before the wind, putting the miles steadily behind her. Through the mist and the cloud Donald saw the tall peaks of the Little Barrier Island, pale blue on the vague horizon. Then they were blotted out.

The rain lay close on the sea, a grey blanket that could hide islands, reefs, mountains, but retreated before them to show nothing but an empty waste of water.

The mainland was there on the chart; Takatau Point behind them now, Kawau guarding its bay of many islands, the long tidal reaches of the Mahurangi River. But the rain and storm hid them, too. It was a strange feeling, to sail on and on, the centre of a narrow circle, surging water confined by ragged cloud.

'Is this the worst storm you've had in the *Fiona*, Roddy?' Donald asked.

'Storm?' Roddy repeated, his blue eyes bright in a wind-reddened face. 'Well, I'll grant that it's not calm, lad, but I would call this a good sailing breeze.'

'Then why not put on more sail and make better use of it?'

'More sail would not help. It would only drive her nose into the sea. We're doing very well as we are, Donald. Don't be impatient.'

Roddy fumbled through his beard, which he had tucked inside his oilskins, and brought out a heavy gold watch from an obscure pocket. Thoughtfully he studied it, consulted the chart, and altered course a few points to the south.

'If you see an island looming up to leeward, let me know. It will be Tiri, the gateway to the inner gulf, and a signal for us to start packing.'

'But we have a long way to go yet, Roddy.'

'Yes, Donald; a long way to go, but a good breeze to take us there.'

Donald strained his eyes through the murk. Dark squalls took on the shape of land, lying close to the sea. They dissolved and formed again, cheating the senses at the first quick glance.

The wind, coming so steadily, flowing over them like a river in spate, was lulling to the senses once he had accustomed himself to the rhythm of the movement. But now from a more westerly quarter came a sudden, vicious gust that set the mainsail quivering and made Roddy whip the tiller sharply around.

'Forward to the stays'l, Donald: We'll have to gybe.'

The *Fiona* came up in her tracks and seemed to pause, shivering, until the mainsail boom swung over. Donald, struggling in the wind, secured the staysail on the new lee side and went back to Roddy.

The wind came again, a tigerish gust from the west that plucked at his face and clothing with harsh fingers. And then, for a moment, there was calm. As if a restraining hand had been lifted from it, the sea began to churn and dance wildly, a tumult of waves with no rhyme or reason. The *Fiona* lost way. One great wave, coming from nowhere, paused indolently above her bow, then crashed down and swept her deck. The sky had momentarily lightened, but far to the south, as the *Fiona* shook herself clear of water, Donald saw black clouds boiling over the horizon. And from them came a fierce, biting wind; a cruel wind that made the other seem to have been a summer breeze. On their starboard quarter, a mile or two away, was an island backed by a long, hilly tongue of land. It showed for a few minutes, then was lost in the rain squalls. They had left Tiri behind them.

'Where is Auckland now, Roddy?'

Roddy pointed. 'Straight in the eye of that wind,' he said.

'So what can we do?'

'Sail there,' said Roddy simply. Donald saw that he was vastly enjoying himself, in spite of wind, sea and the water he occasionally combed out of his beard with one big hand.

'This is where one must advance by devious means. We cannot sail straight towards Auckland, and so we must tack. Slant across the wind as close as we can to the sou-east, then whip across her face until we are heading sou-west – but always, I hope, making some distance in the required direction.

'Your sailing lessons are coming with a rush, like this next squall, Donald!'

Donald tried to remember what he had seen on the chart. They were in the broad entrance to a channel that stretched for more than twenty miles to the harbour entrance. It was bounded to the west by the coast, protected by reefs that made close sailing dangerous. To the east were scattered groups of islands that gradually hemmed in the open water until, at the harbour mouth, it was no more than two miles across. Down this channel, pursued by the devils of the wind, the great waves came racing at them.

Thunder of water, shriek of wind, jar and crash and heave of straining timbers. As they plunged down the streaming back of a great wave, Donald was for a moment stark with fear. Once again he was standing on the kauri log as the dam burst and the river fell away with a roar at his feet. He gripped the rigging with a desperate hand, and looked round at Roddy for reassurance. The *Fiona* spun dizzily – so it seemed – up the flank of a wave that curled but did not break. Roddy, with one eye shut, the other crinkled against the weather, leaned on the tiller and kept the *Fiona's* bowsprit close against the wind.

He was concentrating, but not overburdened with care. One part of his mind – a smaller part – seemed able to deal adequately with the problems of the storm. For the rest, he was wearing a meditative, reflective air, as if there were other things to think about. His eye opened suddenly, a blind going up on a sunny morning, and he grinned at Donald.

'Come back here, lad. It's warmer, and just as wet!'

Donald huddled down in the shelter of the cabin top. The *Fiona* was travelling easily enough, but now and again a wave caught her in mid-flight. She would falter for a moment, and then the wind would press urgently and she would slice through foam-laden, hissing seas.

'I wonder what they would be thinking at Waipu if they could see you now, Donald. Is it as bad as you expected? Would you like better to be back in John McKay's boat, going home after a hard day's fishing; dry, warm and ready for dinner?' The mainsail shivered and Roddy eased her slightly off the wind.

'And little Jessie, now: Would she be worrying, do you think?'

'Probably not,' Donald said. 'Her father was a seaman, too, and in sterner waters than these. She would know I could come to no harm in the sturdy ship *Fiona*, with Captain Roddy McKenzie at the tiller!'

Roddy laughed back at him. 'At moments like these, Donald, I think of the years wasted while I grew vegetables in my garden and shivered under the minister's scorn. But it was not until my father arrived that I realised just how low I had sunk. He looked at me pityingly, Donald, as one who had resigned himself to death in life. And I couldn't stand too much of that.'

He slapped the tiller affectionately. '*Fiona*, my girl, I have much to thank you for.

'And what are you going to do about Christy Cameron? You were very concerned before we left, but I haven't thought to inquire since.'

'Nothing,' said Donald. 'It's none of my affair, and it is better left for herself to work out.'

The wind cut Roddy's words away: 'And did you hear who was the man?'

'No,' Donald answered, 'but from what they were saying in the bush, it could have been Johnny Bain. I couldn't ask Christy, of course, and indeed I have not seen her since I came back. There is another thing I wish to know for sure: whether the baby is still alive. She told me that it was, you know, but could I take that for truth?'

'Johnny Bain?' Roddy's thoughts were definitely moving away, for he was staring intently into the wind. 'I saw him last time I was in Auckland. An enterprising young man, I should think, though he seemed a little down in his fortunes. He didn't mention Christy to me.'

'He may not even know about her yet,' Donald answered. 'In any case, it's out of my hands now – if it was ever in them – and I'll cudgel my brains about it no more. Living is an adventure, and our responsibility can at times be limited to ourselves.'

Roddy laughed, a merry devil glinting in his eyes. He buffeted Donald on the back with his free hand. 'That's what I've been hoping to hear you say, Donald. And now, relax and enjoy your blessings. After all, if the *Fiona* were to take a plunge, you would not want to go with a tear in your eye, would you?'

Even as he spoke, Roddy was listening to the wind and the sea. And there came to Donald's hearing also a deeper note in the roar of the waves.

'Time we went on the port tack,' Roddy said. 'There's an island or reef up ahead. Can you hear the surf breaking?'

As they came up into the wind, every beam and plank in the little *Fiona* seemed to be groaning with the weight of water. Then Donald, perched on the streaming, slippery forward deck, mastered the staysail. The wind filled it and they moved off heavily to the south-west. He did not join Roddy again for the moment, but stood watching, his face turned from the wind. There were currents here that disturbed the pattern of the waves; tide movements, perhaps, that made the *Fiona* fight hard. But what a fighter she was!

To Donald, a landsman with only a slight smattering of sea knowledge, her motion seemed chiefly up and down; or even, when a great wave thrust against her, backwards. But the sails, reefed down to a fraction of their full size, never stopped drawing. Her bow buffeted the sea and subdued it. The wind was her ally, although at times it seemed more likely to be her master.

He clung to the rigging when a wave crashed against her bow and sped hissing across the deck. The little dinghy was holding well, he noted with satisfaction. Then, as the *Fiona* gathered strength in the trough between two waves, he ran back to where Roddy sat, the tiller firmly under one arm.

There came a blinding rain squall, the wind eased for long enough to take three deep breaths, and then it hit stronger than ever. Roddy frowned at his big watch, and shrugged his shoulders.

'We'll not be in tonight, I'm thinking. This wind has upset my plans, for what they were ever worth. We don't want to be still tacking back and forth when night comes, and that's just what we'll be doing at this rate.

'Well have to run before it, Donald, and find somewhere less exposed to lay her to!'

'And give up the distance we have made?'

Yes, indeed, and a little more as well, perhaps. You can't afford to be miserly with sea miles in a situation like this, Donald. With such a wind behind her, the *Fiona* will be like a horse with the bit between her teeth, and if we can find no good place to stop her, we must just let her run. Are you ready, Donald?'

Roddy watched the waves with a careful, considering eye. A hundred yards ahead Donald could see them starting to take form. The water seemed to run together, mounding into a ridge that heaved and struggled as it came towards them. Sometimes it would smooth away and go easily under them. Sometimes it would mount higher and higher, towering as if it must surely break in a swirling, shapeless torrent. The *Fiona* would climb gallantly, and survive.

But those were the waves they had to watch. Roddy did not speak. Often, as they ploughed through the trough between the waves, Donald fancied that he could see the words forming under Roddy's beard, but they did not come. He tried to see if there was a regular interval between the seas, something to guide Roddy's timing. But they came choppily, and with unpredictable viciousness. Then, before he could see it, Roddy had brought the tiller hard up and they were around. The big boom came across and he jumped at the staysail sheet, hearing the roar of a breaking wave that foamed below them and ran away far ahead.

He went aft and grinned at Roddy: 'I don't know where we are going, and I find I don't much care!'

Roddy laughed into the wind, his beard streaming like a comet's tail. There was a recklessness in his eye that matched the elation which Donald realised had suddenly possessed him. 'Let the sea roar, let the wind blow. We have the beating of them!'

The next few hours were a confused running together of sharp impressions. As night approached the gale shrieked louder, the clouds darkened and the sky shut down about them. Donald seemed to be looking down on the *Fiona*, seeing her in his mind's eye as a tiny chip of wood in a vast, raging sea. Not lost, although her surroundings dwarfed her. Driven along by wind and water, but still under firm control. With the early darkness, too, there came a creeping cold. He made a hot drink, and they gulped some food. It helped to cheat the cold and the damp.

* * *

'We could run all night, Donald, with nothing between us and South America. But it would be a long way back.' Roddy had said this when the last light was draining from the sky and they had crept into the shelter of an island. Round into the wind again; staysail down, tiller lashed hard over with the mainsail keeping them steady. The *Fiona* rode smoothly enough on diminished seas, although she groaned restlessly with every wave. In turn they went below and had some sleep.

This is a battle worth the fighting, thought Donald as he crouched in the darkness. The night was alive, full of fierce and unexplainable sounds.

Over it all the drumming of the wind seemed to call in different voices, meaningless but strange and exciting. His eyes were hot in a face that was stiff with fatigue and salt spray, but his exhilaration stayed with him. The storm would pass – that much he knew – and with this thought came a momentary flash of regret.

Roddy emerged from the cabin a little before daybreak. Together they watched a pale line show in the eastern sky, and gradually the moving darkness took form; a wilderness of tossing sea, grey clouds sweeping low on either side of them, the island still there but distant now. Roddy moved stiffly forward. He sniffed the air like a tired and bedraggled dog and then returned to the shelter of the cabin.

'We'll have some breakfast, Donald, and by then, if I'm not sadly mistaken, this wind will have blown itself out.'

Streaks of pale blue sky showed in the south. Gusts became spasmodic, as if they were losing heart. 'We'll shake a reef out of the mainsail,' said Roddy after they had eaten. 'It will be quite different sailing today.'

* * *

And now the wind flowed freshly from the north again; a cheerful, buoyant wind that carried no threat of storm. It swept the heavy clouds away and soon, incredibly, the sun was warming them.

'How quickly it can change,' said Donald, looking with wonder at the sparking sea. It had been a stout battle, indeed, and now that the sun was shining, he felt his strength coming back with the autumn warmth, his weariness replaced by a keenness of spirit that sharpened his enjoyment.

Roddy was brisk and businesslike, impatient to reach Auckland. 'Jib and stays'l out,' he said. 'We'll give the canvas a good airing.' The *Fiona*, emerging from the world of storm, foamed along with her wake marking the waves. The seagulls had returned, too, and now as they passed Tiri in the clear, rain-swept morning light, white-winged birds swooped and wheeled about them, enlivening the air with their raucous cries.

Donald found himself looking forward to seeing the town.

* * *

Chapter Thirteen

AFTERWARDS, WHEN HE ALLOWED HIMSELF TO THINK ABOUT HIS one eventful day in Auckland, Donald wondered how much of it had come about by chance and how much by design – Roddy's design.

It began as they neared the narrow waters, and a great four-masted ship, a swift sailer on the London run, came past them with a magnificent surge and sweep. Roddy sighed. 'It's a great pity that you will never know that life, Donald. You're too old to learn now. A few dull trips back and forth between Waipu and Auckland and you'll bid farewell to the sea forever.'

'I hope not,' Donald replied. 'I must surely see more than that – and in your company too, perhaps.'

Roddy's face was all innocence as he answered, 'So you might, it is true. So you might.'

He spoke casually, as if uttering idle thoughts. 'Do you think Christy loves this fellow, Johnny Bain? But I'm forgetting. You couldn't know. But she might, if he is indeed the one. And, again, she might not.

'And what about Johnny, himself? It would be interesting – and informative, perhaps – to see his reactions when told about Christy. I think you should ask him, Donald, if we happen to see him.'

'I'm not interfering, as you well know, Roddy.'

'So you have said. But I've been thinking about those people back in Waipu. They didn't spare you, did they Donald? It would be grand to put them in their place – to produce a blushing bridegroom and show that, after all, he was not so reluctant.' He laughed softly to himself. 'And I wonder what Christy would do if we brought him back and laid him at her feet.

'But enough of that. Let us think of other things.'

They rounded North Head and Donald's heart leapt at the sight he now saw. A brisk sea danced against the hulls of ships lying impressively at anchor, and gave sprightly life to a host of smaller vessels that criss-crossed the harbour like floating dragonflies. A clear sky-line after the storm, and every building in the little town sharply defined in the afternoon sunshine. Grand houses above the cliffs of the nearer bays, church spires and circling windmills, lines of commercial buildings clustered thickly on the waterfront, then straggled, a little forlornly, up the hills. Red gashes in the cliffs below the fort, the gleaming slate roofs of the barracks above the centre of town. Shipbuilding yards where wooden vessels stood in the slips. And the wharves!

Here was a sight to dazzle Donald's unaccustomed eyes. A spider's web of rigging and running gear; masts as thick as trees in the forest. There were tall, full-rigged vessels, barques, schooners and brigs. Beside them the wharves were busy with teams of horses with wagons and men. Work was going on steadily, and the noise of it came across the water to the *Fiona* as she sailed discreetly past.

Roddy brought his cutter to a humbler wharf. He threw ashore mooring lines that were secured by willing idlers. Snugly, the *Fiona* settled to her berth, while master and crew made everything neat. 'She may be only small, Donald,' said Roddy, 'but she'll be as smart as any other vessel I've had!'

He lowered a wooden bucket over the side and washed down the deck. The brass was shining satisfactorily, the sails stowed trimly. 'I sometimes wish she was a schooner, with fifteen knots under her stem and cargo space to match. Then we would truly go a-trading, Donald – and a few other good men with us. But she's not, and we're not complaining.' He slapped the cabin top with a hard, affectionate hand, and they went below to change into shore clothes.

* * *

Now that he was part of it, the town seemed more impressive in size. They walked off the wharf, past the open beach where Maoris waited patiently beside heaps of produce and goods. Donald adjusted his long stride to keep pace with Roddy's short, rapidly moving legs. They stopped frequently while Donald was shown the sights of the town.

The ground, firm though he knew it to be, heaved strangely at times, but the feeling of elation, the sense of adventure had not deserted him.

He laughed to himself as he watched loungers in the street; men, and women too, walking idly from one group to another of the same kind.

'What do they all find to keep themselves alive?' he asked.

Roddy grunted: 'They're business men, mostly, taking in each other's washing, as the saying goes; and their wives. Having no other occupation, the ladies come in to town to sip tea and talk scandal, much the same as the rest of their sex all over the world. But we can thank them for much, Donald. The money that they have, they spend on food they cannot grow for themselves. And we're the ones who bring it to them.'

Roddy grabbed Donald's elbow and steered him into a dark little shop that was rich with the smell of food and commerce. 'Now to business,' he said. 'Stand by and you'll see how it's done.'

A small boy, almost submerged in an apron of spotless white cloth, pencil behind one ear and wiry hair slicked over to one side, approached and smiled at Roddy. 'You want to see him?' he asked.

'Yes,' said Roddy. 'But first I want you to meet my friend Donald. This is Silas More, Donald; a little fellow with a big future. And now, Silas, tell your master he has visitors.'

The boy disappeared through a door in the back of the shop. Roddy walked round looking at the crowded shelves. 'Would you not like to work here, Donald? Plenty to eat and no garden to dig?'

Young Silas reappeared, and Donald followed Roddy through to an untidy office with a big desk and half a dozen chairs. He had time to see that there were books everywhere, account books bound in rusty black, a litter of papers that covered the shelves. The sun shone palely outside the solitary window.

'Good afternoon Mr McCaul,' said Roddy in his most impressive voice. Then, for the first time, Donald saw that the room was not empty. Mr McCaul came towards them from the shadows: A round little man, stooped, with eyes that peered mildly and incuriously at them over thick spectacles. He walked with short, mincing steps – like a beetle, Donald thought – leaning on a carved walking stick. A praying mantis, that is what he resembled, said Donald to himself, while Mr McCaul extended one of his feelers and shook hands softly.

'Mr McCaul was one of us,' Roddy explained, 'but he chose to enter the world of commerce when we came to New Zealand, and he has never known the joys of life in Waipu. A dealer in many things, and some of them profitable – or so I am led to believe. Is that not so, Mr McCaul?'

The little man smiled. 'Donald McKinnon,' he said thoughtfully. 'That would be Alex's son. Tell me, Donald, what are you doing at sea?'

'He is my friend,' Roddy interrupted, 'and is ready to go wherever I wish to take him. You see, Donald has decided that it's time he learned about the world.'

'You'll do that well enough, I'm not doubting,' said Mr McCaul, his eyes still weighing the young man. 'And do you like what you have seen already?'

Donald began to reply, but Mr McCaul had turned now to Roddy.

'You have more freight, no doubt? What is it this time?'

Roddy produced a list. 'Read it for yourself,' he said, and laughed as Mr McCaul went carefully through the various items.

When he had finished, Mr McCaul nodded briefly to himself. 'We'll manage it on the same terms. Silas!' he called. An alert pair of eyes peered through the door. 'Take this list to our carrier. If he hurries, he should have it unloaded within the hour. And then there'll be other cargo to go down.' He turned to Roddy. 'You saw Kenny?'

'Yes,' Roddy replied. 'And all is well.'

'And what about Donald, here?'

'It will not be interesting him, I suspect.'

Mr McCaul nodded and turned back to his desk, his tiny feet flickering across the floor. He hung his stick on a heavy brass hook and sat down.

'Don't be standing there. You must be tired, both of you, after your long journey.'

Donald found a chair and looked from one to the other of the men. He was puzzled, but had to restrain an almost irresistible temptation to laugh. Roddy, with his bristling beard and mad blue eyes; Mr McCaul, who could surely never be called by any more intimate name, sober but quietly affable, discussing him as if he were a pawn in some strange game of chess. From outside came the noise of traffic; the rumbling of draywheels on cobblestones, the sharp crack of whips and the clamour of numerous voices. A rowdy town, and all the time there was the feeling that something new and exciting was happening.

In the back of his mind there was still the savour of their struggle with the sea, the roar of the wind and the crashing of great waves, and further back still the memory of the quiet, green land that he had left behind. But these were only faint echoes against the new excitement that beat about him.

'What doesn't interest me, Roddy, and how can you be so sure?'

Roddy shook his head solemnly. 'We'll see,' he remarked. 'You can never tell. Can you now, Mr McCaul?'

But Mr McCaul was busy fumbling in a cupboard awkwardly placed behind his chair. With much effort he produced a black bottle and held it up against the light. He set it carefully on his desk and brought glasses from a drawer. He wiped them with an immaculate handkerchief.

'Roddy, you will know that it is not my custom, but I think we should have a wee drink.' He poured the whisky, carefully filling each glass to the same level, and handed one to each of his guests.

'Surely the best way to do business, Mr McCaul!' Roddy raised his glass to a Gaelic toast, which the surprising Mr McCaul repeated fluently. The neat spirit was warm and not unduly harsh. Donald sipped his slowly and the world still seemed a good place.

'Your father,' said Mr McCaul, 'would still be enjoying his occasional glass, I'm thinking, but would make sure that his boys did not see too much of it. A very wise man, your father, when I knew him. Sober in his pleasures, but no crow at a wedding feast.'

Donald was still holding his glass, but Roddy and Mr McCaul had refilled theirs. The little man's impeccable English had gained a lilt that Donald had not noticed before.

'The minister hasn't wooed him away from it, I don't suppose?'

Donald shook his head. 'No,' he replied. 'My father is one man who seems to keep clear of his power. I don't know how he manages it. Perhaps he keeps quiet enough for the minister not to notice him?'

'That is the way to be,' said Mr McCaul. 'Donald, to look at me now you would possibly never think it. But the minister and I, when we were both younger, had some terrible encounters. He could talk louder, and so he won. And that is why I stayed in Auckland when he went to Waipu. But he's a great man for all of that,' he added dispassionately. 'A strong man and a zealous one'

He studied Donald with a speculative eye. 'It is possible, perhaps, that he is not unconnected with your visit to this town. Many a young man he has driven away.'

'No,' said Donald. "And I must say that, for the most part, I agree with him and his ideas.'

Mr McCaul looked at Roddy and shook his head. 'Well, well,' he said, as if not fully convinced. 'In that case, you could have chosen better company.'

Roddy did not speak. He was gazing thoughtfully into his empty glass.

‘And now,’ said Mr McCaul briskly, ‘we’ll have one small drink each, and then you must away. This will be the time, I imagine, Roddy. Will you be calling before you sail?’

‘I must have a word with Donald, here, first. I’ll see you tomorrow.’

The whisky had made Roddy look more innocent than usual.

‘What is this all about?’ Donald asked.

‘Don’t be impatient, Donald. There are important matters afoot, and you will learn about them in good time – that is, if you are interested.’

Mr McCaul was already leading the way through the shop, past perky young Silas More, who was busy piling parcels into a large handcart. Donald found himself following, until he stood once again on the sidewalk of the narrow street. Mr McCaul shook hands softly and went back to his office.

* * *

‘That’s part of our business done. Not so unpleasant, was it, Donald? Are you enjoying yourself, lad?’ Roddy reached for his faithful watch, eyed it fiercely and set off with great haste down the road.

Donald kept pace with him, but his attention was continually being distracted by the sights and sounds of the town. Shutters were going up on the shop fronts, but the doors were still open and a brisk trade being done. There were fewer wagons and drays about. Instead, cabs and handsome gigs, drawn by high-stepping horses with slim legs and fiery eyes, sought a way along the crowded road. In some of them sat formal-suited businessmen; merchants, lawyers, wealthy traders no doubt, going home to a peaceful evening with their families. For others, the day was just starting. A party of soldiers came swaying past them, singing and laughing together. ‘They’ve been drinking,’ Donald said to Roddy, ‘and to tell you the truth I’m feeling quite cheerful myself.’

But Roddy didn’t answer. He was striding along with a preoccupied expression on his face. Donald looked at him with affectionate amusement, and then began to whistle cheerfully to himself. Three shopgirls, plainly but neatly dressed, smiled at him as they walked past. He looked back, and they gave a friendly wave.

‘These townsfolk are not so stiff as I have heard,’ he told Roddy. ‘They seem quite pleased to see us.’

'That's so,' Roddy agreed. 'But whatever happens, Donald, watch your pockets. There are always rogues about, ready to get the best of simple country lads!'

Donald stopped in astonishment. 'But surely they wouldn't be able to tell?' He held out his long arms and invited Roddy to inspect his black cloth suit and polished boots. 'There's nothing wrong with all this, is there?'

Roddy looked at the tall young man. He laughed: 'No, Donald, you are surely a model of fashion. But remember this, too, that no true townsman would speak to casual strangers if he could avoid it. He keeps to himself, for he knows that other men can be his enemies. And again, Donald, they are shrewd at summing anyone up – they have to be. They would look at you and say: "He's browned by the sun, with big, workman's hands, but he's not dressed like a town labourer. And he carries himself as if he fears no-one and calls nobody his master. A farmer or a bushman just come to town to spend his money," they would say. "A bird good for the plucking!" So be on your guard, Donald. Keep your mind alert and your tongue quiet in your mouth!'

They began to walk again, around corners, along tortuous alleys packed with small houses and shops, changing direction so often that Donald lost all sense of where he was. Buildings shut out sight of the sea, and the sun had also disappeared.

'And now, my lad, let us eat.' Roddy pushed against a narrow swinging door in a large, plain wooden building that rose on the edge of the footpath. A dimly-lighted hall was empty, but from an adjoining room there came a blare of talk and a smell of tobacco such as Donald had never known before. Roddy walked boldly into the crowded room with Donald following him.

A big room, with a carpet on the floor and rich curtains masking the windows. Men and women sat at tables or on long couches that filled every corner. There was a piano but no one was playing; the music would have been harder to hear than a piper at a ceilidh. Roddy caught a steward as he went hurrying by with a tray. He ordered a bottle of good wine and two glasses, which they carried to a couch that had just been left empty.

'What a splendid room!' said Donald. 'I should not have thought to find anything like this in Auckland!'

'It is, indeed, a pleasant, well-ordered place,' Roddy replied. 'I have had meals here on occasion, and find the service reasonable. We'll have a glass of wine, and then dinner.'

* * *

This is indeed life, Donald thought as he followed an elegant waitress between rows of white-coloured tables. And what food! Until this moment he had not realised, for excitement, that meals had been rare and short since the night at Kenny Omaha's. How long ago that seemed! He belonged now to another world, packed full of cheerful, honest folk who were kind and hospitable.

They had another glass of the wine that Roddy had brought with him from the parlour. A genial drink, not harsh nor yet too sweet. He felt his goodwill mounting as the wine reached his stomach. Roddy was talking, but apparently he did not expect answers, for he kept on without pause. Donald enjoyed the sound of his voice as a background to the vastly more important task of eating and drinking.

'There's a shortage of good beef and vegetables,' he said. The waitress brought them another helping, on clean plates of fine china. Roddy was making good play with his knife and fork; nor did Donald need any urging. They ordered apple pie, with cream in a silver jug. And only when that had gone did Donald lean back in his chair and look about him.

'I'm bewildered, Roddy,' he said. 'Who would have dreamed that one night we should be tossed in a great storm, and the next eating in such comfort?'

'Life is like that,' Roddy replied. He used a toothpick with considerable satisfaction. 'Ups and downs are the spice of existence. And who knows; there may be even more in the future.' He looked at Donald as if about to add something. Instead he rose from his chair. 'Come, now, we'll sit in the parlour for a while and have a talk before going back to the *Fiona*. She'll be ready for sea again now, or I don't know our Mr McCaul!'

'Has he an interest in the *Fiona*, Roddy?'

'He has an interest in many things, Donald. Half of them I do not know myself, although I'm learning all the time. But remember this: I'm the one who says where the *Fiona* sails, and what she carries. I'm the master, and I have enough power to keep it that way!' His eyes sparkled fiercely, and then, as he sat back in a comfortable chair, he grinned at Donald as if there was some joke that only he could fully enjoy.

Donald was content enough to sit back and relax. While they had been eating their dinner, most of the crowd had disappeared. The air was clearer of tobacco smoke, but the room was warm and soothing to his mind and body. Roddy produced his pipe, cleared his throat and then put his pipe away again. Four men came to the door, hesitated, but did not come in. They spoke among themselves and went away. Donald heard the outside door squeak as it was opened, and then two other men came walking into the lounge as if they owned it. They were smartly dressed, with carefully tended moustaches, and their hands did not look like those of men who worked. They lighted cigars, ordered drinks and sat talking quietly while their eyes roved round the room.

Roddy jumped to his feet. 'There's someone I must talk with,' he said. 'It will not take long. I'll see you again in about an hour.' The last words came over his shoulder, for he was already half way to the door.

The bright lights were swimming pleasantly, and Donald was not perturbed at Roddy's sudden going. An hour, he thought; perhaps more, perhaps less. He felt no great curiosity about what might be happening.

A smooth, masculine voice broke into his thoughts. 'Would it worry you if we sat here?' it asked. Donald jerked his eyes open and nodded hastily. The two men who had come into the room a little earlier lowered themselves elegantly beside him. 'I always find the light is so much better in this corner of the room,' said the other. 'And besides, one can see who is coming in, cannot one? Perhaps you have discovered this in the past, too?'

Donald pulled his thoughts together. 'No,' he replied. 'I hadn't noticed that. But this is my first visit here.'

One of the men was attending to his cigar. Donald looked at the other, and was surprised at the concentration over trivial chatter that showed in his black, glistening eyes.

'Ah,' he said, 'a visitor. From Australia? No? From our homeland, then?'

'And where would that be?' Donald asked bluntly.

A flush touched the swarthy cheeks of the man beside him, and there was a humourless sparkle in his eyes. But he answered with an easy laugh:

'England, of course; the nursery of this delightful young land. The country to which out thoughts constantly turn.'

'No, I'm not from there either,' said Donald. 'To speak the truth, I suppose I'm a Nova Scotian. But my home is at Waipu.'

'Yes, yes indeed,' his new friend remarked. 'A very fine place. I was there once myself.'

'Where?' Donald asked. 'In Nova Scotia, or in Waipu?'

'Both, as a matter of fact, but it was so long ago. Charming places, however, both of them. Charming places.'

He turned to his companion whose cigar was now burning satisfactorily.

'Edward,' he said, 'our young friend here is from Waipu. He is a Nova Scotian. That's interesting, isn't it?'

'Exceedingly,' remarked Edward, with a delicate irony that Donald did not fully appreciate. 'And where the hell is Waipu?'

'Your ignorance, Edward, never fails to amaze me. Tell him, young man, tell him.'

'About eighty miles north of Auckland,' said Donald. 'We came down by cutter.'

'Big town?' asked Edward indifferently.

'Not exactly. It's not as big as Auckland. In fact, it's much smaller.'

'That could well be so,' said Edward. 'But aren't you going to introduce yourself?'

'No harm in giving your name away,' said Edward's friend with a cheerful, hollow laugh. 'Edward Smith; Robert FitzJones – that's me – and…?'

'Donald McKinnon.'

They bowed to one another. 'A good Scottish name,' said FitzJones. 'No wonder you scorned my suggestion that you were from England. You are, I suspect, a Highlander. A noble race who have never had their desserts in this world, I fear. Are there many of them in – ah – Waipu?'

'It is full of them,' said Donald simply. 'There is no room for a Sassenach in the place.'

'That's very good; very good indeed,' said Robert FitzJones, laughing heartily as if at a subtle joke. Donald joined in, for it all seemed delightful and amusing. He noticed, however, that Mr FitzJones's laughter did not reach his eyes, which were remarkably cold and calculating for such a high-spirited gentleman. Edward Smith had lapsed into deep thought and was looking at the door, paying no attention to the conversation.

'Did you hear that, Edward?' said FitzJones with a chuckle. 'Waipu is full of Highlanders. It must be a grand place.'

'You're not laughing at me?' asked Donald, wishing that he could understand this strange Auckland brand of humour. 'It is a very good place to live, and I would not wish to hear a word spoken against it.'

If he had not felt so content, he might have become angry with them. He wished, momentarily, that they would take themselves away, and then was ashamed of the thought. After all, they were only being friendly to a stranger.

'And what do you do at Waipu?'

'We work in the forest and on the farms. We fish, and we enjoy a quiet life.'

'Plenty of rich farmers up there, I should say,' observed Edward, showing more interest.

Robert FitzJones nudged him openly. 'Be quiet, Edward,' he chided. 'You should know that no gentleman speaks of money.' He turned his knowing eyes on Donald again. 'And are you here on holiday, ready to see the sights of our little town? And your friend will be coming back, no doubt?'

'He'll be back in an hour, or less,' said Donald. 'He had a little business to attend to, but it should not keep him long.'

More people were coming into the lounge now. They were well dressed and gay, as if ready for an evening's entertainment. The stewards were busier, too, darting in and out of the room with trays. But the number of guests never became great, for as some came in, others went away.

'You will join us in a drink, I am sure.' Mr FitzJones did not wait for an answer, and a steward was already hastening to his imperiously-raised hand. 'The spirit of the land of your fathers, Mr McKinnon, or something more mild and mellow? A glass of wine, perhaps?'

Donald nodded, not caring greatly what should come. It proved to be wine, pleasant enough to the taste. Mr FitzJones produced some silver and paid with a flourish.

More drink was paid for by the taciturn Mr Smith, who still gave the conversation only half his attention. And then Donald, thankful that he had his purse well filled, gave another order to the smirking steward.

'Still enjoying the wine, Mr McKinnon? Is it to your taste?' Mr FitzJones laughed like a half-tamed animal, but quickly subdued it with a cough. 'Perhaps when your friend returns, you may care to accompany us to the play, or to some other entertainment. Auckland is very bright at present, growing more like Sydney all the time, what with the war and the soldiers.'

'He'll probably want to go to bed,' said Donald, 'but we can see.'

'That is excellent,' said Mr FitzJones heartily. 'Edward, perhaps you could discover just what there is to amuse us.' Edward rose silently to his feet. 'Indeed, I'll come with you.' He nodded pleasantly to Donald. 'We will not be long.'

They glided smoothly across the carpet to the door, and Donald watched them go, amusement mixed with an indefinable irritation. Their company for a whole evening would be burdensome, he thought, and yet they were good-natured. But he was feeling sleepy. His bunk on the *Fiona* seemed a very desirable place. If Roddy returned before the two men, they would not wait. Perhaps he might see them again, another day, and he could make his apologies then.

But he was not allowed to rest. As he sat idly in his quiet corner, watching the door, expecting all the time to see them return and hoping that Roddy might come first, a girl came in and paused uncertainly. She was alone, which seemed strange in this crowded place, and her eyes were lowered demurely, which seemed even stranger. He watched her with interest.

A slight, youthful figure, a well-fitting gown in bright colours, hair that reflected the light. She seemed to sense his eyes upon her, for she looked at him directly. Then, with a pleasing shyness, she came over.

'I do not wish to intrude,' she said, 'but I had hoped to see someone here that I knew, and one feels so obvious standing by the door. Might I sit here for a few minutes? It is the only quiet place in the room.'

She pointed to the chair that faced Donald's. He jumped to his feet, feeling that he was the champion of womankind in distress, and hastily urged her to sit down.

'It is very kind of you,' she murmured, raising her eyes. 'But then I have been told that handsome young men are the most courteous.'

He felt himself blushing. 'Anyone would have done the same,' he assured her. 'It is little enough.'

She sat forward, her hands clasped on her knees, and looked anxiously around the room. 'She has not come yet. I waited outside for as long as I dared, but could not see her.'

Her bottom lip quivered, a rosy lip in a face that, he felt, was made for laughter rather than tears.

'Can I be of any help?' said Donald.

'I do not think so,' she replied, with a quick smile of thanks. Her face became sober again. 'I do not see how anyone can help, if she does not come.'

The steward was at their shoulders. 'Gin for you, dear?' he asked the girl with what Donald thought an excessive familiarity. 'And the same for you again, sir?'

'I'll have some whisky,' Donald said shortly. The unaccustomed wine was over-sweet in his mouth. He wanted no more of it.

The steward went away and Donald turned to his companion.

'I cannot guess what it is all about,' he said, 'but why not tell me?'

The girl fumbled for a crumpled handkerchief and patted her eyes with it. Her fingers, he noted with concern, were grimy, and the nails were not cared for.

'My brother went to Australia from England three years ago,' she said, sipping her gin with as much interest as if it were water. Her eyes looked at him frankly, so sadly, that he felt his protective instincts rising fast. 'My mother and I were to follow him when he had made a home. But just before we were to sail she became ill. I nursed her night and day but she did not recover, and died. What was I to do? The voyage alone at such a time frightened me. But it would be worse to stay in England with no family or friends there. And so I decided to go.'

She sipped delicately at her gin, and Donald watched her breathlessly.

'The ship came to Sydney Harbour, but my brother was not there. He had gone away to the gold-diggings at Ballarat. I followed him, but someone on the fields told me that he had left a month before, and gone to New Zealand.

'I was lucky to find a ship sailing to Auckland. I thought it would not be long before I found him again. But New Zealand is a bigger place than I had thought, and so far I've heard nothing of him.'

She sighed. 'I have had to work, and life has not been easy. Today I received an answer to an advertisement, offering me a position as companion to an Auckland lady. She was to meet me here tonight, but now it seems that I have lost that chance, too.'

Donald expressed his sympathy, and the steward was there again with an inquiring look on his face.

'Would you care for another drink?' Donald asked. She hesitated, and then nodded.

'Perhaps I should... I feel so depressed and unhappy!'

'You'll have to be careful, although it might be wrong of me to say it. You're a young girl, and drink may seem an easy way to make your troubles less serious. But it isn't, you must know!'

She nodded sombrely. 'I understand what you mean, and thank you for your advice. But it isn't really necessary.'

What a tender, frail little creature to have been buffeted around the world like this, Donald thought. Life could certainly be cruel, but he felt an excitement that was not merely the result of his adventurous day, of his unaccustomed surroundings and of the drink he had himself taken.

'Your brother, you are beginning to think, is nowhere about Auckland?'

She bowed her head, and then threw a quick glance at the door. 'I fear I have lost him,' she said.

Donald continued boldly: 'Would this suggestion please you? I do not live in Auckland here. My home is at Waipu, and we return there by cutter tomorrow. They are good people in Waipu; kind to those in distress. Come with us, and I can promise you will have a good home. You'll be able to help with the daily tasks, and you'll have no time to brood over your misfortune. And then, if anything is heard of your brother, you will not be too far away.'

Her eyes were startled, and it was as if she were looking at him for the first time.

'The country is better than the town,' he went on. 'It may be quiet, but it is healthy and your mind will not grow dull.'

'Do you mean all this?' she asked. 'But what would your parents say? And have you no girl of your own?'

'I have, indeed; or I hope so,' Donald answered. 'But it would not concern her. And I know my mother would help you in every way she could.'

She was still watching him with incredulous eyes. They softened, and then, while he waited for a reply, they became as hard as diamonds. She darted another quick glance at the door, as if in desperation.

'Of course I couldn't do that, you poor fool! Leave the towns – even a one-horse dump like this one – and go mouldy miles from anywhere? You must be out of your mind! And what would be in it for you? You can't get a girl as easy as that!'

And now for Donald the lights were really swimming. Was the devil possessing her? His jaw dropped in bewilderment, and he could say nothing to stem the flood of abuse. But puzzlement still kept his anger at bay. What he had suggested was plain and simple enough, and she should have guessed, if she was the girl he thought her to be, that there were no conditions to his offer. And those tears did not seem to be caused only by her fury.

'If you want to come, but cannot, there is no call for such talk,' he said.

The hardness had gone from her eyes. Donald followed her swift glance to the door and before she spoke again had time to see Mr FitzJones and his friend Edward Smith standing there, grinning wolfishly.

'I'm sorry that I have to do this, my friend, but I'm sorrier for myself than for you.'

He was leaning forward, trying to force some clear thinking into his brain, when her hand slapped hard against the side of his face. He shook his head dazedly. She screamed twice, with startling power, and then slumped back into her chair.

Donald was on his feet, watching Mr FitzJones and the silent Smith advancing towards him. Everyone else in the room had stopped talking. Their eyes were on him.

The girl pointed with a trembling finger. 'He…' She stumbled, but the accusing finger still held Donald as the target for their eyes.

'Mr McKinnon!' exclaimed FitzJones. 'What is all this about?' There was not even a pretence of friendliness in his face now. 'Are not our young girls safe from you?'

Donald's mind was in chaos. He noted, dully, that Mr FitzJones, in spite of his dandified ways, was wearing a pair of broken shoes. He had hungry hands, like the claws of a bird. The man, he thought without great surprise, would never have been my friend.

'This sort of conduct is not allowed in our city,' said Mr FitzJones in a loud voice, and Mr Smith nodded disapprovingly, moving closer to Donald.

The girl was quiet now, lying back with her eyes closed. Donald, with strange objectivity, studied her. Streaks of crude make-up showed in the bright light. Her fair hair had a brassy tint, and was dark at the roots. Now that the alcohol was losing its power, he could see that she was a common little creature, her brightly-coloured dress soiled at the neckline. And her neck, too, was in need of a good scrub. A sudden pity came over him, while the men stood watching and the whole room seemed to hold its breath. He moved one hand and touched her cheek with his fingers. Such delicate bone; a face and figure that should have held a man's reverence, not his scorn. How had she come to this? What was she doing, a stray in the jungle of the town? Was there any truth in her story, or was it all an elaborate pretence?

She did not move, but Mr FitzJones reached out. As he touched his arm, Donald shook himself, and suddenly his bewilderment stiffened into anger. It was a conspiracy. From the very beginning FitzJones and Smith, with the girl, had aimed at trapping him.

'We'll go along to the police,' FitzJones said to Donald. His tone was confident, his manner condescending. This man was small fry, he seemed to be thinking. 'You must learn, Mr McKinnon, to control your baser instincts when you come to our fair young city.' There were murmurs of agreement from the bystanders.

Anger had mounted to Donald's brain; a bitter anger that he knew would not easily die. He looked again at the girl, a pathetic little figure. He wished he could help her, but that was impossible now, and she would not listen to him in any case. Forget her for the moment and think of yourself, Donald, and of the awkward spot you have placed yourself in! His brain met the challenge of fear and anger. Do nothing now, Donald; act as would the flustered country simpleton that they think you are. Wait your chance, when there are fewer people about.

Smith was at his other shoulder. He hung back momentarily to see what would happen, and Smith jerked him contemptuously along. He allowed his muscles to go soft and was led to the door.

He was thinking clearly; calculating the time to escape. They would not be allowed to get away without something to remember him by. But first of all, he must make sure. 'They told me, in the bush camp, that there were men who lived on women, but I would never have believed it,' he remarked softly.

FitzJones laughed his jackal laugh. 'What are you talking about, my boy? Any money we have, we truly earn – as you will find out!'

Smith tightened his grip on Donald's arm. This man is the dangerous one, Donald said to himself. He doesn't waste time talking.

They were nearing the swinging door that led on to the street. 'I don't believe you are taking me to the police. You wouldn't dare to face them.'

'Careful, Smithy. Don't let him worry you,' said FitzJones nervously, his smooth accent disappearing. 'We can't do it here. Wait your chance.'

Smith gave a short laugh, but did not reply. His grip was firm on Donald's arm. They moved out into the street, sparsely lighted with lamps.

'You're not taking me to the police,' Donald repeated. He stopped and the two men jerked at his arms. Smith, he saw, was reaching into a pocket under his coat.

'Keep quiet and you'll come to no harm,' said Mr FitzJones.

Donald jerked himself free, and punched at the white mask of Smith's face. The man staggered back. FitzJones aimed a vicious kick. Donald caught his leg and threw him to the ground. Smith was coming in again silently. With cold anger burning in his brain, Donald hit him solidly in the stomach and then, as he collapsed, caught him with another blow to the chin. Smith went down, his legs and arms wavering weakly, scrabbling at the gritty footpath as he tried to rise.

Donald began to run down the road, remembering vaguely the way he had come, and hoping that his sense of direction would bring him quickly to the waterfront. He had gone only a few paces when he heard cries from behind him. 'Stop him! Hold him!' shouted Mr FitzJones, whose strength had apparently returned. 'Don't let him past!'

Donald checked in full stride. A roistering party of soldiers straggling up the road had heard the calls and were collecting themselves for action. It was no more than a game to them, but one which would be far more interesting that wandering the streets. A corporal, or someone more enterprising than the rest, marshalled the men into a formidable group and they came at him, yelling with excitement.

There was no time to waste. Donald jumped straight at one man and bowled him to the ground before he knew what had happened. Then he was through, seeking the shadows at the side of the road, his heart thudding and all his senses on high alert. The alarm had spread far already. He could not keep on this way, fighting past group after group of men who, even if they had no personal interest, would combine against a fugitive.

A narrow lane, badly paved and unlighted, led off to the right. Donald turned along it, stumbled, but quickly recovered. Mr FitzJones's triumphant voice sounded from the mouth of the lane. He plunged deeper into the darkness and glanced over his shoulder to see his pursuers moving in, carefully, after him. A high paling fence was on his left; behind it the shadow of a big tree and a pale light shining through a curtained window. The lane was beginning to climb. It probably ran to a blind end, and then he would be caught. He sprang to the top of the fence, feeling a splinter catch his good trousers at the knee, and dropped cautiously to the ground on the other side.

The hunters went past like a pack of wolves and then came back, trying gates and knocking on doors. As Donald crept by the house, straining his eyes in the darkness, he heard the sound of heavy boots from inside. He began to run, careless of the noise he made. Over another fence, a lower one this time, and through long grass that masked uneven ground. Into the small backyard of another house, where he lurched against a brick well-head and, before he had fully recovered balance, tripped and fell headlong against a small wooden shed – a privy, judging by the noisome smell that filled the air. A stone wall that was easily climbed; a path outlined with white lime that led him past a tall, narrow house where no lights showed. A wrought iron gate opened onto another street.

He listened. Behind him, but coming nearer, were the sounds of voices. Keep away from the roads, Donald, because they know the place better than you do, he counselled himself, and ran back along the path behind the house.

He hoped that he was not losing his direction. But all he could do was to keep on steadily, following the fall of the ground toward the sea. The forest was no more confusing than this. Men, when they had laid out the town, had brought no order to it. There might be gardens and well-painted fronts to many of the buildings, as he had seen earlier in the day, but the way he was forced to follow gave no sign of that now. Here he found cesspools, heaps of rank garbage, the rubbish and filth of a town that had not fully organised itself for decent living. He felt a loathing for Auckland rise in his throat. 'If I get away,' he swore, 'I'll never come back!'

And now it seemed that he had outdistanced his pursuers. Most of them, he guessed, would have dropped out of the hunt long before. But he could not see all of them giving up. What had FitzJones and Smith wanted of him? Surely they would not have gone to all this trouble for the few shillings he might be carrying? But there did not seem any other reason.

He struggled across the broken clay of an empty allotment, slid down an excavation designed for the basement of a house or shop that had never been completed, and peered cautiously through the fence. The road was quiet. He was back in the shopping area now, and the long narrow street was lined with small buildings with boarded fronts. No hotels in sight, no theatres or houses, and no people or sign of any activity. He brushed his grimy clothes – how proud he had been of them so few hours before – examined the tear in his trousers with concern, which lessened when he found it was not very noticeable, and stepped softly out.

The road curved around the foot of a steep bluff and suddenly he saw the masts of shipping against the night sky. He quickened his pace.

Be bold, Donald, he told himself. No fugitive now, but a seaman going quietly back to his ship. He even mustered a whistle as he walked along, keeping to the centre of the road and stepping carefully to avoid the horse droppings that showed how busy the waterfront had been during the day.

There was no difficulty now. The ships at the wharves were quiet and the watchman called out a friendly 'good-night' as he went by. The pursuit had died away, or else FitzJones and his gang were hunting in a different direction.

The big ships were left behind. He skirted the sandy beach where the Maoris had been waiting that afternoon. Soon he fancied he could see the *Fiona* at her berth, her mast swinging in the light swell that the night wind raised on the harbour.

He hurried now, wondering whether by any chance Roddy had already returned. And so, as he stepped on to the wooden wharf, the quiet voice took him completely by surprise.

'Good evening Mr McKinnon. I thought you might be here.'

He stopped and peered at the figure standing as still as a shadow near the edge of the wharf. It was Mr Smith.

Donald stepped closer, and he did not move.

'What do you want?'

'To give you a warning,' Mr Smith replied. 'You have caused us a lot of trouble; more trouble indeed than you are worth. I told FitzJones to keep away from you, but the man's a fool and cannot resist plucking even a sparrow. Now remember this, McKinnon: Keep away from the police, say nothing to anyone else, and you will fare well enough. But if you go talking, you will be sorry. We on our part are prepared to leave it at that.'

He moved one arm, as if to offer Donald his hand, a gesture so unexpected that Donald did not accept it. And suddenly, in the murky light, he saw Smith whip his arm quickly up. In his hand was a bludgeon, weighted at one end, that whistled down towards him. Donald threw himself sideways and the stick glanced off his shoulder, sliding harmlessly down his left arm. Smith cursed and tried to recover himself for another blow. In the pale, reflected light his teeth glinted between lips drawn back like those of an animal.

Donald twisted his body and caught Smith's upraised arm in his right hand. Smith jerked savagely, but Donald had him in a firm grip. There was a trapped ferocity in the way Smith struggled, and in his eyes a sudden spark of fear.

The club rattled on to the wharf planks. A sharp thrust, and Smith spun across the wharf, trying desperately to regain his footing, and then disappeared. There was a splash; a mighty flailing of water.

'And now, Mr Smith, don't be coming near me again,' Donald called softly. 'And here is your wicked weapon.'

He flung the little club far out over the water and turned away down the wharf.

But the splashing continued and Smith, in a choked voice, was calling for help.

'The poor fish cannot swim,' Donald said to himself. He grinned and unbuttoned his coat, folding it carefully and placing it on the wharf. 'My trousers are spoilt in any case.' He jumped into the water, and its freshness cleared the last fumes of alcohol from his brain. What a day it's been! he thought as he searched for the dark blot of Smith's head in the water, seized him by the hair, and dragged him to the steps that led up onto the wharf.

'You'll live to be hanged, Mr Smith; and your friends too.' But Mr Smith was already squelching away, the water dripping from his forlorn clothes.

Donald shook himself and combed his streaming hair with his hands. The men – and women – that there were in this world, even in the town of Auckland! But now he was cold and, interesting though they might be, he'd had enough of them for one day.

He was turning to pick up his coat when a familiar voice stopped him.

'So that's where you are, Donald,' said Roddy. 'I have been wondering when you would be back. In fact, I was about to go looking for you. And indeed, young Donald, you should know better than to go pushing a man into the ocean like that, on your first day in port!'

'But I pulled him out again!' Donald replied hotly.

'That still doesn't make you guiltless,' Roddy replied with a soberness that suddenly dissolved in raucous laughter. He flung his head back, that tremendous beard jerking with the measure of his mirth. Donald felt a great temptation to tug it hard, and bring the old rascal back to reality.

Instead, he gripped his shoulder and asked: 'Where on earth did you get to, Roddy? I waited and waited for you, and then things began to happen and soon half the town was chasing me through backyards and alleys – including that villain I had to douse. Why didn't you come back as you said?'

'I was delayed. A matter of business.' He gave a solemn nod. 'But now, come along and change your clothes. And you must hurry. You will be a hunted man now, from what you have said. No stranger can offend the peace of Auckland and get away with it so easily.

'It's lucky that the breeze is freshening, and we'll be able to make sail immediately.' He glanced back along the wharf. 'Were they hot after you, or had you thrown the police off your track?'

'The police weren't concerned – at least as far as I know. And in any case, I was in the right!'

'Now don't you be worrying, Donald,' said Roddy tranquilly. 'The magistrates would doubtless make allowances for your youth and inexperience. But right or wrong, you are a marked man, and the sooner you're away from Auckland the better.' He jumped spryly across to the *Fiona's* deck and Donald followed. 'Now down below with you, into dry gear, and remember, no lights!'

* * *

They ghosted their way down the harbour past a sleeping town. There were no signs of activity on shore. The big ships dreamed at the wharves, spidery rigging and slender masts tracing a pattern against a cloud-smeared sky. Donald listened apprehensively, but heard nothing to suggest that Roddy's fears were well based.

Mainsail and jib drawing discreetly, the water gurgled at the *Fiona's* counter and North Head loomed dark ahead of them. Roddy seemed in excellent humour. He hummed disjointedly under his breath, and then, as they rounded the Head into the brisker water of Rangitoto Channel, he turned to Donald. 'You're safe now, lad. And should you not tell me what it's all been about?'

Donald told him; he listened with interest and enjoyment.

'And none of it would have happened if you had been back as you said. Did your business go well, Roddy?'

'Yes; and it might go better still. We'll see soon. And now that we're out of danger, should we have a hot drink and perhaps a bite to eat? It will soon be morning.

'And while you're about it,' he called down to the cabin, 'you might see how our passenger is faring. He will probably be asleep.'

Nothing could surprise Donald now. He turned up the lantern, but its flickering light showed nothing.

'Try the ladies' cabin,' Roddy suggested. 'For lack of suitable cargo I put him in there.'

Donald opened the door, bumping his head in his haste as he looked inside. A bed was made up neatly, with a man of about his own age deep in sleep. Donald blinked in astonishment. Nothing that this crazy day had produced seemed more improbable than this. He looked at the dark hair, the thin handsome face with wide-open mouth, the sinewy, well-muscled arm that lay outside the blanket.

He went quickly on deck and confronted Roddy. 'Wherever might you have found him? What kind of game are you playing?'

'No game at all,' Roddy replied. 'But while I was away this night I happened to come across your friend Johnny Bain the worse for liquor and very unhappy about things. He couldn't be left like that, and so I had him taken down here. He doesn't know where he is, nor is he caring much, I think; but he'll learn soon enough when he wakes in the morning.

'A silly young fellow, but sound enough. And after all, Donald, he is one of our own people, and I couldn't leave him.'

Roddy spat mournfully over the side into water that was slipping past swiftly now. Donald studied him carefully in the grey half-light.

'I wish you would be one thing or the other, Roddy,' he said. 'What are you trying to do? Sometimes I think that you have goodwill for everyone. Then I catch a glint in your eye, and you seem nothing but a cunning, mischievous old man.'

'And what about yourself, Donald? What's real under that tough yet soft hide of yours?' He prodded Donald affectionately with a gnarled finger. 'Is Norman McLeod's harsh God your God too, or do you still mean to help your unhappy friend Christy?'

'So that's why you brought him here – to remind me of Christy,' said Donald softly. 'Yes, I forgot too soon. I've been busy, Roddy, and I've enjoyed it. But soon we'll be back home again, with old Norman telling us what is good and what's bad about the world. But in spite of him, I'm thinking it's a wonderful place – sad and happy, cruel and kind. I wouldn't want it to be very different.'

A chill breeze came at them from the east, where the black bulk of Rangitoto Island still brooded on an horizon dark with night. The *Fiona* seemed to sail on blindly, no man caring, like a phantom on an endless quest. But the breeze, coming out of nowhere, spoke to Donald of a world stirring slowly from slumber.

'And now for that drink,' said Roddy. 'Bring it up here, Donald. We'll let young Johnny sleep a while yet.'

They ate and drank in silence. Donald, for his part, was vainly trying to remember where he had been only twenty-four hours before. But his brain was drunk with lack of sleep, and he could think no consecutive thoughts. And what deep plans were stirring in Roddy's mind he could not attempt to fathom.

He was relieved when Roddy yawned heavily and looked at the lightening sky. 'I'm worried about them pursuing you, Donald,' he said. 'Once they know you have escaped by sea, a fast police cutter could easily overhaul us. We'll lie up for the day, out of the road, and catch up with our sleep, too.'

'Is that the real reason, Roddy?' murmured Donald sleepily. 'I'm beginning to distrust your motives; but just at present I'm too tired to care.'

* * *

The bay was secluded, screened from the open gulf by low hills. Before he lay on his bunk Donald looked in at Johnny Bain, who was still sound asleep. Will this mean anything or nothing? he wondered. Conscious that Roddy was watching him with quizzical eyes, he shrugged his shoulders and grinned. 'Good-night, Captain,' he said, and let sleep take him.

They did not stir until mid-afternoon. And Donald discovered that, while his mind and body were refreshed, his doubts had not settled themselves.

Johnny Bain may have been surprised to find himself at sea when he awakened, but he did not show it. 'I must have been drunk,' was his comment after Roddy had explained how he had been found half asleep in a hotel lounge, his bag open beside his chair. 'They've taken anything worth stealing,' he added. 'In any case, I've had enough of Auckland; it's time I went to work again.'

He's a philosopher, even if he is a rogue, thought Donald as he watched Johnny's imperturbable face, which not even the effects of too much liquor and God knew what other debauchery could make jaded and drawn. And then he thought: Perhaps he is not being philosophical about it; perhaps he just doesn't care?

He felt a sudden temptation to say the name 'Christy Cameron' and see what the result would be. But he resisted the impulse.

Instead, he turned to Roddy. 'Why did you decide to take cover here?' he asked. 'Smith was a villain. No police or right-minded man would listen to any charge he laid. In fact, I should have been thanked if I'd left him to sink in the harbour!'

'You're wrong, Donald. Johnny here will bear me out. A city is very conscious of its dignity, and anyone who offends against it must be reproved. Smith, or the girl, or his other accomplice, is just as much entitled to the city's protection as its mayor or leading citizens. They are all bound together, in defence or aggression, against those who come from outside. You were a lucky man to escape, Donald, and I hope you've learned your lesson. And a city has a long memory. Don't go back there too soon!'

'That is all very well, Roddy, and possibly true, but I keep thinking that you had some reason of your own for stowing us away here for the day.'

'That's not so, Donald,' Roddy said quickly. 'These cities... Auckland is not the only one. Sydney, over in Australia, is even worse. And this is where you must be careful, too. A city is like whisky. You visit it, take a wee sip, as it were, and decide you like it. Before long, if you're not very careful, you can't keep away. You know it's wicked of you, spoiling your health, ruining your enjoyment of life, but you keep on tasting it and tasting it again, until your brain is befuddled and you can't enjoy anything else.

'Take old Mr McCaul, for example. There he is, day in day out, in his dusty little office, working like a spider in a dark corner. Would you say he was really living? And yet he was a fine man once, in Nova Scotia. Get him away from a city now, and he would die of boredom. So Donald, listen to me, and keep away in future.'

'You are talking so much, Roddy, that I feel sure you are hiding the truth; but let it be. And being so ready with good advice on what not to do, Captain, if you were me, what would you be doing in any case?'

Roddy stretched his legs more comfortably along the deck and looked innocently at the two young men.

'There's one suggestion I could make. A long sea voyage. To New Caledonia, perhaps, or even to the New Hebrides. And I don't mind saying it would convenience me greatly if you could do it.'

'In this boat?' asked Johnny, startled out of his habitual silence.

'And why not?' said Roddy. 'Donald, here, will bear witness that *Fiona* is a grand seaboat. Ask him – sometime but not just now – to describe the tremendous storm she weathered only two nights ago.

'And neither of you, I imagine, is in a great hurry back to Waipu. Jessie can wait for a few weeks, Donald. And you have no reason to get there urgently, have you Johnny?'

'No,' said Johnny flatly, while the others watched him closely. 'Waipu means nothing to me. I would just as soon never see it again.'

'Now that's no way to talk about your own people,' said Roddy cheerfully, 'but we'll let it pass for the moment. We have stores in plenty on board – a cargo loaded by our good friend Mr McCaul – and the wide open sea before us. What's your answer, lads?' Roddy's eyes were sparkling with a calculated excitement, and Donald found that, once again, he had no great desire to do anything but go along with the plan.

He reached out and shook Roddy's hand. 'I'll be glad to come with you. But first, just so that I have it clear in my mind: You've planned this a long way back, Roddy. Even when we were at Kenny Omaha's you were thinking about it. How exactly did you know that it would turn out? And did your plans include Johnny here?'

Roddy shrugged his sturdy shoulders as if the question had no great importance and sprang to his feet. 'Let us say, Donald, that the plan may have been there, and that the details have fallen into place quite happily.

'But I am serious about this. Don't come with me unless you want to. I can always call in at Omaha and pick up some Mackenzies as crew. But I would be grateful for your company. There may be danger, of course, but that is likely to creep up on us wherever we are, even in our beds. We need not fear it.'

He paused. Johnny studied him with no great interest. 'How long will we be away?'

'A month, or not much more.'

'That will suit me well enough,' Johnny replied, and spread his languid body on the deck.

'And is there anything else you wish to ask, Donald?'

'Only that I would have liked them at home to know where we are going.'

'Write a letter, and we'll pass it to the first boat we see. And now we'll make sail. The wind is round to the sou-west – the proper quarter for a passage to the Islands. So let's not waste it.'

* * *

Chapter Fourteen

A LINGERING SUNSET, PALE WITH AUTUMN'S TRANQUIL COLOURS, found the *Fiona* dipping steadily through choppy seas far up the coast. Donald's letter had been written and given to the skipper of a fishing boat beating back to Auckland. They had passed the Whangaparaoa Peninsula, flying now before the wind where once the storm had held them captive. Roddy had pointed to the narrow entrance leading into Omaha, where Kenny's house lay sheltered from the world. Their course took them well outside Bream Bay, away from the menacing rocks of the Whangarei Heads, and, in the blurred sunset, the mountains behind Waipu were faint purple smears above a ruffled horizon.

Johnny Bain was a competent seaman, as even Donald, with his short apprenticeship, could easily see. There was no disposition for fair-weather sailing about Roddy now. The wind was steady, as if bent on serious business a thousand miles away. It came from a great emptiness behind them, submerged the little cutter like an invisible wave, singing an eerie tune in the tense port rigging. Donald himself watched and tried to learn, noting the economical movements of the other two men, the workmanlike way in which the *Fiona* was handled. Roddy was holding all his sail; staysail and jib drawing well, mainsail on a long rein, and the little gaff topsail giving its mite of thrust to their forward drive.

As the light left the sky, black clouds piled slowly up behind them. The sea took on a pale, unearthly hue, and then began to lose all colour and form in the darkness.

'We'll lower the tops'l and take a reef in the main,' Roddy announced. 'And then, Donald, you can take a turn at the tiller. I'll stay with you for a while, and Johnny can be cook tonight. With less sail on there should be no chance of her jibbing, but you'll have to watch the wind and the sea.

'There'll be no heaving-to this night, my lad. And in a couple of days, all going well, we'll have sailed into summer again.'

The *Fiona* was responsive even to an unskilled hand, Donald thought. He was uncertain at first, but gradually he began to feel the delicacy with which the rudder fused the forces of wind, sea and sail. He experimented with tentative movements of the tiller until the *Fiona* was sweeping in long, flowing arcs. A satisfying sense of power made him certain that nothing was quite so pleasant as controlling a boat in a good sailing breeze.

'And now,' said Roddy, breaking sharply into his thoughts, 'we'll attempt to follow a course that might bring us to where we want to go. Steer by that star. And don't go losing it, or dreaming of wee Jessie back in Waipu, or steering by the moon instead; or else we'll all be ashore and walking the long way home.'

Roddy slapped him on the shoulder and went below. Donald concentrated on the star, prickling in the sky that had once again been swept clean of cloud. The moon was a pale, weak ghost, but a strange luminosity seemed to come from the moving waters. The sound of the steady wind dominated the small, recurring noises that the *Fiona* made as her bowsprit dipped in the trough of the waves and then came slowly upward, rigging and timbers seeming to complain, though lightly, under the strain. The bow gradually was lost in the growing darkness.

Was the *Fiona* actually moving, or was it indeed that this waste of water, too strong to be resisted, was holding her in one place, or even sweeping her back? It was an uncanny feeling. To counter it, Donald forced his thoughts back to the land he was leaving, skipping over his bewildering hours in Auckland, remembering the quiet Waipu landscape. He had told his mother in his letter that he had Johnny Bain as companion on the voyage. What would Jessie think when she learned that?

He could imagine her wondering and wondering as she went about her daily tasks. She would be hoping, no doubt, that he might be able to help Christy Cameron; but she would not be sure that he wanted to, and neither was he. Not, at least, until he knew Johnny Bain better, and had found out the full story.

There would be time for that to come out during the next few days – or weeks. Meanwhile he must keep his mind on his work. The star had wandered off the line. He looked guiltily towards the cabin, half expecting Roddy's angry face to appear, and eased the *Fiona* back on course.

Roddy relieved him while he went below for a quick meal. Whatever else he could or could not do, Donald decided, Johnny was a good cook. Donald spoke to him several times during their meal, but his answers were short and to the point. Donald studied him briefly. Was he worried about something? His face did not show it, and when he had finished eating, he stretched back on his bunk, relaxed and comfortable, before gathering the plates and mugs together and dousing them in a bucket of water.

Donald went back up on deck none the wiser about the man. He said to Roddy: 'How do you think we will fare?'

'Very well,' Roddy answered. 'Tell me, aren't you enjoying yourself?'

'I am that,' Donald admitted. 'And what about Johnny?'

'As far as I can see, he is too. The silly young chap. He had himself in bad company in Auckland, you know, and now that he's away from it, I'm sure he is wondering why he stayed there so long.'

'Do you think he has heard anything from Waipu about Christy Cameron?'

'I suspect he has not,' said Roddy. 'None of his companions in the city were Nova Scotians. But you can never tell with these quiet ones.'

A different note entered Roddy's voice, and Donald could have sworn that he was grinning in that irritating but likeable way of his. 'Why don't you ask him yourself? Remember what you said to me once: "I'll go and hunt down the man responsible for Christy's situation and bring him back to her from wherever he's hiding" – or words of that sort. Surely now is your chance. Make him admit his guilt; watch him like a hawk when we're out of sight of land; tie him up and row him ashore when we return to Bream Bay! That's what you could do, Donald.'

Donald shook his head. 'Nothing seems as clear and simple as it did on that day, Roddy. We'll wait and see. Something will work out of it in time.'

Roddy grunted non-commitally. 'I must admit to being a mite disappointed, Donald. When I found who my companions were to be on this voyage, I had hopes of a pleasant, eventful journey. But now I am not so sure.' He heaved a sigh. 'Life can be tedious, if the mixture isn't stirred up now and again.'

'You've done enough stirring, Roddy, in your own cunning way. Why not let things simmer for a while?'

'Yes. We could do that, too.' Roddy laboriously lighted his pipe, and then looked up at the clean, black sky, listening to the rushing wind. 'If there wasn't the likelihood of meeting other ships, I would be tempted to let the *Fiona* sail herself tonight, and we could all have a good rest. But this coast can be too busy. All the traffic from Britain, Australia and the Islands comes down here, and we must keep our little *Fiona* attended.

'Go down and have a sleep, Donald. You'll probably find Johnny dead to the world already – in the ladies' cabin! I'll wake him later, and then he can call you for the last watch of the night. Sleep well.'

* * *

It was, Donald realised, as he pulled his blanket over him, his first night at sea since the journey out from Nova Scotia; and that was so long ago, and the conditions were so different, that it might have concerned a different person.

Here there was no escaping from the sound and feel of the sea. His bunk moved softly in time with the creaking of the cutter's timbers. When she struck an unexpected wave, the slap of the water, the movement of her recovery, was unmistakable. It was all very strange but none the less soothing. Wind and sea were not so very different from a rainstorm in the forest. His mind went back, with a sharp visual impression, to the night when they had filled the dam; the last night that he and his friend Norman would spend together. But that also seemed to belong to a different life. He would always remember Norman, but there was nothing he could do now to bring him back. And he himself must keep going for whatever God or the fates held in store.

He slept dreamlessly, and did not stir when Roddy came softly down to shake Johnny into wakefulness. Roddy looked at his sleeping friend with something of wistfulness in his expression. He stretched and yawned prodigiously and began to prepare for bed. He folded his clothes and slipped into a long nightshirt, combed his beard carefully outside it. A careful, methodical man, oddly pathetic when his defences were down. He climbed into his bunk. I'm getting old, he thought. What on earth am I doing here, on this wild, harum-scarum trip, when I could be growing vegetables at Waipu, and being scolded every Sunday at church? I'm not only old; I'm an old fool. But that is something I cannot easily change.

Roddy eased his head into a more comfortable position and went to sleep.

* * *

Alone at the tiller during the last hours of night, Donald saw the *Fiona's* bow gradually form out of the darkness; the sails gain a ghostly pallor in the dawn. The stars wasted away like dying embers. It was a sight that he had seen often enough before from the firm base of the land, but now a welter of restless water encircled him, save for a dark needle of rock to the south-west.

That would be Cape Brett, he thought, remembering the chart he had examined with Roddy, and as it disappeared he could say goodbye to New Zealand.

The wind had held all night. The cutter, tireless but docile under his hand, swept on with an easy, unforced gait. He wondered whether he would shake out the reef from the mainsail but his confidence was not great enough. It would be as well to wait for Roddy.

And now the sun was breaking through on his right. It glittered like molten gold on the sea's edge, blinked a ferocious eye and was swallowed by a thin belt of cloud. But its magic could not be denied. The grey eastern sky filled with colour, long streamers of light that flickered and frisked to high heaven. Then there was broad sunlight, dancing on the crests of waves while night shadows still lingered in their depths.

The wind came steadily on his left side, and he glanced occasionally at the *Fiona's* wake to admire his immaculate steering. And then Roddy came up from below, smoothing his shaggy hair and asking if all was well.

* * *

Chapter Fifteen

TWO DAYS LATER, AS RODDY HAD FORECAST, THEY SAILED BACK into summer. And still the wind blew, day after day. Roddy grew suspicious of its benevolence, cocking an eye at the clear horizon over which it came, frowning whenever he took a sight and calculated their position. 'I don't like it,' he said. 'It's unnatural. We should have had a gale or a calm by now.'

Donald was lying at the tiller, a good breakfast under his belt, his mind at peace in a way he had never known before. The choppy coastal waters were far behind, and now the *Fiona* rode easily over a long ocean swell.

'Why worry about it, Roddy?' he asked. 'I'm sure I prefer this to either a gale or no wind at all. We should be grateful for it while it lasts. What say you, Johnny?'

Johnny Bain was stripped to the waist. He had tied a mirror to one of the backstays and was shaving with his usual care. As the mirror swayed with the cutter's motion, he followed it with slow movements of his head and shoulders, intent and preoccupied.

'What's that?' he asked.

'Nothing,' said Roddy blandly. 'We were just gossiping.'

Johnny grunted and scraped tenderly at the point of his chin. He wiped his razor clean and put it away. The other two watched him. He dipped a bucket over the side and sluiced his head and shoulders in the water; then, applying himself to the mirror once again, began to comb his dark hair carefully.

'You need a haircut, Johnny,' said Roddy.

Johnny combed away in silence. 'I don't think so. The last one will serve for a while yet. And no doubt there will be barbers in the New Hebrides when we get there.'

'No doubt there will be,' Roddy replied. 'But you must be careful lest they take your head off as well as your hair. That's what happened to Kenny Omaha's eldest, you know. They ate him.'

'Will we be among cannibals, Roddy?' Donald's knowledge of the Islanders' habits was sketchy, and he was always ready to learn.

'Well,' Roddy replied, 'you could certainly call them cannibals. Much of the time they are happy enough hunting each other, but now and again they decide to vary their diet with a bit of tender white flesh, and that is when visitors – traders and suchlike – need to be on their guard. If the impulse to eat white flesh coincides with the arrival of a trading vessel, the battle is likely to be a little one-sided.'

Donald digested this information, lolling casually and comfortably as far away from any such hazard as a human could conceivably be. He noted with one eye how blue the sea had become; bluer than ever Bream Bay was, sparking with an inward fire, glittering like a jewel. The flying fishes were out in force. One landed on the deck and Johnny, dropping his comb, sprang on it with a panther's speed. 'A nice addition to our fare for tonight,' he said.

'Tell us this, Roddy,' said Donald. 'You are most communicative on matters that are of no moment, but I would certainly be interested to know something else. What cargo are we carrying to the Islands, and what are we likely to bring back to New Zealand? I'm sure that you and Mr McCaul have not planned this voyage solely for our pleasure.'

Roddy looked thoughtfully from one to the other. 'I am not surprised that you should ask that question,' he said. 'In fact, I have wondered why you have not asked before. Trade goods, for the most part, for delivery to Mackenzie's store on Tanna Island. But we will call in first at New Caledonia and do some commissions for him there.'

'Why couldn't Kenny use his own schooner?' asked Donald. 'It's not for me to run his business, I know, but it doesn't seem sensible to bother with a little craft like *Fiona* when his own ship could carry six times as much.'

'You're correct, Donald, but there is one major problem with your sensible scheme. Kenny, although a very tactful man, does not get on very well with the Frenchmen on New Caledonia. He has had one or two encounters with them in the past and, just between you and me, if they were to see him again, they would either shoot him or lock him in gaol.' Roddy grinned cheerfully. 'But the *Fiona* is a different matter. Why, we could do our work in New Caledonia and be away again before the Frenchmen had heard anything about us.'

'And that is what you plan to do, I suppose,' said Donald.

Roddy's smile broadened. 'Yes,' he admitted. 'That is the plan.'

'And what sort of place is this New Caledonia?' asked Johnny, who had now finished his toilet and was silently inspecting his fingernails.

'A wonderful country!' said Roddy. 'Beautiful fruits, wine and ladies. But don't be alarmed, Johnny: You'll be seeing none of them this trip.'

'When do we get there?'

'That is a question I am not prepared to answer,' said Roddy. 'If this wind kept up, we could be there in less than a week. But of one thing I am sure: The wind must drop soon.'

* * *

He was right. Donald had gone below and was studying the chart on which their present position was neatly plotted, measuring distances, calculating the likely day's run, when he heard the sails slapping overhead. He returned to the deck. The sky was still clear, with a heat haze dancing on the horizon ahead of them, but the wind had died away. The *Fiona*, her sails idle, rolled on a heaving, glassy sea.

'We'll take the sails down,' said Roddy after a while. 'She's only wearing out her gear like this.'

* * *

Now, as the *Fiona* rose and fell gently on the languid sea, the calm that had halted her seemed also to have given Donald his first chance to think connectedly since he had left Waipu. The excitement of learning the ways of the sea; storms, new people and places, action and incident that had no place in his normally well-ordered life. All this passed through his mind as he stretched his arms and looked at the empty ocean. Abstractedly, he rose to his feet and went down for the chart. It was battered and stained from years of use, backed with heavy paper that had worn at the folds. But it showed, on a small scale, what he wanted to see.

There was New Caledonia, lying across two degrees of latitude, carelessly thrown down on a bare patch of ocean. Nothing to the west until you reached Australia; nothing to the east but a speckle of islands; nothing to the south except tiny Norfolk Island and, round the corner, New Zealand itself. To the north there was a scatter of islands large and small, but for the most part small. The New Hebrides not so very far away, with reefs sketched in vaguely, even where the waters had been formally charted. Near the south of the group was the island of Tanna, with an east coast on which every indentation had been meticulously marked while the west coast, a few miles away, showed as a dotted line.

So that's where we're going, thought Donald. His eye moved over the other names: Ambryn, Espiritu Santo, Erromango, Savannah and the Guadalcanal Passage. Fantastic names, their origins beyond his power to detect, but sounding strangely of Spain and England as well as of dark native dialects.

He returned to his seat in the stern, taking the chart with him. Johnny Bain had gone below, but Roddy was sitting idly at the tiller, watching the horizon and casting a cynical glance at the occasional cat's paws of wind that ruffled the surface of the sea.

Donald studied the little map that showed him of New Caledonia. Noumea was cosily tucked in a deep inlet behind a screen of reefs. The light markings of coral continued up the west coast, broken here and there opposite the mouth of a river. He read the worn printing: 'Bourail Channel', it said; and nearby, he noticed with mounting interest, there were depths recently marked in ink – more navigation signs than the rest of New Caledonia could boast in all. And across the lagoon, inside the river mouth, he noticed a red-ink dot with a ring drawn neatly around it.

'How do you pronounce B-o-u-r-a-i-l, Roddy?' he said casually.

'You don't pronounce it. You just sail to it,' the older man replied grumpily. 'That is, if we ever get any more wind!' He looked at his friend thoughtfully. 'I see that you're starting to use the brains that God presumably gave you.'

'I just wondered,' Donald answered, and returned to his study of the chart.

'Would it not be possible for you to talk to me at times?' Roddy asked. 'I had no desire to sail with a pair of deaf mutes, but that seems to have been my fate. Not that you are so very bad, Donald, but you must have noticed Johnny. He has not made one positive statement since he came on board. At first I thought it was a brandy headache that would in time wear off. But now I am very doubtful. Surely, with his reputation among the ladies, he cannot be just bone solid about the ears? He must have said something to them sometimes, if what I remember about my own younger days still applies.'

‘Perhaps he talks only when it is necessary, and doesn’t believe in rattling away for the sake of hearing his own voice?’ Donald suggested.

Roddy grunted and looked suspiciously at Donald. ‘That might be so. But I admit I am growing curious about what there is, if anything, inside his head. And if a wind doesn’t come up soon, I might be trying to find out.’

With the coolness of evening they found a light breeze, but not enough to fill the sails that were quickly hoisted. The *Fiona* whispered through the water and the motion was pleasant after an idle day. They had their dinner on deck, a meal interrupted often as they manoeuvred and fiddled about to make the most of this fitful offering.

It was slow work, and after the first few hours Donald wondered whether it was worth while. A single hour with a good sailing wind would mean more distance than a whole day’s cat-and-mouse playing of this sort. But Roddy was anxious and gave them no rest. He slept little himself. The cabin was stuffy, and when his watch was done, Donald stretched out on the deck, its hardness eased by canvas from the sail locker. And then, shortly after sunrise, the wind dropped again.

* * *

Halfway through the morning, Johnny, who had been down below, came up with a fishing line, which he silently hung over the side. The others watched him.

‘You won’t catch anything while we’re lying here like this,’ said Roddy. ‘You might as well pull it in and have a sleep.’

‘I like fishing,’ Johnny said, ‘and you can never tell what might come along.’

He was drawing the line slowly through his fingers. The hook, with a heavy sinker, came up almost to the surface and then slid away down again. But no fish followed it. After a while he hauled in his line, rebaited it and dropped it down again. His lean, handsome face was immobile and expressionless. He applied himself to his fishing with a concentration that excluded everything else.

‘He’s always busy about something, our Johnny,’ said Roddy in a voice that he did not bother to lower. ‘But I’m sure you caught more fish, Donald, that day I saw you in Bream Bay. That’s the only fishing that would appeal to me.’

'It's always better to feel that something is likely to take the bait,' Donald agreed, watching Johnny as he patiently moved his heavy line on his forefinger.

'Those fish!' continued Roddy. 'They'll be dry now, and stored away till winter. You know, Donald, there are few ways of life better than those people lead at Waipu. Don't you wish you were back there sometimes?'

'Not at present, Roddy. This will do me well enough.'

'But you will be back, no doubt,' said Roddy; and Donald noticed that his eyes were twinkling with something approaching malice. But Johnny was still intent on his fishing.

Donald didn't respond; nor did Roddy seem to expect him to. For he had turned toward Johnny with a benevolent mask of good humour on his face.

'You knew Christy Cameron, didn't you Johnny?' he asked suddenly.

Johnny heard that all right. Startled and wondering, he looked sharply at Roddy, his mouth open. He had forgotten his line, his hands coming up as if to defend himself. And then Donald saw the loose coils begin to whisk over the side.

Roddy had noticed what was happening too, and he jumped swiftly to his feet. 'Quick, Johnny!' he cried. 'You're on to a fish!'

But already Johnny had lunged for the line, testing the strain with slow, steady hauls that he could not hold for long. 'It's a big one, Roddy. Thank God I have a strong hook on. But even that mightn't do!'

The fish was fighting back fiercely from somewhere far below the sea's limpid surface. Roddy, his boredom and ill-humour forgotten, was in danger of falling overboard with excitement. If I were Johnny, I would push him over the side, thought Donald. He, himself, could take the spectator's view while the other two were definitely participants; but even in his mind the edge had been taken off Roddy's surprising question by this dramatic interruption.

'Good lad; you've got him moving,' said Roddy, thumping Johnny on the back in encouragement. 'Where could the monster have come from? A big fish on a calm, dead day like this! And he's not a shark, or he wouldn't have even seen the hook.' He beamed at Donald, his beard bristling. 'Not since we took the big cod off Labrador have I known such a thing. We'll be eating him for days, I'm sure.'

'He's not caught yet, Roddy,' gasped Johnny Bain, his face red with excitement.

'But he's coming now, I swear it.'

Donald looked, but could see nothing, although the line was coming in fast, in long, wet loops.

'Here he is! Donald, take this and gaff him as soon as he gets near the side. And I'll try to pass a rope around his tail.'

It was certainly a monster fish that was drawn slowly to the surface, well-hooked but still fighting against the line. In shape it was like a giant mackerel, but there any familiarity ended with other fish that Donald had seen. He reached out with the gaff, while Johnny kept the strain on his line and Roddy, who indeed seemed to know what he was doing, looped its fanning tail.

'One big heave when I say! Now!' Up and over it came onto the deck. The knives were soon busy. 'We'll eat what we can fresh and salt the rest,' said Roddy. And there was no more time for talk until the fish had been stowed away and the deck washed clean.

'And now, to cap it all, there's a breeze coming up,' the captain said. 'What a grand day it's been. What more could any man want?'

They made sail again while a puzzled, silent Johnny Bain studied his mercurial captain and seemingly waited for a chance to speak.

'I'm thinking it would be a kind of tunny,' said Roddy reflectively when they had settled down to a steady course. 'They are plentiful in the older seas – the Mediterranean and out in the Atlantic, even across to the Indies. But I've never heard of any in the Pacific. And yet I feel I am right; and in that case there should be more of them about, for they move in schools. Why not try again with your line, Johnny?'

Johnny shook his head. 'We have enough to last us for a while, and certainly until we are tired of the sight of fish. And I would not be bothered while we're moving like this. Why did you ask me about Christy Cameron, Roddy?'

He added the question with no discernible pause and it took Roddy by surprise.

'Christy Cameron?' he repeated. 'Yes. I remember. It was just an idle remark, Johnny. Forget it. We've more to think about now than any of the girls back in Waipu, or Auckland for that matter.'

'But why did you mention her, Roddy? It seems strange to me, and calling for some sort of explanation. For you see, I did know Christy Cameron, and knew her better than most. Has something happened to her?'

Roddy laughed, a trifle uneasily. 'You've been away from Waipu a long time, Johnny, and many things may have happened without you knowing. Christy was well when I last heard.'

Johnny was frowning, as if something did not fully satisfy his mind. He wanted to ask more, but clearly, Donald could see, he did not know how to phrase any question. And Roddy, the old villain, did not mean to help him at all. He was staring with great concentration at a bank of dark cloud to the east, whistling tunelessly through his beard.

'These could be the trade winds,' he began, but Donald interrupted him, finding the words hard to say.

'But surely you know what happened at the New Year, Johnny?'

The other man's face showed nothing.

'Christy is certainly well enough, as Roddy says, but it seems that some time before Christmas she had a baby, and the minister called her out before the congregation. But she would not say who was responsible, either because she loved the man or because, as she told me, she didn't want to see him again.'

Johnny was staring expressionlessly at the hazy horizon while the *Fiona*, alone on that great circle of heaving sea, sailed on serenely enough.

'She said that the baby was dead,' Donald added. 'But I feel sometimes that she has it hidden away until she can tend him herself, without the Waipu people pointing their fingers at her. Such things can happen, you know.' Donald rose to his feet uncomfortably, for Johnny had given no sign that he had been listening.

'That's all I can say, Johnny, and perhaps it will satisfy your question. I felt at one time that, if the man could be found, it would be proper and fitting for him to go back to her. But thinking over what Christy can be like, I'm not so sure. It might be kinder for the man, and kinder for Christy too, to let her go her own way.'

Johnny had stood up too. He nodded at Donald, as if in thanks, and then looked measuringly at Roddy. 'You knew all this?'

'Some of it, Johnny.'

'A baby boy did you say, Donald?'

'That's so, Johnny. But you know that I'm not absolutely sure.'

'A sad thing to happen to any girl on her own,' Johnny observed with an attempt at casualness. He was, Donald thought, regaining his self-possession now, but it was not hard to see that the news had affected him greatly. But did that mean anything? Had not Donald himself been thrown off balance when he had first heard it? He thought back, with a growing sense of unreality, to that morning in the church when Norman McLeod had called Christy out before him.

'Is she still living at home?'

'Yes,' Donald replied. 'She's not the kind to go away on her own.'

'I'm not so sure,' said Johnny, with a certain bitterness. 'She may be meek and soft on the surface, but there's something hard about Christy underneath. She'll survive where others go under, I'm thinking. I tried her myself, but she quickly told me when I was not wanted. And that was that.'

Roddy had been listening keenly, studying the young man with his eyes while he gave this surprisingly long statement.

'So you didn't get very far with her, Johnny?' he said cheerfully. 'From what I have heard, that is something unusual for you!'

Johnny did not answer. His thoughts, it seemed, were far away. Roddy looked at him speculatively for a moment or two, shook his head in puzzlement and turned away.

* * *

Donald took his turn at the tiller after a fine fish dinner that night. The steady south-east wind was surprisingly cold – much fresher than he had thought the tropics would provide – and it drove the spray against him as he sat near the stern. The *Fiona* was alive again, carrying her sail buoyantly towards the fading western sky.

Roddy had taken their position shortly before sunset. 'Keep watch as you go,' he told Donald. 'The open sea's safest, and now that we're nearing land we must be on our guard.'

He stubbed his thick forefinger on the chart. 'You can see the reefs that hide the south-west tip of New Caledonia. On our present course we'll be clearing them, and then we'll head in toward Bourail Passage. With luck, we should be there by mid-day tomorrow.'

Roddy lighted his pipe and shrugged down deeper into his heavy coat. He nudged Donald and asked in a confidential whisper: 'What do you think about it now, lad?'

'I think it was a surprise to him, Roddy; a rather cruel surprise, perhaps, but he is still very guarded.'

'Don't waste your sympathy on him, Donald. If you go playing about like he does, you're bound to have some cruel shocks. Age is the only thing to cure it. But do you think he will admit it all, or is he trying to cover it up?'

'I don't know, Roddy. But from what I have seen of him, I think Johnny will say no more than he feels he has to. And what he plans to do is far beyond my guessing. One thing I do suspect: If Christy were to be waiting for him when we arrived in New Caledonia tomorrow, she would have to talk quickly to send him away again.'

'You think he loves her, Donald?'

'I think he does; but whether he will do anything about it is another matter.'

* * *

At daybreak Donald knew that he was indeed in tropic seas, off a foreign land. Even before the coastline was visible they could smell a rich jumble of exotic scents, carried over water that was choppy now, with patches of rank vegetation floating here and there. Birds were out fishing, and their raucous cries greeted a flaring sunrise. Then suddenly, the sea was bright blue again and through a fading bank of smoky mist they could see the land.

Donald did not leave the deck all that morning. They gave the coral reef a wide berth, although he could not make up his mind whether safety from wreck or from observation of the Frenchmen was Roddy's primary motive. Far ahead of them stretched the mountains of New Caledonia, scarred and eroded with red ochre streaks sharp against the purple shadows of vertical valleys. The land seemed to be burning away in the blazing sun. From ground that looked too barren to sustain life of any sort, the smoke of countless fires rose to mix with the shimmering heat haze.

He had not thought so small an island – as it appeared on the chart – could host such formidable mountains. But it was not all mountainous. If he looked hard enough over the rising and falling crests of the rollers he could see patches of greenery on the coastal plain; could even pick out, he thought, the flaunting crests of coconut palms that seemed to rise directly out of the sea.

They were free from the cold oceanic wind now. Donald basked shirtless on a deck that reflected the heat of the sun, warmed by a breeze that had gathered something of the fierceness of the land over which it came.

At mid-day Roddy consulted his chart again, and a black-bound journal which Donald could see contained simple navigational guides. He nodded his head in satisfaction, and altered course until the *Fiona* was running directly towards the land. They shortened sail. Roddy looked at Johnny, who had lapsed into a silence even more profound than usual, and then said to Donald: 'Up to the peak, my lad, and tell me what you can see.'

Even the difference of a few feet above the level of the sea widened his vision greatly. Far to the left and right the line of the reef now showed clear, the great waves heaving and fighting before they broke in foam, the clean green water of the lagoon strangely calm. There was no great distance to the shore now; a white unending beach fringed by a thin belt of palms and behind it gently rolling land, brown and harsh in appearance, that climbed into the foothills. Directly ahead, however, the beach was broken by a stream with a few houses huddled on its banks, half hidden among trees. And not far in front of him the white line of surf was also dissolved in blue-green water. The sea swept through unhindered.

'Can you see the break in the reef, Donald?' came Roddy's voice.

'Straight ahead. Keep her as she goes.'

* * *

The approach was not difficult, with a steady wind into which the *Fiona* drove resolutely, and Donald found it hard to concentrate on his immediate task. How different it was from his crossing of the Waipu bar; so short a time ago, but how much experience he had had in little more than a week! How uncertain he had been that day when Roddy had tried to put the fear of God into his heart – and succeeded! Now he hung easily on his dizzy perch, careless of the dangers there might be, and watched the sea with a fascinated eye.

Here and there the colour of the water changed suddenly. Coral rose cliff-like to near the surface, with deep valleys that could hide a vessel bigger than the *Fiona*. Plateaus with spiny outcrops where the waves eddied and swirled. Red, orange, yellow growths, half vegetable, it seemed, half mineral; and water that varied from blue and green to white, magnifying the colours of the reef. Donald leaned forward, lost in the magic of what he saw.

And now the coral had closed in on either side. Deep blue water ahead, but the waves sounded harshly, like a dam that had just been released, close at hand. A momentary tension caught him, and his fingers clenched on the ropes. How deep and powerful was the water where the *Fiona* was sailing; how bright and treacherous it was a few yards to each side.

'No snags ahead?' roared Roddy from the deck.

Donald started. The channel of deep blue water was clear below the bow, paling slightly until it merged with the lagoon. He could see the sandy bottom down there, and fish darting about on the inward side of the reef. No coral projected to tear the *Fiona's* timbers. They were through, and moving smoothly in towards the beach.

Johnny had unlashed the small boat. They anchored and slid it over the side and then, under the staring mid-day sun, rowed ashore. The air was inert; the silence, after the sounds that the *Fiona* made at sea, oppressive and unreal. The splash of the oars was a soft murmur over a dreaming land. When Roddy spoke, his voice seemed unnaturally loud.

'We'll take her up the stream,' he told Johnny who was rowing. Johnny looked over his shoulder as he strained backward, and the boat moved around until it was heading in the right direction.

* * *

A small wooden wharf, its hewn timbers unweathered by the sun and rain, conspicuous for its newness in this indolent setting. Not a man was in sight, nor even a dog; and as the boat drew alongside and they went ashore, the heat struck at them with a fresh vigour. Donald sniffed with delight the strange scents that seemed to come even from the bare earth.

'Where do we go now?' said Roddy, looking about him and wiping the sweat from his eyes. They turned along a worn dirt track leading towards a grove of trees.

'A door is open in that house,' said Donald; and as they looked the dark shadows were broken by the lounging figure of a man. He bent down to tie his bootlaces, then came slowly to meet them.

'Captain McKenzie, would it be?' he said, extending his hand. Donald watched him with interest, the first foreigner he could remember seeing in a foreign land. Nova Scotia, of course, did not count; nor did Cape Town where they had called on the way to New Zealand when he was a boy.

'The day has been well chosen,' said the stranger. He spoke deliberately, with little accent, as if repeating a well-learned lesson. His slow, careful speech contrasted with his alert face and quick, expressive eyes. He had a fine, dark beard, expertly trimmed, and as he talked he studied Roddy's magnificent, untended jungle of whisker as if he could not quite believe it.

'First you must come and eat.' He led the way across a verandah where the shadows were impenetrable after the glaring sunlight, and entered a wide, low-ceilinged room with comfortable chairs and a big table and desk. He called out a few words in French, and a woman's voice answered.

'Lunch will be served in a few minutes, he said, 'but now, something to drink. I would suggest this brandy.' He rose quickly and set glasses and a bottle on the table.

A slim, bare-footed girl pattered in, glanced quickly at the visitors and set places at the table. Fine china, crystal glasses on a spotless tablecloth. She disappeared as quietly as she had entered the room.

'You seem very comfortable here,' said Roddy cheerfully, and whether deliberately or not, his eyes followed the girl as she went through the door. 'But now to business. As you know, we're in a hurry. How is the cargo?'

'It is ready, Captain,' said the Frenchman, dignity making his face seem stern. 'Indeed, it is being loaded ready for taking to your vessel now. Not great in quantity, Captain, but in quality well up to your requirements!'

'That's excellent Monsewer – what did you say was your name?'

'I did not say, Captain, but it is Napoleon.'

'Excellent, Mr Napoleon. Now, I want to be away again in two hours. Can you manage that?'

'Assuredly, Captain. Will you excuse me for a moment?' He went quickly through to the verandah and ran down the steps, whistling shrilly. Roddy jumped up to watch him through the window.

'That's stirred him off his lazy tail,' he said complacently. 'These Frenchmen and foreigners are all the same. He's got a black boy with him now, and something might get done before the day's ended after all.'

'You're in a hurry, indeed you are, Roddy,' said Donald.

'It's not so much that as the principle of the thing. Let these fellows take charge, and you'll be bowing and scraping and fiddling about for the rest of your life.'

He sat down again quickly, just as the Frenchman returned.

'It is hot,' Monsieur Napoleon remarked. 'It is not so easy to make my men work when the sun is high at this season.' He helped himself to some more brandy while Roddy looked impatiently at the door.

'You shouldn't drink that stuff here, you know,' Roddy remarked casually to his host. 'Whisky I would have thought the most beneficial in this climate. However, it is of little account.'

'Not to drink brandy, but to let it all be drunk elsewhere?' The Frenchman laughed merrily. His English was no less correct, but he had become more fluent. He clapped Roddy on the back. 'Oh, no, my friend. You are a Scotchman, and will have your little joke! The whisky we do not sell here. But the brandy and the rum; that is a different story! Those are the drinks for civilised people.'

'Then where are all your customers?' Roddy asked, his own dignity a trifle ruffled now. 'It seemed to me that the village was dead.'

Monsieur Napoleon was surprised. 'You did not know,' he said, 'about the carnival at Noumea, the celebrations which everyone attends? And I was thinking that there could be found the reason for your well-timed arrival!'

'Yes, I remember now.' Roddy lied grandly, but the Frenchman was not deceived.

'Perhaps they did not tell you everything after all,' he said softly. The girl came in with steaming dishes, and they sat down to lunch.

* * *

Regretfully, Roddy pushed his empty plate away, accepted a small cup of coffee and – more dubiously – a cigar from a large brown box. Donald drank coffee too, but left the cigars to his senior.

Roddy moved to a comfortable chair, eased his belt slightly and stretched his short legs in front of him. 'You are certainly very well looked after here, Monsewer,' he admitted jealously. He rested his head on the upholstered cushion of his chair. He apologised: 'We have had a tiring day. The sea can be a difficult mistress.'

'Yes,' said the Frenchman. There was a touch of malice in his expression as he added casually: 'And now, of course, you will wish to hasten with the loading of your cargo? The men are ready.'

'Tell them to have a rest,' said Roddy grandly. 'It is not wise to work in the hot sun, especially after such a splendid meal. I will relax for an hour, Monsewer. Donald, you and Johnny might wish to look at the village. It will probably be your only chance to see how the Frenchmen conduct their colonies, and you should not miss the opportunity.'

He shut his eyes, drew carefully at his cigar and let the smoke spill out luxuriously.

'Be sure to give me a call when the men are ready to start,' he added. Donald looked at him; a comic, irritating, likeable little man. He would go his own way whatever happened, or if he changed his mind, would have a host of good reasons for the change. Let him sleep.

They stood on the verandah with Monsieur Napoleon, who was looking at them doubtfully.

'There is not much to see and it is indeed very hot,' he said, 'but you can go where you wish. I regret that I cannot go with you, but there is work to be done, not unconnected with your Captain McKenzie, for whom I have developed a great admiration.' He laughed gratingly and showed them the road that led towards the village.

* * *

Under the blazing sun, Donald felt his interest in foreign lands melting away with each step he took. Tall gum trees, with bark that stripped off like paper, gave pools of shade in which they were disposed to linger. They looked at the whitewashed cottages, withdrawn and empty, that lined three sides of the village square; and then walked quickly across the harsh, dusty metal that covered the open space, where the reflected heat was as great as that coming direct from the sun.

A road, deep in dust, led them past gardens powder dry now from lack of rain. But the trees and creeping vines were still a vivid green, flaunting their great red flowers to an unseeing world. Another corner, and there was a road like a pale thread looping towards arid hills, featureless and low. In the distance the mountains had retreated behind a light blue haze. The stillness was doubly oppressive now. They stood there, two men alone, and felt the weight of the fierce land thrusting upon them.

'We could walk a long way there and see nothing,' said Donald. 'We'll go down to the river. It should be cooler there.'

The line of the stream was marked by trees. They found a track leading down through gardens. Unexpectedly, from in front of them, came the sound of voices. They stood in the shade and watched native women washing and beating clothes on flat stones by the water's edge. Across the stream they could now see the thatched roofs of huts, a village keeping its distance from the houses of the white invaders.

'Those would be kanakas, I suppose,' said Donald. They squatted there talking vigorously, their shapeless cloth garments wound carefully around their bodies. They were almost coal black, with thick features and masses of curly hair shining with oil. Their faces shone too, with white teeth showing as they talked and laughed, not knowing that they were being watched. An incongruous thought struck Donald, and he laughed too.

'You know, Johnny, they are not so very different from the women folk at home. You must have seen your own mother washing the clothes down by the stream in much the same way!

'And yet, you know, many people who have had much to do with them do not think they are human. They can be killed like useless animals, or whipped like disobedient dogs. Have you ever heard of the Blacks that were hunted in Australia by men on horses, just as if they were kangaroos or foxes?'

Johnny had sat down on the ribbed root of a tree, and was mopping his face as he studied the kanakas abstractedly. 'They could be animals in woman's shape, with no human feelings, and so it would be natural to treat them as animals,' he said.

'Yes, but see those young ones? Slim bodies, laughing eyes; they look like youngsters anywhere.'

'Yes,' said Johnny, 'and no doubt if you lived here long enough they would seem as fair as any red-headed Scottish girl. But not yet, as far as I'm concerned.

'Ask Roddy about that, Donald, if you want to. He could tell you of men – some of them living not too far from Waipu – who've found the Island girls comfortable enough. And when we go further, you'll see brindled ones to prove it to you. Don't worry, Donald; they're human enough for some of us.'

'It's hard to believe, certainly,' said Donald thoughtfully. 'But you can never tell.'

Johnny stood up, and the movement caught the eye of one of the women down below them. A quick call, and every one of them was smiling in their direction. Some turned away self-consciously; others, more bold, laughed with flashing teeth and a cheerful wave of the arm. The old ones, Donald noticed, were less restrained than the girls. One of them began a dance that reduced her friends to helpless laughter. Donald laughed too when the dancer, with a comic sense that was as well timed as it was broad, deliberately lost her footing and landed with a resounding thump on the sand.

They walked away downstream, followed by high-pitched giggles and friendly goodbyes.

'I'm afraid they are the same the world over, Johnny,' observed Donald. 'They like their fun, but they get it mostly from their work. Those clothes will surely be clean by the time they have finished; and they probably look on it as a pleasant holiday.'

Donald glanced at his companion. Johnny did not seem at ease with himself. His mouth was set in a tight curve, and Donald had never before noticed what haunted eyes he had.

'Women!' he said harshly. 'They're a poison that infects the blood. No doubt you think, Donald, that I'm the father of Christy Cameron's child. And old Roddy thinks so, too.'

There was a desperation in the glance that he threw at Donald, who tried to think before he answered. But he could not be diplomatic now, not with those eyes watching him.

'That's what we thought, Johnny,' he answered softly. 'Not that Christy said anything, but it just happened that I heard you had been working near their farm.'

'You must be right,' Johnny said heavily, and then paused as they walked slowly along the river bank. 'Even if she had wanted another man, I cannot think of anyone who would have had the chance to satisfy her. And in any case, it is unlikely, with a girl like Christy.'

He turned to Donald with a strange directness. 'Why should it be like this?' he asked. 'I despise them, and go to work to sweat this greed out of my body. And for a while I can. But then they come back into my mind. They do not need to be beautiful, even. I see a girl, and there is something about her that weakens me. I watch her talk and smile, and there's something in the way she moves her hands, or the way her head sits on her neck, or how she moves her lips and eyes. And then she can flick her finger at me, and I'm lost.

'I thought Christy was different. Cool and remote, uninterested in anything at first, as far as I could see. When I met her she scarcely spoke, hardly looked at me. And yet I was conscious of her without wanting to hurt her. Even though she talked so little, I felt that she was interested in what I said. So it went on for a while. She was a great one for walking, and we would go miles up in the hills on Sunday afternoons.

'And then it happened. Don't ask me why or how. I don't know. I didn't see her for a week, but I need not have worried. She was once again as she had been when I first met her – treating me as a casual acquaintance with whom she had nothing in common. And then, one day, she said I should go away. She had found that I had a bad reputation, she said, and her parents would not be wanting her to be seen with me.

'Tell me, was that a natural way for a girl to act?'

'Perhaps she felt ashamed over what had been done,' said Donald.

'No. She told me not to think about it again and that as far as she was concerned nothing had ever happened. So I went. To hell with her, I thought. And that was that.'

The stream was noisy and cool, running over a shingle bed like hundreds of others he had seen in the bush at home. But nowhere at home could one see such a brassy sky, or exotic trees and creepers with such a wealth of bloom. Donald turned his mind to these things, hoping that Johnny had finished. But his voice came again.

'Tell me, Donald, don't you ever feel that the world is a crazy place? How do you keep so level-headed about it all?'

Donald couldn't answer. There was nothing he could think of to fit the case. He looked at Johnny, who was smiling sheepishly now, as if regretting his outburst.

You could never tell what was going on inside a man, Donald thought. He felt sorry for Johnny, but out of his depth, too. And there was something distasteful about the frankness of this unexpected confession. A man should keep such private thoughts to himself.

He considered his own case, a trifle ruefully. Perhaps Norman McLeod's precepts had more value than he sometimes thought, if they could prevent a man from making such a fool of himself.

Donald looked away. One thing for sure, Johnny was not enjoying this. What did he know of the problems that beset Johnny, or for that matter any other man? He was becoming as harsh and ruthless as one of Norman McLeod's disciples: And that was something he had never expected to be.

'I'm sorry Johnny,' he said. 'There's this, though: I should think a man can find more true happiness with a girl that he loves than with a dozen he despises and hurts. If you can't get Christy out of your mind, why don't you go back and marry her? I think you gave up too easily; and there's the possible baby now. Christy will surely be a different woman from the one you thought you knew.'

'Do you think so?' said Johnny bitterly. 'I don't. She has been through hell on her own, and I'm the last one she would want to see now, or ever.'

Johnny turned and faced Donald squarely. 'You've got some soft ideas, Donald. When will you grow up?' There was a bitterness in the question that Donald could not comprehend. 'That girl – the decoy – who nearly led you into trouble in Auckland: What did you think of her?'

So Roddy talks to him too, the old villain, when he's on duty and I'm down below asleep! This thought came to him first, but was edged aside by Johnny's impatience for an answer.

'Well,' he said slowly, 'she seemed a decent enough girl to me, but sadly misled by the rogues she was consorting with. Of course, I didn't believe all the story she told me, but even when I saw the trap that had been laid I felt sorry that she had to have a part in it. I don't think she did it willingly.'

Johnny laughed. 'That's what I thought you would say,' he answered. 'You think of your mother, or of someone else's charming sister who, when you see her, is always tidy and cheerful and on her best behaviour. You fill your head with romantic notions that all women are like that all the time. Or if they aren't, it's the fault of a man.

'Don't you know women are human, just as we are? And that if we have ugly thoughts and anger and desire, they have them too? You say

I'm astray in my thoughts. But if that is so, it's even truer about you, although in another direction.

'Marry her, you say. Talk to her softly; put your head on her knee and you'll live happily forever. I've seen a lot of women, and none of them are what you dream them to be. They could all crack your head with an iron pan, if life didn't go as they wanted it. And if they didn't do it with the nearest thing that came to hand, they would stab you with words, and that can be even worse.

'You say for me to relax and go back to her. But even if she married me, wouldn't this always stand between us? Wouldn't we keep on hurting each other every day?'

'You might, if you didn't love her, and if she didn't love you,' said Donald. 'Even if you love each other there might still be some hurt in it. But you would get over it, and even that would be better than what you are both suffering now.

'I may be soft, Johnny, and I know I've a lot to learn. But I still feel that I'm nearer the truth than you are.'

The path led past a deep pool where the stream gathered in the tree shade before spilling over towards the sea.

'We should have a swim and cool off,' Donald suggested, looking longingly at the fresh water.

'I can't swim,' Johnny replied shortly. So they walked on until they came back to the town.

* * *

They had not been long away. When he crossed the verandah Donald expected to see Roddy fast asleep, but the room was empty. Quickly now they walked down to the wharf. And Donald, for one, had an uneasy feeling. In a foreign land strange things could happen, like the disappearance of a boat; the kidnapping of its captain. But the *Fiona* was still there, and Roddy too, standing at ease on the wharf in conversation with Monsieur Napoleon. A big whaleboat was rowing slowly back from the cutter.

'You're here just in time,' roared Roddy, who seemed surprisingly alert and energetic. 'Monsewer was about to send a search party after you. We feared that the local beauties might have snared you!'

'That didn't happen,' said Donald. 'But what about you? We thought you would still be sleeping.'

Roddy grinned. 'A few minutes were enough to revive me. And then, with all this cargo to go aboard, it seemed that I should be busy checking the articles through – which is not to say, of course, that I didn't trust our friend Napoleon, here!'

The Frenchman bowed, smiling his dislike.

Donald looked at Roddy: 'And also, perhaps, you wanted us out of the way? What is your cargo, Roddy? Or do I ask Mr Napoleon that?'

'You don't ask him, Donald. It's good, respectable cargo, by my standard, and if we are to discuss it further, we'll wait until we are on board.'

'Will you have something more to drink before you go – or perhaps to eat?' Monsieur Napoleon combed one sleek hand through his beard and waited for a reply.

'Thank you, Monsewer, but we have been here long enough as it is,' said Roddy. 'I'm worried about your customs officials, gendarmes and suchlike. If they should come, and us still here, it could be embarrassing for you. And so we'll away while the fair breeze holds.'

They shook hands, climbed into their small boat and rowed back to the *Fiona*.

Donald looked at Roddy dubiously, half intending to resume their broken conversation; but obviously this was not the time.

'Shake out the sails and get the anchor up,' called Roddy, and bustled about like a small tornado. The *Fiona* gathered weigh quickly. Donald, posted once again at the crosstree, thought hard as he watched his captain. He knew Roddy well enough to be sure just how little he did know about what went on in his mind. And yet it was not easy to believe what he suspected – that the old man was up to some villainy. The hatch cover was firmly down, and it was impossible for him to discover for himself what their cargo, so mysteriously loaded, could be. Roddy could tell him, or not, just as the fancy took him.

When he slid down to the deck, with the reef safely behind them, Roddy had settled the *Fiona* on a course that slanted away from the land. The wind was nicely on their port quarter, and the cutter sailed nonetheless lightly for her additional cargo.

Donald approached his captain. 'Now, Roddy, what are we carrying?'

Roddy was wearing his most innocent expression. 'What are you thinking, Donald? Guns, perhaps, to slaughter the harmless natives?'

'That could be in my mind, Roddy. I hope I'm wrong.'

Roddy laughed and slapped him on the shoulder. 'You are wrong, Donald. No one – not the French themselves, or even the kanakas – would take exception to what we have stowed below. Not that they'll have the chance, I hope. We have trade goods, loaded in Auckland, to supply Kenny Omaha's post in the New Hebrides; all fair and above board. And…' – here he looked more guileless than usual – '…selected articles that will be brought back to Auckland unopened and untasted. Bottles, in fact, of rum, brandy and other beverages for which there seems a demand in our homeland. Mind you, Donald, we have erred in one way. There has been no duty paid on them so far. But that doesn't matter. It simply means that the price will be nearer their true and honest value.

'Are you happy now, Donald?'

'You would lose it all if you were caught, Roddy?'

'That's so. But it is a reasonable risk to take. And soon, at this rate, we'll be beyond the reach of any revenue cutter. We should round the tip of New Caledonia tonight, and then it will be clear going to Tanna Island.'

Roddy's expression changed quickly. 'Are you tired of the sea yet, Donald? Do you wish you were home again?' He looked at the young man with what seemed an honest affection. 'I hope you are not. It would be dreary sailing with someone who wasn't a friend.'

'No homesickness, Roddy.' Donald felt this was true enough. 'But as for Johnny, I don't know. He has some strange notions, Roddy. And I'm thinking that the sooner he is home again the better it will be for him. He's not a happy man, and I wonder if he ever will be.'

'So he was talking to you, Donald? I thought he might be. And full of vexation against me, I suppose.'

'I'm not sure that he trusts you, Roddy,' said Donald with a laugh. 'But neither do I; so that makes two of us.'

'And how do you think Christy will fare?' Roddy asked, ignoring Donald's comment.

'I think he will see her again. But what the outcome will be I cannot guess.'

Johnny came up on deck, wrinkling his eyes against the glare of sea and sun.

'We should have taken on some water, and fruit and vegetables too,' he said.

'The vegetables are there, Johnny, in the locker by my bunk. And now that you mention it, a good meal before sundown would make a new man of me. There's some steak there, too, although I cannot guarantee its tenderness. But see what you can do, Johnny, and we'll be grateful.'

The westward-slipping sun still caught the barren, smoky ranges of New Caledonia in full light. But they seemed remote and unreal now to Donald, like the little village they had visited, the kanakas working and playing by the river, and the conversation he had had with Johnny Bain.

* * *

Chapter Sixteen

A CLOUD HUNG IN THE CLEAR SKY AHEAD OF THEM. NOTHING showed between it and the horizon, but Roddy watched it with satisfaction and announced that, in an hour or so, they would see Tanna Island standing beneath it. Donald wondered at his confidence, and Roddy explained that high land, even when it was as small as the island they were seeking, seemed to draw the vapour from the sea winds.

Donald climbed to the crosstree and waited for the land to grow up out of the sea. Early that morning they had sighted a small island to starboard, the first they had seen since leaving New Caledonia, but it had been too far away to hold any individuality. He found that the prospect of a new landfall had its own excitement. New Caledonia had been one thing. What would the New Hebrides hold in store? The name itself had magic echoes in his mind, recalling the Scottish islands from which his own people had sailed so many years before.

The wind lagged – the trade winds could be fickle in this lost corner of the Pacific. They crept up to the land as dusk was falling, fighting fierce currents that ruffled the sea's surface.

'This is as far as we go,' Roddy announced. 'We'll stand off and on during the night, and hope to make Port Resolution with the first light. One thing is sure; we won't be lost. Look!'

He pointed landward, but Donald had already seen the volcano. A pillar of smoke by day, a column of fire by night. Here, too, as in the days of Moses, God was showing His power.

A cone of ash and cinder rose two thousand feet from the rich green hills. At first there was a tentative puff or two of smoke. Then it became a plume, speckled with black dots, drifting away lazily on the wind. But now night was taking over. The cone had disappeared. The lip of the crater was intermittently marked against the night sky, reflecting the rose-coloured underside of the smoke cloud which itself took its colour from the fires burning deep inside the mountain. Soon nothing could be seen but this strange, fearful glow, waxing and waning between earth and heaven.

Donald had made up his bed on deck that night, tucked below the bulwark for shelter, and through all the dark hours he seemed conscious of the volcano, and of the strange land lying below it. Sometimes, before they tacked to head away from the unknown coast, he thought he heard sounds from the direction of shore; low, deep callings from a conch-shell trumpet, like the one he had seen at Omaha; the beating of drums broken up by the surge of the sea. There were flickering fires too, on the beach. He had a picture in his mind of the Islanders sleeping uneasily on the fringe of a jungle that for them also had its terrors.

But the mountain dominated everything else, whether he was waking or sleeping. Early in the morning, while it was still dark, a clap of thunder startled him and he saw a red fire spilling over the side of the crater. Lava, glowing and incandescent, ate its way down through the darkness until it was quenched in the forest of the lower ranges. And once again the mountain flared and paled, flared and paled, like a great log crumbling to ash in the hearth.

They made full sail again in the morning. For a while the steady breeze from the land powdered them with fine volcanic dust. They drew clear of that, and then Roddy sniffed appreciatively as he stood by the tiller. 'That's it,' he said. 'The smell of the Islands.'

There was life, death and decay in the scent that the wind now brought them. Donald felt sickened and attracted by it at the same time: A sense of rich, violent movement toward ripeness and maturity; an equally swift descent back to the earth that nurtured life and then destroyed it.

'Unhealthy country,' said Roddy, 'unless you're the kind who can beat it. Not many can.

'One thing,' he added, 'it's cooler at this time of the year than when I was here before. Midsummer that was, and even the rain was fit to burn you!'

'When were you up this way last, Roddy?' asked Donald.

'I thought I had told you,' Roddy replied. 'Years ago, when you were but a lad.' His face hardened. 'We were after sandalwood and bêche-de-mer then. We lost three men to the savages. There was no profit from that trip. I meant never to return, but things should be better now – or so I've been told.'

No coral reefs here, Donald noted; and the Pacific rollers broke heavily on the cliffs or drove with great power up the beaches. Behind the sand, the forest seemed to press down against the sea. They turned a rocky headland, opening up a small, secluded bay, a shallow crescent of beach with low land behind it. The entrance was broad enough to allow the waves to sweep through, and they set three vessels dancing at their moorings.

'Port Resolution,' Roddy said, and joined the others in examining what lay before them.

Donald was troubled. He was no seaman, but there was something familiar about the schooner lying nearest the land. He turned to Roddy and pointed: 'Does she come from New Zealand, would you think?'

'Most of the craft you'll see here do, unless they're from Australia or Fiji, or perhaps Peru.' He looked again. 'So you know her, Donald? You should. She was in Omaha when you were there not long ago. And if I'm not mistaken, that's Kenny himself watching us.'

Roddy turned the *Fiona* until she was sliding up beside the schooner. 'How are you?' came Kenny's voice. They took down their sail creditably enough under his eyes, and dropped anchor.

To Donald, Kenny Omaha, high on the schooner's poop, seemed to be set against a strange yet suitable background. He wore a wide-brimmed hat and no coat, but his beard was as trim and piratical as ever. Beyond the sturdy spars of the schooner's hamper the volcano puffed ruminative clouds of smoke. A black boy, his skin shining with sweat and oil, rubbed thoughtfully at the brass-work. The lush green forest was closer now, a choking growth that looked impassable except to birds and snakes, and it exhaled into the humid air a rich and burdening scent.

'Where are you now, Donald?' he asked himself silently. 'There are some things a man should not meddle with, and I'm afraid you are going too near them.'

But Roddy was no longer thinking of his sad sandalwood venture. He was talking affably to Kenny, and Kenny was inviting them to come on board and talk things over. There were matters that needed discussion, it seemed; and he wanted to know how New Caledonia had looked.

'How did he get here so quickly?' Donald asked Roddy in a low voice.

Roddy laughed. 'Good as the *Fiona* is, Kenny's schooner could do a journey in half the time. He drives his ship the way he drives his men.'

'And are you one of them, Roddy?'

'I admire him, and work with him, Donald, but I keep my own identity. Even Kenny, with all his power, cannot rob me of that.' Roddy spat emphatically into the oily water, and clambered into his small boat where Johnny Bain was waiting at the oars.

It seemed cooler in the schooner, and the sense of space to spare overwhelmed Donald as he walked across the deck and followed the others below into an airy cabin.

Kenny went to a cupboard and produced a bottle of whisky and heavy glass tumblers. There seems to be a terrible lot of drinking done in these parts, Donald thought as he took a glass and poured himself a small measure.

The heat became suddenly greater, and the sound of the volcano was like an endless surging of water through a great chasm. The air darkened.

Through the porthole, while Roddy and Kenny talked of New Caledonia, Donald saw the water begin to shine like glass, and then it was pitted by a fiercely jabbing rain.

There was no wind, but the rain drummed on the deck above them as if the schooner were driving through heavy seas. Water streamed past the porthole. Then, as suddenly as it had come, the storm passed. The sun glittered on the sea, and the forest seemed to smoke as the vapour climbed slowly out of the trees.

Donald felt restless as Kenny and Roddy sipped their whisky and talked. He looked at Johnny Bain, who sat somnolently in a corner, neither seeing nor hearing.

'Come up on deck with me, Johnny.'

They climbed from the dark heat of the cabin to the blazing heat of the open sky.

Port Resolution was very quiet. They stood and looked about them without speaking. A shot sounded casually in the forest, and was swallowed up in the heavy silence. Then, on the beach at the head of the bay, dark figures ran down across the sand and launched three canoes. They came out swiftly, circling and then flying forward under the thrust of many paddles. They swept under the schooner's stern and turned neatly along the *Fiona's* port side.

'You have some visitors, Roddy,' Donald called down into the cabin.

There was an explosion of sound from below, and Roddy came charging up onto the deck, followed more slowly by Kenny.

'They're Niahoo's lot,' said Kenny. 'Good friends of mine. I'll get them over here.' He whistled shrilly and called a few words in obscure and garbled English. There was an answering yell from the canoes, which gathered speed in a few yards and jostled about the rope ladder dangling over the schooner's side.

'You would like some fresh food, Roddy,' said Kenny. 'We'll do a trade. Mind you, they can get anything they want from my store on the beach, but they like an excuse to come out and look about.' He called to the kanaka who stood watching up forward. 'Bring up two boxes, Charlie.'

Naked bodies, squealing pigs, fowls that squawked discordantly; the smell of oil and sweat, mouths full of white teeth and red tongues; hair that was dressed and teased out so that the great, brown, shining faces seemed small in comparison; clubs and spears and muskets brandished carelessly but – Donald hoped – without malice. The sedate deck taken over by a hoard of savages, men and women, who looked at the new arrivals curiously, furtively, with a timid boldness, and then darted away to talk among themselves. And over it all presided a good-humoured Kenny, unworried by the confusion, directing his kanaka as he took the lids off two wooden crates and displayed the trade goods.

The heat was merciless, heightened for Donald by the noise and movement of the savages. He wiped his streaming face and watched Roddy attempt to bargain with three men at a time. All of them, it seemed, owned part of one small pig, and all had to be satisfied.

Then there was a roar of excitement and trading came to an end as the natives ran to the railing. Donald looked quickly about him as he followed. Johnny had disappeared! The Tanna islanders pointed and howled and danced, and a few of the more exhilarated jumped with a mighty splash into the water, while their friends howled and shouted even louder. Somehow or other, probably jolted by one of the natives, Johnny had fallen over the side.

'We'll have to pull him out. He can't swim!' Donald spoke to Roddy who had come up beside him.

'The lad's in no danger. Keep dry, unless you are wanting to cool yourself off. Just look at them!'

Johnny was indeed safe enough. A small canoe carrying one girl had come out to the schooner. Before any of the others could reach him, the girl had slipped into the water and now had a firm hold on Johnny's long hair. As sleek and smooth as a seal, and as much at home in the water, she towed him to the ship's side until one of his wildly flailing arms grabbed the rope ladder. Then, as he climbed on board, she swam back and pushed her canoe to where the others were moored.

Johnny shook himself and wiped his hands through his streaming hair. Roddy slapped him on the back. 'Take your boots off, Johnny, and you'll be dry again in five minutes.' The natives crowded round, studying his bare white feet as if they had magical qualities.

Kenny watched with smooth, unamused face. 'You all right, Johnny? The Americans say that a man can go overboard for a girl, but that's the first time I've ever seen it done. Now, you must give her a present, or her friends will throw you back in again.'

She was a buxom girl, with a wide, good-natured smile. Her skin was drying now, but her hair, worn shorter than that of the men, clung like wet twine to her head. She came up to Johnny, squeezed his arm with an exclamation of delight at its firmness, and patted his cheek.

'She's adopted you, Johnny,' roared Roddy.

There was, indeed, an unmistakable devotion in the black eyes that watched Johnny unwaveringly – until they turned towards the nearest box of trade goods.

'Shusar,' said the girl firmly.

'She wants something, Johnny. Get busy and find her a present.'

Johnny reached desperately into the box and brought out a length of turkey-red cloth which he held out towards her.

She shook her head and smiled at him. She was not beautiful, Donald thought, but she had a simple determination that would take her a long way. 'Shusar,' she repeated.

Johnny produced in turn a mirror, a large straw hat, a knife, a bright woollen shawl, a pair of men's trousers with a neat pinstripe. She shook her head every time, sometimes with a show of reluctance but always firmly. 'Shusar,' she said again.

Johnny looked around at the row of grinning faces.

The girl smiled at him again, and ran a hand through his long hair. She clicked her tongue in admiration.

'Shusar,' she explained, as if she were speaking to a small and rather backward child. She opened her mouth, plucked with one finger beside her face and with doubled tongue hummed discordantly. Most of the spectators had lost interest by now, and were busy bartering with Kenny and the others; but those who remained applauded her performance. She continued for several minutes while Johnny looked even more puzzled.

Suddenly his face lit up and he scrambled anxiously in the litter of goods still inside the box. 'Could it be a jew's-harp, do you think, Donald?'

The girl nodded vigorously. 'Shusar. Shusar!'

Down among the beads and trinkets Johnny found a box of jew's-harps, strange little instruments that twanged and vibrated when they were plucked between the teeth.

Johnny grabbed three of them, put one back in the box and thrust the others at the girl.

'What's your name?'

'Ouanake, me,' she replied, with glistening eyes.

'For you, Ouanake,' said Johnny. He reached forward and shook hands with her. She took his hand in both of hers.

'And thank you for helping me from the water,' Johnny said, trying to withdraw his hand.

Ouanake smiled and held on. Her expression, Donald thought, was like that of a mother cat that had found a strayed kitten. Johnny was unhappy, but the sadder his face became, the more staunchly did Ouanake cling to him. He struggled, ungallantly, to break away, and the girl slipped on the deck and fell forward on him. Ouanake was giggling now with delight. This new game that the white man played was a happy one.

Johnny fought hard to get his footing, but failed. He had enjoyed other encounters more than this, Donald though sardonically. He grabbed at the girl, but she was as slippery as an eel. And then his hand caught the string holding her scanty skirt in place. It broke, and the jew's-harps, tucked into an open pouch at her waist, clattered to the deck.

This was Johnny's salvation. As quick as light, Ouanake had released him and was pouncing on her precious musical instruments, her skirt lying where it had fallen.

Johnny scrambled to his feet, wiping the sweat from his face and looking, Donald thought, as if he would leap back over the side at any moment. He picked up the skirt by one of its strings just as Roddy's mocking voice showed that he had seen what was happening.

'Come now, Johnny. These girls aren't as easy as some you have known. You must court them, Johnny; court them. Or their brothers will eat you alive!'

Johnny scarcely heard him. He was holding the skirt out to Ouanake, but she was still too preoccupied with her jew's-harps to pay him much attention. 'You good girl, Ouanake,' he pleaded. 'Your skirt. Put it on again please!'

Roddy's laugh jarred in their ears. 'Be patient, Johnny. Woo her as you would a Spanish beauty. She's none of your waterfront sluts!'

But by now Ouanake had gracefully taken the skirt from Johnny's hand. She tied it about her, gave him a glowing glance of admiration, and jumped overboard beside her canoe. She waved with one light paddle and was soon sending the canoe swiftly over the water towards the beach.

Trading came to an end in a welter of incoherent farewells and repeated handshakes. After all, it had been chiefly curiosity that had brought the natives on board. They had observed the new arrivals, and that was enough for the present.

Donald watched one man, older that most of the others, with sinewy arms, loose skin on his chest and shrivelled stomach. He walked slowly to the side of the boat, ushering the rest before him. Then with a slowness that seemed somehow defiant he climbed down into the canoe. Where his companions were cheerful, his eyes as he looked back at them were sombre and unreadable.

Kenny came up beside Donald. 'That's Nifua,' he said. 'He's lost condition since he turned Christian.'

Donald chewed over this remark and waited for Kenny to explain it further. 'He was a great chief and priest; a noted cannibal. He would go out a few miles from his village and lie in ambush beside the track, and jump out when a child came by, seizing him like a tiger. But now the missionary has told him he mustn't eat his enemies, or even their children, any more.'

Kenny paused and wiped his forehead with a fine white linen handkerchief. Donald said: 'Why didn't they kill him? Surely they would not allow a man to hunt them down at will?'

'I told you he was a great priest,' Kenny said, 'He was more than that. He was the god of the sea, and his only rival was the god of the mountains, a black-skinned devil who came raiding them from the jungles far inland. I tell you, the two of them led the people a merry dance, Donald. And what did a baby or so every month matter if their sacrifice meant that disease and hunger would stay away?

'And then suddenly Nifua came to the missionary and said he wanted to go to church. Now he's no longer a god, even the heathens despise him, and he has to scratch for his food like the rest of them.' Kenny shook his head. 'There's no accounting for what a man will do.'

'Where is the missionary?' Donald asked. 'In Resolution Bay here?'

'His house is just out of sight there.' Kenny pointed towards a low, forest-covered spur that came down almost to the water at the head of the harbour. 'But he's away now, and I'm not sure when he's due back. You should meet him, Donald. His name is Hugh Craig and he's a Nova Scotian like ourselves – from Pictou, I believe.'

Kenny was in a relaxed and contemplative mood. He spat delicately into the darker blue water on the cool side of the ship, and they watched the small fish darting and hovering below the surface.

'This is the strangest of worlds, Donald.' Kenny looked at him with thoughtful eyes. 'You were just a lad, and would remember little of it; and what you did remember you wouldn't understand. But a fever seemed to get into our blood back there in Nova Scotia, urging us to pack up our goods and sail away to these southern seas. A few years of wandering; South Africa, Australia, and then New Zealand. And there we settle. The fever dies in most of us, but some still wish to move about. And here we are, in tropical heat, in islands that make the memory of Nova Scotia seem like a drink of cool, clean water. And what do we find? Back there in the land we had left the restlessness has taken a different form. A poverty-stricken church, with no resources except the fervour of its members, decides to send out missionaries across the world to these same islands. Once again we meet face to face. But I'm warning you, Donald, the missionary might be our flesh and blood, but for him the trader is the devil's agent. We are close together, but in truth further apart than if he had stayed in Nova Scotia and we in New Zealand.'

Kenny lit a cigar and puffed smoke that hung fragrantly in the still, oppressive air. 'These are some of the things I think about, Donald. A man must think, you know, and although Norman McLeod never had much power over me, I find it a formidable thought that his religion has come here before us, carried by a man who is like him and yet very different.'

'What sort of man is he?' Donald asked.

'Who? Craig? He's not the only one, Donald. There are half a dozen of them scattered through these islands. Some have their wives and children with them, but it's no life for those who would want the best out of this world.

'Craig is quiet where Norman is strong of voice, but he's just as tough underneath.' Kenny laughed. 'You know, he has had me worried at times. He tells me that I'm not doing the natives any good, and that my Nova Scotian relatives will disown me. I tell him that most of my relatives would be keener for the business than I am; and that if the Scottish traders, and missionaries, were to move out of the Islands, the natives would fare worse from the English and the French. For a moment he looks as if he'll curse me up hill and down dale; but then he laughs and says that perhaps I am right. But I know that he hasn't given up, and that he'll be after me again.

'Some of the missionaries are all right, Donald, but except with Hugh Craig, their love of God has driven away their sense of humour.'

The bay was quiet now. A head showed on one of the other vessels anchored not far away. 'French scum,' said Kenny dispassionately. 'I'm with Craig there. The French are even worse than the English when they get loose up here. They've no manners at all, and make things harder for us.

'Now to work.' He called out to Roddy, who had just come up on deck; a rather tired looking man, Donald thought, but still walking and acting jauntily enough.

Kenny said: 'We'll get the trade goods ashore this afternoon. There's time enough still. And then you'll be able to make a start for Lewin's plantation early in the morning. The whole business should be ended in a few days.'

Roddy grunted a reply, and Donald was surprised to read suspicion and a certain reluctance in his eyes. Kenny laid his hand on the older man's arm in a friendly way. 'You'll have dinner on board with me. I don't know whether you young fellows are anxious to go ashore, but you can go with the boat if you care.'

Kenny was watching Roddy, and there was a forced note in his laugh as he added: 'Be sure you watch yourself, Johnny. You certainly made an impression when you went overboard this morning, and these girls take a power of dodging!'

They left the schooner and returned to the *Fiona*. Three sturdy boys unloaded the cargo under Roddy's supervision, and four others took it ashore in a whaleboat. Johnny went with the first load, but Donald stayed on board. He chatted idly with Roddy who was ticking items off his list with the stub of a pencil.

'Who is Lewin, and what are we going to see him for?'

Roddy looked uneasy. 'It's something I have promised to do,' he said, 'or rather something that Kenny promised I would do. And that's why I don't like it much.

'Ross Lewin's out of our class, and perhaps, although I'm not so sure, out of Kenny's class too. He has a plantation on the other side of the island, and a bodyguard of a hundred natives brought from elsewhere to keep him safe. He needs them too, from what I've heard. He deserted from the navy years ago, and has made his own way since then. And now, to do him a favour, Kenny's promised that he will take half a dozen of his labourers back to their own island. They must be sick, or Lewin would not be letting them go so easily. But, according to Kenny, he hasn't any friends on that island, and if one of his own cutters calls in there his crew might not get away again.

Roddy checked more cargo out of the hold while Donald thought this rather involved statement over.

Ross Lewin, then, was a blackbirder, one of those who recruited natives to work on plantations in Queensland or Fiji or New Caledonia – wherever there was work to be done that white men could not do. Some people called the blackbirders by harsher names: Slavers; pirates; murderers. And sometimes they were right, for their methods could be unscrupulous. Others said it was merely business, and that the natives were improved in mind and enriched materially by their stay on a plantation.

A little blackbirding was done by most traders; Kenny, he suspected, among them. With a few, it was a full-time profession. Donald thought it over soberly while he watched the cheerful black men pull away at the oars. They seemed contented enough, but how thinly hidden beneath that contentment was there a hatred of the white man; an envy and despair at the passing of the life they knew? And how quickly could it be aroused?

Roddy interrupted his thoughts. 'There's one thing for sure, Donald. We're not going blackbirding. This is an honest transaction, a favour that Kenny wishes to do for a friend. And that is all I intend it to be.' He nodded emphatically, and they left it at that.

* * *

The boat was coming back now, its crew pulling at the oars under a sky of molten lead. Frisking around it were the natives' canoes, light, incredibly swift, some of them with sails hanging slackly above the plunging paddles.

Johnny Bain was sitting in the stern, Donald noted. A quick look ashore had apparently satisfied him. Donald saw him give a half-hearted wave. The girl was back again, alone in her small canoe, her eyes fixed on Johnny's face.

There's no doubt about him, Donald thought. I wonder if Christy is in his mind now, or the baby he has never seen, or the other girls he has courted wherever he goes? However, there's not much chance of this handsome brown wench getting a hold on him, for we'll be away in the morning.

Donald felt momentarily depressed. All the plans I've made, the high-flown ideas I have nursed about many different things, and still I am carried along like a twig on a swift-flowing river.

He looked at Johnny's unrevealing face as the young man clambered forward and jumped on board the cutter. To try to pressure him to return to Waipu might not only be useless; it might be unpleasant. How much easier to let matters rest, and see what happened. If he were to meddle with Johnny's life, come to think of it, there was no reason why Norman McLeod should not interfere with Donald's own. And that, at times, was something he was not disposed to allow.

But on the other hand, one man was bound to influence another. Take Roddy for example, spinning a web around them from his own artful simplicity – and sometimes becoming entangled in it himself. Or Kenny, manipulating from a discreet distance the threads that make a hundred others move to his command. Or this man Hugh Craig, intruding, on God's account, into a way of life that had existed for long enough without the intervention of God or white men.

'You're not going ashore, Donald?' Roddy's voice broke into his thoughts. 'This will be the last load.'

Donald shook his head. Two heavy cases were lowered by slings into the whaleboat. The *Fiona* seemed even now to ride more buoyantly. She's shaken off a weight, Donald thought, and is the better for it. And so must I, he added. No more vain worrying. Let the river carry the twig along: It will get somewhere in the end.

* * *

Chapter Seventeen

ARMED WITH VAGUE BUT SUFFICIENT INSTRUCTIONS AND OBVIOUSLY refreshed after a quiet night, Roddy roused them before dawn in an optimistic mood.

'There's a breeze coming up that we can't afford to lose,' he said cheerfully. 'We'll waste no time.'

It was a black world, with glimmering streaks of white on the water and in the sky. A world drained of colour, except for the blood-red puffs of smoke that came spasmodically from the volcano. Light increased imperceptibly, and then with breathless speed. But until the sun shone, it was a flat and empty world, resting for a few minutes before the sun woke it to life.

The night had been calm, but now the volcano's plume streamed low across the hills. There would be wind in plenty outside, and even in the bay there were gusts that would fill their sails. As they slid easily away, Kenny's head appeared above the deck of his sleeping ship and he waved them farewell.

The wind was warm even now, but there was life in it, and Donald felt the exhilaration that always came with movement and novelty. Under light sail the *Fiona* danced happily, then dipped her bowsprit down as she met the open sea.

Donald was busy with the jib when he heard a call of amazement from Roddy. Hard across their bows came a small canoe. It turned swiftly along their course and its only occupant, judging the moment perfectly, jumped onto the deck. The canoe drifted rapidly astern.

Roddy stared in choked silence until the slatting of the mainsail made him adjust his course, and at the same time broke the spell. 'What's this?' he spluttered.

The girl smiled ingratiatingly at them all, but her eyes turned back to Johnny, who was as surprised as the rest.

'Mallicollo Island home belonga me. Not this.' She pointed at Tanna's rocky coastline with a vast contempt. 'I know you go there. I come too.'

Roddy looked accusingly at Johnny. 'Did you arrange this? No; I'm sure you didn't. How did she find that out? But of course, word soon goes around. What do we do now?'

The perturbed Roddy was asking questions and answering them for himself so readily that no one else spoke. 'We must take her back. It will be hard in this wind, but we certainly cannot bring her with us. People would talk!'

The humour of the situation suddenly made his eyes sparkle. 'I can see the report in the Auckland newspaper: "Captain Roddy McKenzie found guilty of kidnapping." That would give them something to talk about back in Waipu!'

The girl had been listening, and now attempted to frame words urgently. 'No,' she said. 'Nifua angry because he' – she pointed to Johnny – 'gave me shusar. He take them away. Now, if I no go, maybe he eat me!' She nodded in emphasis.

Trouble, trouble everywhere, thought Donald. Roddy was obviously undecided, and he was getting no help from his crew. Johnny did not even seem very interested. Meanwhile the *Fiona* sailed steadily on, with Roddy glancing from the tiller in his hand to the rough coastline in a fine fever of indecision.

The girl looked around their faces, smiled and sat down gracefully. Roddy gave the tiller a hearty cuff. 'For God's sake, Johnny,' he said, 'find her another jew's-harp!'

There was no coral reef on this coast either, Donald saw. The jungle, unbroken on the rugged spurs, deep in blue shadow in the valleys, left little room for its human inhabitants. Any cultivation that the natives did, any villages that gave them shelter, must have been well hidden beneath the screen of growth.

The west coast of Tanna opened before them. Ahead now was a tangle of islands, all green on the burning blue sea, free of the metallic haze that had marked New Caledonia.

'Which is Mallicollo?' asked Donald.

'It must be about the only one we can't see yet,' replied Roddy. He studied his crude chart. 'You know, Donald, no one has done much to survey these islands since a Sassenach sea captain, James Cook, came this way about ninety years ago. He was good,' Roddy added glumly, 'but I feel he can't have been right all the time.'

He pointed to the small round circle that was Tanna.

‘Here is where we are going,’ he explained, ‘drawn by no less an expert than Kenny himself. Captain Cook apparently didn’t see these parts. He called at Port Resolution and gave it that name, but then he went off up north. Not that he was missing much, I’m sure. However, we’ll find out soon enough. And as for Mallicollo, no doubt our passenger will be able to help us when we get there.’

* * *

Ross Lewin’s plantation was cut out of the forest, straggling over low hills in a wide bay. There was an anchorage far too exposed for Roddy’s liking, a collection of native huts varying in size, and a more ambitious house that must surely belong to Lewin himself. Fortunately, with the wind off shore, the *Fiona* lay comfortably enough in deep water by the mouth of a small river. They took the sail down and were preparing to anchor when a whaleboat came out to meet them. There were eight rowers, disciplined in their precision, and a white man seated at the stern.

‘That doubtless will be Ross Lewin,’ said Roddy studying him keenly. The native rowers, big men wearing what Donald could only describe as blue kilts, shipped their oars on a quiet word of command and the boat glided up to the cutter’s bow. Lewin stood up. ‘Prepare to take a line on board,’ he called. ‘We’ll tow you in. The channel is too narrow for you to sail.’

The girl had been sent below and had gone willingly enough. The three men sat by the tiller as the *Fiona* slid easily behind the whaleboat. Lewin was sitting down again. He took no further notice of them.

‘The notorious Ross Lewin – that’s what the missionaries call him,’ said Roddy. ‘But he looks harmless enough to me.’ Donald himself, who had been expecting someone spectacular and piratical, was also surprised. Lewin was below average height but squarely built, a man well past middle age. His face was calm and assured. His crew, Donald saw, jumped to every word in his quiet voice.

They were a seamanlike lot, whether through training or instinct. The *Fiona* was brought alongside a wharf that jutted out into the stream and quickly secured. Lewin came over and jumped down. He shook hands. And then the girl’s head appeared through the cabin door.

‘What’s this?’ asked Lewin brusquely.

'A stowaway,' Roddy said. 'Heard we were going to Mallicollo and came aboard as we were leaving Port Resolution.'

Lewin nodded, obviously not greatly interested. 'You've been up here before, Captain McKenzie? You know your way about?'

Roddy was ready with an answer, but Lewin had already gone on in his level voice: 'First of all, there have been changes in the plan I discussed with Kenny. You're not going to Mallicollo. That business has been done. But there are four of my labourers to be returned to Efate. Let us look at your chart. You'll make for this bay here, just south of Vili Island. Dump them off there. And the girl, too, if you're wise. She'll find her way home easily enough.

'They can sleep on deck. And there are two men of mine who can go with you as well. I want them to see what's going on up there, and report back to me.

'Stores are ready. You won't need much. You're clear of cargo in the hold?'

'Kenny's goods have been unloaded,' Roddy replied with a certain reserve.

'Good,' said Lewin. 'And, by the way, there's a new missionary prying around in these parts. But he won't get in your way. If he does, talk to him nicely. They are harmless enough so long as you palaver to them.'

Lewin rubbed his hands together briskly. 'That's all clear, then? How is Kenny?' He did not wait for an answer but added: 'If you should run into trouble, my two men will see you through it. Now come ashore and have some food. You'll not be wanting to delay, with about eighty miles to cover yet.'

Donald was startled by hearing Johnny's voice. His silence had been unbroken for a long time. 'What about the girl?' he asked.

Lewin answered briefly: 'My men will see that she's fed. Now come along.'

As he followed the stocky figure, Donald felt a rebellious spirit rising in him. And along with it was a distinct feeling of distrust. This man, quiet mannered though he may be, would talk his way over or through any obstacle. He might, if he were allowed, drag Donald along behind him like a dog on a lead. There was in his manner an assumption of superiority that jangled in Donald's independent frame.

Roddy, however, seemed less perturbed now than when he had sailed from Port Resolution. He took Donald by the arm and allowed the active Ross Lewin to draw ahead.

'Don't be worrying,' he said. 'I'm sure now that he's planning some trick. It is better to know definitely than to be uncertain, as I was before. We'll keep our guard, lad, and all will be well.'

Roddy darted a malicious glance at Lewin's back. 'The only thing I'm not sure about,' he added, 'is whether Kenny is in with all the scheming. But that's something we'll find out, too; all in good time.'

Lewin ate well, but hastily, and his guests followed suit. Before long they were trudging back down to the wharf, the glare of high noon about them, even the dogs unwilling to stir from dark splashes of shade.

Roddy grunted, his beard stiff with suppressed anger. He nudged Donald. 'Our passengers, evidently,' he said.

The natives were lounging on the forward deck, and two white men, their wide-brimmed hats, beards and light coats giving them a strange uniformity, sat comfortably by the tiller. They had rigged a sail to give protection from the sun. They nodded to Lewin but ignored Roddy, who was almost bursting with indignation.

He said to Lewin: 'I see our consignment has been delivered. It looks well enough.'

Lewin spoke to one of his men. They had climbed to their feet now. Donald saw that they carried guns and cartridge belts. 'Everything is in order? Well, there is no need to delay. Captain McKenzie is ready.' He gave a casual wave and turned away. The girl, who had been waiting on the wharf, came hesitantly on board.

The full tide was ebbing now. 'My men will tow you out,' Lewin called, 'if you need them.'

Roddy looked at the water and sniffed the breeze. 'We'll manage right enough,' he replied shortly.

* * *

And now they were out at sea again, and the air seemed the fresher for it. The islanders had made the foredeck something of a marketplace, with food and their small possessions littered about them. Up there, also, were Lewin's two men, and not very happy about it.

Roddy had handled the situation with a delicacy that had delighted Donald, even if it did not altogether surprise him. As soon as they were clear of the coast he had called the guards – for that is what they seemed to be – before him. He had suggested that the proper place for them was with the labourers, and added that the girl would have to be kept away. For that reason she would remain aft, and they would see that their men kept out of the road. Nor, he had added, would their help be required in sailing the cutter, and he expected them to obey any orders he gave without delay.

The men looked surly, but said nothing. They had, it seemed, become accustomed to discipline. And Donald, watching Roddy, had not felt any surprise at their meek acceptance; for the little man who could at times appear comical and harmless was now the reverse.

Donald looked from Roddy's set face and shrewd, angry eyes to the two men. They were surly, but disciplined enough to contain their feelings.

'You're hard on them, aren't you, Roddy?' he said.

'I don't trust them,' Roddy answered. 'And I trust their master less. Why should he have sent them? Men like that? I don't like it. And until I find the answer, they will not move a step without my knowledge.' Roddy was never an apathetic man, Donald thought, but now, as his mind tackled this new problem, he seemed more alive that ever.

He grunted, and smiled at Donald with his old cheerfulness. 'There's little they can do in the meantime, unless they organise a mutiny. So we must relax.' His brilliant blue eyes turned towards Johnny, who was sitting as usual with a remote look on his handsome, empty face.

'Did you find another jew's-harp for your girl, Johnny? Why not ask her nicely if she will play us a tune?' Without any further encouragement, Ouanake began to pluck at the instrument; a nasal twanging reinforced by a dirge-like chant.

'Better than the bagpipes,' Roddy pronounced, but he did not seem over-enthusiastic. The girl was enjoying herself. The time at Lewin's plantation, the undercurrent of ill-feeling on the cutter, had made her feel uneasy. But now Johnny was smiling as he watched her obvious pleasure, and the bearded man was no longer frightening her with his fierce eyes.

She played even more zestfully, and the kanakas on the forward deck joined in with strange words and gestures. Roddy filled his pipe for the first time since leaving Tanna and sat back against the tiller.

'There's one thing sure, Johnny,' he remarked. 'She might win herself a lover in other ways, but I'm afraid she would lose him quickly enough if she began to sing. But perhaps your tastes are different to mine! Tell me, Johnny: Does she measure up to the other ones you've known? Christy Cameron, for example? Or the waterfront tarts at Auckland? Donald met one there, you know – or hasn't he told you about her?'

Before Johnny could speak, Donald broke in on Roddy's mocking question. 'I don't know what you're trying to do, Roddy, but I wish you would stop. There's a fit and proper way to talk, as you well know.'

Donald was going to say more when he saw a flicker of amusement cross Roddy's face, like a sudden blink of sunshine on a grey day. And then he felt Johnny move forward from beside him.

Johnny spoke in a low, tense voice, and Donald was shocked to see that his mouth was quivering and his eyes were moist. 'Why did you say that, Roddy? Why do you keep going back to Christy? Are you trying to shame me? Or goad me into doing something I might be sorry for?'

His hands clenched and unclenched. His mood seemed a mixture of anger, desperation and self-pity. Pity, too, perhaps, for Christy Cameron. Or was that too much to read into his face and actions?

Roddy sat there stolidly, quite unconcerned, while the two men forward studied them with well-schooled, inscrutable eyes.

Johnny reached one hand towards Ouanake, who had stopped singing and was watching them now, troubled and startled by their attitude, like a child whose parents begin quarrelling before it. 'And why make fun of her, Roddy? She hasn't done you any harm!'

It was strange, Donald thought, how a weak man like Johnny could suddenly gain dignity when he forgot about himself and let someone else command his emotions. But was Johnny weak? And who was he to make a judgement of that kind on another man? There was no doubt Roddy would find it hard to wriggle out of his present situation with his colours flying. Johnny had fixed him with his eye, and was waiting with a strained face for Roddy's answer.

Roddy puffed reflectively at his pipe, then turned to Johnny. 'And is that all you have to say?'

'If you weren't the captain of this boat,' Johnny continued, 'I might say that you were a cunning old fool, a man who made trouble to satisfy his own curiosity. But I can't say that, and so I'll keep quiet.'

Donald was startled to discover a pity for the man growing inside him. A sense of desperation, too, that was something he had never felt before. What strange, contrary tides ebb and flow within a man's heart! Once he had seen Johnny as a thoughtless despoiler preoccupied with his own selfish pleasures; a man who lived happily without a conscience. And now he was sorry for him. How could anyone be judged black or white when such complexities went into his making? I could never be like Norman McLeod, Donald thought; but how simple the world must seem to those like him.

The girl had stopped listening to them, and the other men, lying sprawled now on the deck, were watching with increased curiosity. Ouanake was giving all her heart and mind to the music, watching the kanakas whose voices now roared louder than ever.

Over their heads the mainsail shivered suddenly, and Roddy bore down on the tiller.

'Ease that sheet, Johnny,' he commanded. Johnny, his face relaxing, had obeyed the order before giving himself time to think. Then he returned, but the tension had gone. Roddy smiled. 'In the heat of our debate,' he said profoundly, 'the wind must have come round. We must watch our seamanship, especially now we have a critical audience.' He looked forward with unfriendly eyes and then studied Johnny speculatively.

'If I wasn't pleased, Johnny, I might have felt disappointed in you. When I brought you on board I had hopes that we were shipping a roistering rascal, a careless devil who would bring variety to our days and a certain cheerful dissipation to our nights. But I was wrong. You're not cut out to be a seducer, Johnny. You are, I fear, that dullest of all God's creatures; the home-making man – just like your friend Donald, here. So why in His name don't you accept what you cannot avoid, and marry the girl?' He laughed at them irrepressibly and stood up. 'You'll take over, Donald. And Johnny can try his housekeeping talents on dinner.'

Johnny stood still, out-talked and groping for words, overwhelmed but only partly defeated.

Roddy had halted as if struck by a sudden thought. 'This girl. We can't set her ashore and send her home like this. How could she expect to find a husband with no gifts to offer him? It wouldn't be right.' His eyes rested for a moment on the other natives. They were as naked and ill-equipped as if they had never worked for a white man. 'Lewin has not been generous with his labourers, I notice. You would almost think they weren't going home.' He brooded on this strange circumstance. 'Johnny, bring up the trade box, and see what she would like.'

The girl was watching with intelligent eyes and came quickly over when Roddy signalled her.

'Now help yourself,' he said genially. 'The selection may not be wonderful, but we'll do the best we can.' He produced a length of turkey-red cloth which Ouanake seized with delight and wound about her shoulders. 'A hat? This seems the only one. Your size, my dear?' he held out a small, hard bowler, with curly brim. She clicked her tongue in wonder, and thrust it on her head. Roddy scratched his beard reflectively. 'Now what else? Stockings, perhaps.' He grabbed a pair of brightly looped stockings as gaudy as a barber's pole. 'No footballers up in these islands, but no doubt they will serve.'

Ouanake was puzzled for a moment, but then pulled them over her bare feet. The effect seemed to please her.

'And now, if we can, to find a coat.' Roddy rummaged deep in the chest and came up with a long tail-coat which he held out to her with a flourish. 'Not this season's, perhaps, but still sufficiently in the vogue.' Ouanake turned it about with her hands, made a half-hearted attempt to put her arms through the sleeves, and then triumphantly reversed it, tying the tails firmly about her waist. She stood up in great excitement, parading about the limited space, as proud as any woman in Auckland when the new fashions arrived from London.

Roddy looked on the result with a moderate satisfaction.

'Something else is needed.' He frowned into the box and brought out a small umbrella, with gay red cloth and ornamental handle. Ouanake's delight was obvious. She opened the umbrella, set it over one shoulder and twirled it nonchalantly. Roddy nodded. 'You'll pass muster now, there's no doubting that. What do you think of her, Johnny?'

Johnny's face was still troubled. 'It's not right to make fun of her ignorance,' he said stubbornly.

'Make fun?' Roddy echoed. 'You have some strange ideas, Johnny. Just try to take those things away from her. There's nothing could please her more than what she has right now. In case you haven't noticed,

Johnny, these folk are different from us. They have simpler joys, more natural pleasures. Don't spoil them, and for the Lord's sake, stop worrying.'

Ouanake thanked him, including Donald and Johnny in her beaming smile, and folded her gifts away carefully. But she still wore the bowler hat and carried the umbrella, taking it down from her shoulder now and then, studying the cheap design on the handle with a humble admiration.

* * *

Roddy had given the problem a good airing, and now we could put it away and forget about it, Donald thought; and that suited him well.

In the last hour before nightfall the *Fiona* was sailing quietly and kindly across a sea of fading colours. Efate Island was somewhere just over the horizon. The harbour entrance was not an easy one, Roddy had explained. They would wait until morning before going in.

The *Fiona's* passengers were moving about on the cramped deck, the two white men in close conversation with one of the natives. He was a handsome big fellow, Donald noted, with arms and legs as sturdy as trees. One of the white men was doing most of the talking in a voice that reached Donald as an indistinct buzz of sound. The others listened intently, nodding their heads at times and glancing aft to where Donald sat alone at the tiller.

Donald watched them with a mounting distrust. I'm with Roddy in this, at least, he thought. We must be on guard in the morning.

But now, in the warming sun and the wind that went past him like a great torrent of air, he found that his worries kept sliding away out of mind. And, rather to his surprise, he discovered that he was looking forward to the next day and to the excitement it would certainly bring. He might have something to talk about after all when he was back in Waipu. It was not unlike that moment when you waited for a tree to fall, when axe and saw had done their part; or that instant when a dam had been tripped, and the water seemed to hang behind the flying gate before it hurtled down into the stream-bed.

And, once again, as the damp, cool scent of the forest came to his nostrils, and he thought of Norman and Jessie, a feeling of unreality took charge of him.

He gripped the tiller more firmly and shook himself back to the present. This was he, Donald McKinnon, sailing towards a savage and unknown island, with nothing certain about his future: And not caring greatly about what fate might bring to him.

* * *

Chapter Eighteen

THE BAY AHEAD OF THEM WAS EMPTY OF LIFE. THE *FIONA* sailing smoothly with a fresh breeze, clouds scudding across a sky that had not yet lost its morning freshness to the hour-old sun. A black arrow of birds pursued the clouds across the *Fiona's* steady topmast. From a mountain spur a few miles ahead Donald heard the sound of drums, slow and melancholy. They spoke briefly then were silent.

Joe Black, who seemed to be the leader of Lewin's party, called out to Roddy and pointed to a coral-white beach off their port bow. 'That's where they are to be landed,' he said.

Then, as if by magic, the bay held a fleet of canoes that raced towards the *Fiona* and circled her at a cautious distance. A big man, bristling with weapons and ear and nose ornaments of carved bone, daubed all over with black and red paint, stood in the stern of one canoe and called out in English.

'Man stealers!' he yelled. The other canoes still circled them, as swift as gulls surveying a lump of carrion before they dived in.

They could have been creatures from another world, Donald thought. And he would not have been surprised if they had vanished as suddenly as they had come, leaving the bay open once again to the morning calm. But they showed no sign of going. The paddles flashed in the water and the warriors studied the *Fiona* and her crew with fierce eyes. How long would a missionary – or even a trader – last among this lot? he wondered. Even Norman McLeod's personality would find it hard to subdue them. And yet, he remembered suddenly, it was to this island that Lewin had said Hugh Craig, the man from Tanna Island, had gone. Could he be still alive among such as these?

Roddy was talking to Ouanake. 'Tell them, in your language, that we do not come to steal men but to return these ones to their village.'

She lifted her shoulders. 'I can say nothing to them. They do not know me. But I try.'

'Surely the men could speak for themselves, Roddy. That would be the best. Why not ask your friend Black to see what he can do?'

Roddy gave Donald no answer, but rubbed his cheek with an uncertain hand.

'Look at them. What do you think, Donald?'

They certainly did not look like exiles glad to see their native land. They lounged in the shade of the sails, apathetic in the face of these new excitements. Black and his mate stood casually by.

The big savage waved his spear as his canoe came under the *Fiona's* stern and turned away like a chip of wood in a strong current.

'Man-stealers!' he shouted again, but half-heartedly now. Black strolled back to where Roddy sat at the tiller. He spat over the side.

'Don't let these crazy bastards worry you. We'll make for the beach and get it over.' Like his companion, Donald noted, he was wearing a pistol and carried a rifle. The *Fiona* sailed on serenely, with its strange escort concentrating now on reaching the beach before the white men.

Roddy said: 'Do we stay long? Are your men ready to go ashore?'

Black gave him a careless glance. 'That's not your worry. Do as you're told and you'll be all right.'

'But it is my worry. I may have been persuaded to bring you here, but the *Fiona* is still my ship!' Roddy was swelling with indignation.

'Is it?' was the uninterested reply. 'Anyway, we have more to think about than that. Bring her into the beach and anchor there.' He pointed a casual finger. 'And if I were you, I'd find a rifle for myself and these others.'

He strolled away, his lean face and tawny eyes preoccupied now. His glance that flickered at Roddy had seemed to say: 'You had your moment last night, keeping us penned out on the open deck. Now see how you enjoy some of the same medicine.'

Roddy said, as much to himself as to Black: 'We'll take you in, but I'm dropping no anchor. And I'll ask you to be quick with whatever you have to do.'

If Black heard him, he gave no sign.

* * *

The *Fiona* turned into the wind, her mainsail slatting. Roddy growled: 'Johnny, go down and bring out weapons, but I'm not planning to use them.'

Most of the canoes were on the beach again; light, swift, straw-like craft that could be easily handled. But two kept edging in towards the *Fiona*, their crews watching carefully.

'They could be hostile, or again they could be friendly,' Roddy muttered. 'But we've no way of telling. Those men on the beach, for example: That dance they are doing could be a cordial welcome, or it could mean that they want to knock our heads off. What do you think, Donald?'

Donald was watching Black and his companions unlash the small boat and manoeuvre it into the water. He had no time to answer, for Johnny had returned with weapons and ammunition.

'This, I hope, will frighten them as much as it does me,' said Roddy. 'I have no pleasure in powder and shot. Johnny,' he commanded, 'it is for you to see the young lady ashore. You should be safe enough with our thugs up forward there. Donald will stay with me to guard the cutter.'

Johnny nodded and climbed down into the boat. Roddy gave the girl a polite farewell. He seemed happier now, Donald thought, as if the situation were no longer beyond his control. But his eyes snapped when he saw the boat ready to pull away.

'What are you doing, Black? What about these other men?' He pointed to two of the natives who were still on board.

Black grinned sardonically. 'Don't you be worrying. We'll be back for them.' The boat slid away, the girl waving to them cheerfully.

* * *

Whatever Black was planning, Donald decided, he and his party did not seem to lack experience. As the boat grounded they leapt out and dragged it half out of the water, then stood in a compact group facing the natives. Ouanake slipped away from them, attracting little notice from the other natives. She approached them, but was waved away. She stood hesitantly in the shelter of the first forest trees, her bundle of clothes under one arm, the umbrella hanging forlornly from the other.

Black was speaking now, and the natives were listening intently. Apparently he could speak the dialect of this corner of Efate. He pointed to the two kanakas who had come ashore with him, and who still stood there silently. Then he turned and waved towards the *Fiona*.

'He's spinning them some fancy tale,' Roddy said to Donald, 'and they seem to be listening. What's he meaning to do?'

The natives were not dancing or calling out now. Most of them moved in closer to the white men. The big native spoke and Donald could see, across the narrow stretch of deep water, that he had not completely lost his suspicions. He stretched his spear towards the ship. Black answered him and the other savages laughed and howled with glee.

The talk went on and Donald found his attention wandering. Further up the bay there were two more canoes, dwarfed by the distance but moving in their direction. He watched them crawling like insects across the water, and then looked back to the beach. Ouanake had come back again. She spoke to the natives, then went up to Johnny and patted him on the back, ignoring Black and his mate. She pointed out at the *Fiona* and shook her head violently.

Black spoke again, his voice sharp. One of the Efate warriors roared like an animal and, in a pantomime that was half-comic, half-serious, chased the girl away up the beach. She went unwillingly, but eventually disappeared along a track through the trees.

Roddy was muttering to himself, and Donald tried desperately to work out what was happening.

Black signed to three of the savages who were nearest to him. They followed him gingerly into the boat. Johnny and the other white man scrambled over the side while the two kanakas pushed the boat out from the beach and jumped on board to take the oars. The distance between the boat and the *Fiona* lessened rapidly.

It was a picture that, with its fierce, stark colours, was to remain in Donald's mind; a picture that kept changing until it was blurred in a sudden confusion. Blue sea, brassy, heat-ridden sky, dazzling sand and cool green forest. The sweating bodies of the savages, barbarically adorned, weapons that made him remember suddenly Kenny's collection at Omaha, and the grim tales he had been told there. Joe Black and Lewin's other man, as quiet and dangerous-looking as the guns they carried.

The boat grated against the *Fiona's* side, attended now by half a dozen canoes that ranged up on her flanks. Black was quickly on board, followed by the three savages. The others waited expectantly.

'Some presents for them,' Black explained, and began to uncover the forward hold. He disappeared, but returned in a few minutes with three antique muzzle-loaders which he handed over with much ceremony. He could not resist adding in English: 'Use them, my friends, and you'll blow yourselves into small pieces.'

He waved to the other canoes. The men threw themselves on to the *Fiona*, nearly a score of them, filling her small decks with confusion and a babel of strange speech. They reached out like boys fighting over a prize for the guns that the others held, and tugged and tussled until Donald expected them to fall apart. But they were good-humoured, in a violent way, with an eye on Black in the hope of further presents.

Now it was a world of smells as well as of strong colours: warm, heavy and earthy; oily, musky, sweaty, rich and revolting to his unaccustomed nostrils. Great horny feet padded across the deck, mops of black hair jutted against the white, trembling sail; the blue sky. It seemed impossible to see beyond them, beyond ears and noses, distorted by ornaments of shell and bone, chests scarred by battle, disease, or unspeakable rites. Strange men, but invincibly human in spite of that, showing the normal qualities of envy, greed and mischief.

Donald and Johnny stood together, hemmed in, ignored and momentarily overwhelmed. Roddy was by the tiller, and a glance at him showed his bewilderment, his almost comic perturbation.

Black shouted a few words in the native dialect. The savages listened and then swarmed forward to the open hold, jostling for a front position. Black smiled an invitation, but his eyes, Donald saw, were calculating and merciless. And his henchmen stood tense and alert.

Eagerly they spilled over into the hold, their weapons for the most part thrown aside. 'Presents for all,' said Black mockingly in English; 'but of a kind you don't expect!'

He waited, his attention on the last of the natives. The din from the hold became deafening.

'Now!' he cried out suddenly. 'Billie, up with the sail! The rest of you know what to do!'

And as they began to move swiftly about the *Fiona's* deck, Donald understood the whole plan, and marvelled at his dullness. Black had baited a trap cunningly. This was no mission to return labourers whose working terms had expired. Black was recruiting new slaves for his master!

The sails were beginning to draw now. Black and two of his men had seized the cover and were hauling it over the open hatch. The other white man had brushed Roddy aside and taken the tiller. In what seemed a flash of time Donald had seen all this, had seen too that Roddy was standing slack-jawed and at a loss, his eyes for the first time those of an old man. No comments could come from him.

And now Donald felt anger boiling up inside him; not only at the evil actions of these men, but also at the way they had ignored him and his friends, as if they were of no account.

'Johnny, they are kidnapping these poor devils, and using our ship for it, too! Come on!'

The imprisoned natives had realised what was happening also. There were howls of anger and fear, and two long spears had been thrust through the open hatch before it could be fully sealed off. Black's kanakas heaved in vain, and Black himself, pistol in hand, was crawling carefully towards the edge, calling out threats in a cold voice that was drowned in the din.

Donald was quick, but Johnny was quicker. He pinioned Black with one long arm and sent his pistol flying with a wrench at his wrist. Donald caught a glimpse of his surprised and furious face as he heaved at the hatch cover, the kanakas offering no opposition.

'You fool!' shouted Black, wrestling in Johnny's grip. 'They'll murder the lot of us!' He wriggled vainly, his eyes fixed on his pistol lying on the deck. Donald held his breath as the natives erupted from the hold. But they had had enough of the white men and their ways. In a few seconds they were over the side and swimming towards the drifting canoes, leaving the *Fiona's* deck littered with their weapons.

Donald picked up Black's pistol. 'Hold him, Johnny,' he said and went aft to where Roddy and Lewin's other man were by the tiller, glaring at each other now like two dogs disputing a bone.

'Roddy, you should take over again, and then perhaps we can decide what to do about our passengers.' He looked at Black's companion who clung doggedly to the tiller as if in that way alone he could keep his fate under his own control. 'Give me your pistol, and get up there with the others.'

'Why not come and take it?' the man suggested. Roddy shouted at him not to be a fool. But Donald had already flung his own pistol aside and jumped at the helmsman. They grappled across the tiller, while the *Fiona* began to steer all over the bay. Roddy hovered ineffectually on the fringe of the battle. Donald had a firm grip around the other's throat. He hauled him to his feet, reaching for the gun that was thrust in his belt, and tripped. They fell in a heap. The main boom swung suddenly across as the *Fiona* settled on a new slant of her erratic course. Roddy tried to reach the tiller, but flying arms and boots kept him away. To Donald he called advice, unheard in the blur of action.

The *Fiona* was sailing now on a line almost parallel with the coast. Roddy looked frantically ahead for reefs, thumped the fighters on their backs to move them away, and grabbed vainly at the tiller. But Donald knew nothing of that. The hard contact of muscle and sinew absorbed him. His eyes were open, but he fought by feel rather than sight; the blood racing through his body, the air sucking fiercely into his lungs. There was in him no hatred for his opponent, but a delight in the spilling of energy as great as when – years ago it seemed – he had wrestled a log down from the hill into the river.

A jarring fist shook his head, but there was no pain, only an upsurge of the fighting lust that possessed him as madly as any love could have done. The *Fiona* heeled, and they rolled over and over in the restricted space. The enemy who was not an enemy grunted as Donald's fist crashed into his stomach. The pistol lay on the boards, unnoticed. Donald felt the other's body arch below him. He let the fellow come, and then with all his strength dashed him down again, just as a cold, clear thought entered his brain: 'This is madness. What am I doing?' And then he realised that the man lay still. The fight was over.

Sweat filled his eyes. He wiped one hand across his face and knelt beside his victim. He was breathing, and his pulse was strong enough. Black and his four kanakas had been herded together towards the bow. Johnny had collected weapons and had the situation well in hand. Roddy said: 'You finished him just in time, Donald. We would be on the beach, or piled on that reef, if it had kept going much longer.' He looked at Donald with a strange expression: 'But don't fight again, lad. For a moment I didn't recognise you there, and feared that worse might happen to him. But all's well that ends well, and now we can get back to Tanna.' Roddy nodded complacently. He was once again in command.

Donald was happy to let it stay that way. He noted with surprise that they were still off the beach where Black had attempted his kidnapping, but it was empty now. The natives were keeping under cover, fearing perhaps another raid. The two canoes he had seen earlier were close at hand, but the *Fiona* would soon leave them behind. He reached over the side with a bucket for water to bathe his cuts and bruises; then thought again, and splashed it over the unconscious man's head. He shivered and opened his eyes.

Donald's elation had gone now. He looked sadly at his opponent, regretting the joy that the fight had brought him. He might easily have killed the man. 'You're comfortable enough?' he asked awkwardly. The man nodded, and Donald began to wash his own cuts in the warm salt water.

* * *

At the first instant, the sound seemed to fit his mood: a harsh grating below the *Fiona's* bow, then a convulsive leap, a straining of timber. The *Fiona* stopped, her mast groaning. The waves as they passed did not move her.

Roddy was on his feet yelling orders and carrying them out himself. 'All sail down, quick!' he yelled. Even Black jumped to help. The wind was light and the mast still stood; but for all that the *Fiona* was firmly aground.

Roddy's face was a picture of dejection. 'All's well that ends well,' said Donald lightly, and clapped him on the back. 'We're not done yet. But we should see if she is taking any water.'

'We'll know soon enough,' said Roddy. The *Fiona* trembled and heaved, like a horse caught in a bog. But she settled down again, and they could hear the rock grinding under her stout keel.

'My poor *Fiona*,' Roddy lamented, busily uncovering the after hatch. 'You have been sadly mistreated! How firmly are you held, and how are the tides? Bring the boat alongside, Johnny, and take soundings all around her. Ah! No water in here, yet; and the forward hold is clear, Black? It's bad enough, then, but it could be worse!'

Johnny reported: 'Deep water under the bow, Roddy, and at the stern.'

'She must be held on top of the reef,' said Roddy, 'and the tide is nearly full. We must work quickly.'

And then, in a day that had had more than its share of action, Donald received the biggest shock of his life. A voice said: 'What can we do to help?' A voice that sent a cold tremor down his back, for in accent and tone it could have belonged to Norman Finlayson, his cousin long since dead in the New Zealand bush, and buried in the sight of Donald himself and many others. It was a voice with a hint of humour in it, an urbane and authoritative voice, but, as Donald saw when he jumped about and looked seaward with startled eyes, it did not belong to Norman Finlayson. The two canoes had crept up unseen in the confusion. Sitting in the stern of the foremost one, surrounded by savages as barbaric as those who had just escaped from the *Fiona*, was a white man. While the paddlers held his canoe steady, he stepped forward and studied the *Fiona*.

'You're there, Joe Black, I see. Rightly I should leave you to drown, but the devil looks after his own and you'll live to be hanged, or eaten.

'May I come on board?' He did not wait for an answer, but leapt nimbly from the curved bow of the canoe on to the *Fiona's* deck. 'Who are these others? More of Ross Lewin's scourings?' He wore a light suit and deep-brimmed hat; closely-clipped black beard and his blue eyes were of a startling brilliance in his sallow face. 'But there's a mystery here. How did you come to lose your victims? It's not like Lewin to employ incompetents – and why should rogues fall out?' His glance dwelt momentarily on Donald's battered face, and then turned to the other man sitting awkwardly by the tiller.

The voice was like Norman's – uncannily so. But now that he saw its possessor there was a difference. An easy good-nature had been Norman's, but here the humour, he felt, was laid over a rock-hard core. Even his laugh had a sting in it as he spoke to Black. He might smile, but he would never deviate or compromise. And yet the echoes of a remembered voice kept ringing through Donald's mind, recalling what had past and, strangely, why he had come here. How far he had fallen, brawling with a stranger, consorting with rogues and savages!

Roddy stepped forward, and a glance at his face showed that, for the moment, he had forgotten that his beloved *Fiona* was perched firmly on top of a rock. He spoke with dignity, in a reproving tone.

'You may know these men, sir, but you do not know us. I am Captain Roderick McKenzie, and these are my friends, Donald McKinnon and Johnny Bain. It is by no wish of ours that we have taken part in a blackbirding raid, and indeed my friends here have just made certain that the raid will go no further.'

Roddy's formality, in serious moments, always gave a stiffness to his speech.

The stranger's eyes twinkled, but he replied with an equal punctiliousness. 'And I am Hugh Craig, and these are my friends.' He waved towards the natives in the two canoes. 'There is also Dr Murray who you may meet later.'

Donald noticed then that, in the second canoe, another white man, unkempt and darkened by the sun, was lying slumped across the stern boards. A doctor, perhaps, but he seemed more in need of medical care than capable of giving it.

But now Roddy was briskly in command. 'We are pleased to meet you, sir, and your friends. But at this moment I'm more interested in getting afloat again, and away from these God-forsaken islands.'

'God has not forsaken them,' Craig said slowly. His voice had deepened. He looked at Black who quailed before his piercing eyes. 'But the devil is still strong in his works. There is much to do.'

This must be the missionary that Kenny told us about, Donald realised. The man who had come from Nova Scotia to Tanna Island. A kinsman of their own, but how widely separated from them in outlook and conduct!

Roddy had been brooding silently. 'You're the missionary. That doesn't mean much just now, but when we are clear of this worry, I will take pleasure in a talk with you, and perhaps in hearing how our folk at home in Nova Scotia are faring. It's a strange thing, Mr Craig. We go to New Zealand for our own good, you come from Nova Scotia to these islands for their people's good.' He bowed grandly. 'And we meet like this. And the quicker I'm away, the happier I'll be.'

The *Fiona* was nudging and squirming as she felt the tug of the newly running tide, but she stayed firmly on the submerged reef.

'She doesn't mean to move on her own account,' Roddy observed, 'and if we don't do something she won't move at all. She's held by the stern, and that's where all the weight is. The forward hold is empty. We'll start by moving our cargo from the after hold into it. Then, I fancy, she should slide off into deep water. Now smart is the word!'

The cargo came up quickly, box after box of brandy and rum, cases of wine. 'Watch Black and his friends,' Roddy muttered to Donald. 'I wouldn't be putting anything past them, even after the beating they've had.'

'This is your cargo, Captain McKenzie?'

Hugh Craig was speaking, and there was something in his tone that made Roddy jump as if pricked by a needle. 'Yes,' he replied defensively, watching Craig with suspicious eyes. 'But it's not for these islands. I'm no trafficker in liquor, any more than in men. It's merely a drop or two for some friends in New Zealand.'

'You're playing with dangerous goods, Captain McKenzie. I've seen others start in this way, and their end is sure damnation.'

'But I'm no trader in spirits!' Roddy exclaimed. 'This is no commercial venture! Why, the stuff won't even pay duty when it gets to New Zealand! It will be whipped ashore one night at Omaha, when the revenue cutter's well away, and no one will be any the wiser, except those who take it. And in any case,' he added stubbornly, 'drink in moderation is all right, in its place.'

Even Hugh Craig was baffled by this argument, and he looked at the little man with a milder eye. 'There's only one place for this cargo, and that's over the side! Look! It's all been moved, and you are still held fast. Throw it over, Captain McKenzie, and the evil it could bring will be no longer on your conscience.'

Roddy listened, the beginning of a grin showing under his beard.

'You couldn't do that!' cried Black, startled out of his silence.

'Be quiet,' Roddy snarled. 'It's no concern of yours. I can do as I please, if it's a matter of saving the *Fiona*.'

'And when it's out of the way,' Craig continued, 'my men here will have her off; that is if she doesn't clear it on her own.'

Roddy gave a mighty chuckle. 'You know, Donald,' he said conversationally, 'the further we have gone with this affair, the more it smells in my nostrils. It's not so much what we're doing, but the way we've been led into it. That blood-sucker McCaul back in Auckland, Lewin, even my friend Kenny. They have been devious with me. Not that I hold any of this against Kenny. He has a family to keep, poor man. And whatever I do, they won't be able to say a word! Over the side with it all!'

It seemed a shocking waste to Donald, and he could not bring himself to help. But he watched as the cases were broken and thrown into the bay.

'I never thought to see you allow a thing like this,' he said to Roddy.

Roddy looked down his nose. 'I'm tired of the whole business and, who knows, Craig may be right. Anyway, I suspect Mr McCaul has an interest in Lewin's affairs, and this will be a judgement on him. We'll go back to Waipu just as we came away. No richer, certainly, except in experience. But that is something, isn't it Donald?'

They climbed into the small boat and made ready to try and tow the *Fiona* off. The canoes interlocked under her counter. Half of Craig's natives heaved at the stern. The others ran quickly forward to the bowsprit. Easily, as if she were moving down a slipway, the *Fiona* slid into deep water and lay there rocking gently, as if all her worries were over.

* * *

Chapter Nineteen

LIKE A MAN – OR WOMAN – OF PERSONALITY, THE *FIONA* SEEMED to attract about her an increasing number of people with little in common. At first, Donald remembered, there had been only Roddy and himself. Now, as the evening stillness settled on the sea and the last light seemed to battle against the darkness, he looked around and studied the others.

A quiet lot they were just now: Johnny, whose handsome, brooding face seemed full of thought but who, he realised now, accepted most things passively; Black and his still nameless friend, surly but acquiescent; the kanakas, disciplined by Lewin but away from his eye, incapable of any initiative; Hugh Craig, his work on Efate now ended, content to relax on the deck, his eyes hooded in a calm, untroubled face; and Dr Murray, a dark shadow behind the missionary.

Donald watched him curiously. Since he had come on board after the *Fiona* had been refloated and Craig had said goodbye to his native friends, Murray had not spoken. He lay there now, seemingly in a light and restless sleep. Donald looked at his fine hands, his intelligent head, the sick eyes and grey, distorted features. He must have been a big man once, but his muscle had run to fat and now, as if his condition had fallen suddenly away, the flesh hung on his face in shapeless folds.

'Where did you come upon him?' asked Roddy, pointing with a stubby finger.

Craig did not answer directly. 'You have not heard of Dr Murray, any of you?' Roddy shook his head. Craig looked at Black. 'You must have heard his name?'

'I know about him,' replied Black.

'Murray's story should be burnt into your hearts,' Craig said in his soft voice. 'I found him in a hut in Efate, sick and dirty, cared for by the natives he had betrayed and killed. His own people had rejected him.'

Murray stirred, and his eyes opened.

'You should know his story, Captain McKenzie; and more particularly so should you, Donald McKinnon and Johnny Bain. Nor will it harm our other friends to hear it from his own lips.'

The night was gentle now, mild and calm and beautiful. The *Fiona* sailed softly through a sea that flashed with fire. Donald could only just distinguish the doctor's features as Craig spoke to him:

'James,' he said, 'tell these folk about your voyage on the *Carl*.'

Murray was silent for a long minute, and then said abstractedly: 'They wouldn't keep quiet. They kept calling out and quarrelling among themselves down there in the hold. All one day and the next night and the next day again. Some of the wild ones were trying to break the hatch down and get out, and the others were stopping them. So we had to fire at them. Wilson was smart. He threw lights down into the hold to direct our aim. We kept firing among them all night. At dawn, when Scott volunteered to go down and pacify those who were still alive, one of them wounded him in the chest with a long sharpened pole. But they gave in soon after that.'

'Start at the beginning,' said Craig quietly. 'They don't understand what you're saying.'

But Murray didn't seem to hear him. 'And then we threw the dead ones over the side, and the badly wounded too. And we cleaned and whitewashed the hold and scrubbed the deck until all the blood was hidden. I didn't know black men could bleed so much.' A shudder grated from his throat, and Donald saw his staring eyes glinting in the light reflected from the sea.

Hugh Craig shook him. 'From the beginning, Dr Murray,' he repeated in a louder voice. Murray had begun to mutter unintelligibly to himself. Donald's mind tried to grapple with what he had just heard. He felt a mingled revulsion and pity, and yet it was difficult to realise that Murray was talking about himself and not objectively about someone else.

'Where did you sail from in the *Carl*?'

Murray's voice was flat and unemphatic. 'I'm sorry, my mind was on other things. We sailed from Melbourne. We tried for days to recruit the blacks in the usual way, but they laughed at us. They didn't want to go to the Fijis, they said. So there was our ship empty, and no matter what we promised them they shook their heads, threatened us and went away. We even dressed Wilson as a missionary, but that bait was useless.

'Then we threw pig-iron into their canoes, or ran them down off the beaches, and fished them out of the water. They were hard to pick up, and sometimes we had to club them before we could get them on board.'

'Tell them what Wilson said you did before you attacked the natives.' Craig's voice was the voice of impersonal judgement.

'Wilson said I would read prayers before we went among them. And later, when we were killing them that night, he said I sang Marching through Georgia. That's what he said in Court when I turned Queen's Evidence, but I don't remember singing, and in any case, I never liked that song.'

'How many natives did you load on the *Carl*?'

'About one hundred and twenty. Then we set off for the cotton plantations in the Fijis.' Murray paused, his whole body drooping wearily. 'I've told them the rest.'

'Tell them it all.'

Murray shivered, and his voice was trembling. He was far away from the mild tropic night that enveloped the *Fiona*. No glittering stars, serene and inscrutable, looked down to comfort him.

'When we tried to open the hatch there was a roar of anger and hate. It was as if we had trapped a host of wild animals that were about to escape and devour us. We fired a shot or two, and told them to be quiet. They took no notice. We fired again and again and again. They were screaming with pain and fright, but there were still some who seemed more angry than afraid. And we had to keep shooting down among them.'

'How did it end?' said Craig inexorably.

Murray groaned. A dark shadow, to Donald's heightened fancy, seemed to lie now across his face.

'After daybreak they became quiet. We told those who were alive to come up. Five climbed out of the hold. We looked down below. A few were moving, but most of them were still. Two of our men went down. They found many badly wounded, and a few who were only slightly hurt. There were piles of dead.'

'How many?' said Craig.

'I know you are a man of God,' said Murray, 'and also a kindly man.' His voice had the dignity of deep feeling in it now. 'Could you rid me of this devil that will not let me sleep at night, that jabs in my mind like a barbed spear?' He groaned, and Donald seemed to groan with him.

'Only God can do that, in His mercy and in His own time.' Craig placed a hand on Murray's shoulder. 'Now tell the rest, and then perhaps you will sleep. How many were dead, Dr Murray?'

'We brought out fifty bodies from the hold, and threw them over the side. About ten who had superficial wounds I treated. There were eighteen badly wounded. Those we threw into the sea also. Some struggled, and we had to tie their legs together first.'

A gruff voice broke in on the mounting horror in Donald's mind.

'He's had enough,' said Roddy, 'and so have we. For God's sake let him stop, Craig.'

Hugh Craig turned towards Roddy, and Donald saw that his face was a mask of pain.

'Can't you see, Captain McKenzie? He must go on, and we must listen! Only in that way can he be cured and we be warned.'

His voice took on a new passion. 'There are some today who mock the devil, and say he does not exist. But he is still ravening abroad. Here were these men, light-heartedly starting an adventure, not dreaming how it would end. But they gave the devil his entrance. Fear, greed, lack of self-control, envy perhaps – these took hold of them, and the devil had possessed them. We must all of us, always, be on our guard.'

Murray was still speaking, conscious, it would seem, of no listeners; walled against their words by his own dreadful preoccupation.

'Even those who were near death struggled, their eyes rolling in despair, begging us to save them in words that we did not know. But we had to be rid of them, and over they went. Their blood streams in the water. Their blood marks the deck, and the sails, and our hands, and the sky itself.' His voice had fallen away, and now died.

Donald shook himself, as if to throw aside the nightmare. A deep fear held him. How close were we to the same thing? he wondered. If the natives enticed onto the *Fiona* had not swum away – if they had revolted when the *Fiona* was out of reach of the land – what would have happened then? We would have had to kill or be killed; and though many would have thought us justified, it would have been a hard thing to convince ourselves in that way.

So close to every act does evil lie. Or the devil, he added grimly. It could indeed be that Hugh Craig was right.

The missionary had covered Murray with a blanket, and he seemed to be sleeping. Donald studied Craig's fine-drawn face. He must have been familiar with the story, but its repetition had shaken him. The soft reflected light was lost in his dark beard, and his eyes were caverns.

'When I came here from Nova Scotia,' he said, 'I felt my first task would be to convert the natives to white men's ways. When they could think and act as we do, I thought, it would then be easy to teach them the Gospel. But soon I saw that it was harder for a white man, educated in evil, to renounce his life than for a savage blind in his ignorance. Yet God loves one just as much as the other, which makes my work no simpler.'

'Why did he come back to the Islands?' Donald asked.

'Who can answer that?' said Craig. 'After the trial he had no friends in Australia. Not because of what he had done to the wretched natives, but because he had informed on the captain and crew of his ship, and in this way dodged a charge of murder. He came up here on a trading schooner, and left it at Efate. When I found him there, the natives were looking after him, but as you can still see, he was sick in body and in soul. I hope that God can cure him, and pray that his mind might be eased. But all that is in God's hands.'

They were silent, and the *Fiona* idled along through the gentle night.

'And why did you yourself come here?' asked Donald. In his mind's eye, made keener by the events of the day, he could imagine young Hugh Craig growing up in a Nova Scotian valley, which in many ways would not have been very different from Waipu itself. He would have worked on the farm, or in the forest, or with the fishing fleet, perhaps. And for sure he had gone to church, under a minister who might have been not over-different from Norman McLeod. A youth spent much as he, Donald McKinnon, had spent his. And yet Hugh Craig had made a bold decision, and he himself was still floundering in uncertainty. What was the germ that made men grow so differently?

Hugh Craig was looking at him in surprise. 'I came here because I had to. I heard what God said: "Go ye into the world, and preach the Gospel to every creature." He said: "You may perish, but I remain. And I have sworn by myself that the whole earth shall be filled with my glory!"'

The words, thrillingly spoken, seemed to hang in the air and echo in Donald's mind. It was as simple as that for Hugh Craig, he thought. A sentence or two that he had heard as a youngster, and his course of life was decided. How pleasant it would be to have no flickerings of doubt or moments of self-distrust!

Roddy spoke. 'That is a good, simple, honest reason, Mr Craig. I wish you well. And from what I have seen of the world, you have plenty to do, and not only among the black heathens. But now we must have some rest.'

* * *

The night air was mild and pleasant after the day's fierce heat. But Donald found it hard to sleep. He watched Craig go over to Dr Murray, who was moving restlessly. Craig spoke to him, his voice like a benediction. He wrapped him up carefully and set a blanket under his head.

Johnny, who had already been sleeping, awakened and took the tiller. The *Fiona*, it seemed to Donald as drowsiness overtook him, drifted like a ghost ship through a milky sea.

Donald found himself pondering the words that Hugh Craig had quoted: "The whole earth shall be filled with my glory." What did they mean? All about him was the glory of God's handiwork, the more impressive through contrast with the ugliness and evil that lived within it. Could evil ever be removed from the world? And if it was, would goodness and beauty shine with the same brilliance? He must ask Hugh Craig what he thought about it; but for himself, a world of absolute goodness would seem dull. And yet it would be free of the monstrous deeds like those Murray had described.

He tossed and turned on the hard deck, but his mind refused to become quiet. He seemed to hear again Murray's voice, recounting so quietly its chapter of horror. Pictures of death and violence burned before his eyes. Why had Hugh Craig forced the man to talk? Surely he did not think Donald could have become like Murray?

He turned over again, watching the tall mast reaching across the star-filled sky. He watched and watched until, suddenly, the world seemed a very small place, the *Fiona* a speck lost in a profound immensity, the men on board her too small to be regarded: But, his mind insisted, not too small for God's care. Perhaps some part of that Being was even now pondering the story of Dr Murray, the murderer with a conscience.

He glanced across to where Hugh Craig was lying. He seemed to be asleep. But as if he felt Donald's glance he turned his head and smiled. 'Get to sleep, young Donald,' he whispered. 'There's another day tomorrow.'

Hugh Craig lay back again, his face towards the sky. Donald studied his profile; the black beard softened in the dim light, the slightly aquiline nose, the forehead that gave power and delicacy to the face. There was an all-encompassing serenity about the man, but a toughness too. He would spare himself less than he spared others. His spirituality would feed his companions while his tongue chastened them.

I would like to know him better, Donald thought. And then he was asleep.

* * *

A great white gull was hurtling down towards him with wings widespread and savage beak outstretched. It screamed hoarsely, and whirled above his head. Donald awoke in the black night, climbing painfully back to consciousness from his restless sleep. The scream had been real.

Beside him Hugh Craig was on his feet, and Roddy, back at the tiller, was calling out. Donald saw that Murray was no longer in his place.

The hoarse cry still seemed to echo, but there was no other sound.

'He went over there.' Roddy pointed back. 'I'll bring her round.'

Donald shivered. The *Fiona* could not have sailed far. He jumped down into the sea. Even as he jumped he saw that Craig was coming too. Donald swam quickly back along the *Fiona's* wake and then lay floating. Hugh Craig came up beside him and they listened intently. The sea and sky were without form or substance. The *Fiona* had sailed out of sight and hearing. There was nothing but their own breathing and the sighing of the sea.

They swam on a little further and trod water, straining their ears. But they heard nothing. Then Roddy's voice hailed them. They answered. The *Fiona* loomed up suddenly against the sky, and other hands hauled them on board.

Donald was shivering violently as he changed into dry clothes. He wondered why, for he was not cold; but a chill seemed to have descended on his spirit as he thought of Murray choking to death in the sea. The light breeze had dropped, and the *Fiona* lay there with her sails down. As dawn came he looked at the strained grey faces of his companions. Black and his friend were silent; the kanakas too. They were staring at the sea, the leaden, impersonal sea that had swallowed Murray.

'Why should he have done that?' Donald asked Hugh Craig.

The missionary answered: 'I do not think he meant to. He was hanging onto life too grimly to throw it away.' Craig's face was grave and troubled, and he added uncertainly: 'I think his will could not have overcome his conscience and his dreams. Just as the Gaderene swine were dashed to pieces, so the devil inside Murray, wrestling for his soul, hurled him to self-destruction.' Craig sighed. 'I do not know. We can never know. But that is how I think it was.'

And so, with the sun lighting the all-concealing sea, they sailed back to Tanna Island. Roddy told Black tersely enough: 'We're not taking you to Lewin's plantation. You'll be able to find your way home from Port Resolution.' And Black agreed with a nod.

They sailed into an empty harbour.

Roddy cleared his throat gruffly and looked at Donald. 'Kenny's away. That's unfortunate.'

'No doubt we'll wait until he comes back,' said Donald.

'If he comes tomorrow, well and good. But we'll sail for New Zealand on the following day. I'll be seeing Kenny soon enough for his liking. Indeed, knowing Kenny, I suspect his absence is deliberate. He was always one to set things in motion and then let them run along under their own power. But this time, he'll find, they've taken a different course. We'll load stores and water and then it's back home for us. Are you pleased, Donald?'

Donald thought it would have been easy to agree, but now something held him silent. Roddy watched him curiously for a moment, but did not press for an answer.

* * *

Chapter Twenty

IT MAY HAVE BEEN THE RESULT OF A SLEEPLESS NIGHT AND unsettled days, but Donald felt defeated. The loss of Murray, the fact that a high-spirited adventure could become no more than a cheap kidnapping attempt, these were all part of it. He had seen Roddy, the serene and inscrutable, become suddenly – for a short time – a fumbling old man. And what of himself? He did not think he had won any laurels on this voyage.

The feeling persisted on the next morning. They had talked late on the dimly-lighted verandah of Hugh Craig's house, a patter of insects against the screens, the flying foxes barking in the trees. They had talked of Murray, of Lewin and the blackbirders, of the future of the Island people and of Craig's work. The heat had been oppressive without the sea breeze to cool them, and no one had slept well.

But this morning was clear, with a taste of freshness; and when Hugh Craig suggested that they should climb the mountain, Donald had accepted eagerly. Roddy looked dubiously at the smoke pillar rising from its peak and shook his head. 'Johnny and I will have enough to do here. Does that suit you, Johnny?'

'The quicker we're away from here, the happier I'll be,' he replied. 'And the *Fiona* needs some cleaning up.'

'What did I tell you,' Roddy muttered in Donald's ear. 'A perfect husband, sadly gone wrong.'

* * *

The forest was a maze of narrow tracks that wandered casually under a dense green roof. Two of Hugh Craig's natives had come with them. They set an easy pace and Donald, for so long confined to the *Fiona's* small deck, found it pleasant to idle along behind them, dipping down now and again into a valley, but for the most part climbing steadily.

They spoke only rarely. But when, after an hour, they stopped for a drink of water at a stream that ran merrily as any near Waipu, Hugh Craig said: 'What do you think of our island, Donald? It's a paradise, isn't it?'

Donald nodded. A lush and violent paradise, but more beautiful than anything he had ever seen. The trees were not so tall now, and he could see patches of blue sky. Light came down stirring strange flowers to bloom, as large and ornate as the butterflies and birds that moved across the water.

'We come to a village soon,' Craig said. They splashed across the stream and followed a track along its other bank, climbed a shallow spur and dropped down again to another valley. They were in the village before Donald knew it was there. Craig stopped and Donald stood beside him.

A foot-worn square of bare earth, overhung with great trees; half a dozen small huts, squalid in the forest's gloom, and another larger one, long and narrow, that stood apart.

'That's the kava house,' said Craig, 'where the men of the village meet.' He called out, but there was no answer. They walked on a few paces. There was a platform near the big hut, covered with a fine netting of vines.

'That is their food cupboard,' Craig explained grimly, 'but used only on special occasions.'

There were bones on the platform, Donald saw; white and bare for the most part. But flesh still hung from some of them. Human flesh; decaying and unclean.

'They are still cannibals, even here,' Donald said, horror making his voice slow and thick.

'They eat their dead, if they have been notable enough,' Craig answered softly. 'They know no better.'

The village was quiet as a grave, oppressive as a house of the dead. Donald seemed to feel curious, hostile eyes watching him. He looked around but could still see no one.

'They do not know me yet,' Craig said, 'although I have visited them in the past. We'll leave my two men here, and they will talk to them and tell them a little about that new life that God can offer them. Some day they will be ready to listen to me.'

They climbed for another hour. The air was clean now and the village far behind them, but Donald could not rid his mind of what he had seen. They stopped for another rest. The volcano was still hidden, but the roar of its breathing was louder now. They could not be far from its base.

'Those natives,' Donald said. 'What can you do about them?'

Craig's face was weary for a moment, but he spoke with confidence.

'Some people would try to destroy every trace of their old ways, rubbing off the slate everything they had seen and done. They would teach them a new way of life, with Christian faith only a part of it. I think that is wrong. A Christian must stand or fall by his own belief, and the doctrine is simple enough, and strong enough, to capture even a savage's mind.

'Make them understand what Christ taught – that the soul is immortal and the body that houses it is a sacred temple – and their evil will fall away from them like a ragged cloak. That is all they need to know, and all we need to tell them.'

'And how does that work out with these men?'

'I believe that, in time, they will come to God.'

He stood up, as if impatient to grapple with the devil and all his host; and then his eyes smiled: 'Come on, Donald. Just now we have a mountain to climb, and that should be enough.'

* * *

Suddenly they were out of the forest and the bare brown cone rose above them, a cinder-laden column of smoke towering from it into the sky. The roar was deafening now, and the intervals of silence strangely unreal. They struggled through a soft and shifting ash, sliding back a little with each forward pace.

Craig wiped his streaming face. 'When the wind is in that quarter,' he said, 'they can hear the volcano on Aneityum, forty miles away. Yet we are beside it and still live. How much more powerful is God's secret voice.'

He did not seem to expect an answer. He had spoken simply, as if stating an obvious truth.

Donald climbed doggedly a yard or two behind him. Everything he thinks and does is governed by his belief, he thought. Everything he sees is a sign of God's power and love, or of the devil's hate.

It was a habit that could spread. Those little pink flowers, for example, the only living things in this waste of grit and ash, could be likened to unquestioning faith in a harsh and bitter world; where men died for no reason and savages lived blind, unthinking lives.

He might even say that their slow, laborious climb up this mountainside was like man's progress through mortal life: a vivid illustration, and one that could stand some elaboration.

His thoughts were swept aside by the blast of another eruption. This was no theoretical discussion, but a display of God's power that made the heart almost stop beating and then sent it racing violently. Donald stood still while the sky darkened above him. Molten lava, red-hot stones, a column of smoke that seemed carved from dark-flecked rock. A quick glance showed Hugh Craig standing unperturbed. A boulder, plunging downwards, struck the crater rim not far above them and buried itself in the soft ash. But most of the rubble fell back out of sight, and the smoke was bending away from them before the wind.

Hugh Craig moved on again. No closer, surely, thought Donald; but he followed tamely. Now they could see down into the crater. The ground was hot under their feet, and white jets of sulphurous steam hissed into the air and drifted past them like a ground mist. At the far side of the crater there were deep chasms, from which steam escaped in a frenzy. The chasms seemed bottomless – the gateway to hell – and from their depths came the sighs and strangled sobs of those held prisoner; the grunting of the demons struggling for mastery. Then, once again, while Donald's mind shrivelled with fear, the mountain hurled itself into the sky with a paralysing roar. A boulder deflected by some freak of force spun out of the column and down the mountainside. There was silence again, and out of the silence the subdued complaints of those imprisoned deep inside the mountain.

Hugh Craig spoke. His voice was small in Donald's ears.

'I find it rewarding to come up here sometimes. If hell lies that way, what is this?' He pointed out over the sea. Far away there were islands, some blurred by the distance, others bold in their outlines. They rested on a tranquil sea, and over each there floated serenely a white crown of cloud. No violence, no passion, no movement; the islands of the blessed. An almost intolerable vision of beauty.

They slid quickly down through the volcanic ash, the mountain booming and reverberating behind them. But before they disappeared into the forest, they halted in the sunlight and looked out once again over the land and sea.

A cutter after the style of the Fiona, seen here drying her canvas sails on a calm day. Typical of the boats that plied coastal waters, these were fast, sturdy sailers that could be handled by one man and a boy. — Tyree Photo.

Maori Market of Auckland, 1873.

The trader arrives at a coastal village.

"The Hopeful on the New Guinea coast capturing slaves for Queensland; subsequently captured by HMS Swinger, 1884."

"The Alloet on the Maicasa River, New Guinea, 1884."

"Interior of the hole [sic] of a Queensland slaver. Slave trading, New Hebrides."

"Native coastal village."

Far from the shores of home.

Perhaps Hugh Craig was right, and God's will could be read in every aspect of the physical world. Such a thought attracted and repelled him. He brooded on it without gaining any satisfaction.

'Why did you come to the Islands, Donald?' Craig was watching him thoughtfully.

'Why did I come?' He tried to find a simple answer. 'Chiefly because Roddy wanted me to, I suppose. I was curious about them, too, and wanted to get away from Waipu. And I had some notion of finding out what sort of man Johnny Bain was. But that's a long story, and it wouldn't interest you.'

'It might, Donald. There's no knowing until I hear it.' There was no curiosity in his voice, but a detached friendliness that encouraged Donald to talk. As he spoke, he found that the whole business was becoming clearer in his own mind.

'There was a girl in Waipu who had a baby. We felt sorry for her, angry perhaps that no one showed her more sympathy. She wouldn't say who the father was. I thought I might find him, and tell him what had happened. I was ready to drag him home by the nose, and confront those stiff and starchy folk with him, and see him marry her and be as good as they were.

'Before I found out who the man was, and where he was, I had second thoughts. Who was I to interfere? Perhaps the girl should suffer for her sin – if sin it was.

'But Roddy, I can see now, put two and two together quicker than I did. It was his turn to act as God, and before I knew it we were all sailing for the Islands – Roddy, myself and Johnny Bain, the man who had fathered the baby.

'And now, with it all nearly over, I've decided that, as far as Johnny is concerned, I should have stayed at home. I can't have any part in it. Not because I think the girl should suffer. But I've taken too much on myself. God can manage these things better than I can.'

Craig nodded. 'So now you'll be away home again, Donald. Perhaps some day I'll go to New Zealand, and see this wonderful Waipu that I have heard so much about.'

He paused. For a moment his well-disciplined face seemed to drop, and he looked lonely and sad.

'You would indeed be welcome,' said Donald. And then he found that, although one part of his mind was still dissenting, he had arrived at a firm decision. It was coloured no doubt by what he had seen that day and earlier: natives, traders, slavers or blackbirders – call them what you would; the village like an evil sore in the island's flesh; the contrast between the volcano's violence and the sublime tranquillity of the distant view.

'I would like to help you with your work here, Hugh. Would there be room for me?'

Craig said: 'What makes you ask that?'

Donald answered: 'You showed me the village. I have seen what the blackbirders are doing to the natives, not only here but on the other islands. Yet it seems that they suffer most from their own ignorance and superstition. Your task in fighting against that seems too much for one man. Perhaps I could help.'

'How would you help, Donald? By going away and training as a missionary, and then coming back?'

'That would take too long, Hugh, when there's work crying out to be done. We could make a start in that village back there. Destroy those filthy huts, fell timber, build new houses, grow crops. Teach them our way of living; teach them to speak English so that they can meet the traders on even terms. Kill their superstition with knowledge, and soon there would be no cannibals left, no baby killers, no disease-makers.'

'And that would be your mission, Donald?'

'That is what I would try to do.'

Craig was silent for a long time, his brooding eyes fixed on the farthest islands. The mountain roared again, but it was now only a background to their thoughts. Finally he turned towards Donald, opened his mouth as if to speak, and then looked away again. This is indeed what I want to do, Donald, he told himself stubbornly. What would Jessie think about that?

'You have a girl back in Waipu?'

Donald jumped. Was this man reading his very thoughts? He nodded an answer.

Craig reached out one arm and touched his shoulder. 'Go back there and marry her, Donald. Make a home and raise a family. But don't expect her to be without faults all the time!' He smiled, and his eyes were warm with friendliness. 'You have an endearing habit, Donald, of reading virtues into people which they may not possess, however much they would like to. But all of us are human, Donald, with weaknesses that we sometimes try to conquer, with frailties that we sometimes do not even know to exist.

'I would gladly have you here with me, Donald, but your faith differs from mine, and eventually you would be disappointed in me. Your belief is in the goodness of people; mine is of the power of God to overcome human error.

'As for these people among whom I work: They may be cannibals, drowning in a sea of false belief. But I would prefer them to be cannibals, Donald. The sins of ignorance are lighter than the sins of knowledge. As savages they will understand and accept the Gospel more easily than if they have been partly educated and partly trained in the white man's ways, with cunning, deceit and hopeless ambition added to the evils they already own.'

Donald looked at him soberly. Hugh Craig was still smiling, but his face was firm and his eyes serious. 'So there it is. I'm grateful to you, Donald, but there is no place beside me for you to work. You'll find, soon enough, your own niche in the world outside.'

They walked back towards the sea, where Roddy and the *Fiona* would now be almost ready to sail. Half-heartedly, Donald began to frame words of argument. But they died in his mouth. He realised, suddenly, that his spirits were higher than they had been for some days. He felt that Hugh Craig was wrong, but that was only his own opinion, and he was by no means infallible. And now he would not have the chance to put it to the test.

* * *

Early next morning Roddy was stirring, impatient now that there was nothing to keep him occupied. 'I have left a note for Kenny, acquainting him with the facts; and doubtless Hugh, here, will amplify it where necessary. He can also let Kenny know what we think of his friends – Ross Lewin in particular.'

Donald felt a familiar excitement mounting in him. New Zealand seemed closer now that they were ready to leave. His mind was constantly turning back to Jessie, to his family, to the well-loved land that harboured them and the ones he had known since childhood.

But his eyes also turned to Hugh Craig's imperturbable face, which could at the one time be strong and tender. He felt, in a moment's uneasiness, that he was a deserter. Craig's battles might not be his, but Craig would now have to fight them alone. They shook hands. 'I wish you well, Donald, and know that you wish me the same.'

Donald followed Roddy into the boat. He would be leaving something of himself in these islands, but he knew also that he would be taking more away.

* * *

Chapter Twenty-One

JOHNNY BAIN WENT ASHORE AT AUCKLAND, BUT DIDN'T COME back. And they sailed for Waipu without him.

'I was hoping he would have seen it out to the end,' said Donald. 'I can just see Jessie's face when I tell her we found him, and then lost him. And what will it mean for Christy?'

'Don't be worrying about that,' Roddy said. He added airily, but with an underlying seriousness: 'You know, Donald, neither Johnny nor Christy are very important. I can tell you what will happen. Johnny won't be able to escape her. He'll come drifting back to Waipu, or to some place where he'll be able to hear how she's getting on. And then he'll go away again. But he'll be back, and Christy will know what he's doing, and she'll be interested, whether she admits it or not. And then someday, when they've past their youth and Johnny is tired of his footloose life, they'll be married.

'Some people are passive; they receive and never give. That's how I think of Johnny and Christy. Others reach out from themselves, whether they wish to or not, and influence those about them. I've sometimes thought I'm like that myself.' Roddy considered his friend with a thoughtful eye. 'What are you planning, Donald? Is it time to settle down now?'

Donald didn't answer directly. 'Roddy, could a man who was neither missionary nor doctor do anything for those people up in the Islands? Some day, no doubt, the traders will be different. They'll make an end to robbing those that they do not take as slaves. They'll help them to buy axes for clearing the land, rather than for cutting off their enemies' heads. They'll teach them to live together and dig and plant and sow and fight back against death, their oldest enemy. But when will it start?'

'No doubt there'll come a time,' said Roddy dryly.

'But do you think there would be room for me there now?' Donald asked. 'Hugh Craig would have none of it, but I'm not convinced. We could start a plantation and make it as prosperous as the one Ross Lewin is running, but the kanakas themselves would be the owners, not its slaves. We could grow cotton and fruit and vegetables. We could have our own schooner, and buy and sell on their behalf. And I still believe that Hugh would find it easier to look after their souls if their bodies were better cared for.'

'Perhaps you could,' Roddy agreed. 'We'll see. And if you find you can, you'll not be wasting your life as some might think.'

* * *

'We'll call at Omaha,' Roddy told Donald, 'and be there overnight. Kenny should be back by now.'

Donald nodded. As they turned through the narrow entrance in the later afternoon he looked for the schooner, but it was not there. The cutter nosed up to the wharf and they prepared to go ashore.

Donald was disappointed, and yet relieved, that Kenny was not home. They greeted his wife and went up to the house with her for a meal.

One of the children came running in just as night was falling. 'We saw her from the top of the Big Hill,' he cried breathlessly. 'Kenny will be here soon!' He ran with the others down to the beach.

'There's time to eat your food first,' said Mrs Mackenzie placidly. 'Kenny wouldn't want you to waste it on his account. He'll not be through the entrance for a while.'

There was only a breath of wind in the deep dark night as they stood waiting on the beach. Then a glimmer of sail as the schooner came ghostlike towards them.

'No lights, the rascal,' said Roddy. 'No doubt he would be ill at ease with them showing!'

'Kenny's like a cat in the dark,' his wife said innocently, 'and he'd know his way in here blindfold.'

Kenny was still dapper, but he seemed weary as he entered the lighted room and sat in his chair. He patted the children's heads, taking little notice of their chatter, and told them shortly to get away to bed. He poured himself some whisky and drained it at a gulp while his wife quietly set him a place at the table.

He looked at Roddy, then at Donald, and shook his head slowly.

'I didn't think to see you here. You should have been back in Waipu by now,' he said. There was a momentary gleam in his eye as he added: 'You'll not be going away again, I expect, after that last exploit of yours?'

'I feel that I'll settle down now for a time,' Roddy agreed.

'And so will I,' said Kenny. 'There's a curse on the Islands, and I've had enough of them.'

'What happened, Kenny, to make you talk like that?'

'We had sailed to Nguna to pick up a dozen kanakas. We had a good welcome, better than usual, and the chief brought the men on board. Then they came at us with their clubs and axes. We held them off, but it was not easy. And then I saw that another party of them were scrambling up the bow and cutting at the cable. We had to sink their canoes and shoot a few of them before the rest jumped overboard.

'As you know, Roddy, I don't like that. It's bad for trade. And then I realised that this was something new. They were trying to take our ship! It's bad enough when they ambush and trick you in their devious ways, but they go too far when they aim to take your vessel! They become nothing but pirates. But we taught them a lesson, took the men, and got away safely.

'And then, when we did struggle back to the trading post, there was almighty confusion everywhere. The natives were babbling and restless, and no work being done. Someone had walked into the missionary's house and knocked his head in with a club. It's a messy business, Roddy; too full of uncertainty, and I'm giving it up.'

Donald listened to the casual words, and found he could not accept them.

'Not Hugh Craig?' he asked stupidly.

Kenny regarded him curiously. 'That's the one,' he answered. 'Why?'

'It just doesn't seem possible,' said Donald. 'How did it happen?'

'Everything, it seems, was much as usual. He was sitting inside working at his books. Then a kanaka – a stranger – came in and asked for some rice or flour. Craig probably knew that they were short of rations up in the hills, and he turned to enter the storeroom to get some. One of his own boys came to the door just then and saw the stranger swing at the missionary with his club. Craig went down like a cattle beast, and the stranger didn't strike him again. He ran outside and disappeared.'

'And Hugh Craig was dead,' said Donald heavily.

'No,' replied Kenny. 'He didn't die just then, though they could see he had no hope. His skull was cracked above the ear. He lasted until evening, apparently, and spoke only once. "Let him go," he said. But the teachers he had trained, and other Christians in the settlement, took it very differently. As soon as he was dead, they painted themselves and took their poisoned spears and guns and went off swearing revenge. They hadn't come back when I left, but I'm thinking that, even if they don't find the man himself, there'll be villages burning and plenty of bodies lying about before they finish.

'They're strange people, aren't they, Roddy?' he said reflectively. 'You think they're much the same as we are; and then at the drop of a hat they become savages again. Sometimes I think it would be as well to not stop them killing one another off.'

'What a way to die,' said Donald. His mind was dark. 'Kenny, do you think our meeting with him was the cause of the attack? It will haunt me all my life.'

'No,' said Kenny. 'The native came from the bush far inland, and the killing could be no concern of ours, or yours. He was probably some young buck trying to show that he was a man. You can be sure that none of his family, or tribe even, had ever been kidnapped. So that couldn't be the reason. He just had to kill a white man, and Craig happened to be the one.'

They sat there silently while Kenny began to eat his meal. It was cool now and Kenny's wife had drawn her chair nearer the hearth where a rata log burned slowly away, popping and crackling in clean red flame.

Donald stared at the fire. 'The waste of it all,' he said slowly. 'A good strong man, and his work ends just like that. Why should it be so?'

'It shouldn't be so,' said Roddy with an irritating calmness. 'But it often is, none the less. And you're wrong in one thing, Donald. His work will not have ended. They're a stubborn, thick-skinned breed, these missionaries, and there will be another of them out there, starting where Hugh Craig left off, just as soon as a boat can bring him.'

'I suppose you are right,' said Donald. But now his mind was far away. He could smell once again that rich New Hebridean soil, rioting with life, decaying into death; and with neither life nor death meaning very much. He shuddered at its heartlessness. It's a denial of God, he thought to himself; the God who sees even a sparrow fall. Those words, he was sure, could never have been written in a tropical jungle. Were its inhabitants human? Yes. But their way of life diverged too widely from anything he could imagine for himself.

He had one awful, blinding vision of Hugh Craig lying on the floor of his hut; the insects, the animals, the heat ready to corrupt his body. He thought of the other bodies he had seen hanging in putrefaction in the native village. Eaten like that by these lost children of God; their juices used to infect the tips of spears and arrows.

Were these people always like that, or had degeneration come through contact with white men? Either could be correct. He could never find out. But what he did know was that he could not live there any more. He thought with an almost feverish relief of the cold snows of Nova Scotia, of the untainted wind that blew across the high hills behind Waipu.

Was he running away from something? Perhaps. But he knew he could never go back.

Roddy looked with sympathy and affection at his drawn face.

'It's time for bed, Donald. An early start in the morning, and tomorrow we'll be home.'

* * *

'I feel a certain disappointment about our homecoming,' Roddy observed as the *Fiona* turned to her northward course up the coast. 'How much more daring to come creeping into port, dodging the excisemen and unloading a cargo that would have delighted Mr McCaul's heart and put something of a lining to my own pockets. And here we are instead, poor still and – sad to say – honest. Going home quietly without a straw's weight on our consciences. The sea has been the only gainer from our voyage, Donald; and what use it can make of cases of brandy and rum I find hard to guess.

'There it is,' he cried. They had rounded Bream Tail, and the bay spread before them. 'A good sight,' he added, 'and I'm thinking it will content me for the rest of my days.'

'Are you certain of that, Roddy? If there is one thing I've learned from you it is to expect nothing for sure.'

'It is how I feel at present,' Roddy observed, 'and that is the only thing that counts. And, indeed, I may change.

'But you're different, Donald. Once you've made up your mind, it is as firm as a rock. Have you thought again about the New Hebrides?'

'I've thought about it, Roddy, and I haven't finished thinking about it. That's all there is.'

Roddy grunted.

The *Fiona* ran merrily in towards the river. As Donald saw the green fields and familiar hills spread out before him he felt the love of his new homeland tug at his heart.

'I think, Roddy, that I'm a cold-weather man. Perhaps we're intended to live in lands such as these, whether in Scotland, Nova Scotia or New Zealand. Perhaps, as so often, Norman McLeod was right again when he said God had reserved these empty places for us to add to His glory.'

'That could be so, Donald, but the Scot is mightily adaptable. And whether it's the will of God or the will of Norman, I feel he'll be turning up in some strange places before the world comes to an end.'

'Hugh Craig,' said Donald. 'Look where it brought him. I keep imagining what his parents and friends will feel, away off there in Nova Scotia, when they learn the news. It's cruel, Roddy. He should still be alive!'

'He wouldn't want to be on those terms, Donald. That's true, I'm sure. There have always been men born to be martyrs.'

'Well, I wouldn't want to be one. Why go looking for death? Death can be kind, when it comes at the end of a full life, or as an easing of pain. But when it takes a young man like that, it is harsh and unfair. It was the same with Norman in the forest. There must be accidents, but why is one man spared and another taken? It's done so blindly, Roddy, with no thought for those who remain behind.'

'You cannot rule the world, nor yet explain it,' said Roddy softly. 'I thought you had learned that by now. And there is this too, Donald: You've accepted Norman's death now, haven't you? I remember when you ran away from the forest. You hated it because it had killed Norman, and you wanted nothing more of it. But now, I think, you could walk under those trees, even work with a gang once again, and not feel guilty. It will be the same with Hugh Craig. You're a strange man, Donald. Simply because you had, in your own way, loved those two men, you feel responsible for their deaths. That's true, isn't it now? And then you feel worse because the world can still be enjoyed, even when you suddenly remember they are not here to share it.

'I've told you before, Donald, and I say it again: You worry too much. When are you going to understand that the world goes on in spite of everything; that it's not a romantic dream of someone's making?'

'Johnny Bain said that, too. And so, in different words, did Jessie.' Donald laughed wryly. 'She was angry with me at the time, I think.'

'It's hard to break free from a dream,' Roddy went on. 'But you'll remember this.' He thumped one fist hard into his open hand. 'Whatever you do, decide at once that that's the right thing for you. Go to the Islands if that's what you wish. Stay at home and marry Jessie if that seems a better choice. Come to terms with the world, whether it is the devil or Norman McLeod who is to rule you. But stop tormenting yourself with vain regrets.'

Roddy was so emphatic, his face and voice so earnest, that Donald smiled suddenly at him and clapped him on the shoulder. 'You make me sound a poor kind of man; and doubtless you're right. I can't see the answer yet, but that may be only because I'm excited at coming home again, and perhaps I'll know for sure when we're there.

'Look at it, Roddy. Doesn't it warm your heart?'

* * *

And now the mild rollers on the river bar – so fearsome only a few months before – were lifting the *Fiona* against her press of sail. She seemed to curtsy, and then the smooth river water took her in its grip, and the tranquil banks were flowing past them.

Long before, it seemed, they had been seen from the signal hill that stood between the village and the sea. There were figures waiting at the wharf beside the McKay house. Roddy grinned.

'Perhaps we should tie up there, Donald. It should be convenient enough on all accounts. And we've nothing to interest the excisemen.'

Familiar faces in a familiar setting, and so strong was the impression they made that the past few months in Donald's life seemed, momentarily, a dream.

He called out greetings as he jumped ashore, glancing hastily from the group up to the McKay house on the rise. Jessie wasn't there, nor was she in sight anywhere. John McKay shook his hand, and there was warmth in his welcome. One thing was sure, he thought, Jessie must be well. For one sickening heartbeat he had feared that something might have happened to her, too. The shadow of Norman and of Hugh Craig had darkened a bright day. But the fear disappeared as old John McKay spoke: 'Jessie will be sorry not to have seen you come in. She's been away this hour or two. Off to your mother's, most likely. There's been no news of you since you sailed for the Islands, and we've all been wondering how the voyage was going.'

'I'll doubtless meet her on the way,' said Donald.

'You won't be staying for a meal and a talk?' said John courteously.

'Thank you, but I must be on the road. Roddy, you'll be able to manage now? I'll collect my gear tomorrow.'

Away he went, long striding and more than a little confused.

The two older men smiled at each other as they walked up to the house. Roddy ruffled his beard with one hand. 'It's likely,' he said, 'that you'll be having grandchildren around you before you know what's happened. And you with a baby of your own not yet out of swaddling clothes!'

John McKay nodded slowly. 'You can't stop it happening, Roddy; and they'll be good ones too. I'm hoping they have as much pleasure out of their children as I'm having out of mine.

'I guessed that you would not want to wait long before seeing your father, Roddy. When the *Fiona* came into sight, I sent one of the children to fetch him. We'll eat together, and then we'll hear all the news, and there'll be beds for the two of you.'

* * *

Donald was able to pass through the village without being delayed. There was no one in the street. Through the corner of his eye he could see curtains being moved in cottage windows. His return was not unnoticed, but the watchers were content with that in the meantime. They would understand that he was in a hurry home.

The year was dying quietly into winter, but the land was still green during the lazy, shortening days. A land open to sun and wind, with the sweet-sharp scent of the tea-tree filling his nostrils. How could anyone leave this for the Islands, knowing that they might never see it again?

Gradually his stride became easier, the cramped deck of the *Fiona* forgotten. He wondered if he might get home before Jessie left to come back. And then, after turning a corner on the climbing road, he met her.

They stood, unmoving, a few paces apart.

'You're back again, Donald!'

He nodded, for there was such joy on her face that he felt humbled and at the same time filled with pure delight, and couldn't speak in answer.

'Sometimes we thought you would never be back,' she said. She held her arms towards him, as if not quite sure of what she was doing, and all the time her eyes smiled and danced and feasted on him. He stepped forward and touched her hands softly, and kissed her.

For minutes they stood close together, the quiet sounds of the country a background to their quickened heartbeats. Then they drew apart, but still stayed near enough to feel each other's physical presence.

'And now I know I'm home again,' said Donald.

They smiled and looked at each other, remembering with their eyes the forgotten details that are part of the pattern of love. Jessie glanced down and brushed her frock. 'I'm not very tidy, Donald. I could wish I was wearing silk and pearls to meet you again.'

'There's no need for that, Jessie. And to tell the truth, I wouldn't notice them. Will you come back with me, Jessie?'

She shook her head. 'Your mother will want you tonight, Donald; and we've time enough, haven't we?'

'No,' he said firmly. 'You'll stay with us this night. And mother will be glad of some help in the house, for I'm expecting a proper Waipu dinner after all the strange and scanty foods we've had.'

Jessie turned and walked beside him. 'You are thin, Donald,' she said soberly. 'You must look after yourself. And pale, too. I was thinking you would come back as dark as an Indian.' She smiled and squeezed his arm. 'But in most respects, I cannot say that you disappoint me very much.'

Donald lay back in his deep chair in the familiar kitchen. He felt that he had done a hard day's work; content and pleasantly weary. Jessie had gone to her room, and he watched his mother fussing about as she prepared the house for the morning. She came over by him and tidied the hearth.

'It's good to have Jessie here,' she said. 'I always wanted a daughter, but instead was given three hulking sons. I like her well.'

'I'm glad of that, mother,' he said drowsily. 'I like her too.'

'Are you planning to settle down now, Donald?'

'Yes, but it calls for some thinking about. I'm not sure what Jessie wants yet.'

'You've decided on a wedding, then, Donald? When is it to be?'

'I haven't had time to think about that, mother,' he said sleepily. 'Fairly soon, I imagine.'

'But what about Jessie? What does she say?'

Donald sat up in his chair, his eyes perturbed. 'I don't know. I haven't asked her.'

His mother, more formidable than he had ever seen her, reached forward with one hand and placed it under his chin. 'Do you mean that you haven't asked her to marry you?'

He wriggled free and sat forward in his chair. 'I should have done that! I wonder what she thinks of me?'

He was quite awake now, thinking hard under his mother's penetrating eye. Then he relaxed and looked at her cheerfully. 'Don't worry, mother. It will be all right. I think she knows.'

* * *

Chapter Twenty-Two

DONALD WOKE IN THE MORNING WITH A WARM SENSE OF well-being. He wondered why, and then realised that he was still remembering the dream that had faded with the passing of sleep.

He and Jessie had been walking across green fields, shrill with the sound of birds, mild in the morning sun. It was very early, for they cast long shadows in front of them, shadows that lay close together and skipped lightly over the fields as they moved. Their shadows seemed to stretch out further and further. He followed them with his eye and saw that they ended in a clump of trees with shining green leaves and red berries. Two men, their faces hidden, lay on the bank beside the trees. They did not seem to be talking, although their heads were close together. They seemed to be waiting.

Donald watched them with a strange feeling of puzzlement. He knew them, he was sure, but could not name them. And now he and Jessie were so close that their shadows were lost under the trees; and at that moment the two men turned their faces towards them. He saw, without surprise, that they were his friends Norman and Hugh Craig.

They stood up lightly and smiled, but did not speak. Their hands were held out towards Donald, but Jessie too was embraced in their silent welcome.

Suddenly Donald remembered that they were both dead. But he felt no sorrow, for it was impossible to look at their relaxed, bright faces with anything but equal joy. He tried to speak, but in making the effort must have wakened himself. For once again he was in his little room, and the light was creeping in the window.

* * *

He lay there for a few minutes wondering why this should have come about. Normally, he did not dream, or else his dreams did not persist beyond sleep. In fact, he realised with a shock, he had dreamed little since he had seen himself and Norman felling the great kauri tree. That dream had borne its own dreadful fruit; perhaps this one might do so too. But this had been a dream without darkness or threat. It belonged not to the devil, but to the world of light.

Below him the house was stirring, and he began to dress. It may be only because I want it, he thought, but I feel that my friends are wishing me well in whatever I may do.

Whistling cheerfully, he went down the stairs to the kitchen, where Jessie and his mother were busy with breakfast.

* * *

Now that he was home again, there seemed no need to hurry. They idled away most of the morning pleasantly. The time had slipped by until he realised that lunch was ready and he had not yet collected his gear from the *Fiona*. He had promised to see Roddy today.

Jessie went with him down the soft clay road. He looked at her uncomfortably, and cleared his throat several times before he spoke: 'My mother has reminded me that it's the custom to ask a girl formally if she would wish to marry,' he said, the words seeming awkward and artificial as he said them.

'They tell me so, Donald,' she agreed gravely. But behind her tone Donald caught something of the humour that had confused him so completely on that New Year's Eve so long ago.

'Well, what do I say now?' he asked.

'That's surely for you to decide, Donald. Your mother must be right!' She was mocking him now. I'll never be able to pin this one down, he thought, and for some reason was glad of it.

'First, perhaps, you should tell me your prospects,' she said.

'They're few,' he said. 'But I've strong arms and a willing back, and a desire to use them. I've been pretending long enough, Jessie; deluding myself with vain worries about Norman McLeod and his brand of religion, and Christy Cameron and her fancies in love; even with ideas of living in the Islands and making the kanakas into good, businesslike Presbyterians. I'm running away from all that, Jessie. I'll have a big enough task on my hands here, I'm thinking, and one that will keep me happy.'

Jessie looked at him curiously. 'You've changed, Donald,' she said; and there was still a lively, friendly mockery in her smile. 'But aren't you even interested now in what has become of Christy? You haven't mentioned her since you came back. There's her house, and I don't doubt she is watching us from the window now. And her baby won't be far away, either.'

Donald didn't speak, and Jessie went on.

'There was really no need ever for you to worry about her,' she said. 'You see, I asked my mother about it, and I think she consulted her mother. And this is what she told me. Christy, she said, would always have to be a little apart from the rest of our people. It would be foolish for her to go to the church for a while, or take part in other activities. But if she conducted herself discreetly, the people would accept her and she would be able to live a happy life.

'She would always have to be tactful, my mother thought, and careful in what she said and did. And the baby would grow up with no mark of disgrace on him, and would have his schooling with the rest.'

'But this baby,' said Donald. 'You talk so casually about him, and yet when I went away no one seemed sure if he even existed!'

Jessie smiled. 'I'm not sure if it wasn't the mystery that really attracted you, Donald. But I took my courage in hand and spoke to my mother about that, too. And do you know what she said? Quite unconcerned, she said: "Christy's baby?", and didn't even drop a stitch in her knitting. "Oh, he's still up with Mrs McGregor the midwife. No doubt Christy will be bringing him home when the excitement dies down."'

Jessie looked thoughtfully at the Cameron house they were now approaching. 'I think that was the last straw for Christy,' she added. 'When I called to see her and asked after the baby, and mentioned that my mother hoped he was well, she seemed quite startled for a moment or two. But then she brightened, and the baby was with her before a week had passed.'

Donald grunted. 'It's still true, then. There are no secrets from the good people of Waipu. No doubt, as we stand here, you and I are also being discussed by the womenfolk who know more of what's in our minds than we do ourselves.'

'That's true, no doubt,' Jessie agreed. 'But remember this, Donald. They are very tolerant.'

* * *

Christy had not been inside the house, as Jessie had thought. They had passed the entrance when Donald saw her coming towards them alone. She had seen them too, but gave no acknowledgment until they met face to face.

Donald observed her keenly. She was still pale and thin, but the defensive stoop that had marked her carriage was gone. And when she spoke she looked at him directly.

They exchanged only a few short words, generalities on her part with conventional replies from Donald. But there was, he felt, something that must be said. And at last he said it, not expecting an answer.

'We had Johnny Bain with us, Christy, from Auckland to the Islands and back again. He's well enough, and was interested to hear the news from Waipu. Not that he knows it all, yet.'

There was colour in Christy's cheeks now, but she made no reply until she had taken a pace or two as if to pass them by. Then she paused and said: 'You'll be seeing him again?'

'It's not likely, Christy, but you never can tell. He might be up in this direction again some time.'

She hesitated, but did not speak. But the smile she gave them as she walked away was more spontaneous than Donald would once have thought possible.

'So it was Johnny Bain,' said Jessie softly. He waited for her to say something more, but that was all.

* * *

Roddy had brought the *Fiona* to anchor a stone's throw from his cottage. As they approached his head appeared from the cabin, and in a moment he was waving to them from the deck.

'If I were to be a sailor,' Donald told Jessie, 'I'd want nothing better than her. She's a kind little craft.' But even as he studied her he found that a touch of fantasy had coloured and blurred his adventures on the *Fiona*. She was now part of a finished episode in his life.

'I'm coming ashore,' Roddy called. 'Wait for me and we'll go on up to the house.'

Roddy bowed handsomely over Jessie's hand, then took her arm and escorted her up the white shell path.

'We'll sit in the parlour for a little while,' their host said. 'Roddy,' he called. 'We have visitors.'

Old Roddy's startled face peered round the corner and then took on a welcoming expression. He came to meet them. 'Well, young man, I'm not sorry to see you again.' He held out a gnarled hand while he stared at Jessie. 'And who is this lassie?'

'John McKay's eldest,' explained young Roddy impatiently. 'You should remember her, even if she wasn't home last night!'

'I know her now,' old Roddy replied equably. 'And what's brought you here today?'

Young Roddy interrupted before this difficult question could be answered. 'We'll all sit down and have a nice cup of tea,' he said. 'Father, is the kettle boiling?'

'There's no need to roar at me like that!' said old Roddy cheerfully. 'My hearing has not failed since you were away.' He looked thoughtfully at Jessie. 'Come with me, my girl, and we'll make the tea.'

* * *

'It's no good, Donald.' Roddy had thrown himself down in a chair. 'There's still not room for the two of us in the one little house. I'm looking for a man to go to Auckland with me on the *Fiona*. What about it?'

Donald wondered if he was serious, and decided that it was possible though by no means certain. 'Are you selling her down there?' he asked.

'Selling her? While there's good money to be made from trading?' Roddy laughed hoarsely. 'I'm still sane, Donald, though I might not be if I stayed here too long. No. I'll see our friend Mr McCaul, and if he doesn't set something my way, someone else will. But I'll be back soon enough.'

'No,' said Donald at length. 'I'd like to be with you, but if I don't settle down now I might turn wanderer forever. You'll have to find someone else this time, Roddy.'

'You could do worse than be a wanderer, Donald.' Roddy's eyes dwelt on his face with a flicker of hope, but then he shrugged his shoulders.

'I can see it's no use. Well, my boy, you're doing the proper thing. May you be well rewarded for it.' They shook hands half-formally, half-humorously, but Donald felt a shadow of discomfort under Roddy's quizzical eyes. And then Jessie and the old man brought in the tea and scones.

Donald and Jessie were making ready to leave when young Roddy, glancing through the parlour window, jumped to his feet. He whipped around to his father. 'Heaven preserve us! What have you been up to while I've been away? There's the parson coming to call! Quick, Roddy, for God's sake. Go and fill the teapot and butter some more scones. No; don't bother. He won't be eating this late in the day. Just take the things out of sight!'

Roddy combed his beard down, shrugged himself neatly into his coat, and went to the front door. Donald and Jessie, because there was nothing else they could do, sat quietly in their chairs, smiling at Roddy's exertions.

They heard a slow, firm step on the crisp shell, and then the squeak of the verandah boards.

'He's alone,' Jessie whispered. 'This is unusual, Donald.'

They heard Roddy greeting him at the door, and the minister's soft, measured voice replying. One thing I haven't outgrown, Donald thought, is my awe of the old man. He stood up and moved a pace or two forward as they entered the room.

'Jessie. Donald.' He acknowledged their presence with a nod and a handshake. Then, his eyes alert behind the masking spectacles, he moved firmly over to a chair; a straight-backed chair, Donald noted, that commanded the room.

'This will be more comfortable, Norman,' said Roddy.

The minister disregarded him. He lowered himself carefully on to the chair, and folded his big, knotted hands on his knees.

'Where is your father, Roddy?' he asked. 'Is he well?'

'Yes, indeed, sir. He'll be in here directly.' He looked nervously towards the kitchen, but no sound came from there. Donald suspected that old Roddy had seized the opportunity to take himself away.

The minister looked more like a happy old man, less like a dedicated saint on the edge of death, Donald thought. His face was fuller. It had lost the transparency that, at the New Year, had contrasted so strangely with his rugged, virile frame. We should have him with us for a time yet; and Donald realised that the thought heartened him. More than anyone else, old Norman represented the strength and power of body and spirit that had brought his people across the world. When he had gone, a great chapter in their history would have ended.

Norman had been talking to Roddy and Jessie, telling them the news of his son in Australia. The perfect picture of a minister at ease with members of his flock; admonition, perhaps, just around the corner, the discipline of the church and respect for his calling showing in his firm, assured voice and in their subdued replies. But Roddy was finding his feet now. Constraint was going from his body. With his head jutting forward and beard agitated by the quick movement of his chin, he was telling the minister about the Australian plantations where the kanakas toiled.

'Now that's something your son could write about,' he said. 'The only trouble is that few people outside Queensland would believe that such things can happen today.'

The minister studied him. 'You should clip off that beard, Roddy. It ill becomes you. In the days of Abraham such whiskers may have been permissible, but I have never been one to decry the advances that mankind has made. There are razors now, Roddy. You should use them.'

The light gleamed from his spectacles as he turned from Roddy to glance out the window. Was he smiling? Donald could not be sure.

'But that is by the way,' Norman continued. 'I tire of trying to mend the minor errors of my people.

'I have been told of your voyage to the New Hebrides, and it is for that reason I am here. Hugh Craig. I didn't know him, Nova Scotian though he was. But he had the church's true spirit in him. I dreamed, once, long before I came here, that New Zealand could be the centre of a great evangelising mission to turn the heathen from their sins. It could be a task that Paul himself would not have found unworthy. But now I am too old. I pass the work on to others. Hugh Craig was a great man; a good Christian man.'

Roddy's beard jutted defiantly at something in the minister's voice. 'Hugh Craig would have been a great man even if he were not a Christian, Norman. Can there be no morality unless it is centred on the church? And what is more, there was greater love between him and his black men, even though they only half understood what he would have them believe, than there is between most so-called Christians!

'I preserve my right to choose for myself, Norman! Sometimes I may act as a Christian, but that could be partly by accident. At other times you could condemn me for what I did. But it would still seem right to me!'

Roddy glared at the minister, forgetful of the others who sat there watching him. Norman McLeod unclasped his hands slowly. Then he nodded his head and smiled at Roddy.

'You fight hard for what you believe,' he said, 'but your thinking is confused. I cannot accept it. Hugh Craig was a Christian. It is impossible to say that, without his Christianity, he would still have been a good man. This is what I affirm: Without his Christianity he would have been nothing!

'Can you not understand that goodwill alone is vain? It must be anchored to a strong faith. Then only can it change a man, as many sinners have been changed in the past and will be in the future.'

There was a lull in the argument, and then the minister's eyes swept around to Donald. 'You sit quiet,' he said. 'Have you any thoughts on this matter?'

Donald had found the brisk interchange of talk relaxing. He was only half listening, but as he followed the conversation he thought: Neither of them would admit he is wrong and yet, the more they bluster, the more it seems they are trying to convince themselves. Would Hugh Craig, if he could have heard it, be interested in what they are saying? Possibly. But he would be wondering more what he could do than what he could say. But all the same, Donald thought, if they had ever come together they would have been arguing as strongly as the minister and Roddy were now.

And Donald found that he could smile at the thought. Something had happened. It might have been his return to a familiar world that included Jessie, his parents and the minister, as well as Roddy; it might have been the lingering impression of happiness from his dream of the night before. But Donald found that he had accepted Hugh's death, and could think of him without pain.

So now, while the minister and Roddy watched him, he tried to shake his wandering thoughts into some pattern, feeling as he did so that nothing he said would be very important. He glanced at Jessie and smiled, his mobile mouth and clear eyes making his face seem younger than when he was in repose.

'If I had any sure ideas,' he said, 'I would still not be certain they were right. But this I do feel: that there are many good Christians who can be harsh and selfish, just as there may be heathens who can be kind and generous. You'll say, perhaps,' and now he was looking directly at the minister, 'that there were once societies built as God wanted them. There may have been, although those people living in them may have had different thoughts. But we can't go back, can we, Minister? We can draw on what they did then, just as we can learn from the New Testament. But the world has moved since that time. There's room for tolerance, less discipline, today, don't you think?'

'No,' said the minister. He was definite, but still unruffled.

Donald took a deep breath. 'Then I would say this. If you were a young man today, Minister, you would be different from the one who stormed through the parishes of the Western Highlands and set up a new community in Cape Breton. You had to be stern, dogmatic and ruthless against deviation. You had to discipline your people or they would have melted away like snow after winter. But today, as a young man in this land or anywhere else, you would be different.'

The minister had listened with some attention, and Donald could not decide whether he was offended or not. Once I would have known for sure, he thought, as he waited for an answer.

'You mean I would be softer,' said Norman at length.

'Perhaps. But softness does not always mean weakness.' He looked at the minister. 'You have always loved your people. I can see that now. You have been a strong right arm to them. But perhaps they need gentleness today rather than a stick across their shoulders.' He stopped uncertainly and made to get up from his chair. 'I've said more than enough. I'm sorry if I have offended you. If so, it is only because my respect for you is greater than my fear. Come on, Jessie, we must away.'

The minister signalled with his great right hand. 'No, sit down again, Donald. I must think about what you say for, indeed, something of it has been in my own mind for these last years.' The strong cheekbones, the fiercely curving chin stood out firmly, and yet his mouth was not harsh. 'There is one thing you must know. Whether they are young or old, wise or foolish, weak or strong in their faith, I love my people. If I could save one soul from hell, I would lie on my deathbed for a hundred years. And willingly.'

Donald felt his heart reach out to the old man. There was nothing more he could say, or wanted to say. But before he went he stepped forward to where the minister was sitting, took his hand and, with a gesture that was unstudied and full of youthful dignity, bowed low over it. Jessie murmured goodbye, and together they went quietly out the door.

* * *

The minister sat on, his body immobile but his mind full of thoughts. Old Roddy had come back into the room. From the high vantage point of his ninety years he regarded the minister with a friendly affability. Finally the minister moved, as if his thoughts had come back from some distant place.

'I too must away,' he said. He walked firmly to the door, closely followed by Roddy, and paused on the step while he was helped into his heavy topcoat. Across the river, beyond the steady mast of the *Fiona*, Donald and Jessie were walking towards the village. They did not look back.

'You shouldn't worry about what he said too much,' Roddy ventured. 'After all, the boy's in love, and love does strange things to the mind. He'll grow out of it some day.'

He paused and looked inquiringly at the minister who still did not speak. Roddy went on: 'I've always been interested in Donald, Norman. He has it in him to be a fine man. But he was cramped here, and seemed happy enough to stay cramped. And so I was pleased when he came away with me, thinking that he would learn something from the world.' Roddy grinned. 'He may have at that, but I'm not sure it is what I planned to teach him. All he seems to have learned is that there are worse places than Waipu after all!'

The minister was listening to him now, studying his face as if to find some hidden meaning in what he said. Roddy shrugged his shoulders humorously. 'I can see him in another thirty years time. His wife and children, and his grandchildren perhaps, sitting peacefully in a church. He'll be comfortable, with a good farm and timber mills behind him, and he'll think more of his children and their problems than of his own. He won't be fat – that's something the McKinnons don't become – but he'll be heavier, and slower, and he'll frown a little when anything is done that offends against his ideas of right and wrong.

‘I say this, Norman, that he will be busy and successful. But he will never escape from dullness, and in self-defence he’ll have to make dullness seem worthy in itself.

‘I’m not disappointed with Donald. That would be a waste. But I would rather he had gone amissioning in the New Hebrides, or become a trader in Auckland, than that he shut himself away here. Not that I blame him, Norman, but he’s run away from life; and I think that there will be a time when he’ll feel it like a cold breath on his neck. And Jessie will wonder why he seems to be lost in some world of his own.’

Donald and Jessie were out of sight now, well on the road to the McKay home. The two men stared thoughtfully across the stream.

‘I’m speaking like this,’ Roddy said, ‘because it’s important to me that you should know how I think.’

The minister nodded his head. ‘I understand, Roddy. Better perhaps than you know. For what was I but a rebel against the elders of my youth? I can remember the fire that burns in a young man’s blood – and stays with some old ones, too, until they die.’

There was a melancholy in his face as he looked out across the quiet countryside to the mountains, a melancholy that was devoid of passion or strong feeling of any kind, harmonising with the sober, tranquil autumn afternoon. They stood there for a long time, both in their own way, as old men do, remembering fitfully episodes from their lives that had now taken on a dreamlike quality.

At last Norman turned towards Roddy. ‘You listened as he spoke up there, with the girl watching him? That was a new Donald McKinnon speaking, a man who has thoughts of his own. Donald has grown away from you,’ he added slowly, ‘but he has also grown away from me. And, Roddy, I don’t mind. You’re wrong when you say he has run away from life. He has accepted his life as it is, and surely he will make something worthwhile of it.

‘We’ve had our time, Roddy, and we’ve done what we can with it. But the future rests with those like Donald. And we can only hope that they will not forget us when we’re gone.’

He sighed, and then smiled at Roddy as he held out a hand in farewell. Roddy watched him walk down the path, his shoulders square and his head unbowed; a formidable figure even now.

Roddy waved – a gesture that was at once defiant, humble and oddly pathetic. 'They may forget me,' he said softly. 'But this is for sure: They'll remember you, Minister!'

* * *

THE END

Postscript

ONE DAY, SOME NINETY YEARS AFTER DONALD MCKINNON went home to Waipu for the New Year, Neil Robinson informed his young wife Flora that he had written a novel about the early days at Waipu, the birthplace of his mother 'Polly' Campbell, but that he didn't think he would bother with getting it published.

Neil was working with the NZ Weekly News at the time and had typed his novel on 528 small sheets of journalists' copy paper. He then put it away in a drawer of his writing desk and, although a few adventurous borer migrated from the base of the drawer and developed a taste for the concluding pages of the story, made no further mention of it. The manuscript remained unread by any other until discovered by his son Alistair some months after Neil's death on 18 January 2001.

On another day, also around 1950, his mother's brother Owen Campbell suggested to Neil that he write a history of the 1817 migration led by Norman McLeod from the Scottish Highlands to Pictou in Nova Scotia and, thirty-four years later, to Australia and on to New Zealand. This he did, and *Lion of Scotland* was published in 1952 in time for the Centennial celebrations at Waipu.

Just how long Neil had worked on the novel and what stage it had reached in his own editorial mind prior to its interment in the drawer is not known. The preserved manuscript has been re-worked, quite possibly on several occasions. Division of the text into chapters and subsections was done by hand after typing and although 'Part Two: The Sea' was labelled, no Part One was designated as such. No working title was recorded.

Minor changes have been made in preparing the text for publication, one of which is of structural significance: A chapter break has been inserted at Chapter Twenty-one where no break was marked. Neil's hand-written editorial changes were all clear and unambiguous and have been implemented. A few minor errors were detected and have been corrected, and, more subjectively no doubt, some phrases and punctuation marks have been altered—but only after an imaginary, sometimes quite prolonged debate with the author about the question of 'flow'.

Neil's research for *Lion of Scotland* and his unnamed novel are obviously closely linked, and it seems likely that writing the novel was simply part of the research and development process—an imagined immersion into the lives and times and a getting to grips with the character of Norman McLeod—directed towards his writing of the history. 'History becomes a mingling of fact and fantasy,' he wrote in *Lion of Scotland*, 'and out of this combination there often comes a truer picture than could be gained from a bare recital of facts,' partly because of the tight cohesion and sense of unity demanded by any fictional story. The fact that Flora clearly remembers Neil stating his intent and writing the history but has no recollection of him struggling to produce a publishable novel stands in support of this possibility. And it's quite obvious that Neil thoroughly enjoyed writing it.

Neil was, from an early age, a compulsive writer of stories. He thought in word pictures. 'It is always easy,' he wrote in a short, undated, hand-written attempt at autobiography, 'to build vivid word pictures in the mind, to catch delicate shades of meaning, to bring a nebulous clarity to complex issues. The mind, during a wakeful night, can fashion a short story that is dazzling in its simplicity and truth.' This was the man who, as a small boy, had spent holidays with his mother and grandmother at Waipu, listening to oral histories of the people in the district and of the migration which had brought them there; then going to bed, perchance to dream, every night of the holidays.

Writing stories was not 'work' as far as young Neil was concerned, any more than growing a crop of potatoes in his garden or walking the dog on the beach was work. But in his personal judgement, his own written stories never attained the superlatively high standard of the word pictures he had so vividly imagined: 'But the dream melts away,' he continued in the autobiographical note. 'Try to set any of these things down in cold, unforgiving print and they fade to dust or disappear like reflections on a stream.' Making his own word pictures from other people's stories, however, was a quite different matter, and Neil remained an enthusiastic and insatiable consumer of stories written by others throughout his life.

So we might well imagine that, because of this personal perception, Neil did not consider his own fictional output very seriously. It was a means to an end, not an end in itself. He wrote the novel quite quickly—which does not mean carelessly or thoughtlessly—allowing it to flow freely from his mind and not bothering to record the natural breaks as he proceeded, enjoying in the process a brief foray into a distinctly Dickensian tableau with the merchant Mr McCaul and Silas More and a somewhat Shakespearian exeunt to the scene with the two Roddys in Chapter Four. And only when it was written and he noticed that, even when measured against his own unrealisable standard, he had actually produced a lively and interesting, humanly truthful story, did he seriously consider the notion of publication—and reject it, though not without some reservations.

> 'Well, I've finished the Waipu novel,' he said to his lovely young wife one morning at breakfast. But the smile quickly faded from his face and he felt a slight flush in his cheeks when, noticing the look of puzzled surprise in her eyes, he suddenly realised that he'd omitted to tell her about the task he'd been busily engaged with for the past few weeks. 'Oh, I'm still intending to write the history I told you about, my dear,' he quickly continued, 'and have made some plans for it. But right now, I've finished writing a novel. However, I was thinking it over in bed last night and don't think I'll bother attempting to get it published.'
>
> At that moment, before his wife could respond, their big-eared, one-year-old baby boy, who was busy cutting some pre-wisdom teeth, hurled his empty Peter Rabbit porridge bowl towards his three-year-old sister, vigorously rattled the tray of his blue high-chair, and howled.
>
> 'Goodness gracious!' the father exclaimed as he rose hurriedly from the table. 'Is that the time? If I don't get away immediately, I'll be missing the darned ferry into the city!' And in a flash he was gone.

Neil subsequently revisited the work twice or thrice, numbered the pages, made various alterations, formalised the structure, gave the matter of publication some further thought, added 'A Note to the Reader'—and returned the manuscript to its drawer. If a real writer of fiction had produced this story, he thought cheerfully as he tucked it away again, it would probably be well worth publishing. He felt a strong sense of attachment to this story in its own right, which, together with its usefulness in writing the history, saved it from the fate of fire-starter in the incinerator in his back yard.

Standing in stark contrast to many such disclaimers, in his 'Note to the Reader' Neil made it quite plain that, although most of the characters in the novel are fictitious, any resemblance to persons living or dead was certainly no accident or coincidence. He'd spent a lot of time talking with the sea-faring descendants of Mathesons, Meiklejohns and McKenzies of the Omaha area, half way to Auckland from Waipu (see Chapter Thirteen in *To the Ends of the Earth*), and a quick reference to

Chapter Nine (Men of the Forest and the Sports Field) in *Lion of Scotland* reveals the importance of real-life characters like Willie Kempt in the creation of the lives that Donald McKinnon and his companions led:

> 'My mate Rory McAulay and I had just felled a kauri,' Willie recalled, 'and we were standing near the stump for a breather. Up above us, but well clear, another kauri was brought down. Normally there would have been no danger; but as it fell, it struck a rata tree that forked like the wishbone of a fowl, and sent it crashing towards us. I ran for cover under our tree, knowing that Rory would have seen what was happening. Before I could reach shelter, however, the rata came down, one huge limb on each side of me. I called to Rory but he did not answer. He had run the wrong way and the tree killed him.'

So the likes of Rory McAulay and Willie Kempt, seventy-eight years old at the time when he and his mate Cockatoo, alias Donald McLeod, showed Neil how a timberjack worked, live on in the novel, just as they do in the history. And a comparison of the development of this tragic event in the two books reveals something of the grace of Neil's imagination when it was allowed to run freely under full sail before a brisk wind—a freedom and grace that he did not publicly express in his own words very often, preferring, usually, to adopt a rig capable of a tight and exhilarating beat to windward, close-hauled and tacking along his real life's deep, narrow passage, travelling always obliquely towards his main objective; the elusive source of the human spirit-wind which he felt move him and which showed in his broad, kindly face so keenly.

Like Donald McKinnon and his forebears, Neil was a landsman from a family of Skye landsmen. He never owned a sailing boat and spent very little time on the sea. But he obviously understood a thing or two about the theory of sailing, nonetheless.

Most of the names of the characters in the novel mean very little in themselves, other than that they are authentic names of various Nova Scotian settlers in 1860. Names like "Smith" and "FitzJones" would simply not have done for any resident of Waipu in those days. It is the style of characters and life experiences that count, and which Neil hoped were not too far from the truth. The fictional lives of "Norman Finlayson" and "Christy Cameron", for example, can bear no resemblance to those of Norman Finlayson and his grandmother Christina Cameron, who came to New Zealand as a widow on the *Spray* and who died at the age of 85 on 18 November 1875. But the subtle moulding of the life experiences and real characters of Waipu and its surrounds into the supra-real dream world created by a novelist is what helps make Neil's novel such a vibrant and honest story.

Human social history is a growing thing like a coral reef. It advances on numerous fronts a little further towards the light in each moment of every day. It is the timeless rock fashioned by those people who do not consciously set out to rise above the waves and make history, only to be swept away on the next tide, but who simply live out their own social/solitary, human lives and make their true mark, as fitting for themselves in their times. The omnipotent and personal God inevitably and always plays an integral part in this history, and a deep awareness and quiet appreciation of it is essential to the cohesion, the sense of security, and the survival of any human society. This is the history that Neil loved; the rock that he carefully investigated and described; the history in which individual people with their highly elusive private and public thoughts and their shopping lists and their sermons and the stories they tell and the letters they write to each other are of far greater significance than the reigns of remote kings and queens, the puerile performances of prime ministers and presidents, or the fates of faceless winners and losers in wars and parliamentary debates.

Neil wrote in *To the Ends of the Earth*: 'Most of the [letters] I've seen were designed to pass on news or elicit information. And in almost every case there is a picture of the writer, more revealing than he might imagine or desire. There could also be a touch of dry humour, a subtlety hinting at unexplored depths in the writer's personality.' So it is with this novel, left unheralded by Neil but a significant element in the structure of New Zealand social history nonetheless—that life-sustaining structure to which all New Zealanders of all ages and origins make an equally vital contribution in all walks of life, as extraordinary individuals.

And how did the novel get its name? Flora found it a few weeks ago when reading for the first time the story that Neil had told her fifty years ago would not be published. *The River of No Return.* The words of the song from the 'Red Indians' of Nova Scotia held a kind of music, Flora thought.

Peter Robinson
October 2002